DRAGON LORDS

The Return of the Generals

TRENT R. BINGHAM

The Reading Glass Books
(888) 420-3050
www.readingglassbooks.com
production@readingglassbooks.com

TABLE OF CONTENTS

 # Prologue 

In a large dimly lit misty cave were a trickle of water could be heard dripping into a pool of water in one of the corners of the room. As a tender loving mother was gently awoken by the warm noon sun that shined through a large high crack in a cave. She smiled to see that the sun had raised high enough to wake her up then to have the sun light up her lair. After she stretched, she then walked over to large entrance where she could look out over the lush land and breathed in the crisp air. As she continued to enjoy the crisp air, she suddenly felt a familiar heat source as she quickly pulled herself back further into her lair.

Shortly after she pulled her body into her lair, a large fireball crashed into the side of the mountain where she was standing at. After the heat source went out, she peered out of her cave as she saw two dragons pursuing each other shooting fireballs in an attempt to kill each other. She watched in agony as her children continued to fight each other until one of them prevailed over the other one. As she relived the scene in her mind, she could only hope that her new baby dragons could help to end the war plaguing her land.

As this mother walked in her lair to another part of her cave were this eager mother carefully watched over her great clutch of eggs. She carefully cradled two of the big tubular tan leather eggs, holding them close to her forehead. Without saying a word, she conveyed a message to the unhatched newborn, "It is time." She then set the two eggs back with the others. Soon after, the two eggs began to move and tiny claws began to cut through the leathery shell. When the two babies emerged, they stretched out their tiny bodies and rushed from their mother's side out of her presence ready to fulfill their destined command as they disappeared into the darkness.

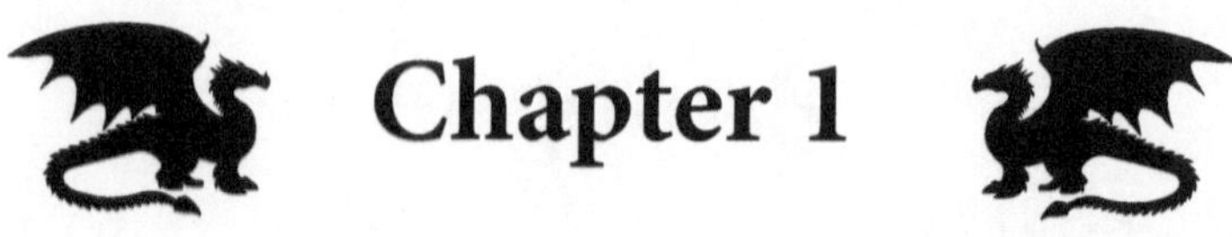# Chapter 1

Ryan Luke was waiting at the corner of his best friend's house so they could go and play in the park before lunch on the bright Saturday morning. As he waited, the smell of a rose bush from a nearby neighbor's award winning pink roses heightened his senses. He heard a pitter-patter of an unmistakable critter. He bent down and was greeted by a very friendly dog named Spot, who was a Dalmatian with a single spot on her forehead.

As soon as she saw Ryan, her excited brisk walk escalated into a run stopping abruptly at his feet addressing Ryan's commands. "Here, Spot, come here, girl." As Ryan combed her slick coat with his hand, she drenched his face with her loving tongue. Ryan pushed her away before he received a second bath.

Spot had nearly pushed Ryan over, pinning him to the ground with her friendly face, when Jerry Thane rounded the corner chasing his dog. Upon seeing Spot tackling Ryan with him loving every bit of it, he said, "Ryan, I swear you are more excited to see Spot than me. You know I'm your best friend!"

Ryan exerted enough strength to push Spot off long enough to get his footing to stand up. As he walked over to Jerry brushing himself off, he spoke. "I'm sorry, Jerry, but you know how my parents are. They won't even let me purchase an aquarium because they say the responsibility will fall on their shoulders. So I have to purchase and read a variety of pet books and enjoy other people's pets to get my love and excitement of owning a pet."

Jerry rolled his eyes as he listened to his excuse. Jerry looked down at his watch, noticing that it was a quarter after ten and knowing Spot likes to play in the park for a couple of hours. He really wanted to go to Ryan's room before it got too late. As Ryan bent down again to pet Spot, Jerry said, "Well, we better head to the park before it gets too late to get Spot worn out for the day."

Ryan got back up on his feet and turned to Jerry saying, "Okay, let's go!" Facing in the direction of the park, two blocks away, they started toward it. With Spot on Ryan's heels, Jerry had fallen behind because he had bent down to tie his shoelaces, so he ran to join up with them. It didn't take them long to walk the short distance to the park.

They entered the park where there was a wide variety of people enjoying the nice day. Several mothers had their children playing on the assortment of park toys. There were couples enjoying a relaxing picnic, and then there were the dog owners enjoying the dog park throwing Frisbees, balls, and other dog toys. When they entered the marked off area, Spot first began investigating the other dogs in the park. As soon as she determined there weren't any dog villains, she wanted to play with her Frisbee and barked and begged at Jerry's feet until he threw it.

This game persisted for close to two hours until Spot began to ignore her favorite toy more and more. This was the opportunity Jerry was waiting for. "Ryan!"

Ryan looked up from the ground where he had discovered several interesting insects that he found fascinating. "Yes, Jerry?"

Jerry walked a little closer to him. "Spot is getting bored and tired. It looks like she wants to take an afternoon nap."

Ryan looked around Jerry and saw Spot laying down with no Frisbee. Ryan responded, "Okay, we can leave. Let's go to your place—"

Jerry blurted out, "*No!* Sorry, rather than my place, let's go to yours."

Ryan said, "Why mine?"

Jerry thought quickly and said, "Well, didn't you say that you got a brand-new dragon game yesterday?"

Ryan's facial expression went from dull and bored to an extreme excitement as he thought about his new game and Jerry's interest in it. Ryan was getting so excited that he almost forgot that it was time for lunch. But his stomach reminded him as he asked, "Hey, Jerry, are you hungry?"

After agreeing with him, they left the park and put Spot in Jerry's house before heading to Ryan's place next door for lunch and Ryan's new game. Ryan unlocked the device mechanism to the front door. As entered, he was aware that his mother wasn't home. Despite this, he decided to call out for her several times. With no response, it was obvious that they would have to make their own lunches. They then continued through the house to the kitchen where Ryan got out two paper plates from one of the cabinets.

He then asked, "So what do you want to eat? We have the ever popular sandwiches, mac and cheese, or I think my mom bought some burritos last night and we could add some cheese for extra flavor."

Jerry sat down on one of the bar stools and rested his elbow on the counter, rubbing his chin as if he was in deep thought, Jerry thought, *What would be the best choice to eat at the moment?*

After Ryan pondered for a couple of minutes, he came up with his reply. "Well, my stomach is pretty hungry, so we need to eat something we can make fast. So I have come up with sandwiches, then after we are done, we can go up to my room and play my new game."

Jerry said, "It's a deal." Jerry reached out to shake hands with Ryan to confirm their decision.

The decision on what kind of sandwich to make was much easier. Ryan was a sucker for peanut butter and strawberry jam whereas Jerry is all for the meat and cheese. Ryan proceeded to make Jerry's first because he could only locate the turkey and ham which was fine for him. After adding a fair share of mayo and mustard, he then added a few slices of turkey, ham, and a large slice of cheese. After Ryan had made both sandwiches, they began to eat their lunch.

Jerry had a thought on his mind ever since they arrived at Ryan's house. He then said, "Hey, Ryan, I know your mom is busy, but where is she at?" Then he stuffed his mouth with a large bite of his sandwich.

Ryan turned around from where he sat to look at the microwave clock, and seeing that it was 4:15 p.m., he then responded, "Well, it's four fifteen on a Saturday afternoon, that means she has to be at the school for Crystal's volleyball game." Crystal is the oldest of three sisters with Ryan being the only boy.

Ryan then went back to eating his sandwich without another thought of what Jerry asked, but Jerry couldn't hold in his thoughts any longer. He then said, "Ryan, I just can't help but think that your parents overlook you."

Ryan had an offensive look on his face as he answered, "My parents don't overlook me at all.

They are very supportive of me."

Jerry just looked at him and raised his eyebrow. "Really? When and what was the last event they supported you in?"

Ryan took another bite of his sandwich. After he was finished, he looked at Jerry and answered, "My parents don't support me in any particular events because I don't participate in any. Besides, what would they support me in a chess tournament? Get real. Besides, my sisters are the athletic ones, not me, so of course, my parents are going to support them more than me. That is a no brainer."

Jerry thought about what Ryan had said and wanted to make another point in Ryan's behalf but also didn't want to make him madder, so he decided to eat more of his sandwich and remain quiet. As Jerry ate the thicker parts of his sandwich, his conversation with Ryan faded into the back of his mind, and he remembered the reason why he was so eager to come over. Jerry suddenly expressed, "So, Ryan, at school yesterday, all I have heard from you was this totally amazing computer game. But I have yet been able to see it."

Ryan's expression went from slightly annoyed from Jerry's last comments to an overwhelming excitement. He then began to stumble over his words, "Oh yeah, this game is so cool. I really think you are going to like it."

Jerry listened to Ryan went on about his new game but what he really wanted was a prized crystal quartz as he began to imagine it in his mind. When Ryan said, "Well, I'm done," it startled Jerry who was still daydreaming about the crystal and made him drop his sandwich. He looked down at his half- eaten sandwich and picked it up. He took a big bite out of it and swallowed it. He said, "Well, I'm full too, so let's go and see this new game of yours, Ryan."

Ryan cleared their plates to throwing them away, then they exited the kitchen turning around the corner to go to his bedroom. But before they began to walk up the stairs, he turned around to face Jerry. His face displayed anxiety as he spoke, "Jerry, you are my very best friend, but I have kind of seen a pattern beginning to develop. You have an interest in a new book, game, or something of mine which you remain fixed on for a short period of time. Then your interest shifts, usually to the quartz I found with you a while back. It's as if my old or new interests are an excuse only to get up to my room and the quartz."

Jerry acted like Ryan hurt his feelings, then with a surprised look, he responded to Ryan's statement, "Ryan, I'm shocked that you would question me on this subject. I am very interested in your books, games, and hobbies. May I also add that my attention span is very short and that is why I get distracted easily." Jerry's quick-witted answer quieted Ryan's suspicion; however, Ryan was correct. Two years ago, Jerry invited Ryan on a camp out and hike with his father. On their hike, Ryan found a huge purple-and-white quartz that isn't worth a dime, but as a kid, it looked like it was worth a fortune. When Jerry saw it, he began to lust after it. Ever since then, he has been using every excuse he could dig up to go to Ryan's room to examine and play with the quartz. While he would further inspect it, he would try and devise ways to steal it and keep it for himself.

Jerry was climbing the stairs picturing the purple-based quartz that he easily compared to his mother's purple pansies that she would plant every year in their flower bed in the front of his house. A little farther than halfway up from the base, it changed colors to a flawless clear crystal quartz. Ryan and Jerry discovered that if the clear side was hold up to a light source, it acted like a prism that would project several rainbows on the opposing wall's surface. They discovered that the brighter the source, the more rainbows it would produce.

They turned this discovery into a game. The object of the game was to see who could make the biggest rainbows on the wall. Sometimes Ryan would win, but Jerry, being very competitive, won most of the time. Ryan and Jerry continued to Ryan's room, and he got really excited the closer they got to his room as he expressed to Jerry, "I think you will really like this game, Jerry. It is a lot like the old warcraft game from the 90s, *Orcs and Humans*, but with dragons and humans."

Ryan kept going on and on. Jerry tuned him out, thinking only of ways to be successful in stealing the crystal. They continued to Ryan's room. They had to go back to the front door in order to go up the stairway. Ryan's room was at the top, the second door to the left. Jerry left him hanging in his daydreams as he got to the top of the stairs. He was again startled by

Ryan waiting at the top when he said, "You know, Jerry, the only nice thing about being the only boy is I get my own room."

Ryan chuckled at his own joke. Jerry gave out a fake chuckle. He must have heard that not-so- funny joke a million times. As Ryan opened his door, Jerry rushed in making a sharp right heading for the computer. His progress was stopped as he stumbled over Ryan's bed.

Hearing the clatter and Jerry's moan of pain, Ryan said, "Oops, sorry, Jerry, I forgot to tell you that my mom reorganized my room yesterday, so my bed is closer to the light switch."

Jerry limped over to the computer chair, rubbing his shin in agony, he said, "Wasn't your bed on the opposite side of the room next to your closet?"

Ryan responded, "Yes, it was but my mom thought it would be better closer to the door and the light switch so I wouldn't have to walk across the room in the dark." Ryan walked around his bed and sat in his other computer chair next to Jerry, and Ryan booted up his computer. Slowly, it began to process itself getting to the log-in screen.

Annoyed, Jerry spoke, "Man, Ryan, this computer is a piece of junk. You seriously need to get rid of it and replace it with a new one."

Ryan looked over at him and said, "Easier said than done. You forget that I have to save up my money and pay for my stuff. I don't have parents that just give me what I want. I have to earn my own keep, as my dad always says. Besides, this was the best computer I could buy at the time."

Jerry was still annoyed but remembered that he requested a new computer from his parents and in a more excited tone said to Ryan, "Hey, I just remembered something. I asked my parents for a new computer since it is outdated by at least a year. It has this dinosaur beat by far, so I'll ask my parents if I can give it to you. I'm sure they won't mind at all."

Ryan also got excited as he spoke, "That would be great. It would help me out so much, but if not, this one gets me by. I only use it for homework and playing games." As the log-in screen finally came up, it took Ryan's attention away from Jerry.

As the computer began to further process the password and begin to load, Jerry couldn't hold in his question any longer. He then asked, "Ryan, as slow as this computer is, how do you play games on it?"

Now it was Ryan who was getting annoyed by Jerry's repetitious questions but chose to answer calmly. "Like I said before, at the time this was the best computer I could afford. As far as games go, I feel lucky that I have a computer that can even play games."

In the process of their conversation, the computer finally fully loaded allowing them to access any information they wanted. Jerry was the first to notice the computer had finished and said to Ryan, "Your computer is done. So what was the name of this game again?"

Ryan's frustration was dissolved when he saw that he could finally access his game. "The name of the game is called *Dragons at War: An Alliance with Humans*! This game is really cool."

Ryan found the icon for the game which was designed by having half of a human face merged with half of a dragon's face. When Ryan clicked on the icon, the game loaded fairly fast. The game started when it finished uploading and began with the icon picture with the title below it. The picture then separated into a human and dragon head. As both continued to separate, they also began to enlarge and cover the whole screen and the title. At this time, the two heads began to rotate to face each other and rammed into each other exploding, creating the menu page. Ryan clicked on the load a game mode which directed him to his saved game where he clicked on and began to load it.

While it was loading, Jerry spoke up and said, "Ryan, before you clicked on your saved game section, there looked to be two other different modes of play."

Ryan turned around on his computer chair to face Jerry as he spoke, "That is correct. There are three different modes of play. The first mode, the one that I have a saved game on, is called Battle of Dominance. The object of this game begins with you as a king defending your kingdom and need to find and defeat your opponent's kingdom. But there is a slight twist on the way of finding your enemy. In your travel, you come across villages or townships of either men, elves, or ogres who live under no flag. Then you have two options at this point, pass on by or attack, to either destroy the settlement or convert it to your side and aid you on your quest to fight your foe. At the same time, your foe is doing the same with the villages he comes across. He can even convert or destroy your own settlements and vice versa until one side is completely conquered.

"The second play mode is called Conquer the Land. In this mode, you are the only player with your kingdoms castle. But you have to cover the entire land defeating your enemies while still defending your castle. You have to fight ogres, trolls, elves, dwarfs, and even other humans. As with the first mode, your foes can join your forces which is what you want or be destroyed.

"The third and final mode is Conquer Your Friend. This mode is set up like the first mode. Only I would be one castle and you would be the other. We would try to defeat each other. This mode allows up to three players, but you must also be connected to the Internet."

Ryan's saved game had finally loaded up and which drew his attention away from Jerry. This would be the perfect time for Jerry to sneak away and find the crystal while Ryan was so intrigued by the game that he wouldn't budge. Jerry's interest in the third mode pushed him to ask Ryan, "How do you play against another player?"

Ryan's progression with his game came to halt as he quickly saved and paused his game and turned around to Jerry with a surprised look on his face as he said, "Are you serious?"

Jerry shrugged his shoulders to which Ryan continued, "Well, if you are serious, then you first need to buy the game. Once it is loaded on your computer, then you need to connect to the Internet as I mentioned before. There is a link with the third mode where you then create a username, then you develop your character similar to *The World of Warcraft* game. Once online, we find each other's log-in names connect, then we try to find and kill each other. So seriously, how interested are you in my game?"

Ryan was expecting a sarcastic answer from Jerry, but Jerry surprised him with his answer. "I really am interested. This game looks really cool plus the fact that I can beat your butt from my house with this game makes it even cooler, so where can I get a copy?"

Ryan looked at the clock on his dresser. It was close to four o'clock in the afternoon. He said to Jerry, "It is getting too late for us to walk to the mall. It closes at eight in the evening on Saturday, plus we have school in two days. Also, we don't have a ride. We will have to go Monday after school, but the name of the game shop is called Mike's Game Room, not a big store, but it has tons of games." Jerry had no choice but to agree and watch Ryan play his game after a short period of time. He then started his own. Before long, Ryan's mom came up to check on them and then asked Jerry if he wanted to stay for dinner.

Jerry said, "Yes, thank you." Jerry then turned his attention back to the game.

Ryan walked over to his mom and in a quiet tone told her, "Mom, he has been on that game for about an hour or two. He is obsessed with it."

Ryan's mom said in the same hushed tone, "Let him play. He probably doesn't have much time to play games with his busy schedule."

Ryan then whispered back to his mom, "Well, I think part of that busy schedule is going to open up. Because he is going to buy this game on Monday, and we are going to have Internet battles. It's going to be really cool." Ryan's mom left, and Ryan had to go to the bathroom before heading down for dinner. Jerry was left to exit out of the game which he did.

As he was turning to leave, he reached for his ball cap which he placed on a shoebox on the shelf above the computer. When he retrieved his hat, the force pulled the shoebox halfway over the ledge. The teeter tottering caused the box to fall over unto the floor spilling the contents all over. Jerry scrambled to the box putting the box back in order. As he did, he noticed that the contents were pictures not of random friends but on just one individual, a girl named Pam Lark. He also saw some love notes addressed to her, but they were never delivered.

Ryan was leaving the bathroom when he looked over to Jerry rummaging through his pictures before leaving his room. Like lighting, he burst back into the room. In a frantic tone, he said to Jerry, "I would appreciate it if you would leave that box and the contents in it alone." Ryan stormed across the room grabbing it out of Jerry's hands finishing, putting the pictures and notes back in the box.

Jerry offered his apology. "I'm sorry, Ryan. While grabbing my hat, I accidently bumped it off the shelf, and while putting back together, I saw the pictures and love notes. I guess I went further than I should have." Jerry had an expression of regret. Ryan couldn't remain mad at him and accepted his apology.

Jerry walked over to Ryan and said, "So, Pam, huh" giving him an elbow to the shoulder and a couple of raised eyebrows.

Ryan instantly came up with an excuse. "It's not what you think." His face getting redder with each passing second. "It's true that I do have a crush on her as does every guy in our school. Including you, I'm sure."

Jerry agreed by shaking his head when Ryan looked over to him. Jerry made a comment. "Then why don't you make a move?"

Ryan's face told the story of a million boys who had a crush on a girl but didn't have the guts to tell her. He said, "She has a boyfriend, jock Brad Steel. Plus, I am not the kind of guy that she would be interested in."

Jerry flapped his lips like he was letting out steam before he said, "Ryan, you loveless romantic, how do you know she isn't interested in you? You have to get over your fears and go talk to her."

Ryan stared at the floor as he said, "Easy for you to say. You can go up to any girl you want and carry on a conversation with no problem, including Pam."

Jerry expressed a confident look by lifting his left eyebrow while drooping his bottom lip down and slightly tilting his head, shrugging his shoulders at the same time. Then Jerry said, "True, I do have the gift of talking to girls, but I also know that if I liked a girl as much as you do to the point of making a love shrine box like that…" pointing to Ryan's box, "then I would muster up the courage to talk to her."

Ryan pondered on Jerry's last comment carefully as he placed the box back on the shelf stepping back, making slight adjustments. Repeating this process until he was satisfied with the positioning of the box on the shelf.

Jerry looked at the box puzzled and asked, "How did you get all of those pictures anyways?"

Ryan turned around from staring at his love shrine and said, "I have yearbooks. She made some news in the newspaper, so I clipped her picture from there as well as social media. I am on the yearbook committee, so of course, I made copies of pictures of her from there, and I have even ventured out to talk to her friends who are also friends with Angela." Angela was his sister, just older than him.

Jerry just stared at Ryan in disbelief as he said, "So you will talk to her friends but not directly to her!" Jerry rested his chin between his right thumb and pointer finger formed in a semi cup as if he was seriously thinking of the latest comment.

Ryan was in no mood for any of Jerry's sarcastic games, so Ryan decided to humor him as he said, "Okay, Jerry, you win. I'll work up my nerves and go up and talk to her sometime in the near future." Ryan now was heading for the door but noticed that Jerry wasn't following. He turned to find him in the same position he was in when he made the challenge.

Jerry slowly lowered his hand as he said, "Fair enough, but I have one stipulation." "What!" exclaimed Ryan.

His response made Jerry give off an evil grin while speaking. "I'm there when you talk to her!"

Ryan was now the one who had to use his wit. Jerry always managed to get his way when he presented a challenge. Ryan thought he came up with the solution. "I'll think about it and get back to you with my answer. Now let's go get some food before it's all gone."

Jerry got off the bed and walked over to the door by Ryan then said, "I want to know soon. It has to be by the end of the week."

They shook. All of a sudden, Ryan's secret love box had now became a challenge for him to talk to the most beautiful girl in the school. Relieved to finally have Jerry off of his back concerning Pam, now his stomach was being tied in knots about the idea of actually talking to his dream girl. It was bothering him so much that he needed his focus to be on something else. During dinner, Ryan was agonizing over the proposed challenge but more he was thinking of a way to either get out of it or make it so that Jerry wouldn't be around to see it. He was afraid of the huge embarrassment he would suffer, not to mention, the possible and most likely enormous beatdown he would receive from her jock boyfriend. His thoughts interrupted his dinner as his plate remained filled even when he asked to be excused.

Jerry had no problem wolfing down his meal and also asked to be excused, and they both headed back to Ryan's bedroom. Ryan watched as Jerry played his own game late into the night. Ryan was waiting for the phone to ring to have Jerry come back home. When it did, Ryan was only more than happy to send him home. As Jerry was leaving Ryan's room, halfway through the door, he peeked his head back in to remind Ryan.

"Hey, buddy, don't forget this weekend you promised to come to my kung fu tournament at the school gym."

As Jerry reminded Ryan of the tournament, his excitement began to rise then came an eerie reminder. "Oh yeah, you have to talk to Pam too. See you tomorrow."

Ryan's excitement dropped at the mention of Jerry's challenge all over again. "Don't remind me!

I am already dreading school on Monday—"

Jerry inserted, "So is that when you're going to talk to her?"

Ryan answered back not so politely, "I didn't say that. It just so happens that we have two classes together, and I will be sweating bullets even more than usual, thanks to you." Ryan gave Jerry an evil eye, staring him down, but it had no effect for Jerry was basking in delight watching Ryan squirmed.

Jerry again attempted to leave. He was stopped by a question from Ryan. "Why is it that you find all of my hidden secrets, then you blackmail me to a point that I have to face them? Answer me, why?"

Jerry gleamed even more. "It's a gift that I have acquired over the years." Jerry was looking at the ceiling with a boastful look on his face. He broke his stare and asked Ryan, "Hey, we are still going to Mike's after school to get me that game right?"

Ryan badly wanted to say no but instead he said, "Yeah, I'll meet you by the flagpole after school.

Don't be late," pointing at Jerry.

To which he replied, "No worries, man, all right. Well, I better go, but I'll see you tomorrow" as he left Ryan's room down the stairs and out the front door to cross Ryan's front yard to get to his house. As soon as Ryan knew Jerry was gone, he grabbed his box and pulled out his favorite picture of Pam.

A five-by-five school portrait, he focused just on her face with that image currently in his memory. He bimagined walking up to her, looking right into her face, and talking to her. He could see the people around him including Pam laughing at him, not to mention the sore black eye obtained from her boyfriend. His thought pattern was disrupted by a gentle knock.

Ryan spoke loudly, "Come in." Ryan had an idea of who it would be and his guess was right.

His mother softly opened the door and entered in, then with a tender voice, his mom said, "Ryan, are you all right?"

Ryan responded by saying, "Yes, mom, I just have a couple of things on my mind is all," hoping this would be enough to have her leave his room.

She persisted and asked, "Do you want to talk about it, son?"

Ryan was getting annoyed but tried not to show it in his response. He said, "No, mom, I would rather not. I just want to be alone right now." He laid face down on his bed covering as much of the bed as he could. His arms and feet hanging over the sides of the bed.

His mom could sense that he wanted to be alone and said before leaving his room, "Well, if you change your mind, you know you can always come to me."

With a muffled voice he could make out, he said, "Thanks, Mom." Even though Ryan didn't want to talk to anyone, his mom left him feeling better like only moms can do. Ryan closed his eyes after his mom left as he was carried away into a carefree world of his imagination. As a knight in shining armor, he was about to rescue his princess when his door slammed open dissolving this world instantly. By the brute force, there was only one person who it could be. "Dad," exclaimed Ryan.

His dad spoke to him sternly, "Ryan, I am going to require a lot out of you this coming weekend.

There are quite a few chores that need to be done. I have a list already. It will only grow larger."

Ryan got off his bed as his dad left his room. "But, Dad, I promised Jerry that I would support him at his kung fu tournament this coming weekend."

Came a desperate plea, his dad answered with no remorse, "I'm sorry, son, but I need you more this weekend than Jerry does. So you'll just have to cancel your get together."

Ryan muttered under his breath, "Just like last time." "What was that?" demanded his father.

Ryan answered, "Yes, sir!"

His dad stared him down as he said, "That's what I thought you said." He closed his door as he left Ryan backed up toward his bed.

When the back of Ryan's legs hit the bed frame, he buckled his knees free falling till he landed on his bed in a sitting potion. He began to stew over his emotions as he continued his heart grew bitter and bitter. Finally, he had to talk to someone.

He left his room searching the house for his mother and found her in the laundry room downstairs, folding clothes.

She noticed him and asked, "What can I do for you, Ryan?"

Ryan entered the room, sat down on one of the chairs by the laundry baskets, then he said,

"Mom, can I talk to you about Dad for a minute?"

His mom nodded and Ryan continued, "Okay, this coming weekend is Jerry's regional kung fu tournament. I promised I would attend two weeks ago, but Dad came to me and said that his chores are more important than my promise. This is the second time I will have to cancel going to one of his tournaments because of Dad."

His mom could see the frustration in his face and asked, "Did you mention your plans to him?"

Ryan answered, "Yes, I did. He said that he needs me more than Jerry does. Can you talk to him and see if I can still go?"

Ryan's mom finished folding the shirt she was working on, walked over to him kissing his forehead as she said, "I can't promise anything, but I will talk to him."

Ryan hugged her and said with confidence in his voice, "Thanks, Mom. He'll listen to you more than he will to me."

She left the room and went to the garage where his dad was working on a small project. Ryan remained in the laundry room anxiously waiting for his mom's return. Ryan only had to wait a short amount of time, but it felt like an eternity.

His mom came back. She walked over to her son and sat in the chair next to him. "I talked to your father, and while we were talking, he got a phone call from some of his old high school buddies. They want to get together this coming weekend, so he won't be able to use you after all. You're free to attend Jerry's tournament."

Ryan got excited and beat her in giving her a hug as he said, "Thanks, Mom, for everything. You're the best." His anger went away, and he suddenly had an urge to play his game. Quietly, he went to his room and began playing. In the middle of the game, he pictured Pam, and just as quickly as the urge came, it left. He almost got sick to his stomach and decided to shut off his computer and just go to bed.

Chapter 2

The next day was filled with a full afternoon with Jerry who was excited to play his game at Ryan's and anxious to get his own tomorrow. Of course, he would not let Ryan forgot about his promise to talk to Pam.

Jerry's parents made him come home early because it was a school night. On the way out, Jerry gave Ryan a little reminder. "After school by the flagpole then to the mall. Don't forget."

Ryan responded, "How can I? You remind me every few minutes. I will actually be happy to get you the game so you stop bothering me."

Jerry laughed as he closed the door on his way heading back to his house. Ryan headed back to his room and looked at his clock on the dresser. It was ten past nine in the evening, and he decided to retire for the evening. As he laid in his bed, he tossed and turned, not able to get his mind to shut down. He decided to think of something that always calmed him down. He pictured Pam's face, and as he admired her beauty, he was able to relax and fall into a deep sleep.

Ryan was having a magical dream of him and Pam. They were dating, and Ryan had taken her on a romantic dinner lit only by candles. As Pam leaned in to kiss him, she said, "If you want a shower and breakfast, you better wake up now!"

His dream was dissolved by his dad's thunderous voice from downstairs. He got up and went to the bathroom. While he was showering, he grew immune to the constant nagging of his sisters. After his shower, he got dressed and rushed downstairs. He gobbled down his breakfast so he wouldn't be late meeting Jerry to walk to school.

Before Ryan went outside, he grabbed his backpack. When he closed the door and turned around, he was startled by an overeager Jerry being right in front of him. Ryan said, "I wish you never took kung fu. They trained you too well in the art of sneaking around in complete silence. I swear you almost gave me a heart attack."

Jerry just laughed and said in an enthusiastic tone, "So today is the day that we go and get my game and possibly the day that you talk to Pam too." Ending his comment with another laugh.

Ryan quickly grew tired of Jerry's laughter, so he spoke up boldly, "As a matter of fact, I think that I will talk to Pam today!" His comment abruptly silenced Jerry. "I don't know when or where I will talk to her, but I plan on talking to her today."

Jerry turned and said, "Well, when you try to make your move, you will text me so I can be right there!"

Jerry's face beamed in delight, but Ryan responded, "Nope!"

Jerry's merry face melted at Ryan's answer. Jerry spoke up. "But you promised me," Jerry spoke bitterly.

Ryan spoke just as boldly as before, "No, I said that I would think about it, and well, I thought about it and decided that you really don't need to be there when I talk to her." Ryan's remainder of the walk was full of joy as Jerry was speechless, and when he would speak, it was a desperate plea to change his mind, but Ryan wouldn't budge.

As they entered the school grounds, Jerry's persistence would not cease. Finally after the bell rang, Ryan said in frustration, "Jerry, give it up. You aren't going to be there. Besides, I doubt she will even acknowledge that I exist, so just drop it. I'll see you at lunch."

Jerry separated from Ryan, still being disheartened by Ryan's decision, as he finally went to his first class.

Ryan also had to rush to his classroom in order to not be late, but luckily, his teacher was running late too. He sat down toward the back and immediately noticed Pam sitting toward the front of the class. He was admiring her long black hair when Mr. Brob, their teacher, entered the room.

He spoke in his nerdy voice, "Sorry, class, for my tardiness today. We will begin a lab project that should take a couple of weeks to complete. We will be pairing up randomly. I will pull out a boy's name, and he will pull out his partner of the opposite sex."

Everyone including Ryan giggled at Mr. Brob motioning sex. Mr. Brob spoke as sternly as he could, "Settle down, class, be quiet!" His comment was followed with a slap on his desk with a yardstick which quieted the class.

Ryan sat back as he thought to himself, *Random partners? There is no way I will be paired up with Pam.*

Mr. Brob began to call out names, and partnerships were being formed.

So far, both Ryan and Pam remained unpaired. Suddenly, Ryan heard an eerie call. "Ryan, it's your turn."

Slowly, he got up and walked to the front of the class walking right by Pam trying not to look at her. He was sweating profusely as reached in the other box and pulled out a name. He hung on to it after looking at it. Mr. Brob had to nudge him with the box to make him read out the name.

He opened the slip of paper; the name on the paper made him sweat even more. He turned to the teacher and whispered, "Can I please pick a different name?"

His teacher just nodded in the negative, so he turned around with the class chuckling at Ryan's performance. Ryan then said out loud, "My partner is Pam."

He returned to his seat and waited for the remainder of the class to get their partners. Finally, it was announced that the class was to get together with their partners. Ryan didn't have to worry about going to Pam; she came to him.

As she got to his desk, Ryan's head was buried in his arm, folded on his desk. His depressing thoughts were lightened by a sweet voice. "Hi, my name is Pam, and your name is Ryan, right?"

Ryan sat upright very quickly. "Yes!"

Pam giggled at Ryan's behavior. She also saw that his desk was moist from him sweating to which she asked, "Are you okay?" She had a very concerned look on her face.

Ryan got a little embarrassed as he said, "Yeah, you know how rough chess matches can get. In my last match, I think I injured my neck, so if I don't keep an eye contact or I rest my head on the desk, that is why."

Pam chuckled at his comment. She then leaned over a desk pulling over and aligned with his. She then said, "You are very funny, but we better get started on our project. It looks like we are going to be together for a couple of weeks doing this."

Ryan, who had opened the packet to avoid looking at Pam, looked and smiled at her and she returned the favor. Pam had opened her own packet and was reading it, so Ryan decided to use this time to scan the room for her muscular boyfriend. He didn't want to get an unexpected elbow to the back of his neck or head. Then he remembered that he transferred to another class because of poor grades. Ryan could now relax and focused on their project.

Pam and him were able to breeze through the packet, and Ryan decided, because they were so far ahead of the majority of the class, to talk to her about something besides the project. Ryan nervously fidgeted with his fingers as he worked up the nerve to talk to her. Finally, he said, "Pam."

She looked up at him. "Yes, Ryan?"

Ryan was even more nervous as he spoke. "I have a question to ask you and please don't get mad at me."

Pam looked at him with her sweet eyes which beckoned him to continue. "Okay, what is it?" Ryan didn't waste any more time as he openly said, "Well, this is kind of embarrassing for me.

But I have had a huge crush on you since the seventh grade, and well, I was wondering if I could ask you out on a date?"

Pam kept her gaze on him as she leaned over the desks toward him to give her answer. Ryan thought, *Maybe, I'll get a kiss too.*

Pam opened her mouth but didn't get anything out because the bell rang disrupting her thought as she began getting her stuff together for her next class.

Ryan still didn't have his answer, so he tapped her shoulder. She turned around and franticly answered, "What?"

Her answer almost discouraged him from asking her. "What do you think about our possible date?"

Pam answered calmer, "That is so sweet, but I am already in a relationship. You know Brad, the quarterback of the football team, and we are pretty serious."

Ryan was expecting that answer, but it didn't make it hurt any less. "Right, my mistake. I knew you were a couple. I'm sorry for asking you and making you question your current relationship. It won't happen again!" He slung his bag over his shoulder and left the room hastily for his next class so he wouldn't be late, not giving Pam any opportunity to dig into his feelings any deeper. As Ryan sat in his class, all he could think of was Pam and their next class together and how awkward it was going to be for him. After he finished writing his homework assignment, he got ready for the bell and his next class with Pam and Brad.

After the bell rang ending the second period, Ryan bolted out of his class and was surprised by a tap on his shoulder. He turned around to see Jerry who came out of nowhere.

He said, "So, man, did you talk to her, and if so, how did it go?" Jerry's face beamed in supportive excitement.

Ryan's face and tone wasn't even close to being excited as he said, "Oh, well, it completely sucked. She shot me down with the boyfriend phrase, and to make the matters worse, I have the next class with Pam and her boyfriend. I am in big trouble."

Jerry now expressed sympathy. "Ryan, I am sorry, man. Hey, my class is right next to yours, so I will be waiting for you in case Brad tries something. Are we still cool for after school and Saturday too, right?"

Ryan looked up with a little more confidence knowing he had Jerry's protection. "Yes to both. I need something to get my mind off Pam." They both walked to their next classes.

Ryan arrived at his class. He crossed the room and sat in the back to avoid sitting in his normal spot close to Pam which was a couple of desks away. He was busy getting out his supplies for his math class as he thought, *Tomorrow, I will talk to Mr. Brob and request a different partner. Pam just isn't going—*

His thought pattern was disrupted by a stern but familiar voice. "Are you busy?" It was Pam, and she wasn't in a good mood.

When he saw how mad she looked, it was almost enough to make him jump out of his seat. He responded by saying in a frantic tone, "I'm sorry. I didn't realize that you wanted this seat." He began to gather his gear together to move, but Pam sat down and motioned him to do the same.

She spoke in a more peaceful voice, "Ryan, you left first period without letting me get another word in. I do like you, but like I said, I am with Brad. If I wasn't, you would be on the top of my list."

Ryan began to sweat all over again as he said, "Do you really mean that?"

Pam gave him a flirtatious smile. "Of course, I do. Now do you mind if I sit here?" She pointed to the seat right next to him. Ryan shook his head no. She sat down next to him, and he began to daydream of them being a couple. Ryan completely forgot about Brad as they finished their work and began to discuss likes and dislikes.

They were surprised to find out they had a lot more in common than they thought and began to develop a friendship around their common ground. After the bell, they were walking out of the room together talking and heading to lunch. Ryan's ear suddenly began to hurt. He grabbed it exclaiming, "Ouch, what hit me?" He turned around to find Brad, not in a good mood.

"That's not the only thing that is going to be hurting!" Brad balled up his fist and was getting ready to throw it at Ryan's face when his forward motion was stopped abruptly by Jerry grabbing his wrist.

Jerry then said, "Hey, man, leave him alone. He didn't do anything wrong." He let go of his wrist. Brad angrily blurted out, "Stealing my girlfriend is doing something wrong, bud."

Jerry looked over to Ryan and found Pam aiding him in his pain. He then turned back to Brad and said, "So it appears that she is with him. That only means that you can date one of the girls you were cheating on with her."

This made Brad furious as he shouted, "After school behind the football stadium, be there!"

Jerry calmly said in a mocking tone, "No, thanks, I have plans, but thanks for the invite and you have fun." Jerry turned his back, and Brad used this opportunity to deliver a cheap shot to the back of the head. He still had his fist balled and threw it as hard as he could.

He was even more surprised to have Jerry avoid it without turning around then he suddenly buckled in pain. As Jerry had thrown his own punch, landing it right on the bridge of his nose causing an instant nosebleed.

Jerry then turned to Pam and Ryan and said, "Come on, we have to get out of here."

They and the rest of the students got up and left the area heading to the cafeteria for lunch. Ryan sat down next to Pam and had a small adrenaline rush. This was the closest he had ever come to being in trouble. He was just waiting to hear Jerry's and his name come over the intercom and be asked to come talk to the principal, but it never happened.

After school, Ryan was surprised to find out that he had beaten Jerry to the flagpole. He didn't wait long as Jerry came running over to him out of breath.

He said in between gasps for breath, "I'm sorry, Ryan, I had to do something for my science teacher, but I got here as soon as I could."

Ryan got up from the cinder block foundation built around the flagpole and said, "It's okay. I really haven't been waiting long."

They both headed toward the curb when they were stopped by a car parking right in front of them. Neither one of them recognized the car, and they were even more surprised to see the window being rolled down.

Ryan was afraid that it was Brad coming to finish what he started, but as the window rolled farther down, he could clearly see inside the tinted windows was Pam.

Pam spoke in a cheerful voice, "Hey, guys, do you need a ride anywhere?"

Ryan couldn't take his eyes off her and thought, *I can't believe she is offering us a ride.* Ryan just stood there.

Finally, Jerry leaned over and said, "Dude, are you going to answer her?"

Ryan smiled at her as he said, "Sure."

Pam smiled right back at him. "Great, where are we heading?"

Ryan was quicker at answering her this time. "We need to go to the mall. Is that okay with you?"

Ryan did his best pathetic look. Jerry just rolled his eyes.

Pam said, "Are you kidding? I practically live there." She stared at Ryan smiling and patted the passenger seat.

Ryan was about to be melted where he stood. Jerry had no problem getting in the back seat and found a comfortable position. Ryan slid into the passenger seat enjoying every part of it.

After he got buckled up, Pam said, "Are you ready to go?"

Ryan shook his head rapidly while Jerry, acting cool, replied, "Oh yeah."

Pam then started heading in the mall's direction. The drive created an awkward silence.

Ryan spoke out of desperation of wanting to break the silence. "Pam, are you sure this is okay with you?"

Pam just smiled and looked at Ryan then said, "Absolutely."

Ryan began to relax when he remembered, "And Brad won't get mad?"

Pam, without any hesitation, said, "He has no reason to get mad. I broke up with him when I found out that Jerry was telling the truth by catching him in the act."

Jerry nudged Ryan to get him to make a move, so Ryan said, "So I guess you are available to go on a date then?"

Pam started to blush. "I would really like to."

Ryan's excitement skyrocketed to the rest of the way to the mall. It was like he was on cloud nine all because Jerry challenged him.

When they arrived at the mall, they all agreed to meet back in the food court in two hours. Pam saw some of her friends, who were just dying to hear all about Ryan. She speed walked over to them.

Jerry looked at Ryan who followed Pam with his eyes until she was out of sight. Jerry interfered with his dreamland by saying, "Okay, lover boy, we'll see her in a couple of hours. Let's go to Mike's Game Room so we can get me that game!"

Ryan and Jerry had to head in the opposite direction of Pam making it was easier to concentrate. They arrived at the game store, and Ryan knew exactly which section the game was in. After scanning the shelves, he finally spotted two copies of the game. Someone had taken one of the copies, so Ryan quickly snatched the last copy and returned to Jerry who was already at the checkout stand.

After Jerry purchased the game, he spotted something in the store across from the store they were in. Ryan was busy looking at different games, so Jerry said, "Hey, Ryan, I need to do something real quick, but I'll be back."

Ryan said, "Take your time. We are in no rush. We still have forty-five minutes left."

Jerry then left the store. Ryan didn't find any games he liked, so he decided to go to the meeting place to wait for Pam and Jerry. When he got there, he saw Pam sitting down enjoying a smoothie. So he casually walked over to her from behind and surprised her when he sat down beside her saying, "Hi, sweetheart."

She covered her chest where her heart was located and said, "You scared me. I thought I was going to have a heart attack."

Ryan apologized, and she accepted. They continued their conversation were they left off at school.

When Jerry didn't find Ryan in the game store, he thought he might find him in their meeting spot. Sure enough, there was Ryan and Pam carrying on a conversation. When he got closer, someone must have told a funny joke because they were both laughing uncontrollably. Jerry approached them from the side and said, "I hope I didn't catch you guys at a bad time."

Ryan tried to control his laughter and had to hold his sides from laughing so hard. "I'm sorry, Jerry. Pam just told me the funniest joke. Do you want to hear it?"

Jerry answered honestly, "No, I would really like to go home and play this game." Ryan noticed a second bag but didn't think much of it.

Pam said, "We probably should go. I need to get home too."

Ryan got up and did the gentlemen thing by holding her chair then he said, "So are we still on for Friday?" Pam nodded in agreement.

Jerry said, "What are you doing on Friday?"

Ryan responded, "It's our first date. Just dinner and a movie." This made Jerry smile.

On the way home, Ryan remembered about Jerry's tournament on Saturday while holding Pam's hand. He then asked, "Hey, Pam, would you like to go to one of Jerry's kung fu tournaments on Saturday with me?"

Pam said, "That sounds like fun. I would love to go."

Ryan got a big smile as he thought, *I got two dates straight in a row.*

Pam dropped them off at Jerry's house, and Jerry had to drag Ryan inside because he wanted to watch Pam drove out of his sight.

After Jerry got Ryan inside, he said, "I am beginning to think that getting you and Pam together was a bad idea rather than a good one."

Ryan smiled as he said, "Jerry, I am glad you challenged me. I found out that my dream girl actually likes me."

Jerry said sarcastically, "Well, you better invite me to the wedding."

Ryan laughed then he said, "Let's go get you started on this game." The rest of the week was filled with Internet playing of the game between Jerry and Ryan.

When Ryan got a free minute, he would use it to talk with Pam. Ryan could barely wait for Friday night. After school, he rushed home, not waiting for Jerry. Boy, did he got an earful when Jerry got to his house, but Ryan didn't care. He continued to get dressed up in some of his nicer clothes. After some proper hygiene, he got the flowers he purchased for Pam and then made the walk over to Pam's house.

When Ryan knocked on the door, he was surprised by her dad who was a very large kind-of- scary guy. Ryan timidly said, "Hi, I'm Pam's date. Is she home, sir?"

Pam's dad was about to have some fun messing with his mind. But was interrupted by Pam sprinting to the door. "Hey, Ryan, I have been waiting," said Pam who was a little out of breath.

Ryan somewhat stunned by Pam's beauty as he said, "You look great tonight."

Pam giggled to herself then Ryan remembered that he had flowers for her. While offering the flowers, he said, "These are for you…"

Pam accepted the flowers, smelling them.

Ryan continued, "Pretty flowers for a pretty girl."

Pam's dad rolled his eyes. Pam quickly put her flowers in their kitchen and came back grabbing

Ryan's right hand as she said, "Let's go before my dad does something embarrassing."

Ryan nodded his head as he agreed with her. Their whole night was magical. Ryan took Pam to the most expensive restaurant that he could afford, then after dinner, they went to the movies. Pam wanted to see a chick flick, so Ryan agreed and actually really enjoyed it.

On the walk home, Ryan was enjoying the star-filled sky and holding Pam's hand, then he asked her, "Are you still wanting to go to Jerry's tournament tomorrow?"

Pam smiled as she said, "As long as you will be there, I will love it, but you will have to explain to me what goes on there because I have never been to one."

Ryan laughed and said, "I'll explain as much as I know." The remainder of the walk was heavenly for both of them. As Pam went inside of her house, Ryan said, "Until tomorrow, have sweet dreams." Pam smiled and slide inside slowly closing the door. Ryan walked away happier than he had ever been. When he got home, he changed into his pajamas and quickly fell asleep. The next morning, Ryan cracked open his eyelids to find Jerry standing over him.

He was about to knock him over when Jerry said, "Hey, champ, are you ready for today? I am pumped. Come on, my parents are waiting outside to take us to the school." Jerry grabbed Ryan's hand and tried to drag him out of bed.

Ryan said, "Jerry, I told you already. Pam is going with me, so she is driving me over there. Then afterwards, we are going for an ice cream. Do you want to come?"

Jerry let loose of his arm and said, "I'll see you over there." He rushed out filled with disappointment and down to his parent's car waiting for him. Jerry and his parents pulled away, and not long after, Pam pulled up to Ryan's house.

Crystal looked out the window and yelled upstairs, "Ryan, there's a red sport car parked out front."

Ryan jumped out of bed and was brushing his teeth. He quickly finished and rushed downstairs pulling his shirt overhead nearly colliding with April, the oldest of his twin sisters.

She blurted out, "Watch where you are going!"

Ryan didn't have time to watch where he was going. His focus was on his second date with Pam.

Pam was in the process of knocking on the door when Ryan opened it, completely surprising her, "Hi, Ryan, are you ready to go?"

Ryan grinned. "Yeah, just let me tell my mom that I am leaving…" He turned around and saw his mom walking into the kitchen. "Hey, Mom, I'm leaving now."

His mom answered back, "Have a good time."

Ryan turned back around smiling saying, "Let's go." They walked to Pam's car both expressing how much fun last night was.

Ryan opened Pam's door for her before getting in the passenger seat. Pam expressed her gratitude. "Thank you, Ryan. You are such a gentleman, unlike Brad at all."

Ryan smiled. "My mom always says treat a woman the way they deserve to be treated."

Pam leaned over and said, "She is a good teacher."

Ryan got tingly all over as Pam hold his hand and drove off toward the school. Ryan saw that the parking lot was getting filled.

"We better hurry if we want good seats." Pam found a parking spot not far from the school entrance as they hurried inside.

When they got to the gym, Ryan pointed to a poster holding a roster of the fighters and a bracket then said, "In this tournament, there are thirty fighters. Each one has to fight within their skill level first, then as they win, they move up to harder fighters. It's a single elimination, so if you lose, you're out. Jerry is in the top of his class. He's a fourth degree black belt." As Ryan looked over the contestants, he saw that Jerry had fought all but one of the fighters.

Ryan then escorted Pam to their seat where they began to watch as the tournament commenced.

As the fights continued, Pam had some good questions. "How is a match winner determined?"

Ryan answered, "A winner is determined by hitting your opponent three times in one of three areas. The first is the head and neck, the second is the shoulder and chest, and the third is the mid waist. Below the waist is a penalty unless you hit them in the legs to knock them down in order to get a hit for a point."

Pam asked, "Is there any other way a match is won?"

Ryan responded, "Yes, a match can also be won by disqualification by too many illegal hits or leaving the circle to many times, but more likely, it is by a knockout. This is when a contestant is hit so hard that they are unconscious. Jerry has won many matches by knockout."

As the tournament advanced, Jerry was easily beating all of his competitors and so was the unfamiliar fighter that Ryan didn't know. As the tournament went on, all the contestants were getting beaten except for Jerry and Jesse Fou, the top ranked fighter that Ryan was unfamiliar with. They would be the last fighters to determine the next kung fu champion.

Ryan had an opportunity to talk with Jerry before his last fight. "Hey, Jerry, how are you feeling?"

Jerry responded, "I'm pretty good but a little concerned about my last fight. Jesse is good. I have been watching him. I just hope I have what it takes to beat him."

Ryan gave an encouraging comment. "Jerry, you're the best fighter I know, and I believe you can beat him."

Jerry smiled and turned around to prepare for his final fight. He stretched out all of his muscles then had his hands and feet tapped before stepping on to the mat. Jesse too stepped on to the mat. The official gave them instructions and started the fight by asking them to bow toward each other than to him.

Both fighters got into their stances. The whistle was blown starting the fight, both fighters began by circling each other. The crowd was silent awaiting the first strike. Ryan focused on Jerry, trying to think how he would attack Jesse. But Jesse made the first move as he rushed forward throwing the top half of his body into Jerry's body, then with lightning speed, Jesse thrust his right fist toward Jerry's face. Jerry studied this move from other fights today and blocked it with his left hand and threw his right hand into Jesse's left side unexpectedly, causing that portion of his body to slightly collapse from Jerry's force.

Jerry was rewarded with one point, and they were asked to go back to their corners before they would retake their stances for the next part of the fight. Jesse had anger flowing from his eyes then through the rest of his body. He had never lost the first round before until today. Jerry gained confidence but still feared Jesse's skill and expert moves. The referee blew the whistle starting the second round. This time, Jesse wasted no time as he ran at Jerry aiming to hit Jerry low at the ankles.

Jerry began to quickly prepare for the blow, but Jesse changed his course and landed a front kick to his face. He did this by anchoring his left foot firmly on the mat and cocking his right leg, then he swiftly unloaded his powerful kick to Jerry's check bone, making him fall to the mat gaining him a point. At first, there was no movement from Jerry. The crowd was getting concerned, but slowly, Jerry began to pick himself up off the mat. This brought relief to Ryan and Jerry's parents. The referee called a time-out in order for Jerry to gain consciousness and determine if he wanted to continue on with the match.

Jesse went to his corner as instructed while Jerry's trainer carried him to his corner and sat him on a chair. Jerry inhaled smelling salts from his trainer, Master Pou. He quickly regained his consciousness.

After a second, Jerry asked, "Master Pou, what happened?"

Master Pou answered by saying, "Jesse has been training some new forms of kung fu. With lightning speed reflexes and having the ability to change stances just as fast and deliver punches or kicks with deadly accurateness as you have witnessed. In order for you to win, you need to throw him off his style and make him fight your style, avoid his attacks so you can deliver your own."

Jerry bowed to his trainer and reentered the circle to engage his opponent. Jesse was eager to beat on Jerry some more.

The referee walked over to Jerry and asking, "Son, are you sure you want to continue?"

Jerry shook his head yes. The referee then asked the two fighters to take their stances and began the third round by blowing his whistle. This time, Jesse circled the mat like the first round. Jerry cautiously watched his movements, as Jesse advanced again toward him, attempting a similar move.

Jerry countered his movements by moving sideways and then landed a kick on Jesse's shoulders with his left leg and another to his head with his right foot. Jesse began to fall downwards by Jerry's first kick. But after the second kick to the head, it sent him falling on his back rolling in agonizing pain. Another point was awarded to Jerry who was now leading the match two to one.

This time, the referee called a time-out for Jesse's trainer to carry him to his corner; Jerry went to his corner without instruction from the referee. Jerry waited and watched as Jesse was gaining his consciousness, then he was just as eager to come after him as Jerry was eager to come after him. Jerry also could tell that he didn't like the counsel his trainer was giving him. Finally, Jesse's trainer walked to the referee giving his permission to allow Jesse to continue fighting. As the fourth round began, the tension in the air was thick for the two fighters and all the viewers.

Jesse and Jerry circled each other, then Jerry made his move first rushing in, attempting the same move that Jesse got his first point from. But Jesse easily blocked Jerry's amateur move and did a counter punch attack. Jerry unknowingly blocked Jesse's punch off to his right with his side left arm knocking Jesse off balance. Noticing this, Jerry threw a punch to Jesse's side which Jesse blocked. Jerry was counting on this as Jesse hold Jerry's hand. Jerry did a cartwheel kick landing square on Jesse's forehead causing him to do a complete backflip landing facedown.

Jerry landed straddling him with his right arm set to deliver a finishing punch, but Jerry's kick gave him the winning point also knocking Jesse out. As the crowd ran from the bleachers to congratulate Jerry, Ryan's momentum was stopped as an eerie feeling came over him like he was being watched by someone or something. He quickly turned around and scanned the rafters of the second story of the gym but found nothing.

Pam came over to Ryan and asked, "Are you okay?"

Ryan turned to her, turning his thoughts from the mystery eyes, and said, "Yeah, I just had a strange feeling is all. Let's go talk to Jerry and congratulate him."

They both made their way through the crowd toward Jerry. Ryan could still feel the eyes looking at him. When they got to Jerry, Ryan forgot all about the hidden eyes. All three of them began to talk about their favorite parts of the fight.

In the middle of their joyous conversation, an announcer began to talk over the loudspeakers. "If everyone could please take their seat, the award ceremony will begin…" Everyone began to shuffle around finding an available seat.

The announcer continued, "In third place is Randy Heath…" The audience clapped as Randy went and accepted his trophy and stood on the third place spot on the award podium.

"In second place is Jesse Fou…" Again, the audience clapped as he too accepted his trophy and took his spot.

Then the announcer continued, "And the winner and champion of the tournament is Jerry Thane." The audience exploded in clapping, shouting, and whistling as Jerry took his well-deserved spot on the podium. Jerry beamed as he basked in this moment and got his picture taken with his trophy and the two other fighters for the local paper.

After all the pictures were taken and Jerry was finished talking to the contestants, especially Jesse, he scanned the gym for Ryan and Pam and found them talking to his parents. Jerry rushed across the gym to talk to them. When Jerry approached them, they all stopped, turning to him. They were all happy for his accomplishment.

Jerry walked to his parents and asked, "Mom, Dad, is it all right if I go with Ryan and Pam for an ice cream?"

Jerry's mom said, "Of course, son, have a good time."

Jerry turned to Ryan and Pam and asked, "Is it still okay if I join you two?"

Ryan smiled. "Of course, it is Jerry. You're my best friend and nothing will ever change that."Ryan and Pam waited outside of the locker room while

Jerry changed. When he came out, he said, "I need to drop my clothes in my parents car before we leave, then we are good to go." Ryan said, "Okay."

All three walked outside of the school. Ryan and Pam waited for Jerry at Pam's car. When Jerry arrived, they got in and began to leave the parking lot.

Before they left, Jerry said, "Ryan, I am so excited for your birthday tomorrow. I have the coolest gift for you."

Ryan got embarrassed, and surprised Pam replied, "So your birthday is tomorrow? Well, I don't have a gift for you yet, but I will have one in time."

Ryan sunk down in his seat as they drove off to the ice cream parlor. As the car disappeared out of sight, two large reptilian figures remained in the shadows watching their every move.

Chapter 3

It was Sunday night as Ryan was all by himself on his fifteenth birthday. Like the usual, his family seemed to had forgotten all about it because his sisters always had more interesting and important matters that took up his parent's attention. While he was leisurely swinging back and forth on one of his sister's swing sets in the backyard looking at the moon, a gentle night breeze swirled around the house by his mother's lilac bush carrying the sweet aroma to his senses. Reminding him of happier days, it was then when Jerry came through the gate to wish him a happy birthday.

"Happy birthday, Ryan. Aren't you supposed to be inside celebrating with your family?" said Jerry.

Ryan looked up from the ground and said, "I was inside, but my bratty twin sisters wanted to play a game. So my parents were more eager to play with them than to pay attention to me. By the way, how did you know I was in the backyard?"

Jerry said, "When I was upstairs in my bedroom, I happened to look outside. I saw you in the swing set, so I came right over to your backyard."

It was then that Jerry remembered his gift, pulling it from behind him. "I really hope you enjoy your present from me."

Ryan eagerly tore into his present from Jerry. As Ryan unwrapped his gift, he saw that it was concealed in another box. After Ryan opened the flaps of the box, it revealed a dragon model. Ryan could put it together and paint it whatever color he wished. Ryan's love of dragons had spread all over his face, and this allowed Jerry to find this gift and thinking it would be perfect for him.

Ryan had purchased many books on this subject and had several figurines and artwork. In fact, whenever he would do any sort of artwork, it mainly consisted of dragons. As Ryan and Jerry excitedly examined the new gift, they were both unaware of two very large reptiles that had approached them. Jerry was the first one to look up from the excitement to discover the scary lizards.

Jerry shook Ryan's shoulder to get his attention. Slowly, he said, "Ryan, we are being watched, look!" He pointed in the direction of the lizards.

As Ryan looked up, one of the two lizards rapidly advanced toward him until one was about a foot away. When he looked over the lizard, he discovered both of them were pitch black and each of the scales were outlined with a forest green. These lizards not only startled Ryan but Jerry too, and as he turned to run, he was stopped when he was face-to-face with the other lizard.

Ryan backed up until he was touching Jerry's back. Jerry leaned over to his left ear and asked him, "Ryan, do you recognize what type of lizard these two are?"

Ryan responded in a nervous tone, "No, I don't recognize them from our Boy Scout manual or any of my other animal books. Unless I am mistaken, the only lizards that have any proof of aggressively attacking and hunting people are Komodo dragons." Ryan not only loved dragons but any kind of animal or creature he could read about or study.

Ryan began to inspect the lizard in front of him. He noticed an enlarged claw five times the size of the rest of the claws. Upon this detection, he leaned back over to Jerry and said, "Jerry, look at the front left foot and the inward toe. What do you see?"

As Jerry began to look over the lizard, he to found the claw. In a scared tone, he mustered, "Ryan, I see a very large scary claw. Do you think they are going to hurt us?"

Ryan was about to answer Jerry's question but was interrupted by a different question. "Are you just going to stand there shaking or can we please get going?"

Ryan was confused, so he turned to Jerry and asked him, "Did you just say that?" Jerry replied, "No, I thought you did."

But then the voice spoke again saying, "You are both wrong. I said it, but don't be afraid. We aren't here to hurt you."

Ryan turned his attention from Jerry toward an open area in his yard, and in a quivering voice, he uttered, "Who are you?"

The lizard in front of Ryan stood up on its hind legs and said, "I will tell you later."

Neither Ryan nor Jerry knew what to do. Jerry was about to turn to Ryan and tell him to run when the lizard in front of Jerry stood up on its hind legs. It then stated in an impatient tone, "Can we please get going! We still have a lot to do tonight."

Puzzled, Jerry leaned into the magical lizard in front of him and said in an eager voice, "Okay, smart-talking lizard. What are you doing here?"

To this the lizard replied rather rudely, "Well, first off, we are not lizards but dragons."

The dragon in front of Ryan began to speak in a much calmer voice, "And you two are dragon leirds chosen by the Dragon Master herself. You may call me Nogar." Upon finishing his comment, he bowed out of respect toward Ryan.

After Nogar's comment, the other dragon piped up, puffing out his chest, and in a boastful tone,

he said, "And my name is Sparcan."

With a little laugh and in a joking voice, Ryan said, "We aren't leirds…" while moving his hands around as if he was royalty. "We are just kids."

Ryan was still continuing to laugh while Jerry was more struck with fear. Nogar spoke up in a peaceful but losing patience voice, "If you two are not indeed dragon leirds, then you will have no problem picking each of us up. Upon picking us up, if our enlarged key claws do not glow and turn a certain color, then we will not bother you any further."

Ryan pulled Jerry aside to speak to him in private. "Jerry, let's just pick them up. Nothing is going to happen. Dragons don't exist. They have to be some kind of a hallucination." Ryan then moved in closer to Jerry and nudged his shoulder with his elbow and said, "You didn't happen to line my present with a hallucinating powder, did you?" When he ended his comment, he was trying not to laugh.

Jerry wasn't as confident, and in a nervous voice, he responded, "But, Ryan, if dragons don't exist, then why are there two talking ones in your backyard?"

Ryan said, "I will prove it by going out there and picking up one of those hallucination dragons." With that, Ryan marched over to the dragon who called himself Nogar reached down and picked him up. Ryan yelled over to Jerry, "See? Nothing happened!"

But before Ryan could say anything more, the enlarged claw began to glow a brilliant green color which made Ryan awestruck. Seeing the reaction of picking up one of the dragons, Jerry decided to pick up the other one. He walked over to Sparcan and picked him up. Just as Ryan's dragon claw glowed, so did Jerry's. Only this time, the claw glowed a deep red color. After each claw glowed, the claws detached from the dragons and settled in both boys' hands. Both Ryan and Jerry were about to drop the claw and dragons. But then the key claws immediately fastened unto each boy's right index finger. Each claws fit perfectly, and they couldn't get them off.

As soon as the key claws were attached to each boy's designated finger, the claws began to glow even brighter than when they first picked up the dragons. As they were gazing at the glowing claws, they were both unaware that the scenery around them was changing until they were blinded by a large flash of light. When the claws both stopped glowing and the bright light disappeared, they both could clearly see.

As the boys looked up, they discovered that they were no longer in Ryan's backyard. They were in a cave lined in with pure gold that was lighted by wooden spiral torches that looked like snake or lizard tails. Each torch had great details in the scale work as they were staggered on top of one another by having the staggered torch six inches lower than the higher ones. The holders looked like skinny arms and hands that reminded Ryan of a goblin's hands and arms. Embedded with gold throughout the cave as there were lots of precious jewels also, Jerry's attention was instantly focused on the gold and gems as he followed a path led by Sparcan.

The path led to a large room with the biggest jewels he had ever seen. As Jerry looked around the room, he couldn't see how the room was lit. Until he looked up and saw what looked like an enormous fire consuming the entire ceiling. As the fire flickered, the light bounced off the jewels creating multiple rainbow prisms just like the ones he would make with Ryan's crystal in his room.

Ryan also noticed the jewels but had little interest in them. As he noticed that the cave wasn't damp like the caves he saw on TV and he also didn't see any water sources. Then he saw something that really interested him—a very large round door with a long dragon made of iron or brass. Which was strange since the rest of the cave was made up of precious metals. The dragon was circling the entire door until the head rested in the middle.

Ryan's interest in the door prevented him from noticing Jerry's disappearance. As Ryan looked closer, he noticed that there were several holes in the door. He also saw that the eyes of the dragon were closed. He silently began to count the holes and his final total was thirty-two holes. As each boy continued to observe the item of their interest, they were unaware of where their dragon friends were at.

When Ryan finished looking at the door, he looked around the cave to try and locate Nogar, his new dragon friend. In frustration, he blurted out, "Nogar, where are you at?"

With a smirk, Nogar looked down at Ryan. He was hovering over Ryan with his newly acquired wings and said, "Ryan, look up. I'm above you."

Ryan then realized Nogar was flying and asked, "Nogar, when did you begin to fly?"

Nogar replied in his old wise voice, "Once the key claw is detached from the dragon claw and attached to the dragon leirds designated finger, the dragon acquires a new set of wings and then the dragon's and leird's minds slowly begin to be connected as we start to think as one."

Ryan got a confused expression on his face; Nogar further explained to Ryan about his new life. Nogar began to explain. "Ryan, as a new dragon leird, you will need to be trained in your new talents. That is why I am here. I am your personal dragon trainer, as is Sparcan to Jerry. As we train you, we will exercise your body and your mind. And as we gain ground in our training, our thinking and actions will merge. Once we have mastered all that is required tasks by the Dragon Master, we too will merge and become as one."

Ryan was even more confused and asked, "I have a question. Tomorrow, I have school and a very important test that I have to pass. So can you please tell me when this fantasy will end so I can go home?"

Nogar replied, "Ryan, your life back in the human world has been replaced by a surrogate copy. As soon as you picked me up and the key claw fastened unto your finger, you chose the life of a dragon leird. When we merge as one, you will be a dragon lord."

Ryan then exclaimed, "What? You mean to tell me that my life, my family, my friends—I will never see them again?"

Nogar then said, "That is exactly what I am telling you, Ryan."

Ryan was frantic as he said, "Okay, how do I get off this train? I want to go back home and forget this whole thing!"

With a sigh, Nogar lowered himself down beside Ryan who was sitting on the floor. He then said, "Ryan, once you inserted your finger into the key claw, you made a choice. You have to follow through with your commitment, but you are not alone."

Ryan replied, "I know Jerry is here too."

Nogar then said, "No, I mean there are thirty-one other dragon leirds and their trainers. You and Jerry have arrived first so there is just thirty more to show up."

Still confused, Ryan said, "What happens when all thirty-two dragon leirds are assembled?"

Nogar proceeded saying, "The Dragon Master will give some instructions, and after she is finished, each leird's key claw will glow. Simultaneously, a hole in the door will also glow. The dragon leird has to place their key claw in their designated hole. This must happen in order for the door to open to the wonderful world of Dragtoneea."

Ryan decided to examine the door again to try and figure out which hole his key claw was designated for. There were no differences in the holes, so he decided to ask, "Nogar, which of these holes does my key claw fit into?"

Hearing Ryan's question, Nogar flew over to the door and closed his eyes while opening them, he began to quote a poem. It was written in ancient text from an inscription written on the top of the door. Ryan did not understand the language at first, but soon after Nogar began to read the poem, the words appeared in his mind so that he could understand it.

"The key you hold will open this door you see,

But only if your key and hole doth it glow so free,

So take your turn and thirty-two will find,

A world unknown to your human mind."

After Nogar finished the poem, Ryan remarked, "So each key claw has to be entered into its keyhole, but how do you know for sure which hole to put it into?"

Nogar quoted a part of the poem. "If your key and hole doth it glow. So by this phrase, it means that if both your key claw and keyhole are glowing, then you know when and where to enter it."

Amazed by what Ryan just learned, he was eager to share this knowledge with his best friend. But he couldn't see him anywhere and decided to ask Nogar if he knew where he was. Ryan then asked, "Nogar, do you know where Jerry is at?"

Nogar responded by saying, "I don't know where he is at, but maybe if you call out his name and look for him, you might find him."

Ryan began calling Jerry's name. While Ryan was calling out Jerry's name, Nogar thought of something. He then said, "Ryan, I don't mean to interrupt, but I just thought of something that might help you find Jerry. Do you see this tunnel?"

Ryan responded, "Yes."

Nogar continued, "This tunnel leads to a beautiful room filled with jewels covering its walls. Let's try to find him there." Nogar hesitated a little bit before he said his next comment. "Ryan, I could be wrong, but in that room are some extremely large jewels that other leirds have tried to remove. He could be trying to remove them too so he can keep them for himself."

Ryan ignored his comment as he thought that Jerry would never do that.

Jerry was completely fascinated by the jewels in the cave. He could see were several leirds tried several times to remove the jewels with their fingernails. Jerry did not want to share any treasure he could manage to break free from the gold wall. Jerry could hardly believe his eyes as he examined rubies, sapphires, and emeralds outlined in silver, but the gem that caught his eye was a huge diamond. It had to be twelve inches in diameter and had to worth a fortune.

Upon seeing the diamond, Jerry said to himself, *I have to get that diamond out for myself.* With this determination, his heart focused on this diamond. He then went to work trying to dig out the diamond from the wall. Sparcan encouraged him to try and get the jewels free even though he knew it was impossible. He also knew that the greedier Jerry got, the bigger advantage he would have over his mind.

But Sparcan had his own objective as he stared at the fire lighting the room. He slowly backed away from Jerry as he didn't want to disturb Jerry's concentration and slowly flew toward the fire. As Sparcan got closer the ceiling, the fire got brighter and hotter but he persisted on. With each failed attempt, Jerry looked around for some advice from Sparcan and found Sparcan flying into the fire.

Jerry thought to himself, *He is completely insane.* He continued to watch Sparcan as he got so close to have some of the flames start to make his scales glow red from the heat. But before he got to the center of the fire, the heat knocked him unconscious causing his lifeless body to fall to the ground. As he plummeted to the ground at an incredible speed, Jerry scrambled to his feet. Once up, he then rushed over to catch him before he injured himself even further. He was also trying to figure out how to help him.

Ryan and Nogar proceeded down the same dim hallway getting closer to where Jerry was as the hallway led them to a brighter light. The hallway began to expand until it led them into an enormous jewel room shining with beautiful gems of all kinds. Ryan's attention was drawn to Jerry who had vigorously tried to dig out the giant diamond but was now at Sparcan's side trying to reprieve him. As Sparcan slowly gained consciousness, Jerry wondered why Sparcan flew toward the fire in the first place but knew that now wasn't the time to ask him about it.

After finding Jerry, Ryan leaned over to Nogar and said, "Looks like you were right. He is trying to get rich quick."

Nogar nodded in agreement, and as Ryan entered the room, he accidently kicked a few pebbles that startled Jerry. Out of pure greed, Jerry left Sparcan and made an attack on Ryan for he didn't want to lose the treasure he had claimed. As Ryan looked at him, Jerry's eyes seemed to be glazed over to the point of almost blinding him with greed.

Once Jerry realized that the intruder was Ryan, his aggression subsided periodically, but he did not want to take any chances that his friend might take his treasure away from him.

Jerry then said, "Ryan, if you help me to extract these jewels, I will share the wealth with you." But Jerry had no intention in sharing the treasure with his friend; he just wanted Ryan to help remove the jewels from the gold. Ryan was inspecting some areas around the jewels and noticed several claw marks.

This wasn't the first time that someone attempted to remove these jewels. After this discovery, he said to Jerry, "I don't think we can get these jewels out. It looks like there have been several attempts already to extract them."

Ryan's remarks only made Jerry more agitated because he thought Ryan knew how to get the diamond out and planned on misleading him so that he could extract it for himself. But he told himself, *I found it first, and I intend to get it out and keep it for myself.*

He immediately began to plot a way to kill Ryan and figure out how to keep all the treasure for himself. Jerry returned to the wall as he continually clawed at the priceless diamond. At this time, they all heard a noise and a bright flash of light from the hallway in the cave from where they had all arrived.

Ryan said, "Let's check it out."

Jerry was disgusted to leave his treasure but agreed. Ryan was more eager to see what the noise and light was. Together they proceeded down the tunnel and came into the key door room of the cave. As they exited the tunnel, Ryan spotted a blond-headed boy with his trainer. Ryan looked around and found several large protruding rocks coming out of the floor a few feet away from the walls. These rocks were just below some of the lowest torches where he decided to hide until he could figure out who he was. Jerry then spotted a brunette-headed boy with his trainer and decided to hide behind the same rocks too on the opposite side of the room. They both had a puzzled look on their faces. Ryan realized that each of the boys had a key claw similar to their own. He then came out of his hiding space ready to greet the new arrivals.

Jerry sprang out from behind the rocks speaking up before Ryan could in a stern voice stated,

"Who are you two?"

The blond boy in a startled response stated, "My name is Bobby Grant, and I discovered that this reptile is a dragon who calls himself Socer."

Then the brunette boy spoke up and said, "My name is Jake Homes, and my dragons name is um…it's umm…"

The dragon hovering over him was getting more annoyed by the second and firmly said, "My name is Agar."

"Right." said Jake. "But before I continue on with any more of my answers, may I ask you a question?"

Both Ryan and Jerry nodded in approval. Bobby then asked his question, "Where are we at?" This time, Ryan spoke before Jerry could. "Didn't your dragon trainer explain any of this to you?" Both of the boys looked at each other and neither one had any answers and looked back at Ryan. This time, Jake said, "No!"

Ryan began to look for Nogar and spotted him several feet away and shouted, "Nogar, can you come here for a minute?"

Nogar flew over to Ryan and the two new leirds and asked Ryan, "What did you want from me?"

Ryan replied by asking Nogar to tell the two boys the information he had told him when they arrived.

But Nogar tapped Ryan on the shoulder and motioned for him to come a little ways from the group. When they were alone, Nogar told Ryan, "I can't speak to those boys. I can only talk and communicate with you right now. The same goes with their trainers. Anything you want to tell them, you will have to tell them yourself."

After receiving this new insight, Ryan returned to the group. He then proceeded to explain to Bobby and Jake the same information that Nogar had given him until everyone had a better idea of what they were doing here.

With this new wealth of knowledge, Jake turned to his dragon trainer and said, "That was what you were trying to tell me, Agar?"

Upon hearing Agar's name, Nogar who was not around when Bobby and Jake introduced themselves, slowly moved in closer. Nogar then said, "Agar?"

Agar then replied, "Yes, and who are you?"

Nogar then replied, "Don't you recognize me? It's me Nogar."

Agar slowly began to examine Nogar, and after being satisfied, he got a much happier expression on his face. "Nogar, I don't believe it."

Agar then grasped Nogar in a hug. Nogar then spoke first. "I thought you were dead," he said as he wiped a tear from his eye. Ryan, Bobby, and Jake were all confused while Jerry had already slipped away back to the jewel room.

Agar responded to Nogar's question, "I survived but just barely. I was captured by a Wapec Lord."

Sparcan heard his comment and crouched a little lower behind a rock so he would not to be noticed. Agar then continued, "The Wapec lord got distracted by a Gunar lord, and I was able to escape. He pursued me, but I was able to hide my young learning leird and then myself. Now that leird has advanced in rank to a captain in the Gunar army." He ended his comment with a smile.

This made Sparcan charged up to Agar from his hiding spot. He stopped just inches from his face and began to look him over carefully. Confidently, he conveyed this message. "Next time I will finish what I started!"

This sudden burst of harassment alarmed Agar. He carefully examined Sparcan too. He noticed a gash over Sparcan's right eye which he received from the Gunar lord who had helped him escape. Agar's own eyes began to expand, and he slowly began to hover backward, cautiously keeping his eyes on Sparcan. As he hovered, he tried to speak but no words came out. Finally, he said, "It was you. It was you who betrayed us all that day. We trusted you."

Sparcan responded in an annoyed tone, "Yes, it was I! As you can tell that stupid Wapec leird that I trained into a lord was killed thus giving me another chance to settle the score and conquer all who oppose me."

Before the rampage could escalade, Nogar flew in between the verbal warfare and spoke in a much calmer voice, "Listen, we all have our own battles. But right now, if we kill each other before the door opens, all of our hopes are lost. Our young leirds will remain in this cave forever, and we dragons will die with no hope of glory."

Agar spoke up before Nogar could say any more, "You Wapecs think you can control everything. First, you trick your young leirds and control their minds, then you want control of all the land. I have news for you! We Gunars will be victorious once and for all!"

Jerry had just returned and heard the last part of the discussion about the controlling of the minds. He raced toward Sparcan grabbing his tails, pulling him down, preventing any more verbal attacks. Firmly grasping his tail, he spun Sparcan around until he rested face-to-face with him. He was not happy as he spoke, "You control my mind?"

Sparcan spoke in a joking matter and with a laugh said, "No, of course not. This Agar fellow lost one of his many brain cells during battle. We don't nor we can control your mind, but if you focus really hard, you do have the ability to control other Wapecs' minds."

Jerry slowly began to soften his grip on Sparcan, and as his grip loosened, he gained an evil grin.

In his mind, he was conspiring an evil plot.

Sparcan focused on Jerry's thoughts. "If I can control the minds of other Wapecs, then I have the ability to discover their wealth and take it for myself." After he ended his thought, he rubbed his hands together in a greedy fashion.

Sparcan began to laugh to himself noticing how easy Jerry was blinded by greed and power. In the middle of their evil enjoyment, another bright light blinded everyone in the room. From that light appeared another leird. This time, the leird was a beautiful girl.

Chapter 4

At first, the four other boys were blinded by the bright glow from the newcomer. It was the same light that brought them all here. Instantly, they were aware that someone else had arrived and sought out this newcomer but were unable to figure out who it was because her back was toward them. They couldn't see her face; however, they could tell that it was indeed a girl due to her long blonde hair and pink outfit that screamed girl. All the boys in the room quietly crept closer to this new girl when she suddenly turned around, startling them all.

She had a bubbly personality which was apparent as she introduced herself. "Hi, my name is Susan, and this dragon with me is Angoree." She offered a hand to Bobby as a token of friendship. Susan then began to talk with the other boys. They were glad to have a girl in the room to talk to but that wasn't what caught Ryan's attention. He was awestruck by her beauty that gave her a radiant glow. Her face reminded him of the rarest, most beautiful flower—the lady's slipper orchid, whose beauty was sought out by most herpetologists.

As Ryan continued to daydream about her, Jerry noticed his friend's concentration was on Susan. He discovered even more that Ryan seemed to be developing a very deep attraction toward her even more so then Pam. This made Jerry angry and jealous. Jerry no longer wanted Ryan to be happy, but he wanted him to be miserable. It became Jerry's intention to steal the heart of this girl. Not because he loved her, but because his jealousy toward Ryan was developing into hatred.

Each boy in the room introduced themselves along with their dragon trainers until she finally got to Ryan and Jerry. As Susan moved toward Ryan, he thought in his mind, *I finally get to meet and talk to this beautiful gem.*

Midway through his thought, he was interrupted by a sweet voice, "Hi, my name is Susan, and my dragon's name is Angoree. What is your name?"

Slightly stunned, he responded, "My name is Ryan, and my dragon's name is Nogar." Before he could continue on with their conversation, he was rudely interrupted with a boastful tone.

"My name is Jerry, and this is Sparcan," pointing to his trainer hovering beside him. Before Ryan could try to continue on their conversation, her attention was stolen by Jerry. This time Jerry said, "Susan, would you like to see one of the most beautiful jewels in the whole wide world?" Before Susan could respond, he grabbed her hand and rushed her away to the jewel room.

After they had arrived, Susan gazed in awe at the beautiful colors of the gems. Then she caught a glimpse of the giant diamond. After being satisfied with viewing the diamond and the other jewels, she dashed down the hallway to the door room and seized Ryan's hand. "You have to come quickly and see the most beautiful diamond you will ever see!"

Pleased that Susan was holding his hand, he softly said, "I'm looking at her right now."

The eager pulling stopped as she turned around to face him with moist eyes. "You think I am beautiful?"

"No…"

Susan lowered her head in sadness thinking she was not pretty, but Ryan picked up her head with two of his fingers and said, "I know you're beautiful!" Slowly they came closer together and edged their lips toward each other as if getting ready to kiss but were stopped when Sparcan rounded the corner from the hallway.

He flew in between them, and in a disgusted tone, he said, "You two lovebirds make me sick that

I want to vomit."

Shortly after, Jerry came around the corner spotting Ryan and Susan together separated only by Sparcan. A hot boiling anger brewed inside of him and more than ever he wanted to hurt Ryan as much as possible. Sparcan could sense the overwhelming anger building in Jerry as it blinded his judgment. He knew that this could be a very powerful technique to control Jerry's emotions and mind and in turn use this anger to control other Wapec lords and accomplish his designs.

After the tension of the situation settled down, another bright flash occurred. This time, it was five times brighter than when Susan arrived. Five more dragon leirds arrived, and the introductions began. There was Lucy Smith and her trainer, Arcan; Justin Timber and his trainer, Forgur; Judy

Turner and her trainer, Furton; Mike Porter and his trainer, Bargar; and Spencer Luke and his trainer, Zorcan.

After the new leirds had finished introducing themselves and asking their questions, Nogar was tapped on the shoulder by Ryan who motioned him to a secluded part of the cave to be alone. He asked, "How much longer is it going to take before we can put our key claws in the door?"

Understanding his eagerness but also realizing that several more leirds had to arrive first, he softly grasped his shoulder and patiently spoke, "There are only ten of the thirty-two dragon leirds here. Once all thirty-two dragon leirds arrive, you will receive counsel from the Dragon Master. Be patient, the last twenty-two leirds will arrive soon."

No sooner had Nogar finished his sentence then another bright flash of light appeared brighter than the previous lights. This time it brought six more leirds and their trainers who arrived in the midst of the other leirds with their trainers.

As with the other leirds, the introductions started with Tommy Lee and his trainer, Porgan; Austin Cal and his trainer, Galit; Summer Long and her trainer, Swecur; Jared Smoke and his trainer, Moucer; Heather Wing and her trainer, Spuny; and David Hide and his trainer, Sporen. As with the other leirds, most of them were not caught up to speed on what was happening. After a long moment of uncomfortable silence, Jared finally spoke up and began to ask the same questions that everyone else had asked which helped stop their puzzling thoughts. Ryan was the main informer along with Nogar feeding him the answers through his mind, answering as many questions as they could answer. After Ryan was done answering their question, Jerry pulled him aside with a question on his mind. "Hey, Ryan, I believe that Susan is getting crowded in here. How many more of these leirds are going to arrive before we get out of this cave?" This was only an excuse for what he was really thinking was, *How soon could he obtain the power and wealth that Sparcan promised him?*

Ryan's response showed how tired he was getting from all the questions he had been answering. "There are thirty-two total leirds and their trainers. We now have half, so there is only sixteen more to show up."

"*Thirty-two!*" exclaimed Jerry. "Now I know for sure I am going to suffocate in here—"

Before he could finish his sentence, he was interrupted by the brightest light that occurred by the door in the front of the cave. With this bright light, eight more leirds and their trainers materialized. Another equally bright light followed not more than three seconds later in the hallway leading to the jewel room. This bright flash also contained the last eight leirds with their trainers bringing the total to thirty-two.

Amongst the first group of leirds were Joe Lake and his trainer, Tarin; Scott Right and his trainer, Poren; Jack Home and his trainer, Sungon; Frank Mee and his trainer, Locur; Triss Small and her trainer, Hamanie; Alice Smart and her trainer, Tudnii; Bryan Strange and his trainer, Garnar; and Jason Hunt and his trainer, Sonrar. Amongst the second group was Alan Big and his trainer, Hanec; Paul Zoom and his trainer, Cacer; Tyson Moore and his trainer, Oager; Chris Bright and his trainer, Falar; Jana Nice and her trainer, Flowy; Allie Bing and her trainer, Deceer; Brandon Mink and his trainer, Nogan; and Jeremy Dark and his trainer, Dungar.

As they waited, Ryan asked, "Nogar, earlier before the rest of these leirds and their trainers arrived, I heard of two groups of lords the Wapecs and Gunars. I was wondering what they are?"

Nogar took a long time before he spoke up. "Well, Wapec and Gunar were some of the first dragon lords loyal to the powerful Dragon Master. As time passed, Wapec grew greedy from all the treasure and power. He collected his lordship over the time while Gunar considered his most valuable treasure his loyal obedience to the Dragon Master.

"Over time, the greed and power possessed Wapec. He vowed to kill anyone who got in his way. There were many who decided to join his cause, and there was only one who dared to oppose him and his army. That dragon was Gunar, he gathered his loyal followers and quickly outnumbered those of the Wapec army. This started the Dragon Lord War that filled the land with terror and death. Through the years, both the dragon lord leaders fell in battle along with many warriors on each side. In memory of these leaders, those loyal to the Dragon Master and her cause of freedom are called Gunars but those loyal to Wapec and his cause are called Wapecs."

Nogar then fell silent to honor and remembrance of his fellow friends and soldiers who died in battle. Nogar then continued, "Ryan, you will learn more of the wars of the past and those of the future through lecture, but mostly through experience. Before you can experience the future, you will need to become a dragon lord yourself. In order to become a true dragon lord, much training of the mind and body is required. This aids you to become a true lord.

"However the Wapec lords are only interested in their treasure, power, and bloodshed. They achieve their lordship through cheating and thus easily transform into dragon lords. They do not have near the power of a Gunar lord. However, some Wapec lords are quicker in battle and have silenced many good Gunar lords."

A little scared, Ryan asked, "But we do fight…I mean, I will fight, won't I?"

Smiling, Nogar said, "Yes, you will, but as I mentioned, the Gunar army is strong and will become stronger with your presence and those who will follow you. You must not rush into battle. It will find you soon enough. Right now, you need only to focus on your future training."

Ryan nodded, pondering on the wisdom of Nogar, but a question still lingered in his mind.

"Nogar, I still have but one last question. Why were Jerry and I the first to arrive today?"

Nogar took another pause that was beginning to annoy Ryan for it lasted much longer than the first two pauses together. He wanted his answer!

Finally, Nogar raised his head and prepared himself for the information he was about to deliver to his leird. With a flap of his wings, he lifted himself off the ground and landed on a rock beside Ryan. He spoke as Ryan looked eagerly into his eyes. "Ryan, the first two leirds of each new generation of dragon lords are the leaders of the forces of either the Gunar or Wapec force. You are the strong leader of the Gunar leirds, and unfortunately, Jerry is the leader of your opposition, the Wapecs."

As the information Nogar delivered sunk in, Ryan's peaceful demeanor was turned into sadness then anger. Ryan bellowed out angrily, "Why must my best friend becomes my worst enemy?"

Nogar felt Ryan's frustration and anger. "We don't choose who opposes each other. We are given commands from the Dragon Master, and we must obey them."

Ryan's anger began to die down as he began to replay the actions Jerry took once they arrived in the cave. Even to the point that Jerry had the look in his eyes that he would kill him.

Ryan continued to swim through his thoughts when Nogar spoke. "Ryan, you do have reason to rejoice. Of the thirty-two leirds here, fifteen are loyal to you and the Gunar force and only nine are loyal to Jerry and the Wapec force—"

Before he could continue, he was interrupted by Ryan. "If only nine are loyal to Jerry, then that leaves seven other leirds. Who are they loyal to?"

Nogar then replied, "They are what we call Lumac leirds. They are unconverted to either side. It is your responsibility along with Jerry's to convert them to either side. If they remain unconverted, they will join the other Lumac lords that remain disloyal to the Dragon Master."

Confused Ryan asked, "Wait a minute, who are these Lumac leirds now?"

Nogar then replied, "I was about to explain this in the beginning. There was a small group of dragon lords who refused to pick a side to join because this group couldn't agree totally with either side. The leader of this group is Lumac. He is the only original dragon lord alive today. The Dragon Master was furious with these dragon lords and banished them to Seven Mile Lake where they have become water dragons. Now these young Lumac leirds have the opportunity to listen to the leaders of both sides and make a choice.

"If they become dragon lords and are still unconverted, then they have three months to decide. Otherwise, they too are banished to Seven Mile Lake. The Lumacs blame both sides for their punishment, and in every opportunity they get to attack other dragon lords, they seized them with vigor, regardless if it's a Wapec or Gunar lord."

Ryan took in all of this information. He then thought in his mind, *I am a leader of the Gunar force, and there are many followers of mine. However, there are many that I will need to help convert over to my side. And then there is Jerry, my best friend, who has become my worst enemy. He has the same responsibility as I have*— Ryan's thoughts were interrupted by a different thought other than his.

Yes, Ryan, it is all true, came a interrupting thought from Nogar.

Ryan then said out loud, "How are you in my thoughts?"

Nogar then relayed a message through his mind. *We are connected in all ways and the most important is the connection of the mind. Ryan, Jerry has shown forth signs of his greed and need for power much quicker than any previous Wapec leird. Just as you have been able to focus your mind much faster and stronger than any other Gunar leird.*

Still trying to take all of this in, Ryan asked, "What do you mean by my mind is growing stronger than previous leirds?"

Nogar turned from facing Ryan in the direction of the other dragon leirds in the room and said,

"Look at the other dragon leirds and tell me what you see."

Ryan moved away from the wall toward the leirds to observe their behavior. "I see them talking to the other leirds in the room."

Nogar then said, "And what of their trainers?"

Ryan then responded, "I see the trainers hovering above them. They are communicating to each other as well."

Nogar then exclaimed, "Yes, normally you and Jerry would be among them, but you especially seemed to be leaps and bounds ahead of schedule, beyond the rest of the young leirds. Perhaps the Dragon Master has special plans for you."

Before Ryan could react, his ears caught a sound that he had not heard before in the cave. He was not the only one to notice the sound. All the other leirds could hear the sound too. The sound was coming from the door leading into Dragtoneea. As they approached the door, the sound became clearer. It sounded like metal rubbing against stone. The source was soon found as one leird pointed directly to the door. Each leird then moved in closer. They could see the metal dragon figure's head moving back and forth, as if it was trying to break loose from the rock. Finally, the dragon's head broke free from the rock and slowly turned in the direction of the young dragon leirds.

Chapter 5

After blinking several times, as if it had just woken up from a deep sleep, the metal dragon fully opened its eyes. Upon opening its metal eyelids, however, Ryan noticed that the eyes were not made of metal but had the physical appearances of a real dragon eyes. It had a long slit like pupil and the iris was reddish orange with black specks like a snake eye with a little bit of a white sclera with visible blood vessels. The eyes mostly have the appearance of a reptile but with a small hint of human attributes. As this metal dragon blinked a few more times, it began to focus its eyes and scanned the room.

It soon found Ryan and Jerry standing together and focused on them. In a soft gentle voice, the dragon began to speak. "I am the Dragon Master. Very soon, each of you will get the opportunity to meet me personally, some a little sooner than others. Each of you have in your possession a key claw given to you by your dragon trainers. When I am finished talking to all of you, I will return to my lair and this metal dragon medium will return to its fixed position.

"Upon which the thirty-two holes will glow in a sequenced order along with the key claw that are designed to go in the glowing holes. As you place the key claw in its designed hole, it will loosen the grip on your finger and remain in the hole until a later appointed time. At that time, you will place your finger back into the key claw and you and your trainer will be transformed into a dragon lord."

There was some stirring comments among the young leirds. Most of them consisted of, "We aren't going home? I thought it would be like Harry Potter. You know, we come and we train or do whatever and then go home in the end."

The Dragon Master could hear their controversial conversations even the ones that took place only in their minds. She then said, "I assure you that if you went back to your old lives, even now, you would not be recognized or accepted. You have accepted your role as a future dragon lord by having the key claw attach to your finger. You have already been replaced by a perfect surrogate replica continuing your life where you have left off."

Some of the dragon leirds understood their decision while some had a near perfect life and didn't want to leave it behind. The Dragon Master continued, "No matter what your reasons are to go back to your old lives, you made the choice to come and you cannot return back." The Dragon Master had to wait for the leirds to calm down and fully accept their new roles in their lives.

Finally, the commotion died down as each dragon leird who may or may not have been thrilled accepted the responsibility that was about to be thrust upon them. The Dragon Master began to further instruct them. "I can assure you that as each of you begin in your training and learning with your dragon trainer, they will become one of your closest friends. Your old life will slip from your memory as you absorb your new life like a sponge. However, this new life will not be easy and at times not safe, still, you will love it.

"In order for you to begin this new life, the key claws must be placed in the door then the door will be unlocked. When it is, it will open a world unlike anything you have ever seen, the world of Dragtoneea. As you enter this wonderful world of beauty, magic, and peace, you will also witness death and destruction. For this world is far from perfect.

"Unfortunately, I am afraid to say that each of you will have to learn this fact firsthand. Now this next part is very important. In order for me to be able to visit with you, you're going to have to go through the door, and this is only the first step. Once you enter into this world, the door will pivot so that when it closes, your key claws will be accessible to you. From here, there is a path that leads to my lair, the Dragon's Keep. Still in front of you are a couple of obstacles that have to be passed through. First is the Death Valley."

Upon mentioning Death Valley, the Dragon Master had to once again refrain from continuing on with her instruction for there was a mixed reaction. The majority of the leirds tried to keep the fear out of their eyes while yet others seemed eager to explore the unknown danger ahead of them. The Dragon Master then continued, "My dear young leirds, do not be afraid. Death Valley is simply just its name for the final resting spot of the fallen warriors who have died in battle."

Jerry began to think to himself in the middle of the Dragon Master's counsel. *This world just keeps getting better all the time! First, Sparcan informs me that I will have loads of treasure, then I don't have to do any more of my chores ever again. Now we will be involved in deadly combat. I am loving this more and more.* At that moment, Jerry looked over to Jeremy and noticed that he wasn't paying attention but instead found a gray-and- black cave slug. He was fascinated by squishing its innards out of it into his hand, so Jerry reached over and lightly hit him on the shoulder and said, "Pay attention."

The Dragon Master reconfirmed their safety by saying, "There is no need for any of you to worry as long as you stay on the path. It will lead you out of Death Valley and then alongside the Valley of Gunar. This is the valley of my loyal supporters, and they will protect you if needed. Just remain on the path, and soon you will see two large rock formations and a wall of water suspended between them known as Seven Mile Lake—"

Alan interrupted her by asking, "Why is it known as Seven Mile Lake?"

To this the Dragon Master responded, "That is an excellent question, thank you, Alan. The lake is much wider and longer than seven miles. But the main reason for its name is because the rock structures are seven miles high and seven miles apart, giving it its name."

Alan's jaw dropped as he imagined the square wall of solid water.

The Dragon Master then laughed a little bit before saying, "Once you have spotted the lake, continue on the path. It will guide you to the second rock formation. At its base is a long flight of stairs leading to a large opening. In that second structure is the Dragon's Keep. As soon as all the leirds and trainers have arrived, I will give each of you further instruction. This advice will help you in becoming a dragon lord and some will even be privileged to receive additional counsel from me personally while the rest of you will have to wait. My last bit of advice to you is this—be careful on your journey, not everything that looks safe is so."

After her closing remarks, the metal dragon looked directly at Jerry which caught Ryan's attention. But he quickly put it out of his mind awaiting for the next phase to occur. No sooner did Jerry's eyes connect with the Dragon Master's, then she quickly put her metal head back in its original position closing her eyes remaining motionless. Once the head had completely stopped moving, the right eye opened revealing a hole instead of an eye, then it began to glow in the color green, the same color as Ryan's key claw. As he looked at the glowing hole, a light caught his attention and caused him to look down at his key claw which was glowing too.

He then walked to the door, and instinctively, he inserted his claw into the designed hole for him. This hole at first was loose fitting, but then it got a little harder for him to fully insert the key claw. As he twisted the claw around, he discovered a small groove in the bottom of the hole that fit the tip of his claw perfectly. Once in the groove, the key claw then slide in easily the rest of the way. Just as soon as he did, the key claw was loosened from his finger. So he removed his finger from the key claw which remained in the door and he return to his trainer, just as the Dragon Master had said.

Jerry was still hanging his head low after the Dragon Master's staring glance at him from earlier. But he picked it up just in time to see Ryan put his claw into the door. This made him even madder than the earlier events despite the fact that his turn was directly after him. Sparcan took note again of his jealous behavior which he would use to aid him even more in his endeavor against the Gunar forces.

As the holes continued to light up, Ryan noticed that the order of the holes lighting up followed the order in which the leirds arrived in the cave until all thirty-two leirds had deposited their key claws. Everyone in the room was anxious as the last leird pulled their finger away from the door. Suddenly, they all heard the sound of rock rubbing together, and they knew the door was opening. Slowly, the door began to lift up in the direction of the leirds.

Once it was fully opened, they all walked through it, and they immediately noticed that they were standing on a tall hill. The longer they stayed there, the more they could observe the wonderfully beautiful world of Dragtoneea. But they also saw the death and destruction of war promised by the Dragon Master when they saw Death Valley that came with a view of a boneyard.

Each of them slowly began to walk down a path on the hill from the key door leading them toward Death Valley. In the distance, they could hear the roaring sounds of dragon lords in battle but couldn't see them.

Curious, Alan saw a less traveled path as he took it. It led the way to a ledge upon which he observed the savage nature of which these dragons attack and kill each other. Not long after, the other dragon leirds also found this path and joined Alan as they observed the intense battle going on.

None of the leirds noticed the key door had closed behind them because their undivided attention was on the battle. After the door had closed, it then spun around so that the key claws were exposed to Dragtoneea. Now the key claws could be retrieved without having to open the door and going back into the cave.

As Ryan continued to watch the horrifying death scene, his focus was interrupted by something bumping hard into his right foot. He then looked down at his foot and discovered bizarre looking pair of snails because two snails were attached together at their heads clear down the rest of their bodies. Ryan instinctively picked it up and further discovered that even the shells were fused together. Ryan had to hold it tight because it was trying to get out of his hands. As Ryan continued to struggle holding these snails, he saw more of them rapidly moving past his feet. The scene reminded him of "the never- ending story," particularly of the racing snails.

Ryan then cupped his hands around the snails and walked over to Nogar who was still interested in the battle. Ryan tried to get his attention subtly. Finally, Ryan blurted out, "Nogar, these snails ran into my foot. What are they running from?"

Nogar seemed irritated as he looked back at Ryan and then at his hands. When he saw the snails, he said, "That is actually just a single snail called a ram snail. If it ran into your foot that hard, it is probably trying to escape from its most feared predator—the wezille."

Satisfied with his answer, Nogar then turned his attention back to the battle while Ryan first began to examine the snail. It had a large black slimy body and the cream double shells had a curl pattern outlined in brown that protruded outward, resembling the look of ram horns. He then remembered what Nogar said about its natural predator and began to look all around, even spinning in circles at times.

Ryan's movements easily caught Nogar's attention as he quickly spun around and said, "Ryan, what are you doing?"

Ryan stopped moving and was a little dizzy from spinning. When the dizziness stopped, he then turned and found Nogar saying, "I'm looking for the weasel that is chasing this ram snail. If snails can look this cool, then I could only imagine what a weasel would look like here. Back at home, they look like a skinny long rat similar to a ferret or mink." Ryan continued his search, looking around the nearby rocks and under the bushes. He even separated several bushes hoping to get a lucky peak.

Nogar was amused with Ryan's determination, then he said, "If you really want to find a wezille then all you have to do is look over by that small pound."

Ryan stopped looking by the bushes and went over to where Nogar was pointing but blocking his view was a large bush. And so just as he had done previously, he separated some of the branches and got his first view of this small pound. Ryan looked around with eagerness while still struggling to hold tight to the snail, but as he did, he couldn't make out any figures, only yellow and blue rocks. Ryan then pulled himself out of the bush so he could walk around it in order to get closer to the pond. When he did again, all he could see were these yellow and blue rocks, but upon closer examination, he discovered the rocks had little spikes on them that reminded him of a sea urchin. While Ryan was observing the rocks, the ram snail was able to slip out of his hand. When it hit the ground, the closest rock began to move picking itself up off the ground. Ryan realized that the rocks weren't rocks at all but the wezille Nogar spoke of. Under its colorful shell, its froglike legs and rest of its body was a dull gray, but it continued to rise. Its face was of bright red.

Ryan was waiting for it to hop over to the ram snail just like a frog would do, but instead, it quickly ran over to the fast-moving snail. Ryan watched the scene and reminded him of the battle scene that disgusted him earlier. When the wezille reached the snail, it opened its large froglike mouth, revealing two rows of blunt interlocking black teeth along with four yellow tusks. Ryan watched as the wezille used its tusks to latch on the shell then, with force, crack it open causing the snail to fall out.

Now with its helpless prey in front of it, the wezille even more quickly began to tear it apart, swallowing large chunks of the snail. After it had finished its meal, its teeth were still covered in the black slim. It licked its teeth and then turned toward the pound. Ryan was expecting it to lie down just as it had done before, but to his amazement, it ran into the water diving deep disappearing out of sight.

Finally after each of the dragon leirds had seen enough of the fighting either being excited, horrified, or straight out sick to their stomach, they all then proceeded down the path and very soon understood how Death Valley got its name. As their path was lined with several large dead dragons, some only skeletons, along with the massive graveyard, only parts of Gunar Valley were visible due to a large surrounding rock wall. As they continued on the path, Ryan looked up at Nogar and asked, "Nogar, why is this rock around Death Valley?"

Nogar then replied, "Well, it is to help keep the dead contained within this specific area, but also, it helps to keep the reeking odor under control. You will understand when we go further into the valley."

True to his words, as Ryan and the rest of the dragon leirds walked through the middle of the valley, the odor of the decomposing dragon lords was enough to knock them unto their backs. The most impressive sight was the large number of dead dragons consisting of freshly killed, decomposing, and bleached white dragon skeletons.

As they followed the path, it was apparent that the valley was split in half separating each side from each other. Several of the dragon leirds could see the vital and fatal wounds inflicted by both sides in battle. This view made several of the dragon leirds sick to their stomach, which mainly consisted of the excited ones from the battle earlier.

As they continued slowly walking on the path, each of them ventured off the path and took their time examining the skeletons. Allie, who took some interest in the study of cetacean biology, compared the skeletons to those of whale skeletons from pictures of whaling camps back in the 1940s. Jerry was getting more annoyed than fascinated by the boneyard and wanted to get out of this stink hole when out of the corner of his eye some movement caught his interest, and he walked in that general direction. As he moved around a large skeleton, he found a human skull which began to freak him out.

He quickly turned to Sparcan after picking up the skull. "Sparcan, do we leirds die here?" Holding the skull out for him to see.

Sparcan turned around and flew back to Jerry for he wanted out of here just as badly. Sparcan said, "Yes, there have been some young dumb dragon leirds that have gotten themselves killed, but that skull, I would actually drop it if I was you."

Jerry didn't understand why he would insist in him dropping the skull until he felt something poking his palm and instinctively he dropped the skull out of fear. Jerry then carefully began to observe the skull as it rolled around until it finally landed with its jawbone on the ground facing him. Then he watched as the jawbones first began to slowly move up and down as if it was chewing on something. Then exactly at the center of both the upper and lower jawbones began to pull apart. As it fully pulled apart, it revealed two large orange with green stripes sharp knifelike cutting claws on each end of the middle bottom jawbones.

Jerry noticed that the right and left colorful claws had a pouch in front of the left and one for the right and on the back of the right one for the left to pull the jaw completely together. Jerry's fascination began to grow as he continued to observe this strange magical skull. When the jawbones were finally pulled apart, Jerry then noticed that they looked a lot like pinchers on a crab or a lobster but made of bone. After the pinchers where completely apart, all that was left was the round part of the skull including the eyes and nose holes.

Then two long red and green eyestalks with two very large black eyes at the end of them came out of each of the eye socket of the skull. Jerry then saw what had poked him was one of six legs joined in three sections that came out of the foramen magnum. These legs then lifted the crab up as it began to move. After a few moments, it moved over to a dragon carcass. Jerry walked over to it and saw at the base of the skull; it looked like something was chipping out two pieces of bone, but in actuality, it was the mouthpiece of the crab. Sparcan could see that Jerry wasn't going to move or leave that crab until he knew more about it.

Sparcan spoke, startling Jerry, saying, "It's called a skull crab because it looks like a human skull when threatened or scared, so it blends in like a camouflage. Those pinchers are very strong and sharp, one of those pinchers could easily take off your finger or toe. That was why I told you to drop it. The large sharp cutting claws are used to cut into these dead dragon warriors and, of course, to mate. The more colorful, sharper, and stronger the pincher and claw are, the more likely its chances to mate and survive. As they tend to kill and eat each other, and they fend off predators."

Jerry gave Sparcan a confused look as he said, "So these crabs do have predators?"

Sparcan continued, "Of course, but there is only one. It's called a kull cat. It has a black coat. In addition, it has a white lining exactly over their bone that makes it looks like a complete skeleton. When it moves, it looks like a walking skeleton but is most apparent at night. However, they are very hard to find. It is more likely that you will survive several years of battle than locate the elusive kull cat."

Jerry began to look around to try and find one of these rare cats, but all he could see in any direction were dead dragons and their bones.

Sparcan continued, "Back to the main use of that claw which it uses to cut off the scales so it can easily cut off chunks of meat and moves it to its mouth."

Jerry piped up and said, "But I thought the dragon scales is made up of the strongest material in the world!"

Sparcan responded, "This is true in your world, but the crab doesn't cut into the scale itself but the skin that is attached to the scale."

Jerry's fascination with this skull crab had isolated themselves from the rest of the group as no one else had located one of the crabs despite being hundreds of them in the area. However, there were two creatures in the area that they couldn't avoid. There happened to be two very large black and red dragon lords transporting one of their dead soldiers to its final resting grounds. Not being able to find a bare spot to dispose of their dead soldier, they dropped him on some decomposing skeletons causing them to crack and break apart from the dead weight of their dead comrade.

These two dragons seemed to be taking the loss of this particular soldier very hard as they sat upon a partially decomposing dragon skeleton spines resting on it until they recovered from the journey. While they were mourning, some of the trainers quietly flew down to their dragon leirds as they quietly got their attention. Being very careful and quiet, they motioned to them to slowly and quietly get off the path and find a hiding spot. But before they were successful, the slight movements of some of the dragon leirds caught the attention of the mourning dragons.

Upon seeing the dragon leirds along with their trainers, it created an even more intense anger which they simultaneously planned to take out on this group. Ryan was heading toward a large pile of bones to hide when his movements were abruptly stopped. When he stopped, the hairs on the back of his neck rose upon end when he heard some intense growling. He soon realized the growling was coming from the two angry dragons.

He then slowly turned around. As he did, he recognized that they were focusing on the group, and not just him, to do what looked like a planned out deadly attack. All the dragon leirds at this point had turned around and could see the angry dragons leaning forward to follow through with their plan of attack. But as they raised their wings to begin their attack, a deafening roar filled the air scaring all the young dragon leirds making them jump. This roar also scared the two dragons even more.

They instead fell off the skeleton that they were perched on but caught themselves before hitting the ground. By using the motion of their wings that was going to aid them in their attack, it instead took them into flight away from the group back into the battlefield. Ryan climbed upon a spinous process of one of the dragon skeleton's spine. Like a ladder, he climbed high in order to get above the wall. When he got high enough, he watched them as they flew off making sure they weren't going to turn around and proceed with their prior plan. He then tuned into Nogar's thought pattern and asked,

What just happened here?

Nogar replied back, *Those were Wapec foot soldiers who were bringing one of their captains who had just been killed in battle. As you just witnessed, they were very upset and angry about it. They wanted to take out their aggression on all of us, but like you also heard, we were all scared by a majestic roar of the Dragon Master. This caused the two Wapec soldiers to fly off, either to their camp beyond the Black Forest or straight back into the fight.*

Puzzled, Ryan said, "So they were just going to start killing us without finding out if any of these leirds where on their side?"

To this Nogar replied, "Yes, you see when a Wapec lord gets enraged beyond control not even their own kind are safe. They only care to protect themselves."

Once Ryan's curiosity was resolved and the aggressive Wapec soldiers had disappeared completely abandoning their previous vengeance attack, all of the dragon leirds gathered themselves back together and began to quickly reorganize themselves by lining up in the order they put their key claws in the door.

Once they finished lining up, they then took a vote on who they felt should lead them the rest of the way. The majority wanted Ryan to lead them out of the valley. Jerry who finally joined up with the group after the near attack was over and learned what had happened was becoming more and more jealous of Ryan. It was also mixing with anger which was taking over his mind more and more, which was exactly what Sparcan wanted. After it was official, Ryan began to lead the group, and they followed his direction and soon they found their way to other side of the valley.

At the end of the trail was the wall with a large opening leading out of Death Valley. Spanning over the exit creating an arch way facing the valley of Gunar stood a large stone-like sculpture of a dragon similar to the two that almost attacked them but was much larger. The detailed work was incredible; each scale was craved so perfectly that they seemed to pop out at them. Ryan walked up to the tip of the tail and saw that it had turned green from a buildup of mold and moss.

Jana who was interested in art and was planning to major in it was also interested in the statue and was also amazed by the specific detailed work. She started at the tail and moved down it, feeling the texture and examining further the brilliant work of the artist until she was stopped by reaching the wall, then she was repelled back by a different intense odor, not like the rotting carcasses in the valley. She quickly plugged her nose as she proceeded under it, exiting out of Death Valley along with the rest of the dragon leirds and trainers. After she got away of the statue, she exclaimed to Ryan, "Man, someone couldn't wait to get out of the creepy valley before farting." The whole group heard and laughed at her remark but no one was owning up to it.

Jana continued, "Man, the artist did an amazing job with a chisel, but I don't know if it's the rocks in this land or if some of the rotting odor mixed with the mold but that statue reeks."

Ryan looked back at the statue and was disturbed by the pose and expression on the dragon's face, the expression. It was full of anger with its mouth open exposing its many sharp teeth. The face also had several defining scars on the snout and close to its eye which lead Ryan to think that the dragon used to make the sculpture was a warrior. As Ryan began to examine the pose of the dragon, he noticed that the dragon was in fact in an attack pose.

He noticed that the left arm was extended to the sky as if it was reaching out at something or someone while the right arm was at its side but slightly bent. It looked like it was getting ready to strike at the object that the left arm was reaching for. Ryan then noticed that the eyes were focused on whatever the left hand was trying to grab. This made Ryan uncomfortable, and he had to turn away. As he did, he walked past the group of dragon leirds who were resting on boulders or logs, and he saw a ledge that looked over the valley the Dragon Master talked about. As he scanned the valley, he remained speechless.

Not long after, many of the dragon leirds realized that Ryan was gone, so they caught up to him. When they reached him, they noticed that he was staring out over the valley, not moving. "He must be admiring the beauty of the valley," joked Jerry in a girlish tone which caused a laugh amongst some of the dragon leirds and more of an annoyance with the rest.

Jerry was finally the first to walk over to Ryan. When he arrived, he also looked in the direction where his so-called friend was looking. He saw the vast beauty of Dragtoneea. The first area that caught Jerry's eyes was a lush rainforest mountain range. Each of these peaks were connected by a clear blue pristine waterfall; however, midway through the range, he noticed that one of the peaks was broken off. This range spanned as far as the eye could see in both directions.

Below the rainforest range stood a tall single mountain completely covered in snow with a large wall of snow around it with only a single entrance on its eastern side despite the fact that the temperature felt like one hundred degrees. To the far right of the mountain was a small established snow village. The inhabitants though tiny looked like they were Eskimos, and southwest of the village was another large single peak mountain. This time, just the tip was covered in snow. At its base was a mining entrance. Despite the distance, he could see a large beautifully crafted wooden door on the southeastern side.

But Jerry's astonishment of this beautiful world was rudely interrupted by the cruel battle roars. As his eyes followed the noise, they took a southwestern direction that led him to a large stone wall. Once he passed by the wall, there was the continuing battle scene that they watched from the ledge but this time the battle was closer. As he watched two very distinct dragon forces, one looked solid green while the other was black outlined in red. Each side was doing all they could to kill each other. It took the smile right off Jerry's face and filled it with fearful dread.

One by one, the rest of the group walked up to the edge and each of them began to further witness the scene of the dragon forces more intensely engaged in a fierce battle. The sky was filled with a red sun with highlights of orange glow from fireballs flung at opposing dragon forces. The young dragon leirds watched as a dragon would get in close enough. It opened its mouth and then it looked like a pillar of fire was delivered at the opposing base of the dragon's head. When the pillar was successful, the unfortunate dragon would fall to the ground lifeless. The victor would dive down and retrieve something from the dead dragon. Then the allied side would move in carefully to retrieve the body which was then brought to join their fallen soldiers in Death Valley.

Again, some of the dragon leirds were intrigued by the gruesome scene before them that they were unaware that the statue wasn't a statue at all but a captain of the Gunar army. He slowly lowered his head toward the group as he practically and carefully laid it on Scott's and Alice's shoulders. He spoke up and startled them along with all the rest of the dragon leirds. "Please don't be afraid. My name is Captain L. Racklin. I bring you a message from the Dragon Master herself. Quickly follow Ryan and Nogar up to the Dragon's Keep…"

As Ryan listened to the captain, he couldn't help but stare at the battle scars that he first noticed covering his face. It looked like he had been slashed by something very sharp. The scars continued to move down the rest of his body. As Ryan moved down its body, he discovered more and more all the way down to his tail that he didn't notice before.

Captain Racklin continued, "I will lead you safely as far as I can but then I must leave you. I need to join my fellow Gunar soldiers in battle so we must hurry. We don't have much time."

And with that, the Gunar captain turned around and headed toward the Dragon's Keep with the young dragon leirds following close behind him. Captain Racklin, as promised, led them down the path that followed the edge of Gunar Valley. Soon the two towering rock structures that the Dragon Master spoke of came into view along with the mysterious suspended lake held in place between them. Before they reached the stairs, a distressing roar came from the battlefield that caught the attention of them all.

However, when Captain Racklin heard it, he said, "I am sorry to leave you, but I am needed sooner than I thought. Continue on the path and right up the stairs. From there, the Dragon Master will give you further instructions." He then turned around and flew straight into the battle. They watched him fly away.

After he disappeared, each one of them had some fear lingering in their hearts even though no one wanted to admit it. They all were thinking, "What did I get myself into?"

Jerry, however, tried to act the toughest, but they all could see the fear filling his eyes as he exclaimed, "Let's move it. We have a long way to go before our journey is over and its getting dark." Jerry then moved to the front of the group.

Ryan then responded, "He's right. We need to climb the stair and enter the Dragon's Keep in order to be safe. Let's all follow Jerry now."

They were all surprised, but it seemed to hit Jerry the hardest. He wouldn't let go of his pride as he rushed to the front and up the stairs without giving Ryan any recognition.

Chapter 6

After shooting past Ryan and the other dragon leirds, Jerry was the first to reach the stairs, again taking the lead as he started his climb up to the Dragon's Keep. As more of the dragon leirds joined in the climb, it was very apparent that the top climbers wanted to turn this into a race. Amongst the top of the racers was Jerry who was very competitive and even bragging that he would be the winner of this challenge. As Ryan approached the stairs, there was something on his mind that he couldn't shake. He felt that he just couldn't continue on without getting it resolved.

Nogar was proceeding up the stairs as he watched the rest of the trainers and their dragon leirds disappearing out of sight. Nogar could sense Ryan's anxiety and turned toward him and could clearly see that he had no intention to move until his concern was addressed. So Nogar flew over to him. As soon as he was close enough, he spoke. "Ryan, what is wrong?"

Ryan answered, "I keep thinking about Agar's comment to Sparcan. What did he mean when he said that it was him who betrayed them all that day?"

Ryan could see the worry in Nogar's face as he had to dig up past memories that happened so many years ago. After a short time, Nogar finally spoke. "This event happened several hundreds of years ago, but the impact of that event is still felt today."

Ryan looked around and found a large flattop boulder to sit on while he listened to Nogar tell the story. Nogar continued, "As Agar said back in the cave, he was in the process of training a new dragon leird as was Sparcan. Sparcan's dragon leird's heart was set on the interest of greed and violence common among the Wapecs.

"But despite the intentions of his dragon leird's heart, they both seemed to distance themselves from the other Wapec dragon leirds and trainers.

Sparcan and his dragon leird finished their training very quickly and then transformed into a dragon lord. But instead of heading toward Wapec Valley as it's a custom. Sparcan went to the Gunar leader who happened to be Gunar himself. Sparcan then pleaded his case that he had a change of heart and no longer wanted to be a Wapec lord.

"Gunar decided to give him a chance to prove himself in battle. During some of the battles they had, Sparcan fought valiantly killing several Wapec soldiers. But the Gunar forces just couldn't seem to overpower the Wapec forces despite the added help from Sparcan. So after a particularly brutal battle, Sparcan volunteered himself to be on scout patrol. After a few nights on patrol, he came back with some vital news. There was a small Wapec camp on the edge of Hoonar Field.

"Gunar was impressed and let Sparcan pick three men that he requested to take off after this small group. When they left the battle camp, Gunar didn't have the best feeling about this nor about Sparcan, so he decided to send five of his best men to monitor their every move. As these five soldiers shadowed them, they discovered that this small group happened to be the entire Wapec army with Sparcan being their leader. He had converted the two of the soldiers and killed the third.

"He took these soldiers with him so that he could trick Gunar and his army in order to make an attack on them when they would least expect it. After the soldiers discovered this army, they sent one back to camp to notify Gunar and the entire army. Agar was on a dragon leird training excursion when he too discovered the Wapec army. He quickly hid his dragon leird in order to protect him and then tried to hide himself.

"However, despite his best attempts, he couldn't conceal himself properly and was soon discovered by a passing Wapec soldier on patrol who brought him back to Sparcan. He ordered him to be killed with his dragon leird together, but first, they needed to find him—"

Extremely interested, Ryan asked, "Nogar, why did Sparcan ordered to have his leird killed with him?"

Nogar answered his question while continuing with his story, "Well, Ryan, in this world as a dragon trainer, there is a responsibility to protect your dragon leird at all costs. When lordship is achieved so is the assurance of that trainer, even if killed, to return again with all the knowledge obtained in their prior lives. Their life source or the dragon's soul will be renewed—"

Ryan blurted out, "Like being reincarnated!"

Nogar replied, "Something like that, yes, but if a dragon trainer and their dragon leird are caught and killed together then that life source is put out forever. We Gunars don't believe in ending life even that of our enemies. We believe in change. Every creature makes decisions. We simply believe some make bad ones, but they can change."

Ryan looked serious as he asked, "Do you believe Sparcan and Jerry can change?"

Without hesitation, Nogar responded, "Yes, Ryan, I do believe they can change, but I also believe that they won't change. Because Sparcan's heart is so dark that not even the brightest lights can light up a corner of it. And Jerry has fallen too deep into his heart to be able to crawl out of it."

Ryan sat for a while, trying to figure out a way to help Jerry get out of Sparcan's heart but couldn't come up with anything.

Seeing Ryan's love for Jerry, Nogar said, "Ryan, I know how you feel. Sparcan is my friend too, but I had to accept his decision and so do you with Jerry."

Ryan tried to get his mind off Jerry and asked, "Nogar, what happened next in the story?"

Nogar continued, "Well, Racklin happened to be the most trustworthy soldier of the Gunar army even though he had only been a dragon lord for three short years. It was Racklin who was the leader of this additional small group. He witnessed the capture of Agar, and he was able to take out the soldiers quietly that were ordered to carry out the extermination of him. Racklin then ordered Agar to take his dragon leird back to the training grounds immediately. Agar didn't need to be told twice and followed out his orders quickly.

"Meanwhile, Sparcan was looking over Gunar Valley and spotted Agar and his dragon leird escaping. He took flight and began to pursue after them. But he was met by Racklin. Agar looked back briefly and saw Racklin confront Sparcan. So he hid himself and his dragon leird again until he determined it to be safe to continue to the training grounds. After a period of time, if hearing no fighting, they took off toward the training grounds and got there safe.

"Sparcan knew he wouldn't be able to stop his victims and chances were good that this Gunar soldier may have already alerted Gunar and his army. Sparcan then began to circle Racklin, sizing him up as he spoke, 'I've never fought you before, but I have seen you in battle. I am impressed. You would make a fine soldier for me and my cause. Join me!'

"Racklin too continued to circle then said, 'I have my loyalty which should be yours too. I will never abandon the Dragon Master. I would die first.' "Sparcan said, 'That could be arranged.'

"Without warning, Sparcan lashed out toward him, inflicting several wounds covering his face. He was not the only one to inflict mutilations for Racklin was able to deliver a deep, penetrating blow to Sparcan. It starts two inches above his left eye and continuing down his face four inches, which sent him straight to the ground in pain. Racklin stood strong in spite of his own injuries as he towered over Sparcan.

"From their fighting, the Wapec army heard the commotion of Sparcan screaming in pain and gathered behind their leader. When Sparcan saw that his followers had gathered around him, he ordered them to attack Racklin and his small group. The Wapec soldiers were all too happy to carry out his orders. As they moved in for their attack on the four weak foes, however, their course was disrupted by several fireballs exploding in the ground sending clumps of grass flying in the air in front of them.

"The unexpected debris in the faces of the several Wapec soldiers who were leading the charge caused them to uncontrollably fall backward. Their fall caused them to collide with their fellow soldiers, stopping the entire progression of the attack. The Wapec soldiers came to their senses and saw that they were now surrounded by the entire Gunar army led by their general. In the confusion, nearly half of them escaped through the Black Forest and proceeded with their escape to Wapec Valley.

"Sparcan was easily captured as he was more concerned with his inflicted gash than to get himself and his army to safety. By order of Gunar, Sparcan was to be executed in front of his remaining army to enforce justice for his crime—"

Out of excitement, Ryan, who was on the edge of the boulder he was sitting on, blurted out,

"What happened to his army that was captured? Were they killed? Did they let them go? Or—"

Nogar now had to interrupt Ryan to take back control. "Ryan, calm down, I was getting to that. The rest of the Wapec army was thoroughly examined. Any captains were also executed to render them leaderless and less effective in battle. They depend on their general and captains so heavily to lead them into and through the battle. Executing them would assure peace. The rest were released, returning to their valley, ending the war that year and restoring peace for a short season."

Ryan enjoyed the story, but he still felt that he could change Jerry's heart. While still thinking of Jerry, he then jumped off the boulder then looked at the stairs. He then felt he prepared himself enough to begin to climb them. As Ryan climbed the stairs, he took his time meditating upon the details of Nogar's story. He would stop occasionally to marvel at the steep wall of water that was mysteriously held in place between the two large rock structures. He couldn't help but wonder how the water stayed in place.

Nogar once again continued up the stairs ahead of Ryan. Noticing that Ryan was not close to him, he turned to find out what was holding him up this time. Nogar flew down closer to Ryan so he could to read his mind easier. He discovered that he was fascinated by the steep wall of water, and he was thinking how it could drown the entire valley. Nogar moved in closer to him to help out his curiosity of Seven Mile Lake by saying, "It's amazing and beautiful, isn't it?"

Ryan replied, "Yes, it is. It is mesmerizing almost."

Nogar laughed. "I guess I could see that with the underwater current waves and their constant motion. Yes, I suppose if you stared long enough, it would almost hypnotize you."

They both continued to stare at the water. Ryan then asked, "Nogar, what holds this water in place, preventing it from breaking through its invisible barrier and flooding the valley below?"

Nogar smiled to himself as he thought, *This one will be an easy, then we will be on our way to the Dragon Master.* Nogar finally answered, "Ryan, this wall of water and its mysterious invisible barrier is actually very easy to explain. The Dragon Master has so much power and authority, and with that power, she controls certain things—"

Ryan couldn't help himself as he interrupted again, "Can she control life and death?"

Nogar held in his frustration as he replied, "Ryan, you really should stop interrupting me. Yes, she can control life and death but she chooses not to. More importantly, she controls this lake. This particular spot is the only spot where Seven Mile Lake does not have a physical barrier, but it is still contained. You asked how is this done? She controls it with her mind—" Ryan was about to blurt out a question but bit his lip to let Nogar continue.

"Ryan, you may not have blurted out your next comment but I can read your mind and I know the question you have. I will answer it. I am sure if you have ever had a fish tank or know someone who does, you have seen the fish hit the clear sides of the tank. Most likely thinking, 'I can escape,' but they realize they are trapped. Similar thoughts go through the minds of the creatures inhabiting these waters.

"They want to explore new places but feel trapped in this lake despite its enormous size. It could almost be called a sea rather than a lake. These animals do realize that the lake supports them and keeps them alive. However, some have jumped out at this very site. They land on the dry ground and die quickly in the hot sun. Most of the animals aren't willing to commit suicide, and they remain in the lake."

Ryan was still full of questions as he asked, "What about water dragons? Have any of them ever attempted to leave the lake?"

Nogar was sure the Dragon Master was going to start without them, but he decided to answer his question. "These questions have lasted longer than I thought they would. Yes, water dragons have been in pursuit of both Gunar and Wapec soldiers, not paying attention to their surrounding environment.

"They were more interested in the possible kill, and as a result, they have broken the lake's surface landing in Gunar Valley. They, like countless other marine animals, have died drying up. Dying by the lack of oxygen is a horrible death. It has largely been from these experiences that makes them stay away from this area."

Ryan was looking at the lake pondering Nogar's story. "So I could reach into the lake and receive no harm?"

Nogar replied, "Yes, there shouldn't be any creatures near to hurt you. But if there happens to be a water dragon close by that sees your arm in their territory, they may attempt to shoot you with a freeze ball—their only defense."

Ryan had a confused expression on his face. Ryan then asked, "Nogar, what is a freeze ball, and what does it do?"

Nogar thought it was obvious but answered, "A freeze ball is the weapon of the water dragons. Since they live in water, they collect water through their gills and suck the water in their mouth through glands. After they do this, the water mixes with their saliva. When it does, this develops into a natural freezing liquid that forms a ball.

"They can use these water balls to attack their enemies above and below along with their prey. The ball only freezes when it hits a solid surface. But if the water dragons were to attempt to spit their balls out of the water once it was to break through leaving the water's surface, the ball has only twenty seconds to hit its target before it would completely freeze and have no effect. Now—"

But Nogar was stopped by Ryan by saying, "Wait a minute, you are going way too fast for me!

Let me ask some questions. You answer them, and we go from there."

Nogar looked up the stairs seeing that the last of the wizards in front of them had finished climbing them. He turned back to Ryan and nodded in agreement.

Ryan then proceeded to say, "First off, thanks for scaring me about the water. Secondly, don't you think you owe me further explanations? Other than the Gunar and Wapec soldiers, what other enemies do the water dragons have? How do you know the time limit of a freeze ball leaving the water? And lastly, why would a water dragon want to kill me?"

Nogar could see that these questions were going to delay their climb even more, so he found a large boulder to the right of him to rest on and relieve his aching wings. Nogar began by saying, "Your questions are very good, and I will try to answer them in the order that you gave them to me.

I know the time lapse of a freeze ball from personal experience. I was being attacked and had several freeze balls fired at me. The balls bounced off me like snowballs because they were exposed too long in our atmosphere.

"If a water dragon does calculate correctly and successfully hits a dragon lord, the water dragon will continue to fire more freeze balls. Each one hitting the dragon lord until it weighs it down enough to either freeze it to death or drag it under the water. As far as the underwater enemies, you will learn of them later in your training. Lastly, the water dragons would love to kill a dragon leird for the same reason a Wapec lord would.

"It would end the life of a future dragon lord thus being one less enemy to worry about. Plus dragon lords tend to fight back and are usually more successful. Even if a water dragon does get lucky and hits a dragon lord, the wounded lord will try to kill their attacker before they suffer their frozen death."

Ryan had an even more confused expression as he said, "You get wounded from a freeze ball?" Nogar promptly said, "You know of dry ice and have heard of liquid nitrogen right?"

Ryan nodded.

Nogar then said, "The similar injuries you would get from these freezing agents are the same that

a dragon lord gets from a freeze ball."

Ryan pondered Nogar's comment, and after comparing, he could see now how a dragon would get injured from a freeze ball.

Confident, Nogar said, "Now that I have answered your questions, I will continue to explain the effects of a freeze ball. If a freeze ball was to hit you, let's say in your arm, the first thing that would happen would be that your arm would begin to develop ice crystals. At first, it would be directly on your skin, then it would instantaneously begin to freeze into your deeper muscles. Until the freezing motion would continue to freeze your entire arm. "Then the water dragon would fire another freeze ball at a different body part to further weigh you down more so they could grab unto you. The minute the first part of your body hits the water, the water uses extreme energy to drag you down to your watery death. However, you don't have to worry about an attack with me here and having us this close to land. The chances of an attack, especially a successful one, are very slim."

Ryan was still a little cautious being right next to the water wall and was not about to put his hand into the water like he was thinking about. Nogar then said, "Ryan, I did not mean for my story to scare you from experiencing new and exciting adventures here. I promise you that no harm will come to you if you want to place your hand or arm into the lake. I will be looking for any and all potential danger."

Regaining his confidence only because of Nogar's reassurance, Ryan carefully began to put his hand into the lake. As he continued to extend his arm further into the water, his progress was abruptly stopped by some force he couldn't see. He looked into the clear lake puzzled by his sudden stop. He was about to ask Nogar what object was stopping him when his hand began to move up and down with no help from himself.

He retracted his arm out quickly extracting it from the water in lighting speed upon examining his arm and finding no harm. He stared into the watery abyss. Suddenly, he was also being stared at by an enormous gray-blue eye that would disappear completely when it would blink. As Ryan continued to stare down at the biggest eye he had ever seen in his whole life, the eye began to slowly turn away from him as it swam away. Ryan could see the water moving over an enormous invisible body.

As it disappeared out of sight, Nogar looked at the puzzled Ryan and spoke, startling him. "Do you know what you were just touching?"

Ryan didn't move or talk. Nogar laughed to himself before he continued on, "That was a Baku or better known as a ghost whale. Because their skin has a natural chameleonlike camouflage that makes them look invisible unless they move. This is one of the water dragon's most feared enemies because the Baku hunts them. A water dragon rarely has an opportunity to kill one of them before they get chopped in half before they even know what is going on. This is a rare encounter and a lesson you got to learn very early in your training."

Nogar expected Ryan to make a comment, but he remained speechless, mesmerized by his experience. Nogar could see that he couldn't break his stare by talking to him, so he decided to splash some water on his face. He reached over and stuck two of his claws into the lake curling them toward Ryan. He quickly pulled them out, sending a large spray of water toward Ryan's face.

As soon as the cold water stung Ryan's face, he began to freak out. He seemed to be trying to scratch his skin off his face. At first, Nogar didn't understand Ryan's reaction to the water until Ryan exclaimed, "I feel my face freezing. I don't want to die, Nogar. Please help me!"

Nogar quickly flew to Ryan's side and grasped his shoulders firmly. He spoke, "Ryan, open your eyes!"

Ryan slowly opened his eyes and realized that he could see in his normal vision.

Nogar continued, "You're okay. I had to splash water on your face in order to pull you out of the state of trance you were in. I didn't think you would associate the flicked water as a freeze ball. I am sorry."

Ryan grabbed the bottom of his shirt to wipe the water off his face. As soon as the warm blood rushed back to his face, he could recognize feeling. Ryan then wanted to strangle Nogar, but he remained calm and kept his composure.

Nogar spoke again. "Ryan, if you are ready, we must finish the climb so the Dragon Master can instruct us all before the real training begins."

Ryan and Nogar began again their climb to the Dragon's Keep where the rest of the group was waiting.

Chapter 7

As Ryan climbed higher up the stairs, he would look periodically over his shoulder, catching a slight glimpse of the Baku he encountered earlier until it completely swam out of sight. Once he realized that he would no longer be able to track the whale, he focused the rest of his time and energy on climbing the stairs. At first, it was easy climbing the stairs, but the closer he got to the top, the harder it became. Ryan reached the top of the stairs and entered into the Dragon's Keep.

He noticed that there were hundreds, if not thousands, of candles starting about four feet from the ground going up to the ceiling. The candles were lining the walls from one side of the entrance to the other. They were all unlit. Ryan thought it was strange, but the natural light from the sun came in from large entrance. It let in enough light to naturally lit the room.

Ryan found the rest of the leirds resting on some stone benches on the wall. As he got closer to them, he could hear their conversation about the race up the stairs they competed in. He got even closer and began to put together his own thoughts of who won the race. Ryan thought, *Well, as I watched them fly up the stairs then struggle, there were about three that weren't struggling as much on the course—Jerry, Jeremy, and surprisingly, Triss. I think the winner has to be Jerry, not because he is my friend but because of his competitive nature.*

As he got up close to the group, he heard Jerry say as he walked over to Triss, "Man, you have to be the fastest girl I have ever seen. I can't believe you beat me."

Ryan couldn't believe his ears. Jerry continued, "Jeremy and I were practically neck to neck, and we had about four steps left when at the last second you"—pointing to Triss—"slide past both of us to pull off the win, but we were right behind you."

What surprised Ryan even more was that Jerry admitted his defeat to a girl. Ryan began to look around the room to locate Susan. He soon found her and walked over to her. She was sitting alone, and when she saw Ryan, her bored atmosphere suddenly sparked with happiness. Ryan decided to sit down next to Susan so he could to talk with her.

As the afternoon grew into evening, all the dragon leirds had plenty of time to catch their breath. The room grew darker and the air grew chiller as it got later into the evening. The young dragon leirds were also beginning to get hungry. Ryan began to search the corners for any sort of hiding space to locate and study the native species of this world.

Scott began to search his pockets for matches, and he found a small book of matches and knew he had a source to light a fire. Now he needed a wood. He began to search the cave for any dry wood to produce light as it was getting dark. He continued to search, but his progress was stopped by movement at the cave's entrance. Scott walked closer and saw the cause—a large wall of fire was sweeping up and down the wall, lighting the candles as it passed.

The fire started on the left side of the entrance and continued its way around the entire room, not harming a single dragon leird or trainer until it had lit every candle. Jerry noticed a hallway previously hid by darkness. Even with candles, the hallway remained dark. It intrigued him, and he was about to question Sparcan about the candles and the hallway, when his view was blocked by a giant smoky blue scaly head. It looked like it had broken through the ceiling.

Ryan was one of the first to recognize that the head was a giant dragon head. The giant eyes seemed to specifically search Ryan out as it stared him down. He couldn't help but think that the eyes looked very familiar. Despite the familiarity, Ryan was in the point of hyperventilating from its stare. He had just caught his breath and was going to use all his energy to scream when the dragon head began to speak.

The head said, "Hello, Ryan and all young dragon leirds, I am the Dragon Master."

Ryan's fear from their sudden encounter immediately calmed after the introduction of the Dragon Master. Ryan's relaxed disposition was also felt amongst all the dragon leirds as the soothing words loosened all the leird's tense muscles from the sudden encounter. The Dragon Master continued to speak after all the leirds had calmed down.

"All of you young dragon leirds have been chosen from around the world for your specific talents. Most of you will jump right into your training with your trainer; however, there are a few of you in this room that I need to talk to before your training and I will ask you to stay."

The Dragon Master ended her comment, and the dragon leirds began to look amongst themselves whispering to each other under their breaths. Amongst some of the comments were, "I wonder if I am one of them?" Others said, "I wonder what the Dragon Master needs to talk about?" Ryan already knew that he was one that would need to talk to her because of the hints he got from Nogar back in the cave. All of the muffled thoughts of the other dragon leirds were brought to a halt when the Dragon Master spoke as some forgot she was still there. "Before I announce who the dragon leirds are that will visit with me, I must give you your training assignments."

At that time, a bright light came from above the ceiling hole and then through the hole came thirty-two dragon scales that were the same smoky blue color as the Dragon Master's. Each of the scales made their way to all the dragon leirds. Each of the dragon leirds reached in front of them to grab the floating scale. They then pulled it in close and began to examine the rough scale and the shallow and deep ridges. As they tilted the scale in the light between the ridges came a bright orange- colored glow. Then all the dragon leirds turned the scale over to expose a smoother side that had some strange characters which looked like they had been burned into the scale and were still burning, leaving a reddish glow.

The young dragon leirds continued to examine the writing and got a very puzzled or even frustrated expression on their faces. The Dragon Master was not surprised at their confusion and said, "You may be a little confused by the strange red glowing characters on the scale training tablets. The reason for your confusion is very simple—the language on the tablets is not familiar to any of you. It is the native language of Dragtoneea called Dragna. With the help of your trainers, this now foreign language will soon become more familiar to you than your native language."

The dragon leirds turned to their trainers, full of questions and confusion. They were so consumed with their questions and the answers they had not yet received that no one noticed that the Dragon Master had retracted her head from their presence. None of the trainers were ready nor willing to answer their dragon leirds questions at this time. They all wanted their dragon leirds to look over the tablet more.

Some of the dragon leirds got discouraged by their trainers, ignoring them and began to look over the tablet more closely. Most were not willing to learn the new language. Others searched the characters and became intrigued by the symbols and wanted to try and learn the new language. It was these intrigued dragon leirds that their trainers came out of silence and began to help them.

Surprisingly, Ryan was amongst the frustrated at first, but then he also began to study the language and found several symbols that began to repeat themselves. He turned to Nogar and asked, "Is the spelling in Dragtoneea the same as my language?"

Nogar looked at Ryan and only shook his head yes. Ryan then began to try to piece the characters together and figure out what some of the training schedule was. Ryan really began to figure out some of the characters by piecing words together.

Jerry wasn't even willing to try at this point and was attempting to get Sparcan's attention, wanting help to understand the tablet and get immediate answers. Sparcan was ignoring Jerry for a completely different reason. He was hiding something he had not yet shared with Jerry. He was waiting for the perfect opportunity to share it with him. Here in the Dragon Master's Keep was too dangerous with all the other telepathist in the room including the Dragon Master.

Sparcan finally caved into Jerry's consistent questions and looked down at him as he asked, "Sparcan, Sparcan, are you listening to me? I thought you were suppose be here to help me out and answer my questions."

Sparcan was not amused by his dragon leird's childish comments. He replied, "Yes, Jerry, I am listening to you. It's hard not to when you complain about everything. I know that you have some annoying questions that are disrupting my thoughts right now, so if you would be so polite and leave me to myself for a few minutes, I will come back and answer your stupid questions."

Sparcan turned away from Jerry to be with himself.

Jerry was dumbfounded and thought, *Sparcan said I'm being childish and stuck up, but he is the one who is stuck up.* Jerry's frustration was converting into anger toward Sparcan as he backed up to the wall and began to pout.

Sparcan came around a rock as he found a semi-flat rock to perch on. It was then that he heard Jerry's thoughts. Sparcan too became frustrated but as he as continued to think about Jerry getting angry with him, he was trying to put together his plan to defeat the Dragon Master.

This he had not yet shared with Jerry. A new thought came to him, *Jerry has a lot of rage building inside of him. As his trainer, I am supposed to help him control these emotions. Instead, these emotions could better help carry out my masterful plan of defeating the Gunar army and the Dragon Master. Maybe now is the best time to reveal my plan to Jerry.*

Sparcan casually slipped off his thinking rock and flew high in the room. When he approached Jerry, he was several feet above him. At this position, he looked down at his unsuspecting dragon leird who was hanging his head to avoid eye contact with anyone. Sparcan said, "Jerry…"

Jerry shot up looking up at Sparcan, startled by his unexpected comment. He then calmed down and sat back down.

Sparcan continued, "I am sorry for my rude prior actions and comments. This had upset you, but as I pondered when I left you, I think I came up with the real reason why you are mad and it's not because of me but something else or someone else. If it is someone perhaps then this person is someone you know personally?"

Jerry was irritated by Sparcan's accusation and stood up to look Sparcan in the face. He then said angrily, "No one has made me—" Jerry froze in place unable to speak, unable to finish his comment as he looked past Sparcan and spotted Ryan and Susan. They were sitting down on the far wall talking or rather flirting with each other. It didn't take long after the discovery of Ryan and Susan for Jerry's calm composure to immediately transform into an enraged jealous and anger.

As Jerry continued to observe Ryan with Susan, he began to flip through his memories and couldn't discover anything that Ryan and he did together where he couldn't beat Ryan. Ryan was always second best. This competition for the hand of Susan was no different. Sparcan continued to monitor the rage building up in Jerry. He was delighted that his plan was proceeding as planned so quickly. He was even more excited that Jerry began to focus his anger on Ryan and considered him more as an enemy rather than a friend.

Sparcan didn't give Jerry too much time to stew over it because he didn't want Jerry to change his mind. He whispered in his ear, "I was right, wasn't I? The person you are really mad at isn't me but someone you know. It's Ryan, isn't it?"

Jerry almost didn't hear Sparcan as his emotions were getting the better of him. On one hand, he was extremely mad at Ryan, but the thought of their friendship ending almost brought him to tears. Jerry had to carefully choose which of his emotions to follow. He continued to watch the interaction of Ryan and Susan and his choice became clear. He then looked up at Sparcan and said, "I believe you are right, Sparcan."

Jerry stood up and continued, "As I look back at my friendship with Ryan, I have always been there for him. I have even used my skill to get him out of trouble and now he has the nerve to go behind my back with Susan without asking me if I liked her or not. He has gone too far. Sparcan, I have grown tired of protecting Ryan. What he deserves is punishment. Will you help me with my revenge?"

Sparcan acted touched by the request of Jerry's and said, "Jerry, I would be honored to."

It didn't take long for Sparcan and Jerry to put together their plot of revenge to destroy Ryan. It fell right in place with Sparcan's evil plan of taking over Dragtoneea. Sparcan spent extra effort into convincing Jerry that his overall plan would eliminate Ryan. Sparcan began to unfold his big plan with Jerry. "My plan not only will help you in the process of destroying Ryan and Nogar completing your revenge but the ultimate ruling of Dragtoneea. The first thing we need to do after obtaining our lordship is restore me to my rightful position as general of the Wapec army. After we get our authority and the respect we deserve, our next objective is to get my long-lost treasure. I will finally be reunited at long last…"

Jerry's eyes lighted up at Sparcan's mention of his treasure. Sparcan had to wait for Jerry to get over his eager daydream of diving into and swimming through the treasure. Jerry's joy was rudely interrupted by Sparcan's loud clearing of his throat. Jerry glared at Sparcan for popping his treasure bubble, but before he could utter his opinion, Sparcan continued on with the rest of his plan. "Now that I have regained your attention, I will proceed. After we accomplish these tasks along with your revenge, we will be set to overtake the Dragon Master with a little help that we need from the water dragons—"

But before Sparcan could continue, he was stopped by Jerry's comment. "Sparcan, why do we want to kill the Dragon Master?"

Sparcan resisted the desire to strangle Jerry for breaking up his speech again. He instead said, "We want to end her life because legends say that the one who can overcome and kill her will then have her power over Dragtoneea. Not to mention the overwhelming wealth of all Dragtoneea including all the treasures of a valley harboring the jewel dragons."

As Jerry thought of this plan, his eyes captured a flame from one of the burning candles, and it looked like his pupils were on fire. As he thought of all the power and wealth he was planning to obtain, he looked up at Sparcan and said, "When do we begin?"

Sparcan just smiled, and Jerry enthusiastically began scheming a way to destroy Ryan and Nogar.

This was going to be the hardest part next to killing the Dragon Master.

As this newly developed partnership proceeded in their endeavor, both were unaware that Ryan and Susan's friendly flirting was very slowly beginning to develop into a deeper relationship. Sparcan was hoping that they were falling in love. This would help his plan to make Jerry hate Ryan. Creating a sensitive hateful area in Jerry's emotions, Sparcan could control him better and ultimately make his entire plan more successful. Jerry suddenly looked back in the area where Ryan and Susan were at and saw they were becoming better friends.

This enraged him even more. Sparcan sensed Jerry's increased anger and said, "Jerry, I know you are having hard feeling toward your friend Ryan—"

Jerry cut Sparcan off as he blurted out, "Ex-friend, Ryan has become dead to me!"

Sparcan gleamed at Jerry's emotional storm as he said, "So I am safe to say you are considering

Ryan as your enemy?"

Jerry hid his face so Sparcan couldn't see his eyes filling with tears but replied confidently, "You are correct."

Sparcan's face filled with an evil grin. "Then we should treat both Ryan and Nogar as enemies. We should keep this plot secret for now, but as the right moment arises, we will move and attack to kill them both."

Jerry was having a hard time fully accepting the evil plot he was entangled in. When Sparcan suddenly alarmed him by saying, "You know, Jerry, these training tasks that the Dragon Master have assigned to you are specifically designed to challenge you and make you take your time. A very long time to help develop your skills as a dragon lord.

"But as a Wapec trainer, I, like the rest of the Wapec trainers, have an advantage over the pathetic Gunar scum. We advance our dragon leirds quicker. Others call our methods cheating while I simply say we are giving you an advantage over the rest of the lesser dragon leirds. For example, look at your training scale."

Jerry looked down at his scale then flipped it over to reveal the strange characters and then looked back up to Sparcan and said, "Yeah, I have been trying to get you to help me understand them."

Sparcan kept his smile as he said, "I understand your frustration, and it's about to end. I want you to take another look at the scale."

Jerry stared at Sparcan angrily for mocking him but forced himself to look back down at his scale. When he did, the characters suddenly changed in front of him, slowly starting at the top of the scale and moving across left to right and down the strange language. As it was being translated into the common English language that Jerry knows and understands.

Jerry was awestruck by the miracle that happened in front of his eyes. He looked up at Sparcan with guilt in his eyes. Then he spoke, "Sparcan, I am sorry that I doubted your word and your power. How did you do this?"

Sparcan had never stopped smiling. He lowered himself to a rock below him where he could look Jerry in the eye. Sparcan then said, "Jerry, this is just the beginning! As your trainer, I will help you accomplish your tasks with ease. The quicker you get through your trainings, the quicker you can focus your attention on more important matters, like your revenge."

Jerry took in Sparcan's words and his excitement grew as he gave in to Sparcan's will and finished scheming out their further plan. Meanwhile, Ryan and Susan took a break from trying to figure out their training scales and were having a delightful conversation. Ryan excused himself. "I'm sorry, Susan. I have to go do something, and I will be right back."

Susan sent a flirting eye wink and said, "Hurry back!"

Ryan almost ran into a large rock looking back while walking away keeping his eyes on Susan. He then focused on looking for Nogar. He found him not far away resting on a rock ledge. Ryan began to do a sneak stalk and was about to let out a loud noise as he would grab and shake his body to scare him.

When without opening his eyes, Nogar said, "I don't appreciate it when people try to scare me.

Hello, Ryan, what is it that you want to talk to me about?"

Ryan was a little disappointed that he didn't have enough stealth and quietness to have a little fun by scaring Nogar. He didn't let this emotion get in his way of asking Nogar about something. As Ryan thought on what he wanted to ask him, he began to rethink his question and got nervous. Finally, Ryan said, "Nogar, how do relationships work in Dragtoneea?"

Nogar smiled as he stretched his stiff muscles, then he said to Ryan, "You and Susan have a crush on each other?"

Ryan began to blush as he said, "I have a crush on her and I think she likes me back but I wanted to find out the rules before I fall head over heels for her."

Nogar leaned in a little closer to Ryan and asked, "Tell me, what are some of the things about Susan that you like so much?"

Ryan hadn't stopped blushing as he said, "I like so many of her qualities I like how beautiful she is and how her face shines when the light hits it just at the right angle. Of course, she has to be one of the nicest girls I have ever met and this next quality almost makes me a little jealous…"

Nogar gave off a confused expression. Ryan ignored him as he continued, "She is so smart. I think she is smarter than me. Also she is really funny, which is good, because I'm really not that funny, and best of all, we think alike. I know to most this would drive people crazy, but to me, it just makes me like her more."

Nogar understood Ryan's position. He added to his comments. "Ryan, I know where you are coming from. You see, I like Susan too—"

Now it was Ryan who had an even more confused look. Nogar quickly added, "But not in the same way. You see, I like Angoree, her trainer."

Ryan let out a sigh of relief.

Nogar continued, "You see, before I became your trainer, she and I were fighting against the Wapecs. We fell in love, and our special bond made us inseparable. Once my sworn enemy found out about my love and his secret love for her, my once best friend sought my life more than ever."

Nogar continued, "It was a warm late summer afternoon and the heat of the battle was getting to both sides. As soldiers began to fall out of the sky without even receiving a wound, they would then continue their struggle of death crawling on the ground. I had just killed a Wapec captain, the general's favorite. This only fueled his rage against me. He launched an immediate attack. I had to separate from my guards. This didn't stop Wapec—"

Nogar's story was suspended by Ryan blurting out, "Wait you and Wapec were friends?" Ryan stopped himself and began to piece Nogar's stories together and calmly said, "Then that means you are Gunar, the future general of the Gunar army." With a pause, he then added, "That also means that Sparcan is Wapec and their general."

Nogar was getting used to Ryan's instant comments that he waited with patience's for Ryan to calm down. "Correction, you are the future general of the Gunar army and Jerry is of the Wapec. You, unfortunately, are in the same situation that Wapec and I were in—enemies after so many years of friendship." Nogar lowered his head, filled with sadness remembering his old friend.

Ryan didn't disturb him. He waited till Nogar was ready. After what seemed to be several hours, Nogar raised his head and was ready to proceed. He did so by saying, "Wapec hunted me down and killed me. That day, I never saw Angoree until this day. Even though I want to be with her, Susan and your union must be taken before the Dragon Master. Her decision is final and lawful. If you disobey, you will suffer her wrath. I don't recommend you make her mad at all."

Ryan nodded, unable to speak for the moment. "How did Wapec kill you?"

Nogar turned away saying, "I cannot tell you any more of this story. In fact, I have said too much already. As you advance in your training more knowledge will be revealed to you."

Ryan turned away disappointed and walked across the room to the dark hallway and found a large inscription on archway. As Ryan studied the characters, he noticed that they were not the same as on the training scale. The more he looked at them, his eyes were opened to its understanding. He turned and yelled loudly across the room, "Nogar, Nogar!"

Nogar looked at Ryan as he continued yelling, "Come over here," beckoning him with his right hand swooping it toward him. Nogar followed his motion till he arrived at the hallway and asked, "What is so important?"

Ryan looked at the archway and asked his own question, "What language is this?" pointing to the inscription.

Nogar carefully examined the writings and said, "That is the personal language of the Dragon Master. No one can read it but her."

He turned to return to his loathing when he was stopped by Ryan's comment. "Then she needs a new language because I understand it perfectly."

Nogar turned around and said, "Prove it!"

Ryan cleared his throat and began to read. "The Dragtoneea Creed. We the guardians are called to serve and protect Dragtoneea and all its living creatures. The land will only be peaceful if peace is kept and a balance kept in harmony. This will lead all to a celestial glory. But if peace is broken, then only one can restore it to its proper balance."

As Ryan finished the creed, an ear-piercing pitch rang through the Dragon's Keep causing all the dragon leirds except for Ryan to buckle over in pain. The pitch echoed off the walls until it rested in the Dragon Master's ears awakening her. Nogar was stunned by Ryan's reading of the creed and couldn't speak wondering what was going to happen next. His question was answered when the Dragon Master lowered her head once more.

She then said, "I forgot to mention which dragon leirds I will be visiting with. As I call the dragon leird's name, that dragon leird and its trainer will come to the center of the room. The rest of you will begin your training. Bobby, Mike, Heather, Frank, Alan, and Chris, I will talk to you in a group. The next names I will talk to individually—Susan, Jerry, and Ryan. The rest of you have much to do with your training. I suggest you get started."

And with that, she removed her head once more from their presence shortly after the dragon leirds began wondering what to do next. When one of the walls began to rumble as it began to split open revealing a large grassy area full of training obstacles. The unselected dragon leirds filtered out with their trainers when the last one exited the wall slammed shut not allowing any of the dragon leirds to reenter. As the nine remaining dragon leirds and trainers waited, they all wondered what would happen next.

Chapter 8

After the wall had closed, the remaining restless dragon leirds were expecting the Dragon Master to immediately reshow herself to further instruct them. They soon realized that the Dragon Master performed tasks on her own timetable. As the majority of the dragon leirds went back to the areas where they were resting prior to the Dragon Master's announcement, Bobby refused to sit, almost pacing a trench in the stone floor, anxiously waiting for the Dragon Master to announce their names and where they were to go.

Ryan finally had enough of Bobby's pacing. He got up and walked right into Bobby's path facing his back. He was getting ready to give him a piece of his mind, but before Ryan could take in another breath to give Bobby what was on his mind, everyone heard a large gust of wind coming from the hallway followed by a large intense reddish-orange light and heat source. Ryan and Bobby were right in the middle of this fire's path and each quickly split going in different directions to avoid getting burned.

The fire got closer, the gust of wind got louder, the heat got more intense, and the light grew brighter. When the fire got within a few feet of entering the room, the wind exited the tunnel causing a burst of wind, which everyone in the room felt. Shortly after, a pillar of fire also exited. Once it reached the middle of the room, it began to expand looking like a tornado until it reached a diameter, well, over twenty-five feet.

The fire pillar stopped expanding and the middle turned from its reddish-orange glow to a bright white radiance. This caught all the dragon leirds attention as they all quickly gathered in front of it. Once all the dragon leirds had gathered in front of the large pillar, they were all intrigued when suddenly the center slowly began to develop into an image. At first, it was fuzzy and hard to make out, but as the image began to get more pronounced, there were features that left no doubt that the image was the Dragon Master. At first, the dragon leirds thought she was asleep because she had her eyes closed. Then without warning, her eyes opened widely, frightening some of the dragon leirds who had moved in closer for a better look.

The Dragon Master made a quick scan of the room then she spoke. "Good, only the requested dragon leirds are here. I am going to talk to Bobby, Mike, Heather, Frank, Alan, and Chris along with their trainers first. If you will, just follow this fire pillar. I will announce the next dragon leirds I will talk to after I finish with this group."

The Dragon Master finished speaking, and the pillar began to retract back into the hallway from where it came. The chosen dragon leirds and trainers followed after it. Not long after the last dragon leird crossed into the hallway, a wall of fire closed off the passage. The fire cooled down as it did were the passageway was is now a solid rock wall.

As the young dragon leirds continued to follow the pillar of fire, one of the dragon leirds wasn't mesmerized by the Dragon Master's image anymore and began to examine the walls. For the first few hundred feet, all that was offered was plain rock walls with no cave pictures or writings. Alan was getting bored by the repetitious walking, but as they neared closer to the Dragon Master, Alan noticed that the left wall remained the same rock structure. But the right side began to develop into the backside of what appeared to be statues.

He could tell that they were dragons by their tails and wings, but the front side of the statues were on the other side and the backside didn't offer much detail. Out of curiosity, he turned to his trainer and asked, "Hanec, what are these figures we are walking behind?"

Hanec stopped in his tracks, turned around, and approached Alan saying, "They are dragons."

He turned back around to proceed on to the Dragon Master.

But he was stopped again by another question from Alan. "Wait, Hanec, who are they?"

Hanec turned around again and said a little more sternly, "That question is better asked to the Dragon Master herself when she addresses us all." He spun around and quickly caught up to the rest of the group. Alan, not moving from his stance, took one last look at the statues and began to count them. His final number was six and finally continued down the hallway. He kept Hanec's advice in his mind so he could ask the Dragon Master his question.

As the dragon leirds were lead further down the hallway, still only Alan recognized the backside of the six statues as they rounded a corner. Alan could no longer see the statues as they moved further down the beaten path. Then the pillar suddenly disappeared through a smaller opening leaving them in the dark. The dragon leirds stood puzzled by the fact that the pillar of fire no longer was leading them.

Mike took the initiative as he slide in between the others coming from behind as he surprisingly and easily squeezed through the small opening and taking very little time. The other dragon leirds were still apprehensive but followed Mike's lead. One by one, they began to pass through the opening. When the last dragon leird passed through the small entrance, they were all awestruck by the beauty of the room they were in. The entire room was completely made out of silver; the shine and the luster were perfect.

Each of the individual dragon leirds began to look closer. They all could almost see their reflections perfectly in this precious metal. It was like looking straight into a mirror. Their trainers had been through this procedure many times and were waiting for the Dragon Master. While the dragon leirds continued to marvel and look around at this amazing room, Heather found a perfectly smooth, perfectly large oval section about five inches thick of silver. It was suspended in the air two feet from the wall. It was not held up by any wire or rope—nothing, just suspended in the air.

The other dragon leirds also found and began to observe the mirror. When Frank slipped in a puddle of water, he grabbed unto the mirror to balance himself. When his touch caused a reaction within the mirror making it bounce around, it moved around in a circle.

Heather walked over to Frank and demanded, "What did you do?"

Frank was speechless, then he and the other dragon leirds watched as the mirror proceeded to spin. Then it slowly began to calm down and an image began to develop within it.

The dragon leirds focused on the developing image. They were all comforted when the image finally cleared revealing the Dragon Master. Then an amazing event began to unfold, the walls in the room began to reflect the Dragon Master's image. Soon all the walls contained her image. Each of the images began to reflect a single ray of colored light in the middle of the room right in front of the mirror. The lights began to develop into a small three dimensional image portal allowing the Dragon Master to walk through the portable, but she was one-fourth the size of her body.

She entered the room with her front right foot. All the dragon leirds were shocked as the Dragon Master's claws broke through the surface of the mirror entering the room with her right leg followed by her left leg then next her head followed by her neck. She then pulled the rest of her body through the mirror, crowding the already little room. A couple of the dragon leirds let a sigh of relief while others remained in awe of what just happened.

The Dragon Master turned her head toward the relived dragon leirds and commented, "Frank, Mike, who or what were you expecting?" Frank and Mike being caught off guard couldn't find words to explain themselves. The Dragon Master ignored their sighs and continued, "Welcome, young Lumac dragon leirds. The reason you are here is to receive further instruction from me. I will permit you to ask me any question on your mind after my instruction to you is finished."

The young dragon leirds were still in stunned, in awe over the three-dimensional image of the Dragon Master and could only nod their heads in agreeance with her. The Dragon Master saw the acceptance of her counsel and decided to continue. "You particular dragon leirds have been summoned to this room to receive my counsel for a very specific reason. All of you are known in this world as Lumac leirds.

"What this means to you is that there are simply two sides in the war of this world. The side that is in support of my cause are called Gunars. They fight for the peace of the valley and the creatures that live in and around it as well as for me. But the opposing force are called the Wapecs. They fight for greed, power, and the thrill of killing for fun or, as they prefer to call it, sport. Your hearts have not prechosen a side to join.

"You must choose a side to join soon. For unless you chose a side by the time you become a dragon lord, you are permitted a length of time of three months before a sentence will be carried out of betrayal. You will be banished to Seven Mile Lake. Your body will begin to change developing gills and webbing between your fingers and toes, adapting to a life solely to be spent in water. You will, from that point and forever, be known as a water dragon.

"You will seek out and join up with Lumac, the only original dragon lord who became a water dragon, and leader of his group or, as he refers to them, his army of water dragons. He is the only original dragon lord general still alive from the beginning of beginnings—"

The Dragon Master was cut short by an outburst toward the back of the room from Heather as

she asked with confusion on her face and in her voice, "What is the beginning of beginnings?"

The Dragon Master was used to be interrupted several times throughout her counsel and always was this particular part. The Dragon Master gave out a small chuckle. After she was finished, she looked in Heather's direction. Then she said, "Heather, I told you to not to interrupt me until I was finished, but I will answer your question quickly before I continue with my instruction. The beginning of beginnings happened almost thirty thousand years ago. It was the beginning of my life and the lives of my dragon lords. I had established peace for almost twenty thousand years. Then about nine thousand years ago, a rebellion took place creating this war. Ever since then, there has never been eternal peace in the valley—"

The Dragon Master was stopped again, but this time, it was by Frank who blurted out, "But, Dragon Master, in the cave you said that this world is a world of beauty, magic, and peace. How can there be peace and war?"

The Dragon Master occasionally had a dragon leird ask her this question. She answered the question with caution. "It is true. The land is at war, and I also said the land contains peace. As dragon leirds in training, you will be surrounded by peace, by the protection of the training walls. Beyond the walls, it slowly turns into a war zone.

"However, even with the war, there are times of peace established, usually with a peace offering given to either side with a treaty containing a specific time period of peace to recuperate each side's forces and rest for continuous fighting. When winter comes, the Wapecs automatically head back for Wapec Valley to wait for spring. This is also a time of peace." The Dragon Master looked around the room at each of the dragon leirds, looking for any more questions the dragon leirds might have. The Dragon Master saw some confusion but none were stepping forward, so she proceeded with the rest of her counsel to them.

"As I said earlier, there are two sides of this war and there are two chosen dragon leird leaders to represent each side. The leaders of these two sides will try to influence you in choosing a side to join so you can help with their cause. For the Gunars, the leader is Ryan and his trainer is Nogar. For the Wapec side, the leader is Jerry and his trainer is Sparcan.

"When you begin your training, both will confront you in different ways, but it is your choice to choose a side or not to choose a side. My counsel is finished now. I will leave you time to ask any question you may have."

The dragon leirds began to turn toward each other and murmured amongst each other. The whispering was broken up by a sudden outburst by Bobby. "How did you walk through that suspended mirror?"

The Dragon Master knew this question would also be asked so she began to answer. "This room is made up of Amvongare silver. In this silver is a chemical called vonga. When it combines with the salt from your sweat, it creates a chemical reaction which allows me, when standing directly behind it, to walk through a portal connected to the mirror. Thus, I could walk through it and talk to you. In order for this to happen, a young leird must touch the mirror before sunset before the chemical reaction can occur."

All the dragon leirds had a confused look on their faces. None of them asked any further questions regarding the mirror or any other subjects. The Dragon Master waited for any other questions. As the time dragged on in silence, she decided to finish their meeting and addressed the group. "I see that all your questions have been answered for now, so I will allow you to begin your training." She pointed to the nearest crevasse to the mirror, and it began to split open creating an entrance to the training grounds, just as she promised.

The dragon leirds began to filter out of the room unto the training grounds all except for Alan. He remained fixed in his position resting against the wall. When the rest of the dragon leirds exited the room with their trainers, the Dragon Master turned to Alan and said, "I have sensed your uneasiness and perhaps you might want to ask me a question while we are alone. We are alone, now ask me your question."

Alan pushed off the wall using his mid-back and shoulders. He turned more directly toward her and asked, "While traveling down the hallway and as we got closer to this room, I noticed the backside of a series of statues. When I asked Hanec about them, he seemed uneasy and informed me to ask you about them. So who are they?"

The Dragon Master herself seemed uneasy, not eager to answer his question. She remained quiet while she was thinking about Alan's question and pondered on her own thoughts. *Alan can see the statues because he is a true Lumac leird observing the negative feelings of Lumac because he was banished to Seven Mile Lake. If he remains unconverted, he will undoubtedly remained fixed on joining with the other water dragons.*

The Dragon Master finally decided to break her silence and answer Alan. "The statues you saw are of my nine council members from the beginning of beginnings—"

As the Dragon Master mentioned the number of statues, Alan counted from his memory and blurted out, "You say nine, but I only counted seven."

The Dragon Master looked patiently at Alan and answered, "You can only see seven from the hallway, but in the council room, there are nine total statues—"

Alan interrupted her again, "Why didn't we meet in the council instead on this cramped area?"

The Dragon Master was getting flustered by Alan's constant disruption every time she was in the middle of her comments. But calmly, she answered his question again. "The reason that I didn't invite the Lumac leirds to the council room is because that room is set aside for more important meetings, but soon you too will be invited to this room to receive more counsel from me."

Alan was upset about the fact that he or the other Lumac leirds were not important enough to meet in the council room. He thought back to her earlier counsel about choosing a side, and he didn't want anything to do with any group who labels a person before they get to know them. He decided to leave and start on his training.

As he was leaving, he was stopped by the Dragon Master who said, "Alan, remember that your choice will affect your whole life, forever.

Whatever you choose, you cannot change so be firm and confident in your final decision but be happy most of all."

Alan pondered her counsel for a minute before he continued on his way. He exited the cave looking back. The Dragon Master was beginning to fade, becoming more and more transparent. As she faded, the wall slowly began to close, leaving Alan and his trainer with the other leirds and their training.

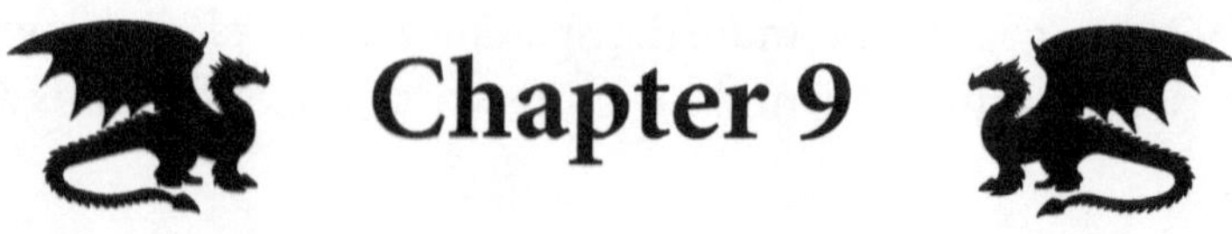

Chapter 9

Meanwhile in the assembly hall or the torch room as Ryan, Jerry, and Susan were calling it, Susan's constant pacing was beginning to annoy Jerry and was making Ryan nervous. Finally, she ended up stopping in front of Ryan then turning toward him, she said, "I wonder what the Dragon Master wants to talk to us about." But what Susan was really thinking was what the Dragon Master wanted to talk to her about. She then immediately picked up her pacing after her quick comment.

As Ryan continued to watch her, he got up and walked up behind her and gently touched her on her shoulders.

Susan jumped from the unexpected contact. She suddenly turned around with murder in her eyes and said sternly, "My brothers were constantly scaring me. They even turned it into a game to see which one could make me the maddest. If you ever do that again, I will hurt you!"

Susan glared at Ryan while Ryan chuckled trying to smooth things over, but Susan continued to glare right through him. Jerry smirked as Ryan's charm was beginning to wear off and he could finally move in.

Ryan finally said nervously, not wanting to get hit, "I've been watching you pace for what seems like hours now. We are all anxious for our turn with the Dragon Master. I'm sure she will be in contact with us real soon."

At the end of his comment, Ryan hugged Susan. Jerry who was listening to the blubbering conversation just rolled his eyes in annoyance. But Susan was truly comforted by Ryan as she held tight.

Their embrace was broken up by the Dragon Master's loud voice. "I will now begin my instruction to the three of you. I will call you by name. Enter the chosen stairway entrance. It will then lead you to my upper chambers and right to me."

Susan turned to Ryan after the Dragon Master ended and asked him, "I haven't seen any stairways anywhere, so how are we supposed to get up to see the Dragon Master?"

Ryan didn't know either and his answer was just as puzzled as his expression. But Ryan responded, "I have no idea. Before you asked me, I was thinking that maybe Nogar knows about it. Let's find him and Angoree and ask them."

Susan agreed, so they began to scan the assembly hall desperately trying to locate Nogar and Angoree so they could ask them where to locate the entrance leading the staircase and upper chambers. The two trainers were spotted high up the east wall on a ledge resting together.

Ryan cupped his hands around his mouth and spoke loudly, "Nogar, Angoree, wake up! Susan and I need to talk to you."

This loud announcement not only woke up both trainers but alerted Jerry as well who went back to his evil plan with Sparcan to take over Dragtoneea and defeat the Dragon Master.

The two trainers glided down to the floor right in front of Susan and Ryan, and Jerry quietly snuck away from Sparcan without him noticing so that he could listen on the conversation. So he went over to a large boulder to conceal himself. Ryan walked right up to Nogar who was turning around to face Ryan and Susan. Ryan was taking the initiative to find out more about the Dragon Master's message. He was acting important trying to impress Susan who rolled her eyes at his feeble attempt.

Ryan looked Nogar right in his eyes saying with authority, "The Dragon Master said there is an entrance to her upper chamber. Susan and I have looked over this entire area, but there's no kind of hallway other than the one the Lumac leirds went through. But it is now sealed close, and there's no ramp or stairs of any kind. So how are we supposed to get to the Dragon Master so we can talk with her?"

Jerry who was still concealed, listened contently in case he could learn something to help defeating Ryan. Nogar was not fazed by Ryan's puffed up performance and gently said, "Ryan, this world isn't like your old world. There is a magic about this place unlike anything you could imagine. You have already witnessed a couple incidents of this magic when the Dragon Master spoke through the metal dragon on the key door. As well as when the entrance appeared for the Lumac leirds. The Dragon Master has her ways in which she wants to run certain matters, but trust me, she won't disappoint you."

Ryan eased up his tensed body instantly as he was calmed by Nogar's counsel and walked back to Susan. Jerry was unaware that Sparcan was right behind just as the others were unaware of him being behind the boulder. Jerry was disappointed that no vital information was revealed that could be used in the defeat of his foe.

Discouraged, Jerry turned around and he had to cover his mouth to prevent his screaming from filling the air from being startled by Sparcan while Sparcan was not amused by Jerry's disappearing act from their secret meeting and expressed his disapproval of his decision all over his face. Sparcan continued to stare Jerry down. Jerry's uncomfortable sense was causing him to sweat profusely. Finally, he dug up enough courage to ask Sparcan, "Why are you mad at me?"

But before Sparcan could respond, everyone's attention was drawn to the ceiling close to where the opening was for the Lumac leirds. At this part of the ceiling came a noise that sounded familiar, a noise heard back in the cave of metal rubbing against rock. The noise drew each dragon leird with their trainers to this part of the cave close enough to the ceiling to see a circular stone rotating clockwise. Jerry walked away from his hiding spot and right up next to Ryan as he was focused on the noise and didn't notice where he had stopped.

Suddenly, just like the dragon, a large metal pillar broke free from the ceiling as the pillar descended in the same clockwise rotation. The dragon leirds could see that the metal base looked to be made of brass. It covered three feet up from the bottom of the pillar. The remainder of the pillar was crafted from a very fine gold and precious gems arranged in a spectacular artwork.

Each of the dragon leirds were awestruck by the beauty of the artwork of three dragons formed from the gold with red gem eyes. They were swimming in a sea of gold waves outlined in silver, each trying to capture the multiple priceless gems—gems of diamonds, rubies, emeralds, and sapphires of all shapes, colors, and sizes.

Susan and Ryan were speechless even after the pillar rested on the ground. But Jerry's mouth watered as he looked at the endless gems and gold, ignoring the art completely only wanting the riches contained in it.

The mesmerized dragon leirds continued to gaze at the pillar when they were all startled once again by the Dragon Master's voice. She said, "The first leird I will speak with will be Susan. Come to the pillar and climb the stairs up to my chamber."

Her voice stopped so Susan obeyed her words but was wondering how she would climb up the pillar. As she arrived at the pillar, her eyes were pulled toward a large purple diamond that looked to be just out of reach on one of the dragon's mouths who was reaching for it. Susan's curiosity got to her, so she reached out and touched the diamond. As soon as she did, unaware of what would happen, this dragon stretched out its neck and snapped at Susan's finger.

She was currently holding her finger on the diamond but the snapping dragon caused her to jump back. As soon as her finger was removed from the diamond, it sunk deep into the pillar until the diamond stopped moving. After this, the same rubbing noise was heard as gold bricks were pushed out of the pillar. The bricks measured three feet wide by four feet long and two feet thick. These bricks started at the base of the copper and continued up in a spiral pattern creating stairs.

When the last brick was pushed out just inches from the ceiling, a strange activity began to happen. The hole where the pillar broke free from began to expand in a folding motion allowing enough space for Susan and her trainer to enter comfortably. Susan looked up the staircase into the vast unknown room above were the Dragon Master was waiting. Susan was a little timid to take the first step.

As Susan prolonged her climb, she began to study the outer parts of the stairs and noticed that the artwork on the pillar once pushed out by the stairs created a new piece of art. Susan noticed that each of the step's art developed into a long Chinese-looking dragon. It was wrapping around the pillar, and like the original piece, it seemed to be chasing gems. Susan was still uneasy about leaving Ryan to talk to an enormous dragon and still procrastinating her first step.

As Susan waited longer, Angoree relayed a message to her through their minds. *Susan, it will be all right. The Dragon Master is just going to give you some more instruction. Everything will be fine.*

Susan's confidence got a big boost from Angoree's comforting words, and she took the first step and began to climb with Angoree right behind her. Ryan watched her climb and worry suddenly appeared and then he began to stress out as the thought of her safety saturated his mind.

Susan stuck her head into the upper room and looked around. The large room appeared to be empty as it was dimly lit with fewer candles then in the lower room. Upon seeing that the room was empty, Susan finished climbing the stairs and stepped into the chamber of the Dragon Master. No sooner had Susan stepped into the room, the stairs sunk back into the pillar then it shot back up allowing no one else to enter. The floor unfolded back into its original position preventing Susan from jumping down.

As Susan stared and stewed over the collapsible floor, she was unaware of the Dragon Master standing behind her. Angoree sensed the Dragon Master's presence and bowed in reverence. Susan was still intrigued by the floor. Angoree raised her head and saw that Susan still had her back toward the Dragon Master. She then hit Susan with her tail on her right ankle just below the ankle bone. Susan grabbed her ankle and hopping then turned around to give Angoree a piece of her mind but instead saw the Dragon Master and bowed, following the example of her trainer.

The Dragon Master reached her arms toward them beckoning them to rise to their feet by slowly raising both arm up. Once both had raised, the Dragon Master spoke softly, "Hello, Susan and Angoree. I am sure you are wondering why I have summoned you to my private quarters?"

Angoree knew, having done this several times, but Susan looked at the Dragon Master and said, "Yes, Dragon Master, I have been pondering why you want to talk to me alone."

The Dragon Master just smiled and turned and began to walk to a different part of her quarters. Susan, a little annoyed, followed after being determined to get an answer. Finally, the Dragon Master stopped abruptly, and Susan almost ran into her from following closely behind her. Susan then walked around her massive body and saw that the Dragon Master was looking into a wooden chest admiring something. When Susan came to a stop several feet away from the chest, the Dragon Master reached into the chest to pick something up. Susan was curious but remained motionless. The Dragon Master then pulled out a perfectly cut diamond in the size of Susan's hand.

Susan was drawn to the diamond like a moth to a light in no time so much that she almost had her face pressed up to it admiring its beauty.

Seeing Susan's interest, the Dragon Master said, "Susan, my dear, you are a very special dragon leird who will become a very important dragon lord."

Susan listened but kept her eyes on the diamond.

The Dragon Master continued, "Susan, do you know why you have such an interest in diamonds and gems?"

Susan broke her concentration on the diamond so she could think into her past. She remembered from a very young age having a fascination in rhinestones and costume jewelry. As she got older, she remembered wearing her mother's expensive jewelry and idolizing royalty movie stars who wore millions of dollars around their necks and on their ears. Susan popped her daydream and answered the Dragon Master's question. "I, from a young age, have always loved jewelry and have dreamed about owning and wearing diamonds. But that diamond tops all my daydreams." And with a very serious look and tone, she asked, "Can I have it?"

The Dragon Master let out a short laugh then looked directly at Susan and said, "You don't need this, Susan." She then she put the diamond back in the chest. The Dragon Master turned to a small peering hole. Then she continued, "Susan, you are a very special dragon leird, and when you become a dragon lord, you will become what is known in Dragtoneea as a jewel dragon."

Susan wrinkled her nose and asked, "What is a jewel dragon?"

The Dragon Master was familiar with all sorts of reactions from young dragon leirds throughout the years and while smiling said, "A jewel dragon is the heartbeat of Dragtoneea. You see, Susan, as a jewel dragon, you will have an incredible gift, the ability to create and produce all sorts of jewels and gems as you please."

Susan's eyes lit up as she heard and pondered on her future gift.

The Dragon Master continued, "But, Susan, you are a Lumac leird and will have to convert to a side either the Gunars or the Wapecs. If you don't, you will be banished to Seven Mile Lake and become what is known as a water jewel and live amongst the mermaids in the Green Sea."

Susan was still daydreaming when she asked, "Dragon Master, am I the only jewel dragon, and am I the only one who has this gift?"

The Dragon Master turned from looking through a peering hole overlooking the training toward to Susan. She then said, "No, my child, there are hundreds of jewel dragons in Dragtoneea. They live in a peaceful place called the Valley of Peace. It is a beautiful place guarded by my strongest and best guards to avoid an ambush by the Wapecs."

She paused then continued, "Susan, you are very special, and I want you to choose carefully. I can't make this decision for you." She stopped and looked at Susan who was pondering the advice she had been given.

After a moment, Susan raised her head looking directly at the Dragon Master and asked, "Which side is Ryan on?"

The Dragon Master puffed out her chest as she answered Susan's question. "He is the Gunar, leader-to-be. I have great expectations for him."

Susan paused for a moment, and with sweaty palms, she spoke up. "Then I choose his side!"

The Dragon Master looked carefully into Susan's eyes and said, "My child, do you have feelings for him?"

When the Dragon Master asked her this question, it was as if all her worries about Ryan went away as she answered, "Yes, Dragon Master, I do. I want to be with him."

The Dragon Master pulled herself back, and with reservation, she spoke clearly, "Susan, you and Ryan are special, and I will have to think this matter over. But for now, you have training to accomplish." With her conclusion, she raised her left arm and pointed to the wall close to the peering hole doing so the wall began to crack open. As it opened wider, it revealed a staircase. When it finished opening, the Dragon Master said, "You may leave now."

Susan was hesitant, but Angoree pulling on her persuaded her to leave and enter the training grounds.

Once the wall had closed behind them, Angoree turned to Susan and asked, "Susan, are you mad at the Dragon Master simply because she won't let you be with Ryan? You must understand that it is impossible."

And with tears in her eyes, she exclaimed to Angoree, "But why, Angoree? I feel a connection with him, and I want to be with him." As Susan turned her head from talking to Angoree, she stopped from descending down the stairs as she was amazed by the stunning beauty of the training grounds.

Chapter 10

As an eerie silence engulfed Jerry and Ryan. They were suddenly startled by the loud voice of the Dragon Master. She spoke loudly saying, "Jerry, I will speak to you next. Enter the doorway that appears."

Jerry smirked while looking at Ryan and said, "I have always been better at everything than you, and now, it's apparent that it implies here too." Jerry was waiting for the same staircase that Susan went up to come down.

As he was looking at the ceiling, he was suddenly startled and taken off guard by two red eyes staring directly at him as they slithered from a dark corner opposite of him. The eyes got bigger as they got closer, and Jerry was backing up to an opposing counter of the approaching beast. As the eyes came into the light, it was clear to see that it was a black dragon with more of a serpent's body with those deep red piercing eyes. Its body was covered in thorny spikes that were striped in black and red. The dragon then opened its mouth and waited. But Jerry remained motionless, not eager to walk into the dragons mouth leading to his certain death.

Sparcan immediately flew into the dragon's mouth and rested on its tongue and then motioned to Jerry to join him. Jerry refused but jumped by the sudden loud voice of the Dragon Master. "Jerry, you must enter into the doorway. The dragon's mouth is the doorway, and you must enter into it in order to come into my chamber for my further instruction."

Jerry cautiously edged closer to the dragon's mouth. He could hear it breathing which made his hairs rose on the back of his neck. He carefully stepped in between the large yellow-stained teeth. Jerry walked inside the squishy mouth and sat down on the tongue next to Sparcan. No sooner had he sat down when the dragon snapped close its mouth and quickly disappeared back from where it came, leaving Ryan and Nogar alone. All Ryan could think was, *The Dragon Master just killed my best friend.*

As soon as Nogar knew that he and Ryan were alone, he flew over to him knowing that he was crushed by Jerry's comment. He then said, "Ryan, I can't say very much right now, but you are about to find out that your feelings regarding this matter are going to change."

Ryan really didn't understand what Nogar meant, so he just waited in silence until it was his turn.

As Jerry sat on the giant tongue, his pants were getting saturated from the saliva swishing around in the dragon's mouth. Jerry didn't understand why Sparcan was so calm while he was still thinking that they were going to be lunch. Finally, he couldn't take it anymore and looked at Sparcan also sitting on the tongue and said, "Why are you so calm?"

Surprised Sparcan said, "What are you talking about?"

Jerry responded, "Riding in this dragon's mouth, don't you think he might be hungry?"

Sparcan now understood why Jerry was acting that way. He started to laugh; this did not amuse Jerry one bit. Once Sparcan got control of himself, he said, "This dragon is the way the Wapec leaders ride in style to receive counsel from the Dragon Master."

Jerry sighed in relief knowing his life for now was safe from danger of being eaten.

As the dragon continued to crawl, Jerry could feel every movement it made. The only cushion available was the soft tongue as it absorbed most of violent jerking motions. Finally after what seemed to be an hour, the giant beast began to slow down and open its mouth allowing steam to escape from his muggy atmosphere. As soon as the mouth was wide enough, Sparcan took flight and disappeared from Jerry's sight. Jerry cautiously took several steps and slide out between the dragon's teeth unto solid ground instantly feeling relief.

Soon after, Jerry began to look around the enormous room, and he began to step away from luxurious ride. Jerry's movements allowed the dragon to close his mouth and backed into the hole that he emerged from leaving their presence. Jerry continued to scan the room and couldn't help but notice a gigantic table for what he imagined would only seat—giants. Beyond the table on the back wall were large dragon statues all in a line.

Jerry was intrigued, so he began the long walk over to equally gigantic statues. As he got closer, he was surprised to see more and more statues emerge from the darkness. What surprised him even more was the fact that each statue was made of pure solid gold. Plus the detailed work on each dragon statue was truly done by a skilled and talented artist. Jerry couldn't get past the craftsmanship as he moved up one of the statues body.

When he got to the lowered head, he noticed that each of the eye were a solid clear diamond. Much larger than the diamond he tried to dig out in the cave earlier which he guessed was close to eighty carats, priceless. He was about to move unto the next one and see if its eyes were diamonds too but stopped when he heard, "They are all diamonds, Jerry," said the Dragon Master. She continued, "Clear stones for those who are obedient to me and red stones for those who fight against me."

Jerry was fascinated by the amount of treasure in arm's reach that he said, "So you have a collection of dragon statues. Those who follow you and those who oppose you. That's kind of weird." Jerry smirked from his comment.

The Dragon Master paid no attention to his smirking and instead said, "These are not just random followers and impostures. These dragon lords were the original members of my dragon council thousands of years ago."

Sparcan snarled under his breath for he was a key member of that council, but his statue was pulled down before completion for his so-called betrayal.

The Dragon Master continued, "This council was created to help develop many of the dragon laws that are still used to this day to help govern Dragtoneea."

Sparcan's rage was building in him as he thought how his statue was torn down despite his advice he gave to the council.

As the Dragon Master moved away from the statues, she spoke, "Jerry, we have much to discuss and we can't focus on the past but we have to look to the future. You are a very important dragon leird for your heart has settled on the side of the Wapecs, but more importantly, you are the leader of your fellow Wapec leirds. Also there are some dragon leirds whose hearts are undecided, and it is your duty to help them choose—"

The Dragon Master was interrupted by Jerry. "If they have to choose, who else is there to compete with?"

The Dragon Master continued, "Ryan is the leader of the Gunars—"

She again was interrupted by Jerry bursting out it laughter.

"*Silence!*" exclaimed the Dragon Master. "Ryan and you are the chosen leaders. Each of you are special in your own ways."

Jerry looked right into the Dragon Master's eyes and said, "What's so special about Ryan?"

The Dragon Master very confidently looked back into Jerry's eyes gently and said, "You're a great leader as is Ryan."

Jerry snickered when he heard the Dragon Master continued to say that Ryan was a great leader.

Under his breath, he said, "Ryan is a follower, and even as a follower, he's a loser."

The Dragon Master heard all that he said and moved in closer to Jerry and said, "Laugh and murmur all you want, but Ryan is a great leader. His heart is good and pure, willing to do anything for those who he loves and leads."

Jerry raised an eyebrow as if to say, "yeah right," then the Dragon Master turned and walked away from Jerry completely satisfied with her answer.

Sparcan then flew over to Jerry and said, "Ryan is soft like a grape, and when the time is right, you will squeeze and squeeze until his head bursts. Then you will know that he is weak and you have always been stronger."

Jerry just looked at Sparcan, not really knowing how to react to his comment.

The Dragon Master returned to Jerry who was being distracted by Sparcan. She was holding a large clear pearly tinted spiraling shell that looked as big as Jerry's head was. While holding the shell, she began to give instructions. "Jerry, this is a medatore shell. I need you to stand on the right side of the shell and Sparcan the left side, and when I give the order, both of you will touch the shell and then, Jerry, tell me what you see."

Jerry thought this was ridiculous but he had seen some amazing things so far, so he decided to go along with it.

"Now!" said the Dragon Master, and both Jerry and Sparcan touched the shell at the same time.

At first, Jerry was joking in his head that he had a crystal ball that will tell the future. But he stopped when the clear shell began to get cloudy, and then shortly after, images began to emerge from the cloud. The first image Jerry saw, he began to describe it as he saw it. "I see myself and Sparcan amongst the other dragon leirds and their trainers. I am speaking to them just like Sparcan has been speaking to me."

The Dragon Maser responded saying, "Good, good, what else?"

Jerry studied the shell a little harder. Suddenly, a different image began to develop. As it did, Jerry again began to describe it. "Now I see a group of us together. We are looking at what looks like Ryan and the dragon leirds he had tricked to join him. I am disgusted and angry at him. Is this right? He's my best friend?"

Sparcan immediately piped up and said, "You have no friend who is your enemy, Jerry. Your world has changed for the better, and I am the only friend you need."

The Dragon Master said gently, "Look again, Jerry."

He took his focus off Sparcan and back on the shell. He then said, "Well, I can't really make out what's in this image. It looks like a battle. It looks a lot like the one we saw from the Valley Death, and if I'm not mistaken, Sparcan is huge. Where am I?"

The Dragon Master spoke, "Jerry, you will become Sparcan. The two of you will merge together and become one in mind and body. Don't you remember my counsel from earlier today?"

Jerry pulled his hands off the shell and backed away from it. "I want to go home now, right now." "You can't," said Sparcan. "You came here with me, and there's no way to get back to what you call your blissful life. This is your life now forever and ever."

Jerry didn't budge for several minutes, pondering on Sparcan's words, and then he walked back to the shell and placing his hands on it, he said, "I'm ready to see the rest of my future."

But the Dragon Master pulled the shell away, leaving Jerry staring at Sparcan. She placed the shell back on the shelf from where she got it, leaving Jerry stunned. The Dragon Master spoke upon her return. "When you retreated from the shell breaking the connection, your desire to leave closed the vision and won't be able to be opened again until at a later time."

"*When!*" Jerry exclaimed.

"When your last vision comes true," said the Dragon Master.

Jerry exclaimed, "But I didn't even see all of that vision. I don't know when it will come true."

The Dragon Master responded, "I'm sorry. That's the way it works, but as for your first vision, here is the interpretation. You're a powerful leader, Jerry. Your influence can and will be heard. You have a mission to convince as many of the Lumac leirds to join your forces and fight for your cause."

Jerry looking down asked, "And Ryan, will he be doing the same?"

The Dragon Master replied, "Yes, you're both chosen to lead your fellow dragon leirds into lordship and then into battle, a fierce and bloody battle. You will command many and lead many, but you will return with less." The Dragon Master lowered her head in reference to the thousands she had lost on both sides.

Jerry waited for the Dragon Master to raise her head to continue to interpret his visions.

Finally not able to wait any longer, he spoke up. "Dragon Master, if you may, can I hear the rest of my known future?"

The Dragon Master raised her head. "Of course, you may, my child. Your second vision is not too unusual for a Wapec leader. It is a hatred for Gunar leirds as they develop into lords, but there is far too much hate and anger. Something is throwing your balance off. Has Ryan done something to you that has hurt you recently?" The Dragon Master asked Jerry seriously.

Jerry shrugged his shoulders and said, "Not that I can think of. I've always won everything we have done together, including getting the girls." Jerry chuckled smiling as he thought of Susan.

The Dragon Master thought for a moment knowing that Susan had already chosen Ryan and chose not to share it with Jerry at this time. The Dragon Master then said, "Well, I'm sure the reason will be revealed at its proper time. As for your last vision, it's difficult to depict when it is really happening. All I can say is that it's a battle, of course, and your target is Ryan and you want to kill him and cause him to suffer as you have suffered."

Sparcan listened carefully and could tell the Dragon Master knew more than she was telling them, so he flew in closer to her where Jerry couldn't hear him.

Sparcan then said, "Dragon Master, I sense you know more than you are telling us. I know you can let Jerry have another vision to help him understand why he is building this anger up. He needs to know no matter how painful it may be. He needs to know."

The Dragon Master turned to Jerry and asked him, "Knowing what you know now, do you have any questions for me?"

Jerry stood in silence for a few seconds then he spoke up. "So I am the leader of my fellow

Wapec leirds, and these Lumac leirds, how will I know who they are?"

"Good question," the Dragon Master said. "Your trainer, Sparcan, will teach you how to tell them apart, and then the rest is up to you."

Jerry was a little frustrated with the Dragon Master for not telling him how to tell the Lumac leirds apart right away and slightly began to clinch his fists together. But his anger was interrupted by the Dragon Master saying, "Jerry, I know you are getting frustrated. Due to all the new challenges here, that's why I am going to let you know why you have hurtful and resentful feelings toward Ryan through a new vision."

Jerry got excited to place his hands back unto the large shell and have a new vision, but when the Dragon Master returned, she was holding a much smaller shell covered with sharp spikes.

The Dragon Master began to explain the new shell. "This is a bitter shell. The visions you get from this shell are bitter and hurtful. It's the only way you will understand your feelings toward Ryan, so when you are ready, place your hands on the shell."

Jerry wasn't so excited now to place his hands on this new shell. But as he built up his courage, he finally placed his hands on the uninviting spikes. As his skin touched the spikes, it was like thousands of hooks dug into him releasing a token to cloud his eyes so he couldn't see anything. Slowly as his eyes began to clear, the first image he saw was Susan which brought a smile to his face. But quickly disappeared as he saw that he was being ignored by Susan to run to Ryan embracing in a hug. The vision continued as they held hands and kissed, turning their backs on Jerry leaving him.

Suddenly his hands didn't hurt any more as he realized his vision was over, and all he could think was how Ryan betrayed him. As well as how he would have his vengeance on his enemy and how enemies' blood will spill on the ground. Sparcan was reading Jerry's thoughts and grinned knowing this would close his heart toward Ryan for good. Further allowing him to plan out his revenge on Ryan and Nogar.

The Dragon Master knew that Sparcan wanted Jerry to see that Susan chose Ryan over him because this was the final straw to turn Jerry completely against Ryan. She also knew that Jerry wouldn't want to hear any more counsel, so she decided to send them to the training grounds. She did so by saying, "Your pain and suffering will continue to build inside of you, and the only way you will get your mind off it is to begin your training."

So Sparcan flew straight toward a wall in the cave which opened allowing them to enter into the training grounds.

But his progress was stopped by the words from the Dragon Master. "Instead of entering the training grounds the traditional way, you will use the abandoned staircase across the room." The Dragon Master was pointing in the direction of the old staircase.

Sparcan had turned around and flew over to the Dragon Master and stopped when he got closer to her. He then said, "The walk of shame. What did we do to deserve that?"

The Dragon Master didn't say another word, just continued to point at the staircase.

Jerry was already heading to the staircase grumbling something, so Sparcan left the Dragon Master and joined up with him. As they walked toward the staircase in an awkward silence. Sparcan ended the silence. "Jerry, you are very angry. I can feel it pulsating through you, just as blood flows through my veins."

Jerry looked at Sparcan with a glare then said, "Of everyone, Ryan. What does Susan see in him that isn't in me?"

Sparcan was acting to comfort him as he said, "Jerry, there are many women out there. Some will like you, others not so much. However, I can tell you this Susan means a lot to you and that backstabbing so-called friend really hurt you."

Jerry acted like dust got in his eyes, and when he was sure there weren't any tears in his eyes, he looked at Sparcan. Acting tough, he asked, "What do you know of my pain?"

Sparcan just smiled then said, "I know all about backstabbing by those you have come to trust."

Jerry was now intrigued.

"Years and years ago when I was much younger, the Dragon Master was gathering gifted dragon lord's to form her council. I was one who was chosen. In this council, we all gave our thoughts and ideas to help improve Dragtoneea. One of my ideas were rejected by the majority of the council. I was furious as were those who also supported my proposal. We left the council and gathered as may dragon lords that we could to fight for our cause." Sparcan flew to a rock ledge to take a break.

Jerry rushed over to him and said eagerly, "What happened next?"

Sparcan was amused by Jerry's energy and amusement. "Well, since I was the lead cause in building our army and establishing our cause, I was given the rank of general. My name was founded as our troop name of Wapec—"

Jerry blurted out, "Wait a minute, your name is Sparcan not Wapec."

Sparcan continued, "My name in this body is Sparcan, but it was Wapec. And upon being a great leader, I was also feared. Now I wasn't able to convince as many as I was hoping for, but the ones I did were strong and ferocious. However, Gunar was chosen to defend those supporting the Dragon Master, and he was made general too. For years, we would have epic battles until one of us meets or death."

Jerry was listening intently as Sparcan continued. "I have waited for thousands of years to be reconnected in a body so I can have my revenge." Then looking at Jerry Sparcan said, "And you're going to help me get mine, and I will help you get yours."

Jerry liked the sound of that as he said "deal."

They then proceeded down devising a plan of their revenge, when Jerry was rudely interrupted by a phrase with a traitorous tone from Ryan. "Good luck, man."

Jerry turned and glared at him with daggers in his eyes before turning around and entering the training grounds with Sparcan.

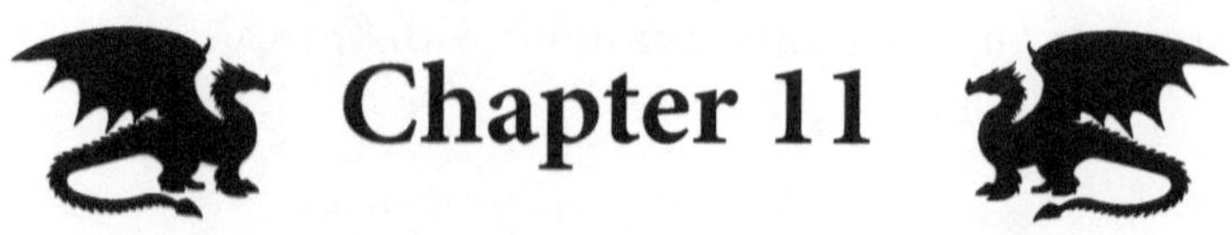

Chapter 11

Ryan began to examine the cave walls, getting awfully bored being alone, and he saw something out of the corner of his eye. It looked like something was hanging on one of the cave walls. So he left the part of the cave he was examining to look at what was hanging on this other wall. As he got closer, he saw that they were scales like the training scales presented earlier. So Ryan called over to Nogar saying, "Nogar, what are these scales on the wall? I can't understand the writing in it."

Nogar flew over to Ryan and knew immediately what they were as he said, "Those are ancient dragon laws created by the Dragon Council that the Dragon Master organized thousands of years ago. These laws help govern Dragtoneea today and only after you become a dragon lord will the writing be able to be read."

Ryan continued to observe the scales trying to focus on the writing to see if he could translate it. Meanwhile, Nogar was aware of the delaying time of Sparcan and Jerry and had a feeling that they were planning something.

Ryan had stopped focusing on the scales and was now daydreaming of the way Nogar and him would be escorted up to the Dragon Master. Would it be on a staircase like Susan or a freaky dragon like Jerry? His thoughts drowned out his surroundings including Nogar. Meanwhile, Nogar was using just about everything to get Ryan's attention sort of hitting him to let him know that the Dragon Master was summoning them. Finally, Ryan came back to reality being startled by Nogar as he was right in his face.

Both of them stopped and listened to a familiar voice of the Dragon Master. "Ryan, if you are ready, then I would like for you to take your turn to come and see me."

Ryan then began to look around and try to find the way they would be going to see her. It was at this point that Ryan saw Jerry and Sparcan were coming down a perfectly camouflaged staircase located in the side of the wall where Susan and Jerry both were escorted to the Dragon Master.

Ryan waved at Jerry, but he was completely focused with Sparcan talking about something and seemed like they were ignoring Ryan and Nogar on purpose. So Ryan waved his hands and jumped up and down, making attempts to get his attention, but he still proceeded to ignore him. Finally, Ryan made one last attempt by saying, "Good luck, man" ending with a smile.

Jerry heard Ryan and turned around, not with a smile but with a glare piercing Ryan's heart destroying his smile, leaving a gloomy feeling.

Ryan looked on with disappointment as Jerry and Sparcan disappeared out of sight unto the training grounds. Nogar who was hovering above Ryan settled down next to him as he spoke, "I'm so sorry to tell you, Ryan, but your friendship with Jerry here no longer exists. He will from here on try all he can to destroy you, but you will always want what you use to have with him."

With tears in his eyes, all he could do was look at Nogar as words were unable to form in his mouth.

In the middle of their tender moment, the Dragon Master spoke saying, "Ryan and Nogar, come forward."

As the two came toward the sound of her voice, they saw the Dragon Master's hand and arm come through the large hole where her voice and training scales came from.

Then the Dragon Master spoke again. "Now, Ryan and Nogar, step unto my hand, and I will lift you up into my chambers."

Just like Jerry, Ryan approached causally not knowing what will happen when he stepped on to her hand. He eventually took the last few steps to get unto her hand, and she gently pulled them upward toward her through the hole. Once in her chambers as she rests her hand on the ground, Ryan stepped off looking around. While Nogar continually gave her his ultimate respect and honor by bowing toward her. As Ryan kept looking, finding Nogar bowing before the Dragon Master, he too bowed himself before her.

The Dragon Master gratefully asked them to rise while they rose as she began to give them her counsel. "Ryan, you are a very important member of the dragon leirds. You are the Gunar leader, and Nogar will be very critical as he will help you make some important decisions."

Ryan was listening but also scanning the room noticing a large area with rounded out sections in it. He had to take his attention away from this section as the Dragon Master was demanding his attention. "Ryan, I am sorry, but I need your full attention as I am giving my counsel. Ryan, the reason you are the last dragon leird to see me is because you are a very important and special—"

The Dragon Master's comments were stopped by Ryan saying, "I'm not special. I'm a loser."

The Dragon Master knew she had to build him up before presenting him with all his new responsibility. She then said, "Ryan, you are not a failure or a loser. You have hidden talents and attributes that you will be surprised by. You are special here for a special reason."

Ryan looked up at the Dragon Master, and for the first time in a long time, he was proud of himself.

The Dragon Master now feeling that Ryan can now handle the responsibility of being a leader, walked over to a part of her chamber where she had shelves on the wall. On these shelves were several weird-looking shells; one was completely covered in spikes. It appeared that a few of the spikes had blood dripping down them. But Ryan didn't have much time to study the shells as the Dragon Master was returning with an enormous clear pearly tinted spiral shell.

Once she got closer to Ryan and Nogar, she began to explain the shell. "This is a medatore shell.

Now, Ryan, I want you on the right side of the shell and Nogar on the left—"

The Dragon Master was cut off by Ryan. "Excuse me, Dragon Master, but what exactly is a medatore?"

The Dragon Master wasn't surprised by Ryan's question as he was a curious boy about many things but especially when it comes to animals. She replied, "Of Course, Ryan, I would be happy to explain what a medatore is. It's a giant snail that lives in a series of ponds called the razor ponds. They have been hunted near to extinction because of the mystical power they have. When one touches the side of the shell, it has the power to predict the future…"

Ryan was fascinated with the story so far.

The Dragon Master continued, "Because of this, the Wapecs have hunted them continually trying and hoping they could gain this power. But unknown to them, one of these snails have to sacrifice itself in order for this power to work. And when I came to them, they saw me having a pure heart. It really impressed them, and one was chosen to do the sacrifice to benefit my cause here in Dragtoneea."

Ryan was completely amazed by the story and couldn't wait to touch the shell.

The Dragon Master gave the same instruction of positioning Ryan and Nogar around the shell then she said, "Once you are both ready, both of you shall touch the shell then describe to me what you see."

Ryan was excited but also nervous. Nogar could sense his excitement and sent him a message.

Ryan, I am ready when you are. I will be here to help you.

The soothing thoughts from Nogar relaxed Ryan, and he said, "I'm ready," and they both touched the shell.

Just like Jerry, the shell went from clear to cloudy. Ryan concentrated on the shell, and slowly, the cloudy began to clear presenting an image that Ryan began to describe. "I see myself and Nogar amongst some of the other leirds and their trainers. They are looking to me for guidance and protection. I don't understand why." That image soon disappeared and another one began to form. "I see something else. I see a few other dragon leirds that weren't with the group in the first image. I am talking with them, trying and pleading with them. Some follow me and one in particular, Bobby, I feel a close bond to."

Once again, the shell clouded up allowing another image to form. This next image gave Ryan a large smile. "I see Susan and me spending time together, and faintly, I see Jerry observing us at a distance. Is that why he was angry with me after leaving you, Dragon Master?"

The Dragon Master looked at Ryan and said, "Yes, Ryan, he has a bitter hate growing between you, and he feels betrayed by you. I am sorry, Ryan."

Ryan was hurt knowing now why Jerry had been distancing himself from his best friend. Ryan didn't have much time to mourn as the next image began to emerge. "I see water, lots of water, as if I was flying above it really fast, but that's impossible because I can't fly," Ryan said smirking, but the image continued. "Now it looks like I have stopped in the middle of this vast water source. I feel Nogar warning me of danger. But what danger? I don't see anything." The image ended leaving Ryan worried and concerned.

Once again, he had to focus on a new image. "I can't make out this one out yet, it looks like your chambers, Dragon Master. I see thirty-two eggs cradled in a stone nest. Most of the eggs are in green color. I only see two or three that are red. The image is changing. It's Nogar. He is huge and flying after Sparcan spitting fireballs at him. Is he trying to kill him? Why?"

Soon the shell cleared and ended its power. The Dragon Master pulled the shell away and placed it on the shelf. On her return, she spoke to Ryan. "You have had many powerful visions. I know you want to know what each one means, but I have to explain them one at a time as you saw them. Your first vision is very important. It shows you as the leader of the Gunar leirds. As their leader, they will look to you for guidance and protection—"

The Dragon Master was stopped by Ryan. "But I'm no leader!"

The Dragon Master continued, "Ryan, I know you don't feel like you are a leader, but you are, just as Jerry is the leader on the Wapec side."

Ryan was still doubting that the Dragon Master called him a great leader as she began to further explain the rest of his visions. "Your next vision is concerning a group of dragon leirds called Lumac leirds. They are undecided to join either the Gunar or Wapec side. If a Lumac leird is unconverted to a side by the time they become dragon lords, they will be banished to Seven Mile Lake where they are destined to become water dragons. This image shows you converting some of the Lumac leirds to the Gunar side.

"One of the Lumac leirds named Bobby, I see you forming a strong friendship. This next vision is pretty clear. Susan and you spend some valuable time together developing another strong bond." The Dragon Master was hesitant to explain the next image, but she finally did. "Your next image is concerning you and your hiecu. It is a weapon obtained as a dragon leird and a symbol as a dragon lord.

"It seems that you are destined to obtain your hiecu over Seven Mile Lake, a dangerous place for water dragons hate Gunar and Wapec leirds and lords alike. I cannot say more of this image. The rest you will have to discover on your own. But your last two visions are very interesting. The image of the clutch of eggs has me very interested. You spoke of the thirty two-eggs and only two or three were in red tint and the rest were green?"

Ryan looked at the Dragon Master and said, "Yes, that is correct."

The Dragon Master smiled, pleased with this vision of Ryan. The Dragon Master proceeded to explain. "As you know, there is a war in this land. Those fighting for my side are the Gunar's while those against me are the Wapec's, and when you saw that the majority of one of the future clutches are Gunar's, it excites me. For it will give us a much needed numbers that we have lost in battle, and speaking of battles, your last vision was of you, not Nogar and Jerry and Sparcan.

"You were both engaged in an intense battle, and it would appear that you have Jerry on the run.

But once more, the vision is cut short, so you will have to wait to see the outcome."

Ryan didn't like the thought of fighting or killing anyone as Ryan continued to think more on one of his visions and the Dragon Master's interpretations.

Then the Dragon Master pulled Nogar aside to speak to him. She then said, "Nogar, I feel that your return along with Sparcan is connected to the prophecy of peace restored to the land."

Nogar spoke, "I too feel that our return is to fulfill the prophecy."

The Dragon Master spoke again, "Nogar, you have to teach Ryan everything. If he is to be the Gunar general, then he must have a vast knowledge of leadership and war."

Nogar shook his head in agreement then said, "Is it part of the prophecy that your last egg clutch will contain so many Gunar trainers?"

The Dragon Master replied, "Yes, it is only with a large and powerful army can peace be obtained through war, defeating the Wapec lords. I feel that Ryan and you are the chosen ones to restore the peace in Dragtoneea, and you will have to fight and kill Sparcan and Jerry."

In Nogar's absence, Ryan began to explore the large chamber and found the large statues that intrigued Jerry. So he too began to explore the vast details of each one. His fascination was only stopped by Nogar clearing his throat to get his attention. Ryan looked at Nogar and then back again at the statues and asked, "Who are these dragons, Nogar?"

Nogar took a moment before he answered Ryan. "These are the dragon lords chosen for the

Dragon Council. From these leaders came much goodness but also much deceit and death. For one of these dragons whose statue was latter cut down rebelled against the Dragon Master and gathered many followers.

"Only those truly loyal to the Dragon Master fought against the rebels until we drove them out of the valley. Ever since then, we have been at a constant war."

Ryan's excited expression turned into a painful hurt. He bowed his head in sorrow.

Nogar, knowing that they are just beginning, said to Ryan, "We have a lot of training to do even for today. So we should get started on it as quickly as we can."

So Ryan who had gotten down into a kneeling position, braced himself by placing his hand on one of the bases of the statues then pulled himself up quickly. Then both of them walked over to the same wall that opened up for Susan to descend down to the training grounds. As the wall opened,

Ryan couldn't believe how green and beautiful the training grounds were. Before they began their descent, Ryan let out a sigh of relief of not seeing any kind of device that hinted war.

Chapter 12

As Ryan continued walking down the flight of steps, the beauty of the training grounds continued to impress him. The grass was greener than any well-taken-care-of lawn Ryan had ever seen. Ryan was barely able to notice a stone wall surrounding the training grounds because it was being concealed by these incredible trees. The bark on the trees were a combination of purple and blue splashes. The leaves were green with yellow stripes. It was stunning and very attractive.

As Ryan focused on the actual grounds, he saw several training obstacles. One in particular was over what looked like a pond that had a clear blue tint to the water. As Ryan looked to his left, he saw what looked like sleeping quarters and a larger building, maybe a mess hall. When Ryan stepped on to the actual grounds, a new sense of excitement overcame him. He then turned to Nogar to express his excitement but noticed something different about him.

Ryan continued to look over Nogar, then he realized that he had grown a few inches, so he asked, "Nogar, you've grown. How?"

Nogar knew he had grown. He also knew that he would have to explain why he was growing. Nogar said, "Your correct, Ryan. I have grown. As a trainer, it is my responsibility to teach you all the training objectives from the Dragon Master. As you accomplish an objective, it transfers from the training scale and is written on my own scales. With each one, I will grow until all the objectives are accomplished."

Ryan thought that was so cool, and he asked, "When the objectives are transferred to you, does it hurt?"

Nogar looked at him and said, "The only way the objectives can be written on my own scales is through dragon fire, and yes, it is an unbelievable amount of pain. Before you ask me what objective we have accomplished,

I'm already going to tell you. Earlier, do you remember when we were communicating through our minds of telepathy?"

Ryan nodded, so Nogar continued, "That is one of the objectives. It usually takes some time to accomplish it. However, we were able to connect immediately. The only reason why I didn't grow until now is all progress takes place when the dragon leird steps unto the training grounds and can't transfer except in here."

Ryan was pondering on this new information when Nogar gave him more to think about. "Each trainer and dragon leird learn at different paces and each trainer grows at different degrees. I have never grown this fast or so big before."

Ryan blurted out, "So big or fast before, I thought you were dead for thousands of years."

Nogar responded, "I was, but before I had a long sleep, I was able to train other dragon leirds in my quest to protect and serve the Dragon Master. When this war began, I was having a hard time finding qualified leaders. It seemed that every time I found one, they would be killed, so I was able to come back and reassign new captains to aid in the war."

Ryan thought, *This is kind like my game only its real life and I never had any desire to enlist in the military.*

Nogar's mentioning of war reminded Ryan of human wars as he pulled away from his thoughts and images that he saw on the news about the wars occurring around the world. Then he looked down at his training scale. He was looking and studying the strange characters when he began to notice the characters changing slowly. They soon began to translate into English, so now he could read them.

Out of excitement, he looked up to Nogar to tell him the good news when he saw that one of Nogar's scales was glowing bright orange, almost red as he continued to watch the scale slowly began to turn back to its normal color. As it cooled down, Nogar began to grow again, gaining a few more inches. As Nogar turned around, Ryan could sense and see the pain in Nogar's eyes and face. After a few minutes, Nogar spoke, "I have never had a leird that caught on to the teachings and trainings as you have, Ryan."

Ryan thought on what Nogar had told him, then he said, "So I have learned a lot so far, but I still have much more still to learn."

Nogar replied, "Yes, Ryan, it's true. You have learned quicker than most gifted dragon leirds, and as the Dragon Master has said, you are a special. You have come here for a special reason. This reason will be revealed at a later time."

Ryan nodded at Nogar in agreement before looking over the training grounds, pondering before further entrance to them. As Ryan and Nogar entered the grounds, Ryan began to look over some of the training obstacles. One had a balance beam with a canopy over it. On this canopy were other beams that looked to fall hitting the balance beam while a dragon leird was on it. Ryan looked across a field and saw yet another one. This one was a large hollow log big enough to have a six foot man run through it comfortably. At the end are two large bags attached by rope that free fall into the log hitting the dragon leirds if they are not aware.

But the one Ryan dreaded the most was a miserable memory of track and field. The one time he tried to be athletic. Ryan fell countless times on his hometown track surrounding the football field. This track in Dragtoneea had steep flowing rises occurring throughout the track. Ryan watched as some dragon leirds attempt a hill and fell down only to get up and try again.

As Ryan and Nogar continued through the obstacles, Nogar flew in front of Ryan and stopped and said, "Ryan, before we begin our training, it's important for me to explain something. It's how to tell apart the Lumac, Gunar, and Wapec leirds along with their trainers."

Ryan looked at Nogar and said, "Okay, how do I tell them apart?"

Nogar, pleased, looked around then said, "Ryan, look to your left."

So Ryan looked to his left and saw Bobby with his trainer, Socer, then looked back to Nogar who said, "Do you remember when we were all in the cave with our key claws?"

Ryan pondered a little before nodding allowing Nogar to continue. "Do you remember the colors of the key claws at all?"

Ryan had to think carefully then said, "Yes, I remember some of the colors, Nogar."

Nogar grinned then said, "I want you to think clearly when I ask if you do you remember the color of Bobby's key claw."

Ryan did as Nogar suggested, searching out the color of the key claw. As he did, Ryan could remember talking with Bobby as he blurted out, *"Purple!"*

Ryan was pleased with his answer so was Nogar. "Correct. Now we don't have the key claws to look to for reference, so we will have to look at the color of the trainers. Now look again at Bobby and his trainer and tell me what color is Socer?"

Ryan looked to his left for a second time focusing on Socer, studying the color of his scales, seeing if he saw any difference, then he said, "Socer is a light bluish-green color, almost like a sea green."

Nogar said enthusiastically, "Very good, Ryan. Now do you remember anything that the Dragon Master said about these dragon leirds?"

Ryan had to really think and focus on the comments of the Dragon Master thinking of the colors.

Then very timid, he said, "Are they by chance the Lumac leirds?"

Nogar beamed. "Yes, they are! Good, Ryan, that is correct. So in order to find the Lumac leirds, look to their trainers, find the sea green-colored scales, and try all you can to convert them to the Gunar side. Also, they tend to stay together until they decide what side to join as you will see so will the Gunar and Wapecs leirds until they achieve lordship."

Nogar continued, "Now, Ryan, do you remember in the cave what color your key claw was?"

Ryan didn't have to think very long as he answered, "Green. I remembered because it's my favorite color."

Nogar nodded then said, "That's correct, Ryan. It is my favorite color too, not because of the mixture of blues and yellows but because of what it stands for. The Dragon Master and her followers wear it with pride and glory."

Ryan could really sense Nogar's loyalty to the Dragon Master as he continued, "Now what color am I?"

Ryan again didn't take long to answer this question. "You're a dark shade of lime green." Nogar again applauded Ryan. "Very good. This is how you will know your fellow Gunar leirds. As well if you convert Lumac leirds, their trainers' color will change to this shade of green as well."

Nogar didn't allow much idle time as he still had another group to discuss. "Ryan, I know you are tired, but I now need you to look to your right—"

Ryan looked before Nogar could finish only seeing Jerry and Sparcan. As he turned back around, he said, "Jerry and Sparcan, I see that Sparcan is pitch black in color," ending with a miserable tone.

Nogar came closer to Ryan sensing his pain. When he got closer, he said, "Ryan, this world is magical, full of beauty. However, something this world takes away is friendships. I know your pain all too well. When I was younger, I had a friend, Wapec. You could say that we were inseparable."

Ryan looked at Nogar and said, "You were friends with Wapec as Gunar?"

Nogar gave a grin saying, "Yes, I was before his heart turned black with greed. He was a noble dragon lord. But when some of his ideas were denied by the Dragon Master, he turned his heart against her, greedy for power and formed his army. Ryan, this friendship you had with Jerry is over. He is a Wapec and our enemy."

Ryan had to control his emotions before he said, "I wouldn't classify Jerry as my friend by the way he has treated me since we have been here in Dragtoneea."

Nogar added, "When someone is used to others being miserable, they can't stand them being happy. So they do all they can in their power to make them miserable again. Jerry has more reason than some to hate you for just like you, he is the leader of the Wapecs. He will do anything to kill Gunar lords, and he will focus on you even more." That was all Nogar had to say for Ryan to understand the lesson he was to learn.

Nogar then said, "Ryan, again I must ask you to remember the cave and to think of Jerry's key claw. What color was it?"

Ryan looked directly at Nogar and said, "It was a bright red, and so I now know how to tell the Wapecs apart by their trainers."

Nogar didn't have to say nor do anything to show how proud he was of Ryan.

Ryan then said, "So Jerry has indeed become my enemy, then I had better learn how to defend and protect myself."

Nogar was encouraged by Ryan's attitude to begin training as he said, "Yes, we will begin our training, but right now, I need to explain something about the Wapec trainers."

Ryan listened intently as Nogar continued, "As a Wapec trainer begins to train their dragon leirds, they cheat in a way. Instead of letting the their dragon leirds learn their tasks on their own, they tell them how to beat it allowing them to control their dragon leird into lordship and the remainder of their life."

Ryan was not surprised by the Wapecs way of teaching their dragon leirds. Nogar then finished by saying, "As your first task, I want you to do is go over to Bobby and try to convert him."

Ryan looked at Bobby then at Nogar and said, "How is going over to Bobby and trying to convert him a training task of mine?"

Nogar smiled as he said, "Ryan, you're not just a dragon leird doing training but a leader in training as well. You have additional tasks and an important one is to gain the trust of the Lumac leirds and converting them."

With that, Ryan turned to the balance beam obstacle that Bobby was training across the field with Nogar behind him. As he approached him, he could see the frustration on Socer's face as Bobby was having a hard time concentrating on Socer's instructions. As the side beams would hit the larger beam, knocking him off unto the ground. Ryan saw this as a perfect opportunity to go over and talk to Bobby.

When Ryan got closer, he offered his hand to help pull Bobby up from the ground. Bobby accepted it gratefully. Ryan looked up at the beam and said, "Man, that's a long way down to the ground. Did it hurt hitting this surface?"

Bobby said while wiping grass off his jeans, "No, it doesn't hurt. This grass is really soft and acts like a giant cushion when you hit. But this balance attack, as Socer has named it, is kicking my butt though. This is the third time I have fallen off. I can't hear Socer very well."

Ryan looked up again at the giant beam as he said, "Well, I can't give you any pointers. I haven't tried it out yet. I think I will try it after you have mastered it, then you can give me some pointers."

They both laughed then Ryan said, "You know, I do think I can give you one good piece of advice I have learned something from my trainer. Open your mind and let Socer in and listen not with your ears but with your thoughts."

Bobby looked at Ryan like he was crazy. Ryan continued, "I know you are thinking that I am crazy, but trust me, look at Socer and listen with your mind."

Bobby decided it couldn't hurt to take some advice no matter how crazy it sounded, considering this had been the craziest day in his whole life. So Bobby looked at Socer with an open mind. He closed his eyes and listened. In the back of Bobby's mind, he could hear something familiar.

As he continued to listen, he recognized the voice as Socer. He was saying, "Bobby, brace yourself when the attack beams fall. It will help you to stay on it and get through the course."

Bobby jumped up unto the beam and looking at Socer smiling as he went through the course for the fourth time. This time as he focused on his balance and saw the attack beams fall, he stopped and braced himself. The beams hit, and Bobby was shaken but remained on the beam and only got off after completing the course.

Ryan ran over to him to congratulate him. After shaking his hand, he said, "Bobby, I am going to be straight forward with you. I am the leader of the Gunar side, and I want to ask you if you have thought on what side you want to join?"

Bobby shrugged his shoulders as he said, "I don't know just yet, Ryan. Jerry came over to me earlier and suggested the Wapec side. So I have been watching the Wapec leirds flying through these exercises. While the rest of us Lumac and Gunar alike struggle to get through one obstacle."

Ryan didn't hesitate as he said, "I will agree with you as far as the Wapecs. They are flying through their training while it looks like the rest of us are struggling. But there is a reason why it looks like we struggle and the Wapecs do it with ease."

Bobby spoke up and said, "Oh yeah, and what reason is that?"

Ryan continued, "I have learned that the Wapec trainers don't want their dragon leirds to struggle with their training."

Bobby looked intrigued, so Ryan continued, "So they give them the solutions to cheat because when they become dragon lords, their trainers still control them instead of letting them go on their own. And as a Gunar leird, your trainer will let you struggle and gain the endurance and knowledge on your own so when you become a dragon lord, you will have all you need to survive on your own. For all these exercises are designed to benefit us when we become dragon lords and to help aid us in a battle."

Bobby reflected on what Ryan had to say when he asked, "Why should I join up with you and the Gunars instead of with Jerry and the Wapecs?"

Ryan looked to Nogar, but he wouldn't give him any help with this, so Ryan thought to came up with a good example. Ryan said, "For me, Bobby, it is very simple—survival and staying alive."

Bobby was a little confused by his response and said, "What do you mean by that?"

Ryan knew he had his attention as he continued, "Well, Bobby, when we first entered into Dragtoneea, we were in Death Valley. Do you remember it?"

Bobby nodded as he said, "Yes, lots of dragon skeletons. Some were freshly killed."

Ryan responded as Nogar had to him, "Correct, and if you don't remember, the valley was split into two separate gave sites. On one side were the Wapec Lords and the other were the Gunar Lords. As we passed through, two Wapec lords had just deposited a fresh kill that piled up far more than the Gunar's side, and I have two simple reasons why."

Ryan waited a moment for Bobby to gain up to speed on where Ryan was heading with his story. When he did, Ryan continued, "The first reason has to do with the training because as they cheat, they don't gain the necessary knowledge or strength to properly defend themselves. Therefore, they are not as reliable in battle as a Gunar lord. And the second reason is this, Wapecs are very greedy for treasure and power. So much so that if another Wapec lord boasts of its treasure, its fellow soldier and maybe friend will kill them for a chance to gain their wealth for its own self."

Bobby lowered his head in thought. After a few seconds, he spoke up saying, "So if I was to choose the Wapec side, I could survive, but it is harder too than if I was to choose your side?"

Ryan countered his response by saying, "Now don't get me wrong, Bobby. Gunar lords die in battle as well. But because they focus on their training rather than just rushing through their training to become a dragon lord as fast as possible only to get thrown into battle with a higher chance of being killed. That's not a gamble that I would want to take."

Bobby really started running the facts through his head and even thought of advancing through his training at a faster pace sounds ideal and easy. But the thought of rushing to his death wasn't so appealing. So he turned to Ryan and said, "I want to be able to survive a few battles, so, Ryan, you got me to go to your side."

As Ryan and Bobby were shaking hands, Ryan turned his head enough to look at Socer, and he could see his color changing starting at his head down to his tail to the Gunar green. Ryan then knew that he was on the right track in his training and in his leadership.

But Ryan was not just here to convert Lumac leirds, he also needed to train on the obstacles. So after their handshake, Ryan left Bobby at the balance attack while heading to the dreaded track. As he walked toward it, he thought, *Maybe this track isn't going to be so hard as I think. In fact, I think it is going to be easy.*

Nogar who can read his thoughts as if he was reading a page in a book just chuckled. Ryan hearing his laugh turned to him and said, "What's so funny?"

Nogar proceeded to explain his sudden chuckle. "Your thought that this track is going to be easy, so once we get over to the track, you can examine it and see how easy it really is."

Ryan thought that Nogar was overexaggerating a little bit, so he will determine it for himself. As he continued the long walk, he remembered the other dragon leirds who attempted the steep rises and suddenly his energy changed. When Ryan got to the track, he saw the dragon leirds who were running on it before were off to the side resting. Ryan stepped on to the track but was hesitant to begin running.

But Nogar just smiled and said, "Ryan, you can't escape this obstacle. All the dragon leirds have to run this as many times as possible in order to build up their leg strength. Because believe it or not, leg strength is very important to get maximum height when taking off when you're on the ground. This is extremely important if you want to get in a surprise attack."

Ryan looked over the track again with no expression on his face. What made it worse was this comment from Nogar, "And you have to complete eight full laps to finish." Ryan studied the track for a minute before he began running. His first two laps were steady, easily climbing the rises on the track. But the next few laps, Ryan was getting tired, having a harder time climbing the mountains. By his last lap, Ryan wasn't running anymore. He was walking but he completed it and he was definitely ready for a nap.

Nogar came over to Ryan who was lying on the ground and asked, "So, Ryan, was it as easy as you thought it would be?"

Ryan barely moved his head for his exhaustion made it difficult to breathe. There was no way he could answer his question. As Nogar could see that Ryan was not able to answer, he said in response, "I'll take that as a no." At the end of his answer, he gave out a loud laugh.

After his amusement, Nogar helped Ryan to his feet and pointed him in the direction to the sleeping quarters. As they continued, Nogar said to Ryan, "You are actually lucky to pick this obstacle, Ryan, because the sleeping quarters aren't very far from here."

As they disappeared over a hill, they were both unaware that their every move was being watched by Jerry and Sparcan. Jerry said to Sparcan, "Ryan is weak and exhausted. We can take him now, let's go."

But Sparcan stopped the overeager teenager by placing his hand on his chest and said, "*No!* Ryan is weak, but Nogar is still strong. We need them both to be weak in order to be successful."

Jerry was furious as he said, "But my so-called friend has stabbed me in the back. I want him to pay hard for it."

Sparcan smiled at Jerry as he said, "Trust me, my young dragon leird, if we mount an attack and are unsuccessful, they will be aware of our attentions. Then they will be very cautious of us thereafter, and any future attempts will be near impossible." Sparcan ended as he stared at the hill Nogar and Ryan disappeared behind.

Jerry was pacing and a nervous wreck and said, "Okay, we will wait until I am stronger and they are weaker. I will get stronger further in our training, but I want Ryan dead."

Sparcan turned to Jerry and said, "Just as I want Nogar dead. We will get them together."

Jerry finally stopped pacing and said, "Fine, but Ryan will die by my hand and Nogar by yours."

Sparcan smiled and said, "Agreed. They will never know what hit them."

Chapter 13

As they both continued to the quarters, Ryan was struggling from being so sore. Nogar eventually had to almost carry Ryan half of the way. When they finally got to the quarters, Nogar became exhausted from helping Ryan, so he decided to take a nap as well. As Ryan saw the buildings, he noticed a common theme of the separation. Each building had a sign over the entrance of black, sea green, and lime green. Ryan knew which building he was to enter and proceeded to the lime green- signed building.

Once Ryan got inside, he saw multiple rooms that also had signs above the doors. Ryan walked to the closest door, getting closer to read the sign. This sign read Austin and Galit. Ryan then went to the next door. Nogar was being patient, but it eventually ran out as he brushed past Ryan and went directly to their room not too far from the entrance. Then Ryan hobbled to the room Nogar entered as he was still very sore.

As Ryan entered into the spacious room, he immediately spotted what his aching body was longing for—a big soft bed with pillow and a cozy blanket. When Ryan sat down on the bed, he looked over to his left and saw a large stone slab and thought, *What is that for?*

He then got a response to his question. "That slab is for me, Ryan, that hard surface to me is more comfortable than your soft bed."

Ryan looked over at Nogar who had not spoken a word and was settling on the slab; Ryan got under the covers and soon was dreaming happy dreams. Ryan's sweet dreams came to a halt due to his aching hungry stomach. Ryan uncovered himself and began to stretch and yawn, not opening his eyes, and began to say, "Man, I just had the most bizarre dream ever. I dreamed that I was surrounded by dragons and other kids my age. We are supposed to train—"

At that point, Ryan opened his eyes and stopped talking. He stopped when he saw Nogar's large body rising up and down from his breathing. Ryan laid back down but was startled by Nogar's voice, "Ryan, you're not dreaming, but some days you really wish you were."

Ryan just continued to lie in his bed until Nogar heard his growling stomach. Ryan rolled on his side, facing Nogar, and asked, "Nogar, what can we eat around here?"

Nogar just smiled as he got up and began to exit the room. Ryan flew out of his bed, following Nogar. As they rushed down the hall and out of the building, Ryan kept hounding Nogar on the subject of food. Ryan got quiet noticing Nogar pushing open a large door to an even larger building with no sign to classify what it was but followed after him.

Once inside, Ryan's nose was introduced to savoring aroma of meat, spices, and vegetables that he was used to smelling on a Sunday afternoon. These smells taunted him before he feasted on his mom's cooking. At this point, all communication had stopped, and Ryan let his nose point him in the direction of this wonderful food. As Ryan continued to drool over the smell, Ryan practically closed his eyes painting a picture in his mind. A picture of a large pot roast cooked to perfection over the course of several hours in a Crock-Pot where the meat would literally melt in your mouth with a good helping of cooked carrots, onions, and potatoes. At this point, Ryan was practically running to the front of the cafeteria setting where the food was located at.

When he arrived, he could see a big pile of cooked meat that looked very delicious. As he looked around, he saw a stone table. On it was a stack of stone trays, knives, forks, and mugs that were filled with water. Ryan reached over and picked up a tray with accompanying knife, fork, and mug which he took a quick sip of the water before placing it on his tray. As Ryan placed his tray on the railing, his nose caught a whiff of the succulent meat that made his mouth water.

His mouth watered even more when he saw some tongs that he used to pick up two pieces of meat and placed it on his tray. To the side of the meat, Ryan saw a couple different varieties of some very strange looking and what he could only guess to be vegetables. He took one of each to try them. Satisfied with the selection of items on his tray, Ryan then turned around from the buffet style of serving to find rows of tables. As he got ready to leave, he saw something move. He turned around quickly to barely see a large furry creature dashed from the meat pile into a large hole in the wall.

Ryan was beginning to freak out, not wanting to eat infested food by rats. Ryan was looking for a trash can to dispose his food. He stopped when he saw Nogar and most of the trainers feasting a pile of raw meat. When Ryan approached Nogar, he noticed that the trainers were all in different sizes. The Wapecs seemed to be a little larger than the other trainers. Ryan remembered Nogar's counsel on the size is according to completion of training goals.

Ryan walked right to Nogar and said, "Nogar, I think this food is contaminated. I just saw the largest rat in my whole life. I saw one dashed from the meat pile back into a hole in the wall. But it happened so fast that I didn't see the animal very well, just that it was furry and had a long fluffy blonde tail."

Nogar was chewing on a piece of meat that he ripped from a larger chunk. After he swallowed it mostly whole, he said, "You didn't see a rat. What you saw was the kitchen help. They are called lermeons."

Satisfied with his answer, he proceeded to tear off another chunk from the same piece of meat. Ryan was still a little confused and began to turn, but just as Nogar thought, Ryan couldn't resist as he turned back around and asked, "What's a lermeon?"

Nogar was getting used to Ryan wanting to know what every creature was. So he said, "A lermeon is tiny furry creature, only two and a half feet tall. They would closely resemble a gerbil in your world. But they have a few differences. For example, they have humanlike hands and faces. But they also can communicate with us. Back when the war began, the Dragon Master rescued them from their lands and homes that were destroyed from the war, so out of gratitude, they live here and give their service to her."

Ryan was satisfied with knowing his food was safe. He then looked down at his tray, and glancing over the meat, he asked, "What kind of meat is this?"

Nogar had torn off another chunk of meat and setting it down on the table. Then he said, "Ryan, you really don't want to know, but I will tell you this. It's really good. You're going to love it."

But before Ryan left and before Nogar could pick up his food, he asked, "Why aren't we given more types of food other than mainly meat and what I think are vegetables?"

Nogar was getting impatient as he snapped back. "You are here to become a dragon lord. A vital part of that is eating like one. We eat meat and only meat." Nogar snatched the meat before Ryan could open his mouth again and turned away from him.

Ryan almost felt threatened by Nogar's comment but turned around to find a place to sit down. Ryan was smelling his meat when he again noticed a theme in the tables as they were separated by color black, sea green, and lime green.

Ryan walked over to lime green table and was going to sit down at the end of it when he heard a familiar sweet voice. It was Susan beckoning to him to sit down by her side by saying, "Ryan, there's a seat here beside me."

Ryan just instantly had a smile come to his face when he thought of Susan and her wanting him to sit beside her. As he proceeded to his saved seat, his smile seemed to get bigger and bigger. When he sat down by her, he caught a sweet-smelling fragrance, a combination of flowers and fruit. There was absolutely no way he couldn't enjoy his meal now.

From the Wapec table, Jerry glared at Ryan. In his mind, he was thinking, *If that stupid Lumac table wasn't in between me and him, I would do some serious damage to him.* As he continued to spy on Ryan, watching as his excitement was growing from Susan's invitation, Jerry was building on his anger for Ryan. Jerry continued to think, *That Ryan is so sly like a fox. He thinks he is so cunning. I can't stand watching him use his tricks to steal away my prize, Susan.*"

A this time, Sparcan had intercepted Jerry's thoughts in between swallowing pieces of meat, and he was thoroughly enjoying them as Jerry was building a stronger hatred toward Ryan. Sparcan wanted to see how committed Jerry was to his thoughts of inflicting pain on Ryan, so he sent him a message. *Jerry, if you're so mad at Ryan for stealing Susan away from you, do something about it.*

Jerry looked around until he spotted Sparcan over by the other trainers and replied with this message, *What do you mean? I'm not going to beat up Ryan. He wouldn't stand a chance against me.*

Sparcan replied right back, *If you're afraid to challenge your weak friend, then maybe I made the wrong choice in picking you in the first place.*

Jerry got even madder with Sparcan's message. He was not a coward. He also knew that if he challenged Ryan, he would buckle. He then returned his focus on Ryan who was enjoying a conversation with Susan while eating. Angry, Jerry got up and began to cross the room over to Ryan by walking on the tables. Jerry never took his eyes off Ryan which made his blood boil as the two were flirting. The constant glare made his eyes bloodshot. Jerry was going to prove to Sparcan that he did make the right choice by challenging the real coward while his anger continued building up inside him. Ryan was getting to know the other Gunar leirds and was laughing at some of the jokes that were being shared by Bobby. Ryan was finally feeling like he belonged here. In the midst of his enjoyment, he felt a light but steady tapping on his shoulder. Ryan turned around smiling that instantly dissolved into panic as his view was obstructed by a hurling fist straight for his face. It was in this moment of need that Ryan remembered some of the techniques taught to him by Jerry about blocking a punch.

By throwing the back of your hand into the attacker's fists while at the same time using the force to move your body away from the attacker.

As Ryan performed this perfectly, it gave him some room advantage in a split second. Ryan saw a tray with leftover meat scraps on it. Ryan reached out grabbing it, and he flung the meat at his unknown attacker. Ryan had hoped the flinging of garbage into the unfriendly face gave him even more time to try and figure out a plan of escape. Ryan was able to slide out from under the table as the thrown food really stunned his attacker.

This move made them back up, wiping the meat off of their face, but this only made them madder too. As Ryan began to back up and away, he was really hoping that this person didn't have any fighting skills because he had none. Before Ryan could get around the Gunar table giving him a straight shot for the door, his attacker revealed his face. Ryan was shocked and scared to see that it was Jerry.

Ryan was now even more cautious knowing of Jerry's superior fighting skills. He continued to back up giving him as much space as possible. At this point, the other dragon Leirds were aware of the confrontation and gathered around them. Ryan had been lucky to avoid the first punch and wasn't too confident in blocking the rest of his moves. In his mind, he knew that his luck would run out.

Ryan vividly remembered some of Jerry's kung fu matches. One contender had to be taken off the mat on a stretcher, countless others had gashes or bloody noses soaking their uniforms. Ryan had no intention of being another unlucky victim of Jerry, but because of the other dragon leirds, Ryan couldn't escape. Ryan still had the tray in his hand, his only means of defense. He then placed it in front of him acting like a shield. His main goal was to stay alive and maybe to wear Jerry out at the same time.

As Jerry stormed toward Ryan, he was trying to reason with him by saying, "Jerry, why are you trying to hit me?"

Jerry wasn't interested in reasoning, only in his revenge that Ryan had no idea what it was about. Ryan was circling the small area keeping out of Jerry's reach, allowing him to catch his breath. Suddenly, Ryan was viewing Jerry inflicting a kick to his torso, and if he were to place the tray three inches in front, it would be blocked.

Ryan without hesitation position the tray in the exact place he viewed in his mind. Amazingly, it was blocked. Not only was Ryan surprised, but Jerry was even more surprised. Jerry began to reposition himself for another more aggressive attack. Ryan also saw Jerry's next move in his mind, so he took a defensive stance to counter Jerry's. Upon seeing Ryan's stance, he got furious and rushed in to do a surprise punch to Ryan's face.

But it was Jerry backing away in pain as Ryan strategically blocked it with his tray. As Jerry's fist throbbed in pain, he was wondering how Ryan could see his every move before he did it. Ryan moved the tray away from his face noticing a crack from the latest impact from Jerry. Ryan himself was baffled by his sudden fighting instinct. It was if Jerry's every move was in slow motion, and Ryan was shown how to defend himself allowing to be more effective in blocking.

Jerry began to shake his hand trying to get some blood flow. As it did, it was easing the pain allowing him to think of new ways to attack Ryan. All he could think of was getting rid of the tray. Jerry suddenly went on a striking spree using mainly his feet to avoid hurting his hands.

In between hits, Ryan yelled out, "Jerry, what did I do wrong?" His attempts were in vain as Jerry didn't let up as Ryan continued to block his blows. He noticed Jerry had stopped hitting only to back up and get enough motion to deliver a more powerful kick.

His kick sent Ryan sliding across the floor and split the tray in half. Ryan got to his feet and continued to yell, "Jerry, what did I do wrong. Why are you so mad?"

With fire in Jerry's eyes and sweat dripping down his face, he stared deep into his soul. As he did, he said with anger, "You took my girl from me. Now you will pay the price for your treason." With the end of his statement, he ran straight at Ryan. When he was just a few feet away from him, he jumped into the air.

The elevation he got gave him the right height to perform a perfect flying kick into Ryan's face. Ryan had watched Jerry perform this kick a hundred times. He was confident that he would not be able to avoid or block this kick and began to brace himself for the painful impact. Just as Jerry was about to the land his kick, an unknown force threw him across the room, slamming him into the wall. Ryan opened his eyes to see Jerry fall to the floor.

Nogar then walked over to Ryan. He motioned for him to get up and behind him. Nogar searched angrily for Sparcan but couldn't find him.

Nogar backed up as Ryan ran out the door unto the training grounds where he felt safe under Nogar's protection. The rest of the dragon leirds cleared the room, leaving Jerry alone. Soon after the last dragon leird left, Sparcan flew over to Jerry. He could see that the only injury he suffered was from being thrown across the room into the wall. As Sparcan handed a towel to Jerry to clean his wounds, he said, "I see you lost the fight, my young dragon leird."

Jerry yelled back, "No thanks to you!"

Sparcan calmly said back, "I told you that we would take them out at the right time. You simply rushed in too quickly, and as the result, you lost."

Jerry spat out some blood as he thought about Sparcan's comment. He then said, "I think I have learned my lesson. I don't want to lose another fight like this one. I will follow your command and win this war."

Sparcan grinned with glee as he began to sink Jerry further in his trap of emotions and told Jerry,

"I have full trust in you, and so you need to have full trust in me, Jerry."

Jerry looked up at Sparcan and said, "I have tried things my way. I am fully ready to do them your way."

That was music to Sparcan's ears.

Chapter 14

Once Nogar knew Sparcan and Jerry weren't following them, he took Ryan behind the Gunar's sleeping quarter where they could have be safe for a private conversation. As soon as Nogar and Ryan got behind the building, Nogar was instantly relieved and began to relax a little. Ryan stayed very close to Nogar, still fearful of what Jerry could do to him completely out of anger. Nogar was positive that Sparcan and Jerry wouldn't be following after, but he kept eyes moving just in case they did follow.

Nogar could still feel Ryan's fear, so he decided to ease his fear by saying, "I don't think we will have to worry about an attack any more tonight. But I do think we will need to be mindful of a potentially deadlier attack in the future."

Ryan had a very simple question. "Why did Jerry attack me? Did I do something wrong?"

Nogar knew about his confusion as he answered, "No, Ryan, you have done nothing wrong at all. Jerry has one of the best Wapec trainer of all Dragtoneea who is able to twist his dragon leirds' minds to do whatever he wants them to do out of fear and anger. He commonly uses this technique to his advantage, such as your attraction to Susan and her to you. Sparcan has made Jerry think that she belongs to him regardless of her decision. Plus the fact that you two were best friends only fuels his fire."

Ryan backed up till his back was against Nogar's side, then he slide down till he was sitting on the ground. He then said, "I guess I can safely assume that I will never be able to trust him ever again." Nogar looked down at Ryan and said, "Ryan, I know how you are feeling about Jerry, and yes, you will not be able to trust him anymore. I am sorry that this had to happen to you, and it isn't the first time this sort of thing has happened."

Ryan didn't feel any better as he looked down at the ground, totally depressed, as the sun was setting. As Ryan stared at the ground, it suddenly began to move as it was covered in a unique-looking caterpillar. This caterpillar had hundreds of long blue spines covering its long eight inches and two inches thick purple body. It moved by using its several centipede red legs to get around at the end of its body. But what caught his eye the most was its two-inch tail that is brightly colored with green, orange, and yellow.

As Ryan continued to watch, the caterpillars turned from hundreds into thousands and from thousands into tens of thousands in a matter of seconds. Ryan, not taking his eyes off the bugs, said, "I have never seen such a colorful caterpillar. I wonder if they are dangerous?"

Nogar smiled because he knew that if he brought him back here, he would see these amazing caterpillars. It was his plan that they would help ease his stress as he said, "I bet you have never ever seen a caterpillar like these. Continue to watch and you will see this tiny bug metamorphoses into a truly spectacular adult form."

Ryan has studied insects most of his life, so he was confident with his comment. "Insects that metamorphose take days or even weeks, not minutes or seconds."

Nogar didn't respond to Ryan as he would soon eat his own words. Ryan continued to watch the caterpillars when suddenly, they all stopped and began to shed the blue spikes. As they did this, they also began to cover themselves with their saliva that hardened quickly as Ryan picked one up.

As Ryan remained baffled by the rapid process of the cocoon, Nogar stated, "In your world, cocoons take days to build and harden then several more days to transform into a beautiful butterfly or moth. But here, these caterpillars don't turn into butterflies or moths. They become a caterpillar beetle."

Ryan was still baffled when suddenly, the cocoon he picked up began to move and a large gray horn pierced through the tough cocoon. Ryan instinctively dropped the cocoon as this new two-inch rhinoceros-shaped horn had a sharp cutting edge. Opposite of the rounded out part of the horn continued to cut the cocoon. What happened next amazed Ryan even more as the beetle started to come out. The horn fully cut through exposing a secondary red-rounded horn located at the base just a half inch long. It too had a cutting edge. This cool horn was attached to a one inch long, one inch thick oval blue head with what looked like a suction cup mouth. If the horns were removed, the head looked like a blue sucker. The top and bottom of the head were completely flat and polished with two antennae, two inches long with a pear-shaped clear bulb at the end. The eight-inch body still had the caterpillar shape, only it looked like a lava lamp. With multiple flowing colors that glowed with blue, pink, green, and orange, the red centipede legs remained the same. Ryan continued to observe the beetle that it had a large clear set of wet wings that needed to dry along with a soften brown shell case that when dried will harden and protect the wings.

As Ryan watched the beetles flap their wings, the process took about a minute until their wings were dry and strong. The protective case took a few more minutes to dry and harden. As it hardened, it turned into dark brown. When the caterpillar beetles had finished and tucked their wings under their shells, it exposed about one-fourth of an inch of its tail. Ryan now understood why it was named so specifically.

The caterpillar beetles started to climb up large rocks, buildings, trees, and any structure that could support their weight. They used these high structures to get enough elevation to begin flying their heavy bodies. As they fill the sky, the clear wings reflect their colorful bodies light toward the ground also lighting up the sky.

Ryan walked under the light show over to Nogar who was resting against one of the building, and Ryan asked, "Why do they perform this dance?"

Nogar had never heard it put in that way as he answered, "These caterpillar beetles are the males of this species. This light show or dance is to lure the females out of their dens."

Ryan watched the spectacular display when suddenly out of nowhere, a large black flying creature snatched one of the beetles out of the sky. It quickly hauled the caterpillar beetle to the ground and vanished into a hole.

Ryan was a little worried as he turned to Nogar who answered his question before he could ask it. "That was one of the females that live alone in their den that they dig in the ground. They look nothing like their mate. The females have a longer ten-inch black body which was also thicker by three inches. They also only have six legs. Their heads were shaped like an arrowhead with one eye at each tip. When they grab a male, they pull them into their den where the female will lay twenty eggs. The males then suck each egg and swallow them. They leave the den and find a safe place to die so they will incubate the eggs for two days when the process begins all over again."

Ryan thought that was totally amazing as more and more females began to snatch the males from the sky. Then suddenly, a yellow-glowing creature twice the size of the male caterpillar beetle males grabbed one of them and flew away in the sky. Nogar was also waiting for this display to happen. With a now more panicking, Ryan looked over at him, waiting for him to describe what just happened.

Nogar smiled as he said, "The circle of life even occurs here in Dragtoneea. What you just saw was a glow bat. They look similar to a bat but are a flying amphibian that survives entirely of caterpillar beetles."

Ryan had socked and confused expression as Nogar got into more details. "The glow bat lives in the monsoon caves near seven mile rock. Their skin is just like a frog or salamander, and they need water to survive but hunts at night when it's cooler and the air is moist."

Nogar unexpectedly clasped his hands together above his head. When he pulled his hands down, there was a sudden glow between the gaps in his fingers. Slowly and carefully, Nogar began to open his hands revealing one of these glow bats. Cautiously and carefully, he began to grab each wing between his fingers. He then began to spread them open, allowing Ryan to study the bat.

Ryan accepted the offer and slowly walked over to the stretched out bat. Ryan observed the yellow body, and the wing structure were exactly like an ordinary bat. With the difference of faint blue staggering stripes on both the body and wings, but the true differences was the head. The first difference was the entire head was shaped like Tokay gecko with tiny sharp teeth filling its mouth. On the bottom jaw, there were three long four to five inches long strands with three black bands varying in length running down each strand looking like a goatee. On the side of its head, there were smaller, almost nonexistent, ears, very different from that of a normal bat. Also their eyes and purple pupils were larger, allowing for better vision.

As Nogar turned the bat around, Ryan continued to observe the backside of the bat for the most part the body still had the yellow glow with blue stripes. But it also had two six inches long black prehensile tails. Ryan looked at Nogar and asked, "Why does it have two prehensile tails?"

Nogar said, "The reason for the two prehensile tails is for them to hang from the roof of the caves where they live in."

That made total sense to Ryan as he also noticed that their feet had a single claw with barbed hook used to pierce their prey then hook them like a fish so they can carry their victim off to a secluded place to dine in peace. Ryan had been studying this single bat for a period of time that he didn't notice that more and more caterpillar beetles were vanishing from the sky by both the glow bats and the female beetles.

When Nogar let go of the bat and it flew away to its freedom, it dive bombed unto an exhausted beetle, ending its life quickly. As Ryan watched the bat flew away, he heard a frantic screech. Following the noise, Ryan looked to the sky were he saw a tiny glow bat flapping its wings franticly.

The sudden outburst drew the attention of one of the glow bats as it changed it course of attack from the beetles to this baby glow bat. Ryan was also aware and saw the tragedy that was about to occur. As he said to Nogar, "That little glow bat is going to be attacked by the larger one. Nogar, what's going to happen?"

Nogar just said, "We will have to wait and see."

So Ryan turned back to the brutal attack as the larger glow bat got closer and extended his two claws to dig into the baby glow bat. When it was about to strike, suddenly a giant yellow-glowing mouth with blue fangs dripping with yellow saliva appeared. It bit down halfway on the adult glow bat. Ryan was very confused as he just turned to Nogar with a puzzled look on his face.

Nogar then said, "What you just saw was a giant deceiver bat. It has growth on the tip of its tail shaped like a baby glow bat. When the growth flaps its wings, it makes the screeching sound just like a baby glow bat would. It uses this deceiving device to attract its prey of adult glow bats to it. Now this giant bat looks just like a vampire bat, only it's entirely pitch black for camouflage except for tip of its tail and when it opens its mouth. At the end of the night, the giant deceiver bat will fly back into the black forest nestle in its nest and bite off the glowing tip of its tail where it will regenerate the next night."

Ryan thought that this was the coolest thing he had ever seen. He then got a little sad as he also thought of Jerry and how if he ever saw an amazing scene, he would share it in detail with him.

Nogar gently cradled Ryan's shoulder and said, "I know you are sad, Ryan. I know you want to share this amazing experience with someone. So I think I can help you with that."

Ryan looked at Nogar confused. Nogar pointed behind him. As Ryan turned around, there was Susan. Ryan instantly turned happy as he walked up to her. When he got to her, he said, "Hi, Susan, do you want to see something totally amazing?"

Susan nodded her head, so Ryan took her hand and led her to the amazing sight. Then he began to explain the different animals and what each one does in the food chain. Meanwhile, Nogar and Angoree also enjoyed the scene together. Their secret love still undetected by Ryan or Susan. They all watched the scene until they both got tired and retired to their sleeping quarters.

Chapter 15

Over the next few days, Ryan trained very hard both physically and mentally on the training objectives as well as on the minds of the Lumac leirds. Susan and Bobby understood the importance of the Gunar position and what they fought for and joined with Ryan willingly. Ryan was also able to convert Frank and Chris, but their conversion was not so willing because Jerry had put a lot of pressure on them to join with him but he was unsuccessful. However, that does not mean that was a complete failure for he had enough over Mike and Heather making his forces a little stronger but still not as strong as Ryan's.

Although there still remained one Lumac leirds who had not been persuaded by Ryan or Jerry, both have tried. But no matter the logic or reason, Alan had no intention of being converted to either side. Finally, Ryan confronted Alan after he had completed a run through the tunnel punch and sat down beside him as he caught his breath while Nogar and Hanec talked about the training their dragon leirds were going through.

Ryan began to speak. "Brutal obstacle, this tunnel punch, if you're not short enough, you have to bend over and run the full ten feet only to be surprised by a leather bag hitting you on your left or your right—"

Alan interrupted, "Or you can listen to your trainer and trust him and jump to the side he said and avoid being hit."

Ryan turned and looked at the log then back at Alan and said, "So that's what I am doing wrong on this one. Well, I will have to trust in Nogar next time to give me a heads-up."

Ryan ended it with a smile, but Alan wasn't smiling. He was just staring at the ground as he said, "You know, Ryan, I have ran this course several times. I've gotten banged up multiple times because I didn't trust my trainer at first. But as I have come to trust him, I don't worry when I train. I know he will be there for me no matter what. Why are you here, Ryan?"

Ryan adjusted his body so he was facing Alan as he spoke. "All the Lumac leirds have chosen a side to convert either with me or with Jerry except for you. My question is why?"

Alan became irritated by Ryan's question and suddenly got a burst of energy as he rose to his feet and began to pace back and forth in front of him. After pacing for several minutes in silence, Ryan was becoming uncomfortable as he played in his mind an angry response from Alan. As Alan began to slow down, Ryan began to brace himself for the worse as Alan slowed down right in front of Ryan. He stopped and turned toward him.

In a surprising calm tone, Alan gave a response to Ryan. "When we all arrived here in Dragtoneea, the sheer beauty took all our breath away. Such a magical and wonderful place we just arrived in. Then as we climbed the stairs to meet the Dragon Master, we all gained a new excitement. Slowly, those already Gunar or Wapec leirds left us to begin their training. And then seven Lumac leirds were called to meet her first. I was so nervous the entire time. As she gave us counsel on needing to convert to one side or the other, I felt torn. Until she mentioned that if we remained unconverted, we would become a Lumac lord, a water dragon.

"I've pondered on converting, Ryan. I did. I was really close to choosing your side, but something is calling me to the sea and so I have decided to remain a Lumac lord where I will join my forefathers and become a water dragon. And then I wouldn't have to be involved in this terrible war that is taking place." With the completion of his statement Alan sat down beside Ryan, confident in his answer to him.

Ryan was also impressed but decided to give some of his own wisdom. Ryan started with saying, "Alan, what you have said makes sense—become a water dragon and there are no worries with this ugly war in the air. But what of the battles in the water…" Ryan turned to Alan, focusing on his eyes as he continued, "The water dragons are a fierce predator. This I am sure of, but in the sea are even larger predators that will hunt you down. Not to mention you will have your natural born enemies in the water. Nogar has told me of stories of the battles in the water amongst the water dragons and the sharkcon. After hearing those stories, I am glad that I don't have to fight in the water."

Alan had a new peak of interest as he said, "Who are the sharkcon? Hanec has not told me of such people in Seven Mile Lake."

Ryan, still looking at Alan, continued with his story. "The sharkcon have the body of a man and the head and tail of shark. They have lived in Seven Mile Lake for thousands of years before they were evicted from their homes by Lumac and his followers.

"This began an endless water war of territory—the sharkcon were trying to gain back what which they lost and the water dragons protecting what which they had taken. The sharkcon live in the deep cavities of the sea bottom plotting their revenge. They vow one day that they will have a big enough army to take back what which was taken from them."

Alan had so many questions that could only be confirmed by Hanec, but Ryan wasn't finished as he continued, "Not mention that the fight in the air doesn't take place just over land but over water too, and if a water dragon attacks, they too become part of the fight. Just because you chose to swim over flying does not mean you are out of danger, my friend." Ryan then got up leaving Alan to ponder on what he had told him as he attempted a run through the tunnel punch.

Alan was still sitting in the same spot when Ryan came over to rest as he took one of the bags to his right eye, bruising it and causing pain. As he sat down, he said, "I should have listened to you, Alan, and followed Nogar's counsel and then I wouldn't have this black eye." Ryan was smirking from his comment as he held his right eye as the pain increased, and it began to swell up, not allowing him to see out of it.

Alan looked over at Ryan still holding his eye in pain and laughed out loud before saying, "Just because you can fly doesn't mean you are clear of danger. When I did get hit, I was smart enough to block it with my arm or shoulder avoiding my face. Watch and learn, Ryan."

And with that, Alan got up, walked to the start, got in the log, and began the run. As he approached the end, Hanec told him to avoid the left. As he did, the bag fell avoiding him. Confident, he slowed down thinking he was finished until the other bag fell catching him in the left eye.

As Alan sat down beside Ryan in just as much pain, Ryan looked through his good eye, chuckled, then he said, "Looks like we are even."

Alan began to laugh at Ryan's comment and looked through his good eye. He was trying to locate the mess hall as he said, "I wonder if the meat here will help with the swelling like it does on earth?"

Ryan, still trying to focus on his one good eye said, "I don't know. I never had to try it. Didn't get in fights or play sports, never had a black eye before."

Alan didn't seem surprised by Ryan's confession. Finally, Alan found the mess hall and said, "I located the mess hall. Let's get steak on our eyes then eat it after we feel better."

Ryan said, "You bet, but first, I want to try this tunnel thing one more time."

As Ryan was getting up, Alan said, "You will have a hard time with only one good eye."

But Ryan ignored him as he focused on listening to Nogar giving him advice. Ryan climbed into the log and began the run. As he got closer to the end, he was listening to Nogar and he heard a faint voice telling him, "There is one coming." Ryan, looking through his good eye, scanned both sides and saw a shadow on his right. So he dodged left and the bag shot past him. Then he heard, "Avoid the left bag." He then dove to his right just as the second bag missed him. As Ryan fell to the ground, he had a smile on his face. When he hit, he did an army roll coming up on his feet in triumph.

In a distance, he heard, "Beginner's luck." It was Alan already heading toward the mess hall but wanted to see if Ryan could do it.

Ryan exited the tunnel and turned around to Alan's voice and ran to him. His eye was still hurting, and he was hungry. What better way to solve both then by putting a steak on your eye then eating it as Alan suggested.

The whole way over to the mess hall, Alan and Ryan were joking with each other on how they both got hit in the eye. As they opened the door to the mess hall, they were both surprised to see Jerry at the Wapec table eating while Sparcan was gorging himself on a pile of meat. Jerry didn't move; he just continued to eat his meal while Alan and Ryan walked cautiously toward the front to get a piece of steak.

After they had both gotten a piece of meat and placed it on their beaten eyes, Alan sat at the Gunar table to talk with Ryan. Jerry raised his mug of water to his face and looked in the reflection. He saw Alan sitting with Ryan at his Gunar table. Jerry was furious for he spent more time on Alan than the other Lumac leirds he converted combined. He grabbed his fork and knife and cut a large piece of meat and began to chew on it in frustration.

As he continued to cut bigger and bigger pieces, Jerry almost choked and had to calm down and stop eating. He got up and walked over to the Gunar, staring at Alan. When he arrived, he looked at Ryan then at Alan and said, "I guess you have chosen a side. After all I told you, you decided to choose the pathetic Gunars who I might add are all going to die when I achieve lordship." Jerry was glaring at Ryan who did not dare to look up at him.

Alan got up and said, "Jerry, I haven't chosen the Gunar side. I am still remaining a Lumac leird clearing up to lordship. Ryan and I were having a conversation. That's the only reason why I joined him at this table."

But Jerry wasn't listening. His glare was still focused on Ryan as he said, "You better watch your back at all times. Because one of these days, I will be there when you least expect it, so watch out." Jerry then stormed out of the building leaving Sparcan behind who quickly followed after him.

Ryan was stuck with fear that left him motionless for a minute, then eventually, he heard Alan's voice asking him, "Hey, man, are you okay?"

Ryan looked at him and said, "Yeah, I am okay. I got scared by Jerry's threat. He doesn't make a threat unless he intends to fulfill it."

Alan didn't know how to comfort Ryan, so he did as any normal teenage would do—he went back to eating.

Nogar walked over to Ryan and said, "You know, Ryan, this could be taken in a good way."

Ryan looked at Nogar and said, "How?"

Nogar couldn't blame Ryan for the way he was feeling and tried to comfort him while he thought that Sparcan and Jerry were going to try something soon. Nogar knew the only way to get Ryan's mind off Jerry was to train even harder and longer and that was exactly what he was going to do.

Chapter 16

After a few days of long strenuous training, Ryan was completely exhausted, and the training today was extra vigorous, so all Ryan wanted to do was to get some sleep.

Nogar could sense Ryan's need for sleep, so he said, "Ryan, tomorrow's training is going to be just as brutal as today. But I am just as tired as you are mentally, so I suggest we get some sleep. Ryan, you're making leaps and bounds. Some rest will really help both of us."

Ryan couldn't agree more with Nogar's suggestion for getting some much needed rest, so he began heading toward his bed. Nogar was right behind him perfectly content to get to bed early today.

Sparcan had been observing Nogar and Ryan for days now, and this was the exact opportunity he was waiting for. As soon as Sparcan was confident that they had fallen asleep, he decided to get Jerry.

Sparcan found Jerry carrying on a conversation with some of the other Wapec leirds while snacking on a piece of jerky, but he stopped when he received this message from Sparcan. *It's time. They are both exhausted and retired early. I am over by the sleeping quarters. Come quickly.* He then excused himself, giving an excuse that he needed to use the restroom, and rushed over to Sparcan who was standing right outside the Gunars' quarters.

As soon as Jerry got to Sparcan, he rested temporarily to catch his breath, and then he said, "Are you serious it's time? Is it really time?"

Sparcan looked up at Jerry as he said, "I watched both of them enter their quarters about an hour ago, giving enough time for them to fall into a deep sleep. So when we go in, which is forbidden for any trainer or dragon leird to enter the quarters other than their own, we need to have our plan ready and carry it out quickly."

Jerry responded by saying, "So right now, they are at their most vulnerable which makes this an opportunity to end both of their lives to accomplish our overall goal."

Sparcan smiled, pleased with how Jerry was molding to his plan when he said, "Remain calm, Jerry, and remember you have to kill Ryan first then I will kill Nogar. The only way this will work is if you kill Ryan first. Otherwise, Nogar will come back with a different dragon leird as a new trainer."

Jerry was completely willing to go along with Sparcan's plan but had one question. "Sparcan, why it's so important to kill Nogar?"

Sparcan took a moment to get control of his emotions, then he said, "Nogar was my very best friend. We did everything together. We even got chosen by the Dragon Master together to be on her precious council. Then one day, I came up with a plan that I wanted to make into a law, but Gunar back then Nogar now voted against it, stabbing me in the back. I rebelled against him and the Dragon Master, and ever since then, I have wanted to get even with both of them. I can kill Nogar today. The Dragon Master will be later, but her end will be soon."

Then Sparcan and Jerry very quietly opened the door to the Gunars' sleeping quarters and slipped in without anyone seeing. Meanwhile in Ryan's and Nogar's room, the exhausted duo lay in their designated sleeping areas. Ryan was snoring loudly that one would think that Nogar was getting very little to no sleep at all. But Nogar was in a deep sleep. He was dreaming of Angoree, the two of them flying through the landscape chasing down a herd of deer.

During this time, Nogar began to feel a new sensation that he knew exactly what was happening to him. A morph that occurs to the trainers when they gain their full trust from their dragon leirds. As Nogar's morph ended, he decided to tell Ryan in the morning when they both were more awake to further explain what had happened and why.

As Sparcan and Jerry walked through the hall, there was the sound of all the sleeping dragon leirds and their trainers, but one sound in particular stood out to Jerry. He turned around to Sparcan and whispered, "That loud snoring we can hear above everyone else is Ryan. He must be totally exhausted. We shouldn't have any trouble sneaking in and doing as we please then getting out unnoticed."

Sparcan toned out the softer sounds and focused on Ryan's snoring, then he whispered back, "I agree with you, but we must be cautious about Nogar, so kill Ryan quickly."

Jerry smiled and added, "With pleasure."

Upon entering their room, Jerry tiptoed quickly over to Ryan pulling out a sharpened knife he stole from the kitchen and prepared to stab Ryan in his heart. Sparcan flew over to Nogar holding a small explosive stone that when swallowed will rupture your eternal organs causing instant death. Jerry slowly got closer holding the knife close to his body until he was in position then he would stab Ryan multiple times.

Sparcan was watching Jerry to make sure he performed his end, unaware that Nogar had woken up instantly alerted to the danger when he saw both of them and knew why they were here. As soon as Jerry raised the knife to stab Ryan, suddenly a large fireball light filled the room.

This bright light startled Jerry as he looked back to see Sparcan but only saw a fireball headed right at him. Jerry had to jump out of the way but still had some of his arm hairs got singed from the fire. He dropped the knife in the process unto Ryan's bed. Jerry ran out of the room with his right sleeve on fire.

Ryan was awaken first by the fireball. Then he saw the knife in Jerry's hand positioned over his heart, so he decided to lay motionless. As soon as Ryan knew Jerry was gone, he got up and out of bed and walked over to Nogar asking, "What's going on?"

Nogar understood Ryan's panic and concern for his life as he said, "What was about to happen here is an unforgiveable crime in Dragtoneea, murder of the worst degree."

Nogar sat down and continued, "You see, Ryan, here when a trainer convinces their dragon leird to commit murder, the trainer deceives their dragon leird in a way to kill an opposing dragon leird first then the opposing trainer will kill their trainer. Because when the dragon leird is killed first and the trainer second, that trainer's soul is lost and dies forever."

Ryan then said, "What happens to the trainer's soul if for example Sparcan and Jerry were successful?"

Nogar took a moment before he replied by saying sadly, "I told you that when the dragon leird and the trainer are killed in that order, the soul dies forever. That means the trainer can never come back to train another dragon leird, and they are also denied their spot in our heaven."

Ryan said, "You have a dragon heaven?"

Nogar sensed a little sarcasm in Ryan's response but answered sincerely, "Yes, we do have a heaven. It is our main goal to obtain our spot in our heaven. But I don't think Sparcan was trying to keep me out of heaven. I think he doesn't want me to obtain lordship and take my rightful rank of general."

Ryan added, "You mean he tried to kill us to prevent us advancing to lordship and from there obtaining the rank of general?"

Nogar quickly responded, "Yes, Ryan, your correct. We will together become a dragon lord. Once together, we will receive the rank of a general. As the Gunar general, we will lead the Gunar army against Sparcan and the Wapecs. According to the Dragon Master, the Wapecs have been slowly gaining ground against our brothers. Without a general, the Wapecs will overcome the Gunar army and win."

Ryan was sorting through what Nogar had just told him after a short amount of time, then he said, "We can't let them win."

Nogar smiled saying, "No, indeed we won't."

Ryan's training from that point was very vigorous, almost to the point of nonstop. Nogar and Ryan wanted to put that night in the back of their mind, plus Ryan wanted to get much stronger. When Ryan would complete an obstacle, he would go through it again several times to perfect it.

Nogar was impressed and pleased with Ryan's progress. He was learning so much so quickly. Nogar knew he was ready for his next big challenge as Nogar watched Ryan breeze through a very difficult obstacle of repetitions. First, doing several repetitions of pull-ups then placing each hand and foot on solid four feet high and one foot in diameter columns. Then do push-ups increasing your repetitions as he got stronger. The purpose was to increase upper body strength. Nogar saw Ryan finished doing fifty repetitions of push-ups, and before he could do his pull-ups, he signaled for him to come over to where he was at.

Ryan was more than happy to take a break from his exhausting workout that he had been doing for over an hour; he felt that his arms and chest were being overexerted. It didn't take Ryan very long to jog over to Nogar. Once he got in closer, he could sense what was coming would be a very difficult challenge. Ryan replied casually, "Hey, Nogar, what's up?"

Nogar responded back, "Ryan, I know you have sensed that what I am about to tell you will be very challenging. But what you don't know is that it will be even more difficult than you can ever imagine."

After everything Ryan had done since he got here, he didn't see how anything could be more difficult. Nogar continued, "Ryan, do you remember in the Dragon Master's Keep you saw visions through the medatore shell about your hiecu?"

Ryan didn't have to think for long as he answered, "Yes, I remember."

Nogar was happy with his response. "Good, this challenge is in relation to that vision. You have grown stronger mentally and physically, so you are now ready. This challenge you are about to perform is not required of by all the dragon leirds but to those dragon leirds who do have such a vision. It is required of them to perform this often dangerous challenge in order to obtain the status of lordship."

As Ryan heard the word *dangerous*, he was having second thoughts and regrets about having this vision. But it's required of him, so he had to overcome his fear and was dedicated to finish this challenge.

Nogar then said, "Before we begin, I must summon someone."

Ryan was getting excited as he saw Nogar using his mind to summon this person. Before long, Ryan could see a streak of brown light moving out of the shadows darting from bushes and rocks until finally it stopped in front of Nogar. As Ryan looked over the creature, he realized that it was a lermeon. He recognized the body structure from Nogar's description and the odd humanlike hands and face. This one was wearing a tattered leather shirt that appeared to have large gashes in it, as if a large predator like a hawk or an eagle attacked it.

As Ryan watched Nogar relay a message to the lermeon, he wondered if this one was the designated messenger for the trainers to use. As soon as Nogar was done relaying the message, the lermeon disappeared just as quickly as it had appeared into the shadows. Ryan kept his eyes on the path the lermeon left, not noticing Nogar approaching him.

Nogar startled Ryan as he said, "Ryan, I know you are curious about what I told the lermeon."

Ryan shrugged his shoulders acting like it wasn't a big deal, but inside, it was tearing him up to know what message the lermeon was carrying. Nogar didn't have the opportunity to tell Ryan as ground around them became dark. Something very large was hovering above them. It didn't levitate for long as suddenly, the large heavy creature landed next to Ryan shaking the ground knocking him off balance. Ryan's heart was racing. He didn't dare look over to see what had landed next to him.

But it didn't stop Nogar as he said, "Marnic, my old friend, it's good to see you."

Ryan remained motionless just as a rabbit would if a fox or coyote was around. Still Nogar moved in giving this Marnic a hug. Ryan started to control his breathing, trying to calm himself down and also trying to gain the courage he needed to look over his shoulder. As Ryan slowly turned to look over his shoulder, an indescribable stench filled his nostrils.

Plugging his nose, he saw a massive dragon that was covered in a strange oily orange liquid dripping down his body. As Ryan began to scan his body finding its shoulder, he saw even more of the orange substance and in larger amounts changing the scales colors. Ryan continued to scan upward locating its back and noticed that several of its boney scutes protruding out of its back were cracked or broken. Ryan followed the back to the neck noticing an unusual amount of scars. Ryan continued until he finally got to the head were the scars began to increase in both number and size. But what made Ryan cringe the most was a fresh wound, a large lesion exposing some of his teeth and gums.

Ryan wondered how he got this nasty wound that's when Ryan heard Nogar asked, "How is the marcouren hunting going, Marnic?"

Marnic responded, "I actually had just killed one and began preparing it when the lermeon you sent summoned me to you. This marcouren was a large bull. The one I have been tracking for a few days now. I found it feeding on a deer. I then got into a good spot to move in for the kill. As I flew down on it, the marcouren flung one of its tentacles at me. I easily bite it off, exposing some of its bone. Before I could severe the jugular, it used the exposed bone to its advantage covering me in its blood before thrusting it in my face giving me this gash." Marnic was pointing to the triangular shaped wound missing from his lip.

Ryan was so confused by his story as he asked, "What on earth is a marcouren?"

Nogar turned to Marnic and said, "My dragon leird, Ryan, is very curious particularly about the animals in this world."

Marnic smiled, opening the wound even more. Ryan had to look away. Marnic was not at all irritated by Ryan's question as he answered, "A marcouren is a very large red with blue spots land squid very similar looking to the squid in the human world. You know that they have ten tentacles so they can move around and climb the mountains. Their heads have the same triangular arrowhead shape, but then our squid change."

Ryan was listening intently Marnic continued, "Their eyes are located one on each tip of the bottom two tips. Its mouth is in the center of the head with an orange beak-shaped like a large pointed oval. When it hunts its prey and goes in for the kill, it opens its mouth where it extends its three fangs. They are similar to a snake having two on the top then one on the bottom. It stretches out its neck where it strikes injecting its venom. The venom paralyzes its victim then it begins to tear it apart while it's still alive, keeping the meat as fresh as possible."

Ryan didn't know if he wanted to throw up or keep on listening to his story, but he just couldn't keep something to himself about Marnic's story and said, "Marnic, I have a question for you. I thought a dragon's armor is among the strongest substance known to anyone. So how did this marcouren gave you that big gash on your face, and why do you hunt them in the first place?"

Nogar quickly stepped in between Ryan and Marnic as he said to Ryan, "Ryan, you first need to understand that dragons like Marnic pride themselves in being marcouren hunters, particular Marnic who is one of the best in Dragtoneea."

Marnic settled down as he continued, "I hunt these red devils for one reason. They are the main source of the Gunar's army's food source. And just as Nogar has said, I am the best hunter there is." Nogar added after Marnic finished, "Marnic's specialty in hunting will help to aid us in this difficult challenge ahead of us. But we need to hurry as the sun is setting and this already dangerous challenge will be even more dangerous at night."

Nogar then turned toward the sleeping quarters as he said to Ryan, "We need to remain in safety at all times. Due to Sparcan's attempt, the Dragon Master has posted guards by each entrance giving us that much needed protection."

Ryan agreed completely with Nogar since the guards arrived the day after the attack. Ryan has felt much safer as they entered.

Once inside Nogar spoke concerning the challenge, "Ryan, this vigorous challenge is a mind- strengthening challenge. I want you right now to close your eyes and begin to relax your body and mind, clearing your mind. As your mind clears, both your mind and body will sink into a deeper relaxation. This is necessary for this challenge to be successful."

As Ryan began to clear his mind, he began to sink into a deep relaxation state. Nogar had to use his mental powers to hold Ryan up, otherwise, he would fall over. He had relaxed so well and so quickly. Nogar noticed that Ryan had reached the level of relaxation necessary in order to perform this challenge. He then communicated using telepathy saying, *Ryan, you have reached the point necessary to safely prepare your mind and body for this challenge. I want you now to picture Seven Mile Lake. Also the only communication allowed will be done through telepathy. Once you see the lake let me know.*

Ryan was exploring deep into his imagination. He began to see images. The first was a brief image of his five-year-old birthday party. Next was a pet turtle he had that died mysteriously. Suddenly, it got very dark, so Ryan opened his eyes in his mind when he felt something brush up against his check. The first thing Ryan saw was a thick moist fog. It felt like Ryan was running through it at an incredible pace. Then unexpectedly, Ryan's body began to tilt downward headfirst. The fog began to fade away until Ryan realized that it wasn't fog at all but a large cloud above Seven Mile Lake.

As he looked over the vast body of water, it began to look more like an ocean. He was in awestruck by the beauty of the scenery. As his descent continued, he got his first glimpse of water dragons. He observed several of these large water dwellers chasing what Ryan assumed were their natural prey. A type of seal or at least the front half looked like a seal, the bottom half looked like an octopus. These strange seals came in a variety of colors—blue, green, purple, yellow, and red with black and white spots.

These seals seemed to school in groups by the thousands when Ryan saw enough savage carnage, he said, *I'm here.*

To his left, he heard Nogar said, *We are too.*

Ryan looked to his left to see Nogar, and to his right, he saw Marnic keeping an eye on the water dragons. Ryan did not understand how a single soldier could fend off an army of water dragons if they got attacked.

Ryan looked over to Nogar and said, "So who is holding me up?"

Nogar smiled at him as he said, "No one is holding you, Ryan. You are flying on your own."

Ryan looked at Nogar estimating the distance. It was well over five feet. Then over at Marnic who was drifting away from him watching the water dragon's activity, making sure they keep their distance. Their descent continued at a steady pace. Ryan was waiting for his body to plunge into water, alerting the water dragon's to their position.

Then without any warning, they abruptly stopped about ten to twelve feet off the water. Ryan was instantly relieved. Ryan's curious behavior began to explore the depths of the crystal clear water. He could see thousands of strange and unique species of fish and mammals feeding on each other.

Ryan's observation was interrupted by Nogar telling him, *Ryan, we now need to proceed to the next stage of this challenge exercise. I see your interest in the abundant underwater wildlife. This is good. I now need to ask you a very important question in regard to the wildlife. Do you see any kind of animal that would alert you to danger by causing you any kind of harm?*

Ryan began to concentrate on the wildlife. He was unaware that this fantastic image was not just a dream in his imagination. But Nogar had used a form of hypnosis that actually transported their bodies to the location in the image.

As Ryan was studying the different life forms, he came across a strangely unique type of jellyfish that had an oval sphere. It had a blue body with deep ridges throughout its leather-like skin. Its body was covered in long thick black spikes for protection and hunting. Ryan noticed that it had one large eye used to locate a prey item, then it would shoot one of its spikes containing a poison. Then using its thick stringy tentacles, it would wrap around it and begin to dissolve it to be able to digest it.

But Ryan saw something even stranger and more alarming looking, even more dangerous—an enormous fishlike creature. Ryan saw several of these fish. They had different shaped shark heads down to their shoulders, then it transformed into a human form. Except on its back was a large dorsal fin and the hips had side fins too. Then their midsections changed back into the body of a shark.

Ryan noticed that there wasn't just one or two but hundreds almost thousands, each was armed with a large variety of weapons. They were moving at a fast pace, eating the fish they could catch, scattering the rest, and not slowing down as they moved in the direction of the water dragons. Ryan, while in a little bit of panic pointing down at the shark-like creatures, said to Nogar, "*Look!*"

Nogar looked down seeing what Ryan was alarmed by and said, "Those are sharkcons, a natural enemy to the water dragons. With their speed and course set right at the water dragons, it can only mean one of two things. Either the sharkcons are starving and need a large amount of meat or they are at war. Either way right now, we are a part of it. But it doesn't matter, the reason for this mission of ours has just became way too dangerous. We need to accomplish our task as soon as possible then head home."

Marnic then said in urgency, "The sharkcon attack has begun. The water dragons are getting more and more agitated by the second. We need to do this right now."

Nogar watched the slaughter of sharkcons to very few water dragons and turned to Ryan and demanded, "Ryan, open your eyes!"

Ryan was confused. If it was only a dream in his imagination, why does he need to end it by opening his eyes? Still confused, he said, "But if I open my eyes, I will lose this awesome dream."

Nogar lost all his patience as he yelled, "*Open your eyes now!*"

Feeling threatened by Nogar's tone and not wanting to disappoint him, Ryan pushed this unbelievable image into the back of his mind and began to crack open his eyes. When he did, it was as if he was waking up from a deep sleep, but he was being blinded from a bright reflective light. Ryan opened his eyes, fully looked around, and realized that it wasn't a dream at all. The scene was exactly the same in his dream.

When Nogar saw that Ryan was fully alert, he said, "This exercise is used for dragon leirds to strengthen their mental capabilities. So that after lordship, their trainers can continue to guide the young dragon lords until they have learned all they need to know. Then the trainer will leave the new dragon lord knowing you're safe and prepared for leadership and battle. However, I am afraid that this challenge that's already dangerous has become way too dangerous to proceed. Normally, you would encounter a known natural enemy and complete a battle challenge. But with the given circumstances of the sharkcon attack on the water dragons, we will have to leave."

Nogar and Marnic moved away from Ryan to discuss a much needed escape route, but Marnic thought Ryan needed to complete the challenge. This caused an argument that had to be settled quickly.

Chapter 17

In the meantime, Ryan continued to watch the brutal war as the sharkcon were dying in mass numbers. At this time, Ryan felt something heavy hanging from his belt on his left side. Ryan reached across his body with his right hand to discover what this heavy object was. Ryan felt a hilt of a sword. He then looked down at the sword. It was a long sword. The hilt was made of local dark brown tree with spirals of silver and gold inlaid in the hilt coming from the blade to the cap of the hilt. The cap has the Dragon Master's crest stamped on it a capital *D* laced in gold with a capital *M* laced in silver in the middle of the *D*.

Ryan grasped it and began to pull it out of the dragon's hide sheath. The blade seemed to be soaked in an oily substance. When it was exposed to the air, it was lit, having a blue tint fading to yellow flame of fire escaped as he continued to pull it out. The blade was of solid steel with a narrow slightly curved structure. The tip expanded looking similar to spear tip.

Nogar was still conversing with Marnic and didn't see Ryan with his new weapon as Ryan continued to look over this awesome sword. He wondered if he dipped it in the water if it would put the fire out. None of them saw that four water dragons spotted them and were heading straight for Ryan. Ryan caught movement out of the corner of his eye and turned in that direction to see the four approaching water dragons.

As Ryan looked at this new threat, he knew why he had received this new weapon and figured this must be part of his battle challenge. He knew he would have to be confident in standing and defending his ground. Ryan watched as one of the water dragons sped up faster than the other three dead set on him. Then this water dragon began to come up to the surface. Ryan had no idea what it was going to do.

Ryan knew now more than ever that he had to rely on his instincts. He also had to apply the training he had done so far. Ryan focused on the lead water dragon holding his sword at his shoulder, height both hands on the hilt. Suddenly, the water dragon surfaced extending its body six feet out of the water firing an icy water ball at Ryan. As the ball flew straight to his face, Ryan kept his eye on it. When it got within swing range, Ryan sliced it in half splashing some of the water in his face.

The frustrated water dragon swam even faster to get closer before he attached again, believing that he had missed an already easy target. As Ryan watched this even more determined water dragon's approach knowing a second attack was evident, then he would have to do his own attack. Just as Ryan predicted, the water dragon surfaced just a few feet in front of him firing two icy water balls. This time Ryan was even quicker to block the two balls of water, and without even thinking, he made a strong slicing swoop until the sword's hilt was resting on his right side.

Ryan looked over right into the water dragon's eyes as they began to slide off its neck as he had severed the head clean off. Ryan watched the head and body fall into the watery depth. Nogar and Marnic were still unaware of the water dragons attack on Ryan until they heard the loud multiple splashes from the dead one slain by Ryan. Upon noticing the other three advancing water dragons still on the attack, they both immediately rushed over to Ryan's aid. But not before another water dragon rushed in quicker to a full attack mode due to being angry from its lost comrade.

This second water dragon lunged out of the water directly at Ryan, preparing to fire at him at such a close range. The water dragon would practically be biting off Ryan's head. The water dragon's mouth was open so wide and so close that Ryan could see water pooling together in a crystallizing ball. Ryan didn't wait for this one to fire before slicing the head clean off at the jaw line. As Ryan watched it too drop to its watery grave, he was freaked out by the terrifying image of the rows of razor sharp teeth before killing it, leaving now only two of the original four water dragons.

One of the water dragons fell back and turned around and headed back to the group of other water dragons to relay what had just happened to their small assassin group. Nogar knew he was heading back for reinforcements. The water dragon had gained too much distance to catch it before it could sound an alarm. Meanwhile, the last remaining one rerouted its course toward Nogar hoping for better success and for a victory this time. For what this water dragon saw was not a dragon lord, only a trainer that means no deadly capabilities an easy kill.

Ryan saw that the new attack subject was Nogar, and without thinking, Ryan did a backflip high in the air landing right in front of the water dragon. With all of his strength, he then thrust the sword straight into its head right above the eyes. The blade only stopped after Ryan had forced the sword's hilt against the dead dragon's skull. It died instantly. Ryan watched as the lifeless corpse slide off the blade, joining his two dead brothers. Ryan then began to scan the water looking for any other dangerous threats.

Ryan noticed calm water after the ripples cleared, then he replaced the sword to its sheath then turned to Nogar asking, "Are you okay?"

Nogar looked at Ryan and nodded in the affirmative. Nogar was thinking of the incredible display. He also thought how greatly impressed he was of Ryan's ability to kill three water dragons. However, Nogar knew that one had escaped and would be alerting the others. There was no way just the three of them could defend themselves against the water dragon's army, so they need to leave now.

Just then, Marnic arrived after the fight was over and said, "Ryan, I am impressed by your fighting skill. Let me apologize that I was not able to protect you. We were both unaware until we heard the splash of the first dead water dragon. I then got a surprise of my own. One of the sharkcon leaders and a few followers decided that I was their enemy and took me off guard. No worries, I killed the leader sending the followers retreating in fear."

Ryan had his fill of excitement for the day. Nogar agreed, so they then left Seven Mile Lake, but Marnic stayed behind briefly just to make sure no other water dragons or sharkcons regrouped for another stronger attack. When Nogar and Ryan arrived and landed back to the training grounds, Nogar first made sure that Ryan and him were in a safe place. When he was confident, he flew to Marnic who had just arrived himself.

Nogar thanked him for all of his assistance, then he gave him a hug before he left. After Marnic left, Nogar walked back over to Ryan having some questions for him, so he decided to ask the most urgent ones first. Pointing to the sword, he asked, "Ryan, where did you get that sword?"

He then added, "Those water dragons could have easily killed you, why did you attack them?"

Ryan looked down at his sword, feeling the smooth surface of the hilt, then he gripped it firmly before looking up at Nogar. He then said, "Just before I was attacked by those four water dragons, I felt something heavy on my left side. I was examining it. I then pulled it out and was awestruck by the beauty of the fiery blade. It was a good thing too as it helped me in defending against the four attacking water dragons. I cannot stress enough that I was attacked, and if I did not defend myself against them, I would be dead. I would rather kill than be killed."

Nogar pondered for a minute thinking about what had just happened and also what Ryan had said, then he said, "So you say the only reason for the attack on your part was in defense for your life? Were you forgetting about the experienced Gunar soldier, Marnic, who was there for your protection for this exact situations?"

Ryan was a little annoyed by Nogar's snappy comment as he answered in the tone he was feeling, "No, I was not. In fact, I would rather he frightened them away or if he had to killed them instead of me. I do recall that you two were a little too busy conversing with each other about what I don't know before I had killed two of them. Then I saved your life by killing the last one before it got a chance to kill you. I had no choice other than to kill my enemies before they could kill me."

Ryan stopped for a moment to take in what he said then asked, "Nogar, did I accomplish my challenge?"

Nogar had some mixed emotions about Ryan's actions which had him needing some answers to his questions. As Nogar was lost in his thoughts, he was thinking about how impressed he was by Ryan's amazing feat by confronting and killing three water dragons. In the history of all of Dragtoneea, no dragon leird had ever attempted to confront a water dragon, little alone kill one.

In the past, if a dragon leird ever came in contact with a water dragon, their fate would be sealed with their life unless they were lucky enough to escape. For it is a law that no trainer or dragon leird were to confront a water dragon. As Nogar continued to weigh his thoughts on this matter, he still continued to ignore Ryan. While Ryan was left in the dark by Nogar receiving no answer and had no clue as to what Nogar was thinking.

Just as Ryan was about to ask Nogar again about his accomplishment, he received a strong signal from the Dragon Master immediately requesting their presence. Ryan noticed that Nogar was too deep in his thoughts to get the Dragon Master's message. So Ryan interrupted him, "Nogar, we have been summoned by the Dragon Master."

As Nogar began to clear his conflicting thoughts, he too clearly received the same message. Nogar then looked at Ryan and said, "You no longer have the ability to fly on your own. I must hold unto you in order for you to fly." With that, Nogar didn't give Ryan any time to respond as he grasped his arm and they took off in the air. While flying he said, "Now we go see the Dragon Master," as he set his course for the Dragon Master's Keep where they will receive of her counsel and wisdom.

As Nogar and Ryan arrived at the Dragon Master's Keep, the Dragon Master was busy performing a task. Nogar took advantage of this circumstance to collect his thoughts to be able to present an extensive presentation. When the Dragon Master had finished her task that she was working on, she turned toward Ryan and Nogar. As Nogar saw the Dragon Master, he was about to present what had happened over Seven Mile Lake.

But the Dragon Master raised her hand stopping Nogar before he started, looking directly at Ryan as she spoke to him. "Ryan, I understand that you were performing a simple training challenge, but then, it turned into a very dangerous situation." Then looking directly at Nogar, she said, "I also understand that at the very critical points, you did not get the aid needed. But I understand that through this all, you have received your hiecu. At this time, I would ask you to present it to me."

Ryan looked at the Dragon Master very confused then he looked at Nogar with the same expression. This is when Nogar spoke to help clear his confusion. "I didn't properly inform you about your hiecu. It is a physical object most of the time. It is a form of a weapon. Your hiecu symbolizes your placement here in Dragtoneea. But more importantly, as yours is a weapon, it also confirms that you have leadership in your blood. Now when you present your hiecu to the Dragon Master, she will confirm your military status."

When Nogar had finished Ryan reached for his sword and pulled out the spectacular glowing sword of fire to present to the Dragon Master. As the Dragon Master began to examine the quality of the sword, she was greatly impressed by this weapon and its symbolism. In the middle of her examination, Nogar got up the courage to say, "My dearest Dragon Master, I would like to explain why I had—"

"*Silence!*" snapped the Dragon Master. She then said, "I have already spoken to Marnic, the Gunar solider, you requested to aid and protect Ryan and you. Now, Ryan, before I let you speak, I want you know that this hiecu represents your true right to be the general of the Gunar army. Now I would like to hear it from you."

Ryan was not prepared to present his thoughts to her. This unexpected request made Ryan instantly became nervous and was covered in sweat as he returned the sword to its sheath. Ryan began to search his memories of this dangerous experience to present the events in the order that they happened in. After a moment, Ryan finally felt comfortable with his collection of thoughts as he said, "Well, during this simple exercise, I was told that a simple battle challenge of a known natural enemy was to occur. I first spotted a large group of sharkcons on the war path toward a group of water dragons. During this battle, four water dragons spotted us and set a war path directly to me. Nogar and Marnic could not aid me as they were discussing a hasty escape route for us. Because it was decided that it was too dangerous to stay. I did not have time to get their attention before I had to defend myself and Nogar for that matter. After it was finished, Nogar took me back to the training grounds when we were summoned by you."

The Dragon Master listened intently to Ryan after he finished, she then said, "Ryan, your hiecu was presented for your safety. It is also the most powerful hiecu I have ever seen a dragon leird receive. Your ability to defend yourself by slaying not one but three water dragons also proves that you have earned your rank and placement in Dragtoneea. Nogar, Ryan has been fulfilling his tasks including this impressive hiecu challenge. Now you know which task you need to do next. I suggest you get started with it now."

With that, the Dragon Master turned away leaving Nogar and Ryan alone to get started on their next task. Ryan was getting a lot of unexpected surprises, this being one of them.

Ryan turned to Nogar and asked, "Nogar, what is the next one the Dragon Master is referring to?"

Nogar was acting very nervous about this new task as he said, "I have to take you to one of the elemental mountains, one that will teach you the respect you need to live in Dragtoneea. The mountain I have to take you to is Snow Mountain, and it is the one that I fear the most."

Chapter 18

As Nogar and Ryan left the Dragon Master's Keep, they turned their direction to the dreaded Snow Mountain. As they headed to the mountain, Nogar shared a very important dragon law with Ryan. "Ryan, for dragon leirds who have attained their hiecu, there is a dragon law. It states that when a dragon leird earns their hiecu, they and their trainer must travel to one of the five elemental mountains where the dragon leird will encounter the natural known enemies when, if needed, they will have to defend themselves. This is one of the last laws a dragon leird must learn."

Ryan listened, then he said, "I have to prove my skill yet again, why?"

Nogar could understand Ryan's confusion and frustration with this new challenge as he said, "Ryan, I completely understand. The Dragon Master already said you earned your placement here when you were attacked over the water. Rarely will any dragon leird and trainer go over Seven Mile Lake, and as a dragon lord, it will be an even rarer occasion. But snow will cover the land every year and the animals tend to roam off the mountain across the land. You will have to know them and know how to defend against them."

After hearing Nogar explain the reasons why they were going to Snow Mountain, he was a little more at ease but still concerned about facing another dangerous encounter. Just before they reached the outer limits of Snow Mountain, Nogar stopped them.

As they waited, Ryan had a fantastic view of the mountain and most of the land surrounding it. As Ryan viewed the landscape, he was stunned by the beauty of the land as the sun reflected off the snow. It was like a thousand rainbows reaching for the heavens.

Nogar looked at Ryan as he said, "Each of the elemental mountains water, wind, fire, earth, and snow have a sustaining ore called racton. This ore is the only substance that can withstand the weight and force of each element. Only the Dragon Master can forge a fire hot enough to shape and mold racton into tools or weapons such as your sword."

Ryan looked down at his sword admiring the workmanship and thought, *At my time of need, the Dragon Master chose this weapon for me.*

Nogar saw Ryan admiring the sword and decided to tell him about what he will see on the mountain, knowing about Ryan's fascination with animals. Nogar said, "Ryan, let me tell you about the animals on this mountain. I want to first tell you about some of the herbivores that call this land their home. A yalea is a white antelope with dark blue stripes, two on the face and one under each eye running down the check and neck until they connect at the middle of the chest forming a *V*. There are several more staggering blue stripes down the body and legs.

"This antelope also has a unique set of horns. They have holes in them, and at its base, the horns can swivel. Depending on the speed of the swivel, the holes in the horns will make a flutelike sound."

Ryan asked, "What would make the sounds coming out become louder?"

Nogar then said, "When the yalea moves the horns then rotate, and the faster it moves, the faster the horns rotate. The calmer they are, the slower they rotate until there is no noise. The noise is the loudest when they are running. The noise can be heard for miles alerting any animal of their presence or the danger that startled them."

Nogar continued to explain more animals. "The zalato is a magnificent white deer with silver spots covering its black body. It also has a majestic set of gold antlers. The yaleas and zalatos tend to herd together for protection."

Ryan then blurted out, "Well, I know what the yaleas can do for protection, but what do the zalatos do?"

Nogar responded by saying, "The zalatos have that majestic set of antlers that not only are gold but can pierce any surface and predators would suffer deep deadly wounds."

Ryan was completely fascinated and then asked, "Is that all that live on this mountain?"

Nogar said, "No, there are others as well like the almi or snow rabbit—"

Ryan couldn't help blurting out, "I know what that is. We have those back at home called snowshoe hares. In the summer, they are a brownish gray and then turn white in winter. Each color phase is a camouflage from predators."

Nogar calmly said, "Well, our rabbits are much different than your hare. This rabbit is completely white with small black eyes. They also have a small horn on their forehead to allow them to dig up food and to burrow into snowbanks. Another difference between your hare and our rabbit is your hare has to make a hole in the ground to make its home. The snow rabbit is made up of snow, and so when it burrows into a snowbank, it becomes as if it was snow."

When Nogar was done explaining the almi, Ryan burst out in laughter as he gasped for air from laughing so hard. Finally sucking in enough air, he blurted out, "You mean to tell me you have jackalopes here that is an urban myth back home. Local taxidermists would kill jack rabbits or cottontails and mount it with a set of horns—a very common tourist attraction. Heck, I even have one."

He then began to laugh again, even snorted a little bit, but his laughter was cut short by Nogar's sharp comment. "I can assure you, my young dragon leird, that almis are very real. In fact, look over your left shoulder and you will see one right now."

Ryan peered over his shoulder, and there was this white rabbit the size of a cottontail with a protruding horn on its forehead. It was digging up plant roots of a white grass that covered the ground. Ryan stopped laughing and decided to listen to Nogar more intently. When Ryan realized that all the animals Nogar was describing were real, he got excited. His excitement grew as he couldn't wait to actually see more of these creatures Nogar was describing to him. Nogar could sense Ryan's eagerness, but Ryan didn't know about all the animals including the dangerous ones.

Nogar did not want to mention to Ryan about the dangerous animals just yet as he continued. "These animals graze on a luscious food source called snow grass. Named so because of where it grows and its white color. This grass only grows year round on the west side of the mountain and only on the north side in the summer. There are a few meadows high up on the mountain that we will not venture to go. But not all the animals here graze on this vegetation for there is a savage predator on this mountain."

Ryan knew that all ecosystems have a series of food chains and at the top were the predators.

With this in mind, he asked, "Nogar, what are these predators you are hesitant to speak of?"

Nogar said, "Not predators, only one predator—the cold ice tiger. A large cat with a body structure very much like a saber-toothed tiger in your world's fossil library. It even has the long protruding front teeth. Its coat is a silky white with silver stripes down its side connected in the middle of its back by a long narrow diamond. Its teeth and claws are completely made up of ice. It has a toxin in its saliva, and it has glands on its paws near the claws to soak them in this same toxin. They use this toxin for hunting their prey that when delivered, the helpless creatures turn into ice which is the only way the tiger can digest its food. They have brilliant blue eyes with slanting green pupils.

"These ice tigers love to hunt snow goats that live high up on the mountain. They look identical to your mountain goats, only they are completely white except for their black eyes. They are large providing large amounts of meat but are hard to get, making them difficult to hunt."

Ryan interrupted Nogar by saying, "Nogar, these ice tigers sound very terrifying, but how do they survive and hunt in this environment?"

Nogar was waiting for Ryan's interruption but answered his question gladly. "This ice tiger is unlike any predator you have ever heard of or seen. The toxin I was explaining earlier also serves a second purpose. The toxin acts like an antifreeze agent as it is mixed thoroughly in its bloodstream preventing it from freezing even in the coldest weather. The toxins warming effect allows the tiger to chase its prey without using too much energy. When the ice tigers go high on the mountain for the snow goats, they are treading very lightly on another predators' domain."

Ryan was fascinated as he asked, "What predator?"

Nogar then said, "The snow eagles live on the highest peaks of this mountain and also hunt the snow goats. They are extremely large. If they catch a glimpse or smell the foul order of these tigers, they will attack and kill as many of them as they can. This is why we will not be going very high on the mountain today. The ice tigers live mainly on the west side of the mountain, making their homes out of the large blocks of ice leaning against each other, creating large cavities perfect for their home."

Nogar then decided to pull the attention off the ice tigers by saying, "You know how some animals display some kind of warning to ward off their natural predators?"

Ryan nodded so Nogar continued, "There is an animal here that uses similar tactics to warn the ice tigers to leave them alone. It is a sheep-like animal called hakuse. These sheep have a pure white wool with spiraling horns about three feet long. When one of these hakuses feel threatened by an ice tiger, they do not panic, but instead if they happen to be attacked, the predator is in for a nasty surprise. Under that thick wool are thousands of spikes laced with a poison that would kill any predator of any size including snow eagles. Because of this defense, the hakuses are completely left alone."

Ryan was very excited to see any of these animals, so he turned around facing the white meadow and began to scan the field searching for any of these animals. As he scanned more carefully and got as close as he could, he began to see several small herds of each of these species that Nogar was describing. However, as he continued to scan the meadow observing the herds and mountain base, Ryan didn't see any ice tigers. This made him less nervous as they began to move in closer to the mountain.

As they flew over the meadow getting closer to the base of the mountain, their movements spooked the herds. As they continued, Ryan, for the first time, heard the flutelike sound coming from the yaleas running around. When they reached the base of the mountain, the herd animals realized there was no danger and relaxed and began to eat the luscious grass again. Meanwhile, as soon as Ryan landed and happened to be on Nogar's right side, he saw a curious mark that he didn't see before. As he examined it more closely, he noticed that it was a scar made out of solid ice crystals.

Ryan was very curious about this strange scar, so he asked Nogar, "Nogar, what happened to your right shoulder?"

This question pulled Nogar's attention away from observing a herd of zalatos as he wondered what they tasted like. He then looked down at his right shoulder acting as if he didn't know what was there. He then said, "A few years ago, I was training a young dragon leird like yourself. He too received his hiecu. It wasn't as superior of a weapon as yours, but he too was required to come to an elemental mountain. We came to this same spot where we are standing now.

"We were observing some yaleas. I was explaining the sound that comes from the horns when I let my guard down. It was then that two ice tiger sneaked up on us. I was shielding my dragon leird to protect him from getting attacked when I got sliced by one of the tiger's massive tooth. Just like you, I acquired the gift of fire which was the only thing that saved my life as I warmed up my shoulder preventing the spread of the freezing toxin. In my weakened condition, my dragon leird had to fend off and even kill one of the ice tigers allowing us to leave quickly. This experience is why I fear this mountain."

Ryan looked over Nogar's shoulder again, stunned by the crystallizing tissue, as he said, "But, Nogar, I've never noticed it before."

Nogar then said while pointing to the scar, "That's because a scar like this one only appears when you're in the surroundings of the creature that gave you the wound. And for some reason, it is really bothering me."

As Ryan thought about the wound and the logic of it, he began to scan the meadow again. Off in the distance, Ryan saw some movement, but amongst all the white, he wasn't sure what it was. As the shape got bigger, Ryan could make some of the striking characteristics of the ice tiger, and it was heading right for them.

Ryan began to tense up a little as he said to Nogar, "I'm sorry that your scar is bothering you, but I think that we really have bigger problems, look!" Ryan was pointing across the field to the ice tiger.

Nogar soon located it as he said, "Do you know why my scar is bothering me? It's bothering me because that particular ice tiger is the one that gave me this scar."

Ryan felt vulnerable as if he had to deal with the past dragon leird's problems.

Nogar was watching the ice tiger as it was stalking a small group of almis. He was glad it was them rather than Ryan and himself. As it was getting closer to them, Nogar quietly said to Ryan, "Get behind me, but do it very slowly just in case the ice tiger sees us and decides to attack us."

As Ryan was getting behind him, he continued to say softly, "We are going to move slowly to that grove of white ivory trees."

Ryan looked over to the white grove of trees. It was thick enough to cover them from the view of the ice tiger. Then Ryan turned his attention back on the approaching ice tiger who still hadn't seen them as they safely got into the grove of trees. Ryan watched as the ice tiger kept a slow but steady stalking pace as it was avoiding some of the larger prey animals. As Ryan continued to observe the tiger, a couple of questions popped into his mind, so he whispered, "Nogar, why is the ice tiger not attacking those deer or antelope?"

Nogar whispered back, "If that tiger alarms just one of those yaleas, this entire meadow will be alerted and would be gone."

Ryan hadn't thought about that, then he asked, "Well, then don't ice tigers hunt in packs?"

This was one fact that did worry Nogar but didn't show it to Ryan as he answered, "Usually, but this one seems to be alone. Which would make sense on why its hunting those rabbits. It wants the challenge of the hunt."

This gave Ryan some relief until Nogar said, "Unless they are hunting as a pack to make the hunt more successful."

Ryan's nerves once again were on edge as he waited and began to scan in every direction, trying to catch a glimpse of any additional tigers joining in the hunt, but he couldn't see any other tigers and sighed in relief but still kept an observant eye on the still dangerous surroundings.

Through the grove of trees, Nogar and Ryan continued to spy on the cautious stalking predator as it got closer and closer to the grazing rabbits. Occasionally, a few of them would chase one another in an act of playful behavior. This situation was great for the tiger as the group of rabbits were engaged in a common daily activity. With this distraction, the rabbits were not focusing on the potential danger approaching.

The ice tiger was now within several feet and was crouching for an attack, watching and waiting for the perfect opportunity. Ryan wanted to shout or scream to warn the innocent rabbits of the danger, but Nogar stopped him by saying, "If you make any loud noises right now, you would save the rabbits from a terrible fate. But in return, your noise will alert the tiger of our position and put us in terrible danger of an angry and hungry tiger seeking us out."

So Ryan had to restrain himself and his emotions in order to remain safe. Ryan continued to watch in despair. As the ice tiger continued to watch the rabbits, he had to cringe at the potential slaughter about to happen. The ice tiger had been waiting patiently in a still crouched position for several minutes just observing the rabbits every movement, establishing a pattern in order to make a more successful attack.

The ice tiger was finally satisfied with its observations as it began to venture in closer to its prey. Soon it was within range of the sensitive hearing and smell of the rabbits. Within a matter of seconds, both senses kicked in as the rabbits began to scatter, diving into snowbanks and disappearing out of sight and out of the hunting range of their attacker.

Chapter 19

Out of the twenty rabbits, the tiger was able to corner three at the base of the mountain. Out of panic, one of the rabbits darted to the left toward an opening and potential freedom. But that is exactly what the ice tiger wanted it to do. The ice tiger immediately pounced on and killed the rabbit with a single bite to the neck. Slowly, the rabbit began to harden into a solid piece of ice then the ice tiger turned its attention to the other two rabbits as the ice tiger paced back and forth looking at the frightened rabbits.

The ice tiger figured it would only get one of the two by pouncing on it. With this in mind, the tiger began its approach on its two victims. As it did, he was trying to judge which direction the rabbits would try to bolt to safety. The tiger did a sudden spring, trying to catch the rabbits off guard. It was successful and killed one of the rabbits with a slice to the jugular. The ice tiger also accomplished nicking the other rabbit in the ear creating a small cut.

This small cut began to fester into a freezing compound, forming a sphere of ice. This would eventually spread throughout the entire body of the rabbit. The ice tiger gathered the other two frozen rabbits and began to tear chunks out of them, swallowing them whole. The ice tiger wanted to conserve its energy and gain some before it began tracking the wounded one as he was planning on finishing it off. This wounded rabbit was searching for a safe place to hide and just so happened to crawl in and hide in the same grove of trees that Ryan and Nogar were hiding in.

After watching the gruesome display, Nogar was surprised to see the rabbit that had gotten away as he looked down on it. He had complete compassion for the helpless rabbit. Nogar continued to look over the rabbit, wondering why it wasn't diving into a snowbank. But soon he found his answer. It had a cut on its left ear. The freezing effect had covered the size of a golf ball and still growing. Ryan too saw the rabbit and also wondered why it hadn't jumped into a snowbank despite the ball of ice on its ear.

So he decided to ask Nogar, "Why isn't it jumping into that snowbank?"

Ryan was pointing to a snowbank next to Nogar when he responded, "The problem with a cut from an ice tiger and these snow animals is their natural defenses won't work. This almi can't burrow into a snowbank for safety so long as it has this ice toxin in that ear. The only way to save its life is to apply heat and cut it out."

Nogar knew he couldn't let this frightened rabbit die in this way, so he gently scooped it up its weak and slowly dying body. Using one of his claws from his right hand, he stuck it in his mouth. Using fire, he warmed up the tip of the claw. Then very gently, he began to carve out the golf ball sized ice out of the ear. The rabbit winced in pain. Once he had completely removed the ice ball, he set the rabbit on the ground right next to the snowbank he was standing next to. When the rabbit felt the loose snow between its toes, it began to crawl into the snowbank until it disappeared.

Ryan looked over at Nogar completely amazed by the operation that Nogar had just completed as he asked, "Nogar, how soon will the rabbit recover and come back out?"

It was as if the rabbit heard Ryan's question because just after he finished his question, the rabbit stuck its head out to look around. Ryan noticed that the golf ball sized cut in its ear was slowly disappearing as its flesh was being restored. When Ryan saw that the rabbit's ear was entirely healed, the rabbit, without warning, pulled its head right back into the bank as if something had spooked it.

Suddenly, the hairs on the back of Ryan's neck began to stand on end as if there was someone or something was right behind him watching his every move. Ryan really didn't want to turn around and look but his curiosity got the better of him and he slowly began to turn around. As he came face- to-face with the ice tiger as it was snarling and had saliva rolling down its large long teeth. The tiger no longer wanted the flesh of an almi but was eyeing Ryan and seemed to hunger for his flesh instead. Ryan could see it in his eyes.

As Ryan stared into death, he was wondering where Nogar had went as he was nowhere to be found. When suddenly, he began to hear an unfamiliar voice in his mind. Slowly, Ryan began to focus in on it. Ryan soon realized that the voice was indeed coming from the ice tiger.

As he realized this, the ice tiger made another comment. *You ruined my lunch. I was not finished with that last almi. I am still hungry. I don't care if I eat an almi or a dragon leird.*

The tiger began to get in an attacking crouch, but before it could attack, out of nowhere, a fireball landed right in front of the tiger causing him to leap backward but not into a retreat. After the fire was extinguished and the foggy steam cleared, the ice tiger gained its confidence back as it sent Ryan another message. *You dragon leirds and your trainers think you can come to our mountain and establish fear in our hearts! Well, I think it's about time that we establish fear in your hearts.*

Ryan gripped his sword, not afraid to use it, gaining his own confidence in his heart but still a little afraid of what the ice tiger could do to him. However, the ice tiger was wary of the trainer that had fired the fireball. But he was still hungry as he again focused on Ryan as it got down in the crouched position. It was at this time that Nogar flew down from the ledge above concealed by some bushes where he was hiding as he landed right in front of the ice tiger.

He had his wings expanded to make himself look bigger, but the ice tiger began to stand up to Nogar. But Nogar kept his wings open as he looked directly at the ice tiger. He then let out a very loud defensive roar that Ryan had never heard before. But the ice tiger did recognize the sound of his roar because he immediately began to look to the sky where he soon spotted three dragon figures approaching quickly to their location. Ryan noticed that the ice tiger was abandoning his original design and was backing out of his attack attempt but didn't leave.

When Ryan saw the tiger backing away, he turned to Nogar and asked, "What was that roar? I have never heard it before and what does it do?"

Nogar said looking to the sky, "It was a distress call…" pointing to the Gunar lords getting closer. He continued, "I was alerting any fellow Gunar lords within a five mile radius. It also gives a precise location to be able to find the distressed trainer and dragon leird." Before the alerted Gunar lords arrived, Nogar turned ever so slightly at just the right angle while talking to Ryan that hit the setting sun rays on his scar that shined in the ice tiger's eyes.

As the tiger began to focus on the source of the light, it saw the ice scar and gripped the ice with its claws to move in closer. As it got in closer to Nogar, it recognized the scar on Nogar's shoulder right away and began to think of how he could use this to his advantage.

Just then, Nogar heard a voice that he really didn't want to hear. "Does it hurt still?" Looking at Nogar's scar and grinning in delight as he admired his handiwork.

The ice tiger's words sent shivers down Nogar's spine as he thought about his scar and how it happened. The ice tiger spoke again to Nogar saying, "So you have returned to the mountain. You're a little smaller than the last time we met. I sense fear from you. Don't worry, I will be quick and make sure I finish what I started so many years ago." The ice tiger began to walk toward Nogar instead of Ryan and said, "You know I haven't forgotten about my brother and what you did to him. You and your dragon leird killed him." The ice tiger glared angrily at Nogar, getting ready to spring an attack on him.

Ryan was still very confused with the reason why the ice tiger wanted to kill Nogar as he had not heard their conversation. He then looked into the sky to see how close the Gunar lords were. They still had at least a mile to go, so he looked back at the ice tiger.

At this point, the ice tiger was still down in his crouched attack position, getting ready to spring while still looking directly at Nogar as he said, "I know you have some of your friends on the way, but they are still very far away, and in that amount of time, I can still cause a lot of damage before they arrive."

Nogar positioned his feet to take an impact blow as he said, "Then what are you waiting for? An invitation?"

Angered by Nogar's insult, the ice tiger was getting very agitated and wanted to attack soon. Ryan noticed the tension between the ice tiger and Nogar and seeing that the ice tiger was getting ready to attack and still gripping the sword, he began to pull it out. The light from the fire on the sword began to repel off all the ice and snow surfaces bouncing in several directions including in the face of the tiger, blinding him and throwing him off balance. Nogar used this to his advantage by shooting another fireball at him but this time in his face, causing him to retreat.

The ice tiger began to retreat knowing he had been defeated but also knowing that the Gunar lords would be arriving soon. When all of sudden, a large fireball lit the area, hitting near the ice tiger and knocked him off his feet. As the smoke cleared, the ice tiger tried to get up but couldn't as he noticed that his left hind leg was useless being seriously burned. As the ice tiger began to look back, he saw a large Gunar lord approaching him. As the ice tiger focused on the facial scars, he knew the dragon to be Captain Racklin.

As Captain Racklin got closer, he noticed that the ice tiger was only injured, and if he got away, he would warn his pack so he had to end his life. Captain Racklin got directly over the ice tiger and shot a solid pillar of fire known as a death pillar, covering the ice tiger's entire body and incinerating the body into a puddle of water. Due to the loud noise, the ice tiger's pack came over a peak as they saw Captain Racklin position himself over their leader and then burned him alive. It was then that they vowed that no matter what, they would get even.

They didn't make their presence known, not wanting the same fate as their leader. They planned to appoint a new leader and attack the Gunar Valley during winter for revenge.

After Captain Racklin killed the tiger, he walked back over to Nogar, and then shortly after that, the two other Gunar lords landed next to Nogar and Ryan. When Racklin saw the other two Gunar lords landed, he walked over to them asking them, "What took you so long?"

Then before they could answer, he turned to Nogar and asked him, "Nogar, Ryan, are you two all right?"

Nogar spoke for both of them. "Yes, we are, thanks to you. If you hadn't arrived when you did, it might have been us dead instead of the ice tiger. I was getting ready to fire another fireball, but it would have only distracted it for a little bit."

Captain Racklin then said, "We are all glad you two are safe. But I know as you do, Nogar, that if any of the ice tigers pack members saw anything that happened here today, they will want revenge. And they will get it as soon as the snow eagles deliver winter to Gunar Valley."

One of the other Gunar lords spoke up. "He's right. We have about three months before winter.

We need to be prepared just in case the rest of the pack attempts an attack on us."

The other Gunar lord added his opinion as he said, "Honorable Nogar, we'll start to prepare the troops for the winter threat, but you will need to continue the training of this dragon leird. Then after lordship, you can aid in the defense of our valley."

Captain Racklin looked to the Gunar lord who had just finished his comment and then to Nogar as he said, "Wise counsel. Nogar, I suggest you stay out of danger long enough to acquire your lordship. I heard about Seven Mile Lake."

Nogar had no comment, and soon Captain Racklin gave the order to the two Gunar lords to head back to the battle in the valley. But not before they secured the area first and made sure Nogar and Ryan made it back to the training grounds.

As Nogar and Ryan split off from the Gunar lords and headed back to the training grounds, Ryan said to Nogar, "That ice tiger spoke to me before you startled it, and I understood him, why?"

Nogar was not surprised as he said, "All the larger life forms in Dragtoneea can communicate with each other. Due to the fact that you understood him means that our minds are connecting a lot faster than I thought. Soon we will earn our lordship and be able to join in the fight of our defense of the Dragon Master."

With this thought fresh on Ryan's mind, it gave him an extra drive to train even harder as they entered the training grounds.

Chapter 20

Ryan's drive and concentration had never been stronger as he constantly had the memories from Seven Mile Lake and Snow Mountain on his mind. He knew that if he was going to survive as a dragon lord that he needed to master his training. That way, he will be prepared for any situation as well as for battle against the Wapec army. Ryan watched as the Wapec leirds advanced to lordship faster than all the other dragon leirds.

The new Wapec lords joined up with Jerry who had attained lordship before them all. He was just waiting for the last one who took a little longer to advance in order to head for Wapec Valley to join their kind. Jerry had also viewed all but two of the Gunar leirds advance. The only two were Ryan and Susan. At this time, it was Susan who found Ryan and walked over to him as he was resting from his training.

Susan said as she got closer to Ryan, "I understand that you have earned your lordship, but you haven't taken the opportunity to advance."

Ryan then said, "It is true, Susan. I haven't taken it yet. I am waiting for all the Gunar leirds to obtain lordship first. Also, Alan hasn't taken his earned lordship. I am hoping that I can still convince him to join our side." And then looking at Susan seriously, he said, "I also understand that you have earned your lordship too. Why haven't you taken it?"

Susan looked into Ryan's eyes as she said, "Well, Ryan, I am waiting for you so we can do it together as we hope we can always be together. Maybe we can't be together physically, but we can always be together in our thoughts and in our hearts." Slowly, Susan sat down beside Ryan as they interlocked their hands together.

Jerry just so happened to be close to the training grounds as his last leird had transformed into a dragon lord. Jerry was getting ready to lead the new lords to Wapec Valley when he glanced over his shoulder to take one last look at the training grounds. It was then when he spotted Ryan and Susan sitting together, just seeing them made his anger reach an all-time high. Since Jerry had become a dragon lord, he had not been able to attempt an act of producing a fireball little alone a death pillar. Without the proper training, it can be very dangerous.

But Jerry was willing to risk his life to be able to avenge his anger. Jerry then went into a full attack planning on killing both of them for if he cannot have Susan then no one would. As Jerry got closer, Ryan spotted him instantly, going straight to his feet and pulling Susan up with him as they were still holding hands.

Susan instantly said, "What's wrong?"

Ryan responded, "Jerry is coming with more anger in his eyes than I have ever seen. I know he has come to hurt us or even kill us."

The two of them ran down a beaten path nearby. It was a large pile of boulders. They were able to slip off the path to be able to hide in this rock structure, hoping Jerry wouldn't find them.

Jerry did not give up his search for his betraying friend and the woman who could have ruled all of Dragtoneea with him after he took it over. As Jerry was closing the gap between them, he came so close to their position, but his path was blocked by two Gunar lords. The same two Gunar lords that came to Nogar's and Ryan's aid at Snow Mountain.

These two protectors were willing to lay down their lives or end Jerry's if he persisted in this foolish attack. Jerry rushed at them several times trying to break through their line, but he was unable to budge them. Since he could not yet produce fire, he had to abandon his attempt for now.

As Jerry returned to his Wapec dragon lords, he would not forget the faces of these two Gunar lords as he planned on ending their lives personally. Jerry then gathered all the Wapec lords, and using Sparcan's memory bank, they took flight to Wapec Valley. Jerry was eager to learn how to fight so he can join in the war and fight against some of the lords they trained with.

As Ryan and Susan waited, hidden from view in the stack of boulders, Ryan didn't understand why Jerry had not yet found them. But he didn't want to venture out just in case he was still searching for them around the pile. Ryan then heard an eerie sound of something very large walking around the boulder pile. Ryan then pulled Susan in close for protection, assuming it was Jerry sniffing them out.

They heard a comforting voice said, "Ryan, Susan, it's all right. You can come out now. Sparcan is gone."

Ryan recognized the voice, giving a much deserved ease of mind to come out, and he reassured Susan that it was all right to come out. As Ryan and Susan exited out of the rock structure, Ryan was never so happy to see the two Gunar lords that aided him before. Ryan saw that one of the Gunar lords was perched up higher than the other, scanning in several directions.

It was as if he asked the one Gunar lord what he was doing as lower Gunar lord said, "Nashure is searching for any other Wapec threats. We were able to turn Sparcan away, but he might have signaled an attack for any close soldiers in the area."

Ryan and Susan automatically began to look in each direction. Nashure looked down at them as if they were scouting right beside him. Once Nashure was satisfied that no other attacks were coming, he stepped down and stood beside the other Gunar lord.

"Nashure, Zodnor, my friends, thank you so much for protecting our dragon leirds." Ryan knew that voice as he said in excitement, "Nogar, where have you been?"

Not only was it Nogar but also Angoree who stood beside him each of them and rushed to their dragon leird, making sure they were okay.

Susan was the first to ask the constant questions from their trainers as she also had one of her own. "Angoree, we are both fine, but where were you two at? We really could have used your assistance earlier."

Ryan too wanted answers as he said with a little anger, "Yeah, here Susan and I were enjoying this last evening together. When suddenly out of nowhere, Jerry who is a deadly dragon lord that decided he is going to try and kill both of us."

Nogar was using a hand gesture the whole time in an attempt to calm Ryan down so he could speak to him and have him listen. Once Nogar knew that Ryan had said all he needed, he replied, "Ryan, I am sorry that I wasn't here when you were attacked. Believe me, I wanted to be here. We rushed here as soon as we could when we received your stress signal. But

Angoree and I were at the key door awaiting your presence as well as Susan's transformation into dragon lords to be done together as you both wished. We also knew you two wanted to take these last moments and spend them before you would be separated after lordship."

Ryan's frustration subsided as he collected his thoughts, realizing that the only reason Jerry attacked was because of his jealously from seeing Susan and him together.

Nogar again said, "I do apologize for leaving you which I know turned into a time of need. But now, it is time for both of you to join your fellow friends as—"

Ryan's frustration exploded as he said, cutting off Nogar, "Friends, friends, my best friend for all my life has now become my worst and most hated enemy." Then Ryan fell silent, folding his arms before saying, "No matter how many times I am reminded, I can't help but think that Jerry really doesn't want the course he has been forced to take."

There was silence for a time that was broken by Nogar, "Ryan, you can't change the past or people and their decisions. You can only look ahead and prepare for what will happen in the future." Ryan was pondering on Nogar's comment before he nodded in approval as he said, "Well then,

I supposed we should head over to the key door and become a dragon lord."

Nogar and Angoree both stepped in closer to their dragon leirds as Nogar said, "And this time, both us will be right beside you the whole way."

At the end of Nogar's comment, Ryan and Susan interlocked their hands back together then turned toward the key door taking steady steps. As Nogar and Angoree followed close behind them holding each other's hands, influenced by their dragon leirds' love for each other.

Upon their arrival to the key door, Ryan saw a very familiar face. It was Alan and Hanec getting ready to place his finger into his key claw. At this point, Hanec was perched on top of the door looking down at Alan. Ryan and Susan had never witnessed the actual process of a dragon leird transforming into a dragon lord. They were both very interested.

As Ryan and Susan continued to observe Alan's transformation, they noticed that Hanec moved from the top of the door to directly behind

Alan. As he was getting closer to inserting his finger into his key claw and as Alan continued to inch his finger in closer to his claw, the movements of Hanec mimicked Alan's every movements precisely. Alan then placed his finger fully into his claw then he pulled it out of the door causing a chain reaction with Hanec first then with Alan.

Ryan observed at the end of his training that all the trainers stood the same height or maybe a little taller than their dragon leirds. But it wasn't until watching Alan place his finger into his key claw that he noticed that Hanec was the same height of him. For Ryan, the next stage totally amazed him at this point. Ryan could only see the backside of Hanec. But he could tell that Hanec's body began to separate first in the arms allowing for Alan's arms to be absorbed then covered by Hanec's flesh. The same process happened with the legs. With each of these processes, Hanec's and Alan's bodies were united becoming one until the entire transformation had been completed. And just when Ryan thought it was finished, Hanec's body began to grow and grow until his body was five to six times bigger than it was before Alan attached his key claw.

Ryan's amazement to this incredible transformation left him speechless even though he only saw the backside of the process. He then noticed that Hanec had finished growing the last few feet, making him enormous. Ryan looked over at Hanec and thought to himself, *Alan, you finally did it. You have become a magnificent dragon lord you were destined to be.* Then Ryan suddenly realized that unlike the other dragon lords, Hanec would not be joining up with the Gunar or Wapec lords unless he can convert him.

Ryan began to walk over to Alan after the transformation had been completed for several minutes when he got over the awe of the spectacular sight. Ryan continued to walk right up to him and noticed that he seemed to be exhausted from the transformation that had just occurred as he was bent over resting. When Ryan got up next to him, he realized that his head was just a little taller than Hanec's knee. It was then that he remembered how dwarfed he was to these dragon lords. As Ryan watched Hanec's breathing, he stepped in closer and said, "Alan, you still have time to choose a side. It's not too late."

Alan looked at Ryan through Hanec's eyes, then he began to lift his body as Ryan followed his head. His neck began to strain as he got taller and taller. When he stood straight up, he looked down at Ryan and in

Hanec's voice he said, "My name is A. Hanec now, and I have made my choice." At the close of his statement, Hanec spread his wings and began to flap them, raising himself off the ground. The force from the wings almost knocked Ryan to the ground.

As soon as he got high enough, he rotated his body by using his tail to face Seven Mile Lake.

Ryan watched him disappear out of sight.

Susan came up to Ryan and asked him, "Are you okay?"

Ryan smiled at Susan then said, "I feel terrible that I couldn't convince Alan to convert. Now he will have to go through a painful process of body and mind of becoming a water dragon. I can't believe how closed-minded he was to all my suggestions."

Susan didn't know how to sooth his frustration, so she decided to change the subject. "Speaking of painful, I guess it's now my turn to transform into a dragon lord." Susan was on Ryan's left side which was closest to the key door as she slightly turned to get a clear view of the door. She saw her key claw glowing a bright auburn color changing once she picked a side. Her claw kept glowing, inviting her to place her finger inside of it.

As Susan took in a deep breath then let it out slowly while doing so, she began to inch her finger closer to her key claw. But before she could place her finger inside, she was physically stopped by Ryan, grabbing her hand.

As Susan looked into Ryan's eyes filled with worry as she waited for him to say, "Are you sure you don't want me to go first?"

Using her other hand, she gently rubbed Ryan's check, thinking how sweet Ryan was, then she said, "Ryan, you are a confident leader. You have made a commitment to have every Gunar leird transform into lordship before you. Ryan, I am a Gunar leird. Please let me become a Gunar dragon lord."

Ryan couldn't argue with someone he cared so much for Ryan was going to miss her. The gentle touch she can only do, the sweet sound of her voice, and even the softness of her skin.

Ryan who now was behind Susan, backed away as Angoree took his place who was just as nervous as Susan was for this painful process. Ryan and Nogar waited aguishly for Susan's and Angoree's transformation to begin. Again, Ryan had to observe the process from behind. He was still unaware of how the dragon leird was absorbed into their trainer. As Angoree began to mimic Susan shaking her hands and arms getting ready to stick her finger in her key claw.

Susan made her final decision to stick her finger into her key claw, not knowing what will happen to her. Just as he was amazed by Alan's transformation, so was he with Susan's as she slowly was absorbed into Angoree. Toward the end of her transformation, Ryan thought that Susan's human existence had come to an end, but her life as a dragon lord had just begun. As soon as Angoree finished growing, Ryan saw her grab at the center of her chest with her right hand falling to her knees in pain.

Ryan was no doctor, but he thought that she was having a heart attack and he didn't know how to help her. After a minute of this tense time, Angoree pulled her hand away from her chest. In her hand was a large octagon-shaped chest scale exposing a large area of bare skin. Ryan's mind was still blown away as something was trying to push through Angoree's skin. All Ryan could think about was the movie *Alien*. As the object got closer, a faint red glow began to shine through the skin.

This light continued to grow brighter as the object got closer to breaking through the skin. Finally, a large red stone broke through her skin, sending a red beam of light into the sky shortly after the light died down. As it did, Ryan saw that this stone perfectly filled the octagon exposed spot in her chest. Ryan was curious what this red stone was and wasn't able to examine it until the beam of light dimmed down. Ryan then looked at this unique stone.

Ryan could tell right away that it was a diamond as he continued to look at this giant diamond. It reminded him of the rarest diamond of all, a red blood diamond. Ryan walked up to her, unable to keep his eyes off this diamond as it had a sort of hypnotic effect on him. Still in awe about the diamond, Ryan pulled his attention away and began to look over her body. As he did, he saw that her scales weren't a solid or even a two-tone color but made up of multiple colors. As Angoree began to move in the sunlight, the different angles produced an array of colors. Ryan barely got out a, "You truly are the most beautiful creature I have ever seen."

Angoree acted as if she was blushing from Ryan's comment, then she said, "It's now your turn," bowing in reverence to her general.

Ryan wasn't sure he was ready, but after Angoree's statement, he was now ready for his transformation. As Ryan walked up the path to the key door, the closer he got to the door, Ryan could see a faint glow which Ryan knew it was his key claw. The glow from his claw was beckoning him to come closer, welcoming him to his new future of dragon lordship. The beckoning only grew stronger. Ryan couldn't help but give in as he began to extend his right hand.

Ryan halted his progress. As he did, he could feel Nogar's breath on the back of his neck and his stomach pressed against his back. As Ryan stared at his key claw, he slowly raised his right hand that he previously stopped and extended his index finger. At the same time, Nogar began to mimic his every move just like the other trainers. As Ryan inched his finger closer and closer, he stopped when his finger was less than inch away.

As he paused, he was trying to prepare himself for what was about to happen. Ryan was unaware of what will happen to his human body. He decided to close his eyes. He then pressed the tip of his finger on the outer edge of his key claw. It then sucked in his finger like it did when he picked up Nogar. The key claw then released from the door when Ryan pulled it out. As he opened his eyes, he could see the door rotating back into the cave, preparing for the next arrival of dragon leirds and trainers.

Suddenly, Ryan felt his personal space being invaded; he then realized that it was Nogar beginning their transformation as Nogar's scales began to crack open to allow Ryan's body to merge in. As the flesh began to separate, it was as if Ryan's own skin and flesh was being ripped apart. He wanted to yell and scream, but before he could, Nogar sent a chemical called nocsias that was only produced in a dragon's brain to Ryan's brain. This acted as a pain killer, instantly calming him down.

As Ryan stood still, Nogar slowly began to move his arms toward Ryan's. As Nogar's exposed flesh felt Ryan's, it hung on. It then began to intertwine into his own flesh beginning the process to become one. Not only did Ryan's and Nogar's flesh merge together, but Ryan's bones began to crack and grow in length and diameter as Ryan's skeleton will replace Nogar's. Ryan could feel his bones growing in the place where Nogar's bones once were.

Ryan didn't remember much of his growing pains as a child, but as his bones began to grow several inches in seconds, tears began to develop in his eyes despite the pain killer. Once his arms, hands, and fingers finished merging in the flesh and filling the joints, Ryan could move the arms and fingers, but his transformation wasn't done yet. Ryan leaned over to watch his legs merge together with Nogar's.

He watched Nogar's legs split open then to see the individual muscle fibers reaching for the human flesh. As the dragon fibers reached Ryan's leg, the human muscle fibers also began to split open as his muscle fibers reached out for Nogar's. As Ryan watched this fascinating development, it looked and felt like ten thousand tentacles crawling over land to connect with each other. As Ryan focused on his legs, he was unaware that the body cavity had already opened and began to expand to allow Ryan's body to fit inside.

Ryan still fascinated with his new legs, not feeling any of the pain as the dose of nocsias was increasing. Because of the amount of pain, Ryan was about to go through it now will be unbearable. Suddenly, Ryan's head flew backward. He was expecting to hit Nogar's chest, but instead, he hit a soft spongy material. Then he noticed the back of his head was soaked in a clear mucus liquid.

As Ryan now began to turn his head around, seeing only solid red walls around him, he then realized that it was Nogar's chest cavity. As if this wasn't enough to freak him out, slowly the chest cavity began to squeeze together. As it did, Ryan's own chest began to expand filling the large empty chest cavity. Slowly, all light was sealed off leaving him in darkness. It was in this darkness that Ryan could feel his blood vessels connect with Nogar's. Then his heartbeat began to increase inside his chest as his panic increased.

Ryan was trying to figure what part of the throat his head was in when he felt his tailbone begin to move. Then the same cracking sensation he felt in his arms and legs, he now felt as his tailbone rapidly began to fill Nogar's own vacant tail of solid muscle. As Ryan was feeling the weird sensation of moving his new tail and beginning to get a hang of it, when suddenly, his head felt like it was in an elevator as his neck was growing.

When his head hit the top of the inside of Nogar's head, he could squint and barely peer out through the eye holes of Nogar's head. At that moment, all Ryan wanted was to have a better view of what was happening. Again, it was as if Nogar heard his every word as he felt his face moving closer to the eye holes. As soon as he reached them, it was like putting on a mask, moving the material around until you can see better through each eye hole. The same was true with Ryan as his eyes adjusted to see through his new eye holes.

At this point, Ryan wasn't aware that his skull was forming into a dragon skull until he felt his upper jaw being pushed out. Then he felt his human teeth being pushed out by his new dragon teeth filling their place. The same process happened with his lower jaw, once both jaws finished growing. Ryan tried to use his tongue to feel his new sharp teeth only to discover a very long lizard-shaped tongue.

As Ryan began to focus through his eyes, he noticed right away that his vision was off as he could only see shades of blue, purple, and red—very similar to a heat vision. But as Ryan would scan the land around him, he also discovered that living creatures had a different heat signature. They stood out having a white three-dimensional figure outlined in black, clearing seeing different animals that previously were hidden from his human sight. As he continued to glance around, he saw Susan who was waiting for him as he turned his focus to explore the full functions of his new body.

He was completely unaware that he had grown a set of ball joints in his shoulder blades in order to use the new set of wings. Ryan continued to determine just how strong he was, but he was still very weak from the transformation that he just went through. As he began to collapse to his knees like the others, he slowly gained his strength back. All he wanted now was Susan. He noticed she was walking to a large rock formation. From that vantage point, one could easily see Peace Valley as it was beckoning her to come home.

Ryan walked closer to Susan and touched her shoulders. As tears were rolling down her face, she replied, "It's my home now, Peace Valley, full of other jewel dragons just like me."

Ryan had tears in his eyes as his voice cracked when he said, "I don't want you to go. I want you to remain here close to me at all times so I can protect you." As he reached down and gripped her hand then pulled it up placing it on his heart, not letting go.

Susan turned toward Ryan with more steady tears falling as she said, "I feel the same way, but my jewel is calling me home, Ryan."

He looked down at her jewel. It was flashing like a heartbeat, and the flashing was increasing the longer she stayed with Ryan. Susan's wings automatically began to beat up and down, lifting her off the ground. Then her body began to tilt forward heading straight for Peace Valley. Her progress again was stopped by Ryan who was still holding her hand.

Susan looked back through her watery eyes at Ryan as Ryan said, "Let's go talk to the Dragon Master. Maybe she can help us stay together."

Susan grinned as she said, "She's our only hope."

Ryan gripped her hand even harder, but Ryan's focus was interrupted by Susan's comment. "We need to hurry, Ryan, because if I don't enter Peace Valley by sundown, I might die."

Ryan focused on Susan's face as he said, "Then we need to leave right now and waste no more time." At the end of his comment, they lifted off the ground and headed for the Dragon Master's Keep to plead their case before the Dragon Master.

Chapter 21

The further Susan got away from Peace Valley, the more her jewel tried to pull her toward it. Ryan had to hold on to her, otherwise, she would have been pulled away. As they continued on watching as the sun got lower almost completely setting, they knew they had to hurry as they began to increase their speed. As they were flying over Death Valley, Ryan was very happy that the Dragon Master gave them an alternate route from the training grounds to the key door avoiding this valley. The entrance to the Dragon Master's lair was visible, and they could see a faint yellow glow coming from lit torches. They automatically knew the Dragon Master was waiting for them.

They both landed on the entrance ledge and together entered into the Dragon Master's lair. They soon spotted her across the room at a table. She was looking over several dragon scales that had the dragon laws written on them.

Without either one of them opening their mouths, the Dragon Master said, "I know why you two are here. My advice to you is to rethink your decision and follow your separate destined path starting with you Angoree heading to Peace Valley."

Ryan stepped forward a little afraid but gaining confidence as he said, "I can't do that if I let my love for Susan slip through my fingers. She will enter into Peace Valley. If that happens, then it is game over for me and her. I won't be able to see her ever again. It's not like we are going off to college in different cities, having the ability to communicate with each other and see each other on the weekends."

"*No*, there are posted guards at every single entrance. They all have very strict orders to keep all non-jewel dragons out which orders came directly from you. So even if I am the general of the Gunar army, I still wouldn't have any special privileges to be able to enter the valley to see her. So again, I stand firm in saying *no*, I don't want to be separated from her."

Susan, with a little more courage, stepped forward by Ryan's side saying, "Nor do I."

The Dragon Master stopped looking over the laws after hearing how confident they were to both stay together. Then she turned around to face the new young dragon lords as she said, "Well, I can see that you two have had time to think this out very carefully. But I want to add these critical points. You both understand that it is physically impossible for you Nogar to enter into Peace Valley or Angoree for you to live outside of Peace Valley, don't you?"

After the Dragon Master was finished, they both looked at each other, and with even more confidence, Susan boldly said, "If I have to die, then I will die in order to remain with Ryan."

The Dragon Master studied Susan as she stood proud. This really impressed her as she said, "Well, I have had several young lovestruck dragon lords come to me. Each of them expressing their undying love toward each other. Coming to me as you have because their love was impossible after a long discussion that typically would turn into a debate. Most of the dragon lords would turn away knowing what they want is unrealistic after hearing the consequences. But there are a rare few, just like you two, that I have a test for them. For this reason, I am going to allow Susan to stay with no fear of losing her life."

The Dragon Master's last remarks gave the loving couple a glimmer of hope. The Dragon Master then said, "Because of your love, I am going to show you something very special to me." The Dragon Master then left the room and was gone for a few minutes, leaving the two dragon lords wondering what was so special. Upon her return, she was carrying a large handcrafted box. This box was made of two different colored woods—a striking white based and deep red based. The two-inch stripes had been woven together leaving no bulges and looking completely smooth. It had a clear piece of glass making up the bottom. The box looked very heavy.

Ryan instantly fell in love with the detailed workmanship as he said, "That is a beautiful box, Dragon Master."

The Dragon Master responded to Ryan's comment, "Thank you. I had the dwarfs of High Mountain make it for me. I gave them the dimensions that I needed it to be, and they made it per my request along with a payment of gold and gems. I did not tell them what I needed the chest for because if they knew the reason for the box, they would try to steal it away from me."

The Dragon Master took in a breath and said, "In this chest is my most prized possession in all of Dragtoneea. When I first acquired this item, some of the dragon lords heard about it, and in their heart a disease developed called greed. Some of those dragon lords made several attempts to steal it including Wapec himself."

The scales on the back of Ryan's neck began to stand up and fire filled in his eyes for he was not only expressing his own anger but the anger of Nogar as well.

The Dragon Master herself was admiring the box as she was gently rubbing it as she said, "This box contains the most unique jewel not only in all of Dragtoneea but in all of the world. This jewel has many tale tells created by dragon lords so much so that if you were to ask other dragon lords about it, they would say it's only a myth and to forget about it. Only those that I have selected to see it know that it's real and have witnessed its power knowing of its truth. Now I am going to open this box and show you two the treasure inside. I call this jewel the half diamond. It's the only one in existence."

Ryan's excitement began to exculpate as he began to imagine a diamond that was perfectly cut in half at a slanting angle. He was getting more eager to have the diamond unveiled.

When the Dragon Master had finished speaking, she waited until she had their undivided attention and she slowly began to open the lid to her scared treasure. When the Dragon Master fully opened the box, there was a faint blackish-green glow that surprised both dragon lords. Setting the box down, the Dragon Master reached in and retrieved a massive square-shaped diamond that easily could fill the topside of a cooking stove.

But that wasn't all, this diamond was a two-toned diamond—half the diamond is a Gunar green and the other half is Wapec black. Completely and totally impressed by the sheer size and coloration but at the same time

Ryan was confused as he asked the Dragon Master, "I am a bit confused about one thing. How is this diamond going to help Susan and I?"

Susan, on the other hand, gazed deep into the jewel as if it was talking to her through her jewel dragon heritage as she said, "This diamond has a remarkable story behind it, doesn't it, Dragon Master?"

Excited by Susan's question and annoyed by Ryan's, she said, "Yes, Susan, it does. I was about to tell you the story behind it and how it will help you when I was cut off by Ryan."

Called out Ryan hung his head in shame from the Dragon Master's comment. Pitifully, he said, "I'm sorry, Dragon Master."

The Dragon Master felt a little bad for criticizing Ryan as she looked directly at him then said, "Thank you, Ryan. I appreciate your apology. Please raise your head while I tell the story."

Ryan raised his head upon her request.

Pleased, the Dragon Master smiled then continued, "Now the story behind my diamond is full of love, war, and betrayal."

The Dragon Master waved her hand around the diamond as if it was a crystal ball. "The story begins a long time ago with someone you are both familiar with—Wapec. When the war had just begun, he was appointed general of his army. As general, the first order of business he declared was establishing his name over the army he leads. But he wasn't satisfied completely as he came to me desiring an heir to his name—an heir of his own blood, one that could carry on his position and all that he possessed. Just in case something should happen to him and he was unable to return.

"I carefully reviewed his request, and my decision was to grant his request. Wapec was only looking at how this would benefit himself and not at some of the consequences that will occur. I tried to explain some to him, but he didn't want to listen to me. He just wanted to go on with whatever he needed to do. So I told him that in order to grant this special request to have an heir in his name, I would need a source of his DNA. I proceeded to instruct him that the area I would have to acquire the DNA from was a very sensitive and painful spot.

"The process requires removing one of the smallest scales on the entire body which is right in between the toes. Once the process had been completed and Wapec's screams had ceased, I was then able to acquire this source of DNA. I then deposit it into one of the eggs being developed that produced a special trainer called Wapar. What made Wapar so special is the DNA donated from Wapec because Wapar is the only trainer to have DNA from a dragon lord. Because of this, he is considered a son of Wapec.

"Wapar was unlike any other Wapec trainer. He did not let his dragon leird cheat but made him train even harder than Gunar dragon leirds. Because of this, he grew very fast in strength, wisdom, and war strategies for Wapec wanted a strong heir and warrior to carry on his name."

The Dragon Master didn't get a chance to catch her breath as Ryan blurted out, "But, Dragon Master, I'm sorry to interrupt you. But I understand that if a dragon lord happens to die, they will be given another opportunity to come back as a new dragon trainer, kind like reincarnation."

The Dragon Master had grown used to Ryan's interruptions as she answered, "Yes, Ryan, that is correct in most cases. But I and the dragon laws make up the choices of who will get that chance. If a dragon Lord does not live according to the laws, then I may not give them that chance right away or at all. Sometimes, even if they break the laws, they may be able to still come back, but it might be in a couple of years or a thousand years. In the case of Wapec, he knows of his treason that he has committed, and he didn't want to take any chances so that's why he asked for an heir.

"When Wapar entered into Wapec Valley as a dragon lord, he would consult with Wapec as he didn't want to fail him in any way. He would show his loyalty by killing anything or anyone Wapec so desired. It was through this loyalty that the name of Wapar became feared and hated in the hearts of all Gunar lords even more so than Wapec himself. In battle, he slew many Gunar soldiers showing no mercy.

"It was through this fear that when he was spotted leading an attack, all fled trying to save their own lives. None were spared, only the fastest survived until he caught even them. Wapar is the only Wapec soldier to ever penetrate Peace Valley several times, obtaining many riches. He even almost caught a jewel dragon. All of these treasures were only shared with his father. It was Wapar who also invaded High Mountain, home to the dwarf race, discovering their talent of craftsmanship with gold and jewels. When he invaded High Mountain, he was able to capture several dwarfs, turning them into slaves that he presented to Wapec again as a gift. Once again, as a display of his loyalty.

"There have been many Gunar soldiers that have made valiant attempts to kill Wapar, but each attempt ended up in the same way—defeat. Because Wapar killed them. However, there was one unknown weapon that the Gunar's didn't even know they had. This weapon weakened Wapar's walls of defense. This weapon was a new soldier called Clamore. The first time Wapar saw her, he was actually stalking her on his way to assassinate one of the Gunar captains.

"But when she turned around and he saw the beauty of her face, her beauty stopped him where he stood as he just stared at her. This pause gave away his position, giving Clamore enough time to alert some of the other Gunar soldiers in the area. Wapar barely escaped as he returned disgraced by failure to his father. Wapec may have gotten the warrior that he desperately wanted. However, no one can control love nor the actions that love produces.

"This first failed mission didn't stop Wapar's distraction after that mission, but each battle afterwards, Wapar would be killing less Gunar soldiers as he did not want to kill this mysterious Gunar soldier that has captured his heart. At first, when Clamore found him seeking her out, she was completely disgusted with him, thinking of the death he caused to her people. As time continued to pass, she tried every way she knew to avoid him but she was unsuccessful.

"Over time, she too began to develop feelings for him to the point that she sought him out as well. They would find ways to meet secretly, sending messages to each other in a code only they understood. These messages would include a particular place and time to meet, usually after a large battle when the other soldiers would be resting. All they wanted was to be together more than anything, but as natural enemies, this is not allowed for enemies can't love each other, or can they?"

Chapter 22

After a short pause, the Dragon Master continued with the story. "It didn't take long for the betraying news to reach Wapec's ears instantly making him furious with Wapar. Through his anger, he called his son to his presence. Once he arrived, he demanded that he end this ridiculous love game and to uphold his devoted loyalty by executing this Clamore. Wapar looking into his father eyes as he agreed to his father's demand, thinking that he must be valiant to his father this time. As he left, he sent a message to Clamore to meet him in their secret place. In his mind, he was planning the fastest way to end his love's life, trying to commit himself to his task.

"But when he came up behind her, locating the kill spot, she turned suddenly smiling at him. At that moment, his heart melted. He told her everything about what Wapec wanted him to do to her. Together they came to me, desiring what you two desire—to be together forever. My first initial thought was to follow the laws, so I began to quote the laws established to keep the order. Of which no two dragon lords of opposing sides could ever love each other or be together.

"But Clamore made a very interesting point that impressed me so much that I later made it into a secret law—the love law. She said, 'Love has no boundaries. Love only has the desire to unite the hearts of those who are in love and to keep them together forever and longer if possible.' Her words brought tears to my eyes, so I told them that I would do all that I could, then I left them to research how they might be able to stay together. Upon my return, I found them holding each other's hands as their love burned deep into their eyes. A love that can't be explained, only witnessed or felt.

"As I was walking back over to them finding what I needed, I was able to see past them through the opening that they came through to see me. I saw an alarming image. Approaching my lair was Gunar and Wapec, flying as fast as they could in an attempt to break up their love. Both wanted to conduct a proper punishment that they felt fit to enforce. I quickly grasped their hands, and before the two generals arrived, I said that if their love is pure then the powers of Dragtoneea will provide a way for you them to remain together forever.

"When I loosened my grip, they both began to glow in their lordship's true colors. As their colors began to glow brighter, they, with no control of their bodies, began to glide toward each other. Once their bodies connected, they began to fuse together, creating an intense bright light filling the room and sending a beam of light out into the night. The two generals saw this beam of light, making them fly even faster.

"It was at this time that a new transformation occurred that had never before occurred which began after the primary contact and fusion. The rest of the process happened very quickly, only taking a few minutes. As they began to transform into smooth sides in their lordship's colors of green and black forming this beautiful half diamond.

"As soon as the light dimmed and then went out, the two pursuing generals arrived completely out of breath, sucking in air as I was picking up the massive diamond. Gunar was the first to catch his breath. When he did, he asked me, 'Clamore, is she safe?' I assured Gunar that she was and would be safe forever. Gunar was relieved and satisfied with my response as he left to return to his army.

"But Wapec on the other hand was not satisfied with my response as he demanded that I return Wapar to him immediately. I told him that Wapar had made a decision that made his demand impossible for I was unable to reverse the transformation. And I refused to turn the diamond over to him. As Wapec tried to figure out where Wapar was hiding in her cave with Clamore, he began to stare at the diamond. As he did, he couldn't take his eyes off it.

"Not long afterwards, greed soaked his heart despite all the treasure Wapar gave him. He wanted that diamond more completely, forgetting about Wapar. The lust for the diamond began to build up as he continued to stare at the diamond as he said, 'Okay, Dragon Master. You refuse me Wapar who is my rightful heir. The only one I can have. So I will take that diamond that you are holding as a replacement for him.'

"I starred angrily at Wapec, not intimidated with him, already knowing my answer as I firmly said *no*. Wapec was furious as greed made him rush at me which was a foolish act as it made me even madder, not thinking of the consequences of his action or what could happen if he made me mad. As he got closer to me, I opened my wings swiftly creating a whirlwind around him, spinning him around upward, making him hit his head on the ceiling, and making him instantly black out.

"I walked over to him to make sure he was still alive. Confirming that he was, I touched his shoulder. Then using the power of my mind, I transported him from my lair to his valley in a matter of seconds. Ever since then, Wapec could care less for Wapar as if he never had a son. He just wants my diamond as he has tried to steal it many times each time he got the same results."

Ryan who was listening very intently asked, "Dragon Master, will Sparcan attempt to steal it now as he was making Jerry attempt digging out that giant diamond back in the cave?"

The Dragon Master then said, "I would say that is most definite, and he might be successful if you don't stop him, but there will be time to discuss that at a later time. But right now, what I have to tell you is very important— the secret law I created in relation to this half diamond. Like I have told you, this law is the only law that wasn't created by a member on the dragon council. This law states that when two dragon lords desire to remain together, they must place their hands on the specific sides of the half diamond. The diamond will then judge the hearts and make the final decision."

Ryan was a bit confused, and it showed when he said, "Wait a minute, just what exactly does that mean?"

The Dragon Master said, "It's very simple, Ryan. Wapar and Clamore inhabited the diamond. When a dragon lord places their hands on the diamond as the law states, the diamond will search their hearts to discover the level of their love. If your love is not pure or strong enough, you're asked to separate from each other because that is what would happen eventually."

It was Susan this time who asked, "Dragon Master, what happens if your love is pure and strong enough?"

The Dragon Master replied, "I have seen many dragon lord couples come and do the test most separated and went their own ways. But a few of them have such pure love that they were joined in the diamond with Wapar and Clamore."

Ryan piped up saying, "So I could potentially be sucked into this giant jewel that is highly sought after by my worst enemy. Oh, he would just love that!"

The Dragon Master then said, "Only the diamond can make the decision, so if you two still want to continue on with the test, just let me know."

Susan did not hesitate as she stepped forward and said, "Dragon Master, I still deserve to be with

Ryan." Grasping his hand, she added, "Forever even if we have to be united in the half diamond." Ryan admired Susan's determination and grasped her hand as well and then looked at the Dragon

Master and nodded, agreeing with Susan.

The Dragon Master then said, "Good, Susan, remember what I told you that you are very special?"

Susan replied, "Yes, Dragon Master."

The Dragon Master smiled then said, "The reason why you are so special is because in Peace Valley, you are the long awaited Jewel Queen. The way I know this is because of your royal diamond." She was pointing to Susan's chest as she continued, "Another reason is because I foresaw your coming along with this exact moment. So I ask you again, Angoree, my Jewel Queen, do you want to continue forfeiting your throne?"

Susan had no desire to change her mind despite giving up her throne in Peace Valley ruling over her jewel dragons. She then said, "I want to be with Ryan no matter what."

The Dragon Master then said, "So be it. I will start. Will Ryan come and stand by me?" Ryan moved over to the Dragon Master.

She continued, "Place your hands on the black side of the diamond—"

Ryan then blurted out in a little bit of anger, "Why the black side?"

The Dragon Master calmly said, "The half diamond is very gender specific and since Wapar was a male and you're a male, then you must place your hands on the black half."

Disgusted with the Dragon Master's demand, he hesitated then put his hands on the black half of the diamond.

Then the Dragon Master turned to Susan saying, "Now, my dear sweet Susan, you come to this side and place your hands on the green half."

Once the two dragon lords had their hands on the designated halves, the Dragon Master then let go of the diamond. As soon as she did, the diamond began to glow so bright on both sides that Susan and Ryan had to turn their heads from the blinding light. While the diamond was still glowing, suddenly an unfamiliar woman's voice came from the jewel. "Their love is strong and pure. The purest we have felt yet. They truly do love and respect one another."

Then suddenly, the voice changed to a man's voice. "Such love is highly sought after. I am seeing Nogar. I see that he is destined for greatness and glory while Angoree is of a royal descent of the jewel dragons."

After a short pause, the woman's voice was again heard. "We will grant their wish of union but not to join us in this diamond."

Then man's voice was heard. "Their path is to be as one with purpose in order to bring peace to this land."

This was all the diamond said, but Ryan nor Susan could release their grip from the diamond as both weren't sure what was going to happen next. Suddenly, Susan was being pulled in closer to the diamond and slowly she was sucked into the diamond. As she did, it was lit up. Slowly, the light turned into two beams of light that searched for each of Ryan's hands. As the beams found them, the light entered into his body. The light began to move up to Ryan's arms until it got to his shoulders. Once there, the light changed course heading to Ryan's chest.

When both sources reached the center of his chest, an intense source of light and heat beamed out of his chest causing an incredible amount of pain. After the beam of light dimmed out, Ryan released his grip on the diamond. He then fell to the ground. The diamond would have hit the ground too, but the Dragon Master was there to catch it.

Just like Susan after her lordship, the scale on Ryan's chest began to push out as a jewel surfaced, but it did not push his scale completely out. Ryan noticed that his scale was still attached by a flap of skin that covered the diamond completely. As Ryan lifted the scale up, he wasn't surprised to see Susan's blood diamond fastened tightly into his flesh. As Ryan continued to stare at his new fashion accessory, he was startled by the Dragon Master.

"Ryan, now that Susan and you are one, you now have acquired her jewel and the powers that comes with it. You now can create jewels through the jewel in your chest. But be careful, Ryan, as creating jewels can drain your strength, so you need to use this power wisely and sparingly."

Ryan looked at the Dragon Master with panic in his eyes as he said, "I thought you said that if the half diamond liked us, we would be sucked into it, not Susan into me." Then with tears in his eyes, he said, "Does this mean that I have to live out my life in Peace Valley as their queen?"

The Dragon Master couldn't help but laugh, then she said, "No, Ryan, your place is amongst the Gunar soldiers. The wisdom of the diamond knows that you are destined for greatness, but they also know that Susan and you were supposed to be together forever. Now, Ryan, I want you to know that you have nothing to worry about. The half diamond would not have done this if it did not know that you could handle the responsibility."

Ryan began to lay the scale back down, covering the jewel. But before he did, the Dragon Master saw in the middle of the red diamond, a slight orange glow. This made her very happy. Ryan nodded, agreeing with her.

Pleased with her wisdom, she then said, "Ryan, go now to your friends that are your new dragon lords. They are waiting in anguish as they need your guidance."

Ryan was still a little stunned from what had just happened, so he decided to take the Dragon Master's advice. Ryan got up and turned around to leave to go to the dragon lords who were waiting for him. But just before he left, he turned around to face the Dragon Master as if he wanted to say something but nothing would come out, so Ryan turned back around and left. As Ryan left and searched for his new dragon lords, he saw a fire just outside of the Gunar battle training grounds which he knew belonged to his new dragon lords.

When he arrived, Hanec was the first to spot to him. As he stood, he said, "Nogar, my general, we have been waiting for you so that we can enter the battle training grounds."

Nogar then landed. When he did, the rest of the Gunar lords stood from their resting positions, giving him their attention. As Nogar walked amongst his new dragon lords, doing a visual inspection, he then addressed them by saying, "I am General R. Nogar. As your general, I will make sure your battle training is just as effective as your dragon leird training was."

All the new Gunar lords were eager as they shouted in approval. As Nogar continued to walk toward the battle training grounds, the rest flew in behind him and entered into the grounds. Nogar began to search for a commanding officer in charge in order to begin. As he scanned, he was impressed by the obstacles that were set up. There were series of targets set up just like a target range. There was another obstacle that had several rings hanging high in the air with corresponding targets. Nogar's progress was stopped as he hit a long pole held by a dragon lord with scars covering his entire body. He was very intimidating looking as Nogar had no words.

The scared dragon finally said, "My name is officer Zar. I will train you, young dragon lords, into battle soldiers. I have orders from Captain Racklin to have no mercy and no breaks. You are here to learn battle strategies in order to survive. I will tell you this that if you fail to learn, you will fail in battle and die. Now to begin, start by flying around this entire battle grounds, *now*!"

With that, the young dragon lords took flight led by Nogar, determined to learn all he could and teach his soldiers if they didn't understand.

Chapter 23

Humiliated by his failed attempt, Jerry looked back one last time at the two Gunar scum sealing in a mental image that he would pull up in the future so he can find and kill them. But for now, he needed to find his new soldiers who have been waiting for him since he left them. He found them just beyond the wall of the dragon leird training grounds. They were observing the current battle in progress. They were far enough away to not be noticed but still close enough to hear the screams and smell the flesh burning.

As Sparcan hovered over his small band of soldiers, he saw how concentrated they were on this battle. Those who were closest to Sparcan were startled as he said, "The Gunar force will crumble under my reign. We will be feared. We will be victorious."

The new Wapec lords just stared at their leader which was annoying him. Finally after a minute of awkward silence, Arcan began to shout and soon was joined by Zorcan. Eventually, the rest of the Wapec lords joined in spreading like a raging forest fire. Their cheers could be well heard in all the surrounding area.

Once he was supported by all the dragon lords, he flew in front of them, then he said, "You will address me no longer as Jerry, that weak human form is dead. But General Sparcan is strong and powerful. I will lead you and the Wapec army to victory. But for now, we must leave for our new home in Wapec Valley. It's a long trip, so we need to leave right now." With that, Sparcan who had lowered himself to the ground during the shouting, lifted himself back into the air, and led his young soldier's home using the memory bank of Wapec.

But before they could reach Wapec Valley, the day grew dark, so Sparcan knew it would be wise to set up a camp for the night. Sparcan immediately stopped flying as he hovered in the air. It caused some of the Wapec lords in the rear to bump into the Wapec lords in front of them. Sparcan turned around to face his confused soldiers and said, "It's getting too dark to be able to continue any further tonight, so we will set up a camp here."

As each of the Wapec lords found a comfortable place to be able to get a good night's rest. As they were all settling down, what everyone couldn't deny was that they were hungry, but it was Sparcan whose hunger made him gave in. As he was looking over his soldiers, he thought, *This is a pitiful group.* But he chose Bargar and Cacer to go out and find food for everyone.

They were both very excited to go and do some hunting as they were both avid hunters in their human life. They eagerly agreed without hesitation. With that, the two of them took flight to go fulfill their mission.

Sparcan watched as they flew together searching the ground them. Suddenly, they split up as if they spotted something of interest. Sparcan soon lost sight of them and then became bored after a few minutes waiting for their return. To try and ignore his hunger pains, Sparcan decided to address the group about what was going to happen in the morning as he began to gather the group all together. Once everyone was within hearing range, Sparcan began to speak very loudly. "Attention, my new Wapec lords, I've sent out Bargar and Cacer to hunt some food for us all. But more importantly, in the morning, we will leave this camp at first light. When after a few hours, we will enter our welcoming home—"

Before Sparcan could continue to address the group, Arcan rudely interrupted him, "And oh, great, powerful leader Sparcan, why do we have to listen and follow you? You know just as much as we do."

Many of the other Wapec lords were agreeing with Arcan while those who knew of his position said nothing, not wanting an early death. Sparcan was furious as he snapped at Arcan, "Silence, Arcan, and stay quiet if you want to live to see another day!"

Arcan could feel his anger and didn't dare say another word out of fear that Sparcan would be true to his word.

Sparcan was still very mad and would remember Arcan in case she decided to act up again. After Sparcan calmed down, he then said, "Now what was I saying before I was so rudely interrupted, oh yes, now I remember.

Our home is very close. When we arrive, there will be an inspection of our tongues."

All the Wapec lords were very confused. Sparcan could see this in their expressions as he further said, "I know you don't understand. I am not completely sure either. It will be a new experience for us all. After the inspection, there will follow a sorting. Now this will immediately be done after the inspection. This is all I know for now, we will now wait for Bargar and Cacer to return, and we will eat and then get some sleep."

One of the Wapec lords then said rudely, "How do you know all of this?"

Sparcan couldn't figure out who said, it but he decided to answer their question anyways. "My trainer told me. You all can know if you want to, just ask your trainer in your mind. They will tell you." Sparcan could see some concentrating, trying to communicate with their trainers while the others trusted him enough to believe in his words. But all were pondering on his words when Bargar and Cacer returned, carrying their prey from a successful hunt.

They walked right past the hungry group to find Sparcan who was also pondering on his own words. It was Cacer who stepped forward to address Sparcan. "General, you will be pleased to know that our hunt was very successful." In each of their hands were four to five multicolored deer that Sparcan wanted to examine further before he ate one.

Sparcan, stepping in closer, said to the two hunters, "You know, Barger and Cacer, if I have learned anything in my past life about colorful animals is it's usually a warning. That they are potentially poisonous, so before I eat one, I would like to know if it is safe to eat."

Upon examination of the deer, he saw no excretion glands that can be found on poisonous amphibians. Pleased with this outcome, Sparcan took one of the deer, leaving the rest of the group to fend for themselves over the remaining deer. After Bargar and Cacer left, he further began to inspect the fascinating deer in his hand. These deer were very large, having a large amount of meat on its body.

Sparcan then began to look over the colorful coat that intrigued him in the first place. The fur covering its body was the color of an ash green. The rump had this same green color, but in addition, it had dark blue spots. Covering it in the center of the spots were lighter blue spots. All four legs were the same bright canary yellow with one inch crisscrossing stripes. Sparcan imagined this was to help confuse predators chasing them on the ground but not in the air. The neck was solid black which accented the color of the head which was a pure blood red.

Another striking feature were its antlers which were unlike any typical deer which tines or spikes coming out the main beam. These had no tines at all. It was just a solid long stump protruding out of the head. With a closer look, Sparcan saw a brown almost bark-like structure with ridges running lengthwise. In between the ridges was a turquoise blue. The top was smooth and rounded surface. Its color was a dark lime green. It had rings like you would see on a tree trunk.

Sparcan began to devour the carcass, aggressively chewing off chunks or stripes of flesh off the bone, leaving nothing in the end but a pile of bones, letting nothing going to waste. Sparcan did not realize that since the other Wapec lords had to fight over the remaining carcasses that they had finished much sooner than he did. With each of them having a full belly, they soon got drowsy, and one by one, they all fell asleep.

In the morning, it was Sparcan who was the first to have the glaring sun force open his eyes. He then shielded them with his hand until his eyes adjusted to the light. He then began to wake all the sleepy Wapec lords as they were so very close to their goal of arriving in Wapec Valley.

As they began to fully wake up, some began to stretch, trying to relieve their aching muscles. The delay began to annoy Sparcan as he told them all he wanted was an early start. Sparcan continued to wait until all the young Wapec lords had finished stretching. Sparcan then said, "All right, Wapec Valley isn't very far from here. If we leave now, we can be there by midday."

Then a random voice asked, "What? No breakfast first?"

Sparcan glared at the group as again he couldn't figure out where the outburst came from. Then without warning, Sparcan lifted himself off the ground into the air turning toward the direction of Wapec Valley taking off quickly. The rest had to increase their speed just in order to keep up with him. As Sparcan continued to fly in the direction Wapec was showing him, he felt something hit his face. It was soft, almost a powdery substance.

As he wiped it off, more and more began to cover his entire body. Sparcan's speed began to decrease then stopped as he landed due to inhaling this powdery substance. As Sparcan caught his breath, he turned his head upward and could see a rolling wall of volcanic ash. Each of the Wapec lords landed with Sparcan. Then touching the Wapec lord next to them, they followed the lead Wapec lord in the front until they found Sparcan. Soon they all saw the volcanic ash wall; each of them were struck with awe.

The silence was broken by a coughing Bargar saying, "What is that?"

Sparcan was still looking at this wall when he was taken away in a memory of Wapec's thousands of years ago. Wapec and his followers were forced out of the lush valley and found this volcanic barrier. Then going through it, he discovered the great valley behind it. He knew the wall would keep out any unwanted intruders. Then Sparcan turned around and shouted, "Wapecs, we have finally arrived to our home."

At the end of his yell, he rose into the air. He was followed by each of the other Wapec lords as they flew in closer to the ash wall. As they got closer and closer, each of them began to feel a tingling sensation in their tongue which quickly turned into an agonizing pain. The pain began to drop each Wapec lord to the ground on their hands and knees. In the same order as they dropped to the ground, they began to stick out their tongues one by one.

They watched as the tip of their tongues began to tear apart blood dripping off onto the ground. The separation created a single fork with two tips looking very similar to a snake's tongue. It was Sparcan who lasted the longest through the pain, but he too couldn't bare the pain any longer as he too dropped to his knees as he followed the actions of the other Wapec lords by sticking out his tongue.

But unlike all the other Wapec lords who had a single fork, Sparcan's tongue developed three forks creating four tips. They were all freaking out but Sparcan tried to remain calm. Sparcan would stick out his tongue but seeing the four tips he would suck it back in spitting out the blood as it filled his mouth. Sparcan then covered his mouth and began to walk away from the group, getting even closer to the wall. Sparcan peered into the thick barrier and was taken back when he saw a pair of glowing eyes coming toward him. Suddenly, it was as if Sparcan's vision was in slow motion as a massive Wapec lord emerged from the ash wall, passing by him moving toward the small group.

Just as Sparcan predicted, this Wapec lord was the designated inspector of their tongues. As he came up on the group, he said nothing at first. He just walked back and forth, looking at each and every one of them. Sparcan fell into line just as the Wapec lord began to say, "My name is Darsan. I am a captain in the Wapec army."

Then Captain Darsan paused his speech as he again walked up and down the line as he looked at them all again before he proceeded with his speech. "I mentioned that I am a captain. Do you know how I know that I am of the rank of captain?"

No one had a clue how he knew nor how to answer his question. When Darsan saw that no one was going to answer, he continued, "I know that I am a captain by my tongue. By now, all of you should have gone through the necessary painful process of splitting your tongue. This process came by means of the Dragon Master so she could separate her followers from us. I am going to now show you all my forked tongue. After I do, I will then ask each of you to show me your tongues so that I can sort you."

True to his word, Darsan stuck out his tongue. It had two forks creating three tips which was unlike all the new Wapec lords except for Sparcan. After he had finished showing all the new Wapec lords, he then sucked it back in. Then very sternly, he said, "One by one, I will approach you. When I do, you will stick out your tongue for me to examine, then I will sort you accordingly. Most, if not all of you, will be place in a battle training. This is determined by a single fork with two tips. In battle training, you will learn the art of war. You will learn from some of my most seasoned veterans, so you will be able to join the fight as soon as possible."

Intimidated by Captain Darsan, each of them began to stick out their tongues where Darsan began to inspect them quickly then telling them to cross through the ash wall. Once on the other, he instructed them to look for a large cleared area that had a series of targets set up, find it, go to it, and wait for him there. Captain Darsan was moving down the line extremely quickly.

As he did, Sparcan knew he would have to show his hideous tongue. As he waited, Sparcan timidly stuck out his tongue only to see the four tips. Seeing them wave in the air, he sucked it back in quickly then covered his mouth with his hands. Embarrassed by this horrible mutation, Sparcan slowly stepped out of line and moved to the very end, giving him a brief moment of relief, but he knew he couldn't hide forever. His prolonged attempt came to an end as Captain Darsan soon approached him as he was the last one to be inspected.

As Captain Darsan stepped in front of him, he said, "Well, soldier, now it's your turn to show me your tongue."

Sparcan was not intimidated by Captain Darsan's threats as he held his hand firmly over his mouth, not allowing his tongue to escape which was a challenge because his tongue wanted to be shown.

As Sparcan shook his head no, Darsan had little patience and lost it all with Sparcan as he said, "Soldier, if I have to I will pry your mouth open by calling in Sezcan, another captain! Now I will only ask you one more time before I will use this force. Now show me your tongue."

Sparcan was prepared to fight to death rather than open his mouth. But Wapec calmed him down by saying, *It's okay, Sparcan, show him your tongue, and you will see the respect that you deserve out here.*

Captain Darsan had summoned Captain Sezcan. Together, they moved in closer to Sparcan to force his mouth open. But trusting in Wapec's words, Sparcan opened his mouth willingly, sticking out his forked tongue.

As Captain Darsan focused in on it and upon seeing the four tips, he fell to his knees then planted his face into the ground. Captain Sezcan did the same. Captain Darsan raised his head only briefly to say, "General, you have returned. I beg you forgiveness for my disrespect. It will never happen again."

Sparcan was now the one who approached the intimidated as he looked down at Captains Darsan and Sezcan he thought to himself, *You're right. You will never ever disrespect me ever again.*

Captain Darsan again raised his head to say, "General, if you will follow me to the captains' quarters. Once there, you will be briefed on the war and the progress we have made so far." Captain Darsan remained lowered with his face planted in the ground, sucking the ash into his lungs as Sparcan walked past him.

As Sparcan once more looked down on these two pathetic Wapec lords, anger filled his heart even more so than when Ryan infected him with it. Sparcan wanted to teach a lesson to these so-called captains because of the humiliation they caused him. He was trying to think of the proper punishment for this act. What he came up with was death. This would show his power and authority. But for some odd reason, Sparcan longed to be in these captains' quarters, and without giving the two lowered lords permission to rise, he left as he flew straight into the wall of ash.

Using Wapec's memory, Sparcan continued to fly blindly through this thick wall of ash and smoke. His blurry vision began to clear, revealing the valley covered by thousands of lava-filled carters. These carters produced large amounts of heat. Sparcan also noticed many lazy Wapec lords resting around some of these carters, soaking in the heat and warming their chilled blood. In the middle of these lava carters was a large lava rock structure. Sparcan noticed that there were two openings toward the top of this large rock. Instinctively, Sparcan flew to this structure and the highest opening.

As he entered one of these opening, it revealed a large room, but rather than exploring it, he saw four Wapec lords lounging around it. As Sparcan began to look them over, he saw that they all had a layer of ash covering their bodies as if they had just recently arrived. Sparcan continued to study them. He noticed that a couple of these lazy lords had gotten so comfortable that they had actually fallen asleep. Finally, noticed by one of these lazy Wapec lords, he was alerted to his presence as he turned around seeing him standing in the entrance.

This Wapec lord sternly said, "These quarters are for Wapec lords of authority. Any one not of authority must leave or die. I don't recognize you. Who are you, and why are you here?" At the end of his questions, he took a defensive stand, preparing for fight. His words also alerted the rest of the other Wapec lords as they took the same stance.

Sparcan was not at all scared as his confidence was boosted with his tongue trick. Instead of getting in a similar stance, he just smiled which then turned into a laugh.

This confused all the Wapec lords who didn't know what to do now. Sparcan, showing no fear, began to move in closer to them. This act alone struck some fear into these Wapec captains.

As Sparcan continued to move across the room, he stated, "I am General Sparcan, and I will be the one asking the questions and giving the orders from now on."

One of the captains mustered up enough courage to say, "If you are our general, then prove it." Sparcan was looking around the room, thinking this place could use a good decorator as he imagined different color schemes. Suddenly, his thought pattern was broken up by a different captain who was a little more demanding.

This captain stepped forward and yelled at Sparcan, "Prove it!"

Sparcan stared him down as he was now losing his patience, and instead of screaming back at them, he just stuck out his tongue. General Sparcan began moving each individual tip one at a time, proving that he is the general.

All four captains fell to their knees. As he came nearer, Sparcan discovered a large stone table. This now took his focus. As General Sparcan walked up to the table, observing the contents on it, he then said, "Arise, my captains, for we have much to discuss in order to catch me up to speed on this war."

Chapter 24

One of the newly humbled captains positioned to the far left of General Sparcan, stepped forward after getting to his feet then he began by introducing himself. "General Sparcan, my name is Captain Zorkan. I am your leading captain. So it would be most appropriate that I be the one to tell you what's happening so far with the war. Right now, we are at a time of peace established by our enemies." Captain Zorkan then pointed to three large chests filled with jewels and gold.

Captain Zorkan then continued, "We are using this time for battle training. We have been fighting for four long months. The three chests are for three months of peace, a token of trust from the Gunar scum. It is a very generous offer. This time will give us ample of time for training and to prepare for the upcoming winter."

Sparcan's reaction startled the captains as he yelled angrily, "You fools! The Gunar army has received a strong addition to their army of nineteen soldiers while we have only received eleven soldiers. Now you're telling me that we have three months of peace before we can attack. I remember seeing a battle right before we came here. We left when the battle was heating up. So tell me, captain, just when you and the army returned here from the battlefield?"

This time, the captain positioned on the far right of Sparcan stepped forward trembling while saying, "General Sparcan, my name is Captain Darmic. The battle you saw were some of our overzealous soldiers in the number of thirty to forty. They call themselves the freedom fighters. I would assume by now that most of them, if not all of them, are dead. Your captains and your army have been here in Wapec Valley for three days. In addition to the battle training, we are taking a much needed rest before we begin our training for the upcoming battle."

After Captain Darmic was done speaking, he stepped back and sat down on the rock ledge he was first resting on.

Sparcan was still very angry but even more annoyed with Captain Darmic as he watched him sit back down. But calmed down as he realized that there was nothing he could do about this peace token he has been forced to accept. General Sparcan decided now was the perfect time for him to use his general authority by saying, "Well, now your resting is over. You will have plenty of time to rest when you are dead. Now I strongly recommend that you all get up and go out and get all these lazy soldiers to begin their much needed training. Now when you return to me having gained a great victory, then I will grant you rest."

At first, none of the captains moved upon Sparcan's demand. Their laziness was really beginning to annoy him as he slammed his fists on the stone table. This sudden burst of aggression from General Sparcan ended their confusion and confirmed General Sparcan's orders. They all left and immediately began battle training. The only comfort General Sparcan got was opening these chests after his four captains left. He then let his greed take over as he examined the plentiful amount of jewels, thinking all of this was his.

In the midst of Sparcan's joy as he was imagining his abundant wealth, he began to hear a voice that sounded familiar. As he looked around, he saw no other dragon lord. General Sparcan went back to his wealth, seeing that he was in fact alone. But the voice began to speak again, but this time, General Sparcan listened to it.

It was Wapec. *Now that we are all alone, grab these chests and let's add them to your already abundant wealth* in my lair.

General Sparcan's attention was quickly drawn from his new treasure to his already promised wealth.

Wapec began to give General Sparcan detailed directions that guided him to coveted treasure into Wapec's old lair.

As General Sparcan continued to follow Wapec's directions, he was led down a long hallway that resulted in a dead end. Sparcan was furious as he thought that Wapec didn't want him to have his treasure after all. He was even more outraged about the dead end as he said, "Wapec, where is the lair? All that's here is a dead end? Is this the promised treasure? A broken promise?"

But General Sparcan's emotions were calmed down by Wapec's soothing voice in his head. *Relax,*

I haven't led you astray. Now take your key claw and run it across the wall.

General Sparcan was a little confused as to why he had to run his key claw against the wall, but he decided to do it anyways. As he raised his key claw and began to run across the wall as directed by Wapec, suddenly he saw a burst of red light that caught his attention. When Sparcan pinpointed the source of the burst of light, he placed his key claw right next to it. He noticed that the light was coming out of a medium-sized hole that his key claw could fit into it perfectly.

As General Sparcan looked at this hole with curiosity, Wapec spoke to him. *Stick your key claw into this hole, and then you will discover your treasure.*

General Sparcan was still a little confused on how sticking his key claw into this hole will reveal this treasure. But trusting in Wapec, he stuck his key claw into the hole. Upon fully inserting his key claw, an amazing thing began to happen. It was like a chain reaction. This tiny hole began to expand, creating a large arched doorway large enough to allow General Sparcan to enter into this mysterious room.

When entered into this room, he discovered that the room was extremely larger on the inside. What impressed him even more was that the walls were covered in gold with very detailed artwork of several dragons outlined in silver in a fierce battle. They were fighting over a blanket of jewels beneath them. In the middle of his amazement, he caught some movement out of the corner of his eye.

He then turned his head to the right were he found eight little men working on his treasure; they were sorting the gems by size, color, and gem type. When the workers saw General Sparcan, they immediately stopped their work in order to address him.

As General Sparcan saw that they stopped working, one of them stepped forward then said, "General, we have longly awaited your return."

General Sparcan then walked up to this worker as he assumed that he was their leader. When he was closer and looking directly at him, he said, "You are all dwarfs. How long have you been in here?"

The same one then said, "In total, we have been in here for over two thousand years, but since you have been gone, it's been a little over one thousand years. But now that you have returned, you can keep your promise by letting us go home to our families."

General Sparcan was not amused as he just let out a laugh. After he had finished, he then said, "You are slaves, and as slaves, you don't get your freedom ever." General Sparcan then turned around. As he did, he saw a huge pile of gold coins. When he saw it, all he wanted to do now was jump into it and swim around in it like a swimming pool. General Sparcan had to use great restraint to resist jumping in the pile of gold as he asked Wapec in his mind, "Wapec, where did all this gold came from?"

Wapec replied right back by saying, *Gold ants. They are a rare ant here in Dragtoneea. They survive by eating minerals that cling to gold. General Sparcan, look to your left.*

General Sparcan turned his head to the left. As he did, he saw a colony of these weird-looking ants. They have a green head with large black eyes and purple antennas. They have a large orange mouth. The middle section was a combination of blue and purple splashes with black legs. The last section was perfectly round and was about one inch in diameter that was flat on the bottom and rounded on the top with green and yellow stripes.

Wapec then said, *These gold ants consume gold in their stomach. They digest everything but the gold. They accomplish by heating up all the particles separating the minerals from the gold. The ants then eat the minerals and discard the gold by compacting the gold into a perfectly round shaped coin, then you can say they poop it out. These ants will actively search out gold pockets. The bigger the gold deposits, the bigger the colony of ants. As I was searching out a spot for my lair, I brought some of my pet gold ants. I then had them search out a huge gold deposit. Since then, they found these other gold deposits, and they have been creating this massive lair. The more my pets eat, the bigger my lair becomes. It is very common for Wapec lords to collect gold ants. We then keep them as pets as they help to create a big part of our treasure.*

General Sparcan then said, "Wapec, I was just thinking that maybe the dwarfs need to be released. It has been over two thousand years—" General Sparcan then heard laughing in his head as he asked, "What's so funny?"

After Wapec's laughing stopped, he said, *You are. What is so funny along with all your crazy ideas? You forget that you are now in my world. From here on and out, you will have to rely on my wisdom just in order to survive as well as to get more powerful and get more riches.*

As General Sparcan was pondering on Wapec's counsel, all he really was thinking about was the power and riches, forgetting completely about wanting to free the enslaved dwarfs. In fact, he was now getting very greedy and wanted to get even more slaves. After a long moment, General Sparcan then said, "Wapec, I was just thinking. If I am going to increase my riches, then I am going to need to increase my slave force. I was also wondering how would I go about to increase my slave force?"

As Wapec heard General Sparcan wanting more slaves, he just began to think how easy it was to warp his fragile mind into doing his dirty work. Wapec then replied by saying, *To increase your slaves could be dangerous. You have to abduct dwarfs, and they don't like to be taken.*

General Sparcan heard Wapec speaking, but the thought of his impressive treasure drowned him out as he began to grab some gold and gems. After examining them, Sparcan asked Wapec, "How do I exit my lair when I want to leave?"

Wapec was also examining the treasure through Sparcan's eyes but replied to his question by saying, *You exit the lair the same way you entered into it.*

General Sparcan then knew exactly where to go and what to do as he walked over to the wall passing by the dwarfs who were angrily at work. When he got to the wall, he saw the same hole that got him into the wonderful lair. Then as before, he stuck his key claw into this hole as the hole began to expand allowing him to exit out of it. General Sparcan then decided that he wanted to go and check on the progress of his troops in their battle training.

Upon exiting, General Sparcan quickly crossed the room. As he got close to the edge of the opening from there, he was able to see his captains actively engaged with the troops in training. General Sparcan continued to observe the training. As he did, he saw a series of targets set up like a target range where the majority of the troops at. General Sparcan figured out that the targets were to help improve their accuracy while others were performing a flying exercise which consisted of two soldiers each of them wearing targets strapped on their chest and back. The point of this exercise was to perform different aerial movements with a designated shooter, but if the other soldiers got a shot opportunity, then they take it.

General Sparcan was so drawn into the training exercises that he was unaware that there was another presence in the room until he heard the soldier clear his voice. General Sparcan quickly spun around, preparing to deliver a death pillar purely out of instinct. But quickly extinguished the fire when he saw that it was Captain Darsan. Despite it only being Captain Darsan, General Sparcan still had fire in his eyes as he said angrily, "What are you doing here? You are supposed to be down there training with the troops."

Bowing in reference, he then said, "Forgive me, general, but the men were wondering if they could have a break from training to be able to hunt for food."

Captain Darsan still remained in the bowed position as General Sparcan approached him looking him over as he focused on the base of his neck. While looking at the spot where the spine connected to the skull, General Sparcan thought about the earlier humiliating incident. All General Sparcan wanted to do now was snap the spot, quickly ending his life. But Sparcan knew that he and the army needed him, so he put aside personal pride and then asked him to rise. After Captain Darsan rose, General Sparcan said, "Give the order to take rest from training in order to go hunting, and Captain Darsan, bring me back some food personally."

Captain Darsan said before he left General Sparcan's presence, "Of course, my general." With that he flew to the edge of the entrance then he bellowed out a loud roar that when heard by all the soldiers, they stopped with their training.

Then the soldiers began to gather into small groups to get instructions from their captains before separating as they all went in different directions to hunt. General Sparcan went back to the stone table to observe the material on it while focusing on the table. It didn't take very long for Captain Darsan to return holding a very large lava eel in his mouth. Captain Darsan then walked over to General Sparcan and dropped this large eel at his feet.

As General Sparcan looked in disgust over the large red eel covered in what looked like tiny spines, like a sea urchin. General Sparcan was about to refuse it when Wapec spoke to him saying, *Sparcan, around here that eel is some of the best food you will get. If you want something different, you will have to send out a hunting party. But that could take several days with the potential of being discovered by the Gunar army and most likely executed.*

After listening to Wapec's counsel, General Sparcan eyed the eel hungrily, then he reached down and grabbed it and began to tear off chunks of flesh swallowing it whole. General Sparcan discovered that this eel has a surprisingly good taste, he then quickly devoured it then demanded more. So Captain Darsan turned around and left to go and get more food for him as well as for himself. As Captain Darsan left, General Sparcan's attention was again drawn to the material on the stone table. But more importantly, a large map of Dragtoneea on the map were several stone figurines of different colors representing the soldiers for both sides.

As Sparcan continued to study the map, he noticed that he was not very familiar with most of the lands as he began to get confused. In the middle of his confusion, Captain Darsan had returned. General Sparcan once again was unaware of his presence due to his concentration on the map.

Captain Darsan disrupted Sparcan's focus as he said, "My general, I have returned with more eels as part of my allegiance to you."

General Sparcan turned around and said, "Captain, I need your assistance and some answers.

Come here and explain this map and its lands to me."

Captain Darsan responded by saying, "Yes, general, right away, sir." As Captain Darsan walked over to him, he carried with him two more large lava eels. When he got over to Sparcan, he dropped them again at his feet.

General Sparcan looked down grabbing one of the eels, then he said, "Thank you, Captain Darsan. I will only eat this one. You can have the second one."

Before Captain Darsan began to explain the map, they both enjoyed their meal. As they were finishing, Captain Darsan began to explain the map to General Sparcan. He explained the different regions highlighted on the map and which ones were friendly to Wapecs and those friendly to the Gunars as well as the few not friendly to both.

With this new knowledge, General Sparcan began to restudy the map. He then confirmed that the black pieces represented the Wapecs and the green ones were Gunars. General Sparcan also tried to figure out how he might be able to claim some of the land for the Wapecs.

General Sparcan then asked, "Captain Darsan, how many soldiers do we have right now?"

Captain Darsan had to swallow his last chunk of eel before he answered, "Including the new recruits, our army has reached an even 126—a fair size for us."

General Sparcan trusted in his opinion. He then asked, "How does our army compare to that of the Gunar army?"

Captain Darsan then took a little bit of time to calculate the Gunar numbers that he knew of. Then he said, "When we left the battlefield, we know we killed sixteen soldiers leaving them only ninety-six strong. Do you know how many recruits they received?"

General Sparcan replied, "Yes, I do know. They have received twenty soldiers. If you want to call them soldiers. This includes their general as well."

Captain Darsan then did another quick calculation as he said, "Those are strong numbers, but we still have the advantage because their number is 116. We still have 10 more soldiers than them which is still a huge advantage."

General Sparcan then had a series of questions to ask. "So I am curious of a few things. On average, how many battles do we have a year? How long do they last as well as how many Gunar soldiers do we kill and how many do we lose?"

Captain Darsan began to laugh to General Sparcan's questions, then he answered in order, "On average, we have two to three big battles a year. Each of the battles generally last two or more months. Sometimes less before winter sets in. Usually, each side loses three to seven soldiers a year, in some cases, more like this year. But now with our larger numbers, we should be able to kill many, many more this next battle as well as this next spring."

Sparcan laughed to himself as he walked away from the table heading toward the entrance, then he placed his right hand on his side. As he looked out over his massive army, he thought to himself, *Nogar, my buddy now my enemy, I am in command of a much larger army than you. Plus I am living in a life of luxury. Now I wonder how are you doing with your small pathetic army that I am going to crush.*

At the end of his thought, General Sparcan let out an even louder and harder laugh than before he had his thought.

Chapter 25

Nogar was working even harder as a dragon lord than when he was a dragon leird in training, not only to be an effective and powerful soldier but also to help the other young Gunar lords with him. Nogar had been pushing himself so hard that he had took a moment to rest from the shooting range. No sooner had he done this, he received a painful kick to his tail. In reaction to the kick, Nogar shouted out, "Aww, what did you do that for?" When Nogar looked up, he saw drill sergeant, Zar.

Nogar pulled his tail over so he could rub it, helping to relieve the pain. Officer Zar had no pity for Nogar. Instead, it made him happy to see him in pain. Still smiling from his recent small punishment, Officer Zar then yelled, "R. Nogar, you are resting on my training grounds. But more importantly, on your own personal training in order to be an effective soldier in this army. You need to be able to master every single obstacle on this shooting range, and I am personally going to make sure you do it right."

Nogar stood up, determined to prove officer Zar that he was committed to his training as he began to head over to the stationary targets.

Nogar didn't get far as Officer Zar said, "No, son, not those ones. Instead, I want to see you do those."

As Nogar turned his head to see Officer Zar pointing to an obstacle all the new Gunar Lord dreaded—the flying shooting rings. Nogar had made a few attempts before but failed each time, so he was a little afraid to make another attempt this time in front of Officer Zar.

Nogar turned toward the rings, trying not to show forth his fear as he turned slightly to salute his officer. Then Nogar took flight toward the rings. In his mind, he was trying to wake up Gunar as he said, "Gunar, I need your help right now."

Alerted to Nogar's anxious tone, Gunar promptly replied, *Nogar, what is it?*

Nogar now knowing that he was awake replied back, "Gunar, I have to do the flying shooting rings right now. To make matters worse, I also have to perform them in front of my officer drill sergeant, Zar, and I am horrible at them."

Gunar was fully aware of Nogar's situation as he has done so many times before—helping to calm Nogar down. As he calmly said, "Nogar, there is no need to fear this obstacle nor drill sergeant Zar. Right now, I want you to first focus on the rings that you will pass through, taking each part of the obstacle one piece at a time. After you successfully pass through the rings, focus on the target that you will need to hit. And always remember, if you don't succeed this time, you will know exactly what to do for the next time you attempt it."

Officer Zar was getting impatient with Nogar's waiting as he said, "Are you going to do it any time in this day?"

Nogar ignored him as he focused on Gunar's advice. When he felt ready to attempt the course, he kept repeating in his mind to focus on one obstacle at a time. As he did, the rings presented no difficulty, and Nogar was able to concentrate on the target. As he did, he was able to hit with precise accuracy.

Officer Zar was very pleased as he flew over to the end of this course where he found Nogar resting on the ground. Nogar was also pleased with his success. Officer Zar landed then walked the rest of the distance over to Nogar, then he exclaimed, "Excellent, Nogar, you are learning fast. Before long, I will be proud to have you beside me in battle in the defense of our Dragon Master."

Nogar smiled at Officer Zar's comment, then he saluted him before he left to check the progress of other Gunar lords. Nogar also changed his course of travel to the stationary targets. He felt a great deal of relief from his accomplishment.

Nogar also knew how to better instruct the other Gunar lords to be more successful on this particular obstacle. When Nogar arrived, there were four other Gunar lords using this range which made him happy because there would be someone there he could talk to. Amongst them was Socer practicing. Nogar naturally lined up next to him waiting until he was done firing before beginning a conversation with him. Their cheerful conversation drew the attention of Officer Zar. He then approached them from behind.

When they both noticed that they were in a shadow, they turned around to see Officer Zar. His presence was all that they needed to see. Then both of them began to focus again on the targets in front of them. Officer Zar left them but would keep his eye on them. Nogar was very accurate on the targets set up at twenty yards and even more accurate at the targets set up at fifty yards. Nogar was having some difficulty with the targets set up at one hundred yards.

Upon noticing Nogar's frustration, Socer turned to him. Whispering, he said, "What has helped me is to take a deep breath, hold briefly, then as I begin to exhale slowly, I fire. It really helps. Try it."

Nogar thanked him, then he thought, *At least I'm not the only one who has to give advice. I can receive it too.* As Nogar focused on the hundred-yard target, he relied on Socer's advice by taking a deep breath, holding just briefly, then while slowly letting it out, he fired hitting the target. Both Socer and Nogar were excited for his success, having a little celebration small enough not to be noticed by Officer Zar. Nogar continued to use Socer's advice. He was able to hit the target three times in a row. Nogar was feeling very confident.

As Nogar focused on the far target for a fourth time, he suddenly had a hot sensation in the back of his throat. Slowly, Nogar noticed where the hot feeling was coming from—a valve flap opened near where his tonsils would be that he couldn't control. As these flaps opened, Nogar felt a hot liquid flowing through a tube-like duct to lead to the front of his mouth. There was another set of flaps in the check area of the mouth. This liquid began to fill a triangular gland. Despite the hot liquid, it didn't burn him.

Nogar noticed that he could control these check glands. As he opened them, he immediately spat out the liquid. Nogar looked down at the substance that came from his mouth. It began to harden. Nogar picked it up. It was as hard as a rock. Nogar was turning this rock over. He even tried to break it in half. As he was doing this, the hot liquid began to fill the glands of the check again. Nogar decided to let the glands fill up, not freaking out this time, knowing that the liquid won't hurt him.

The glands filled in the triangular shape in a manner of seconds. Once the glands were completely filled, his saliva was secreted unto it, cooling it down and also hardening it. The steam was vented out through his nose. Suddenly, Nogar had an overwhelming urge to shot a fireball. When he shot a fireball, he realized that these mysterious spikes exited out with the fireball heading straight for the target. Nogar watched as the spikes rested inside the fireball, glowing bright orange until it hit the target making a loud thud echoing in the training grounds.

Because the spikes stayed within the fireball, the spikes began to get real hot. As the spikes hit the target, they penetrated deep into the target causing excitement by all those who saw it. Nogar was extremely surprised that those spikes came from inside of his mouth but even more so by the damage they inflicted. In ancient times, Gunar developed the idea of these indestructible targets made of racton but only one dragon could produce fire hot enough to forge the metal. When Gunar presented the idea and design to the Dragon Master, she thought these targets would last forever and decided to forge them for Gunar.

Over the course of thousands of years millions of fireballs and death pillars have drilled these targets, none have been able to be damaged the surface at all.

Captor, the range captain, was resting but was awakened by a loud commotion on the target range. He was enraged and tore out of his lair to find the source of the noise. As he rounded the corner, he followed the noise until he discovered all the Gunar lords, including Officer Zar, were in a huddle.

Captain Captor marched directly into the huddle, pushing the young dragon lords out of his way until he got to the middle were Nogar was being praised. Captain Captor was getting more and more irritated as he marched straight to Nogar and got right into his face. Captain Captor yelled, spiting in Nogar's face, "R. Nogar, what is all this noise about? I am trying to get some rest."

Terrified Nogar said nothing. He only pointed to the target he had damaged.

Captain Captor was not impressed. He then found the nearest Gunar lord asking, "This mute won't talk to me. Now tell me what happened."

Captain Captor just happened to be standing next to Agor, one of the few Gunar lords congratulating and cheering loudly for him. Agor had no fear speaking as if it was him who had done it. "Nogar here has an awesome weapon that broke one these targets. It was amazing."

Captain Captor ignored Agor's comment as he knew it was impossible to even dent one of these targets. He then pushed his way through the crowd on his way to personally inspect the so-called damaged target. When he got closer to the target, he could see two rock shards that seemed to be glued to the target. He thought to himself, *This is a dumb trick*. When Captain Captor tried to knock off the shards, they wouldn't budge. He then grabbed them and tried to pull one of them out. He then picked up the target to look at the back of the target. He saw two tips protruding out of the target about an inch. The discovery that this was not a prank but that the targets were actually damaged made Captain Captor furious as he carried the target with him when he flew directly to Nogar. Captain Captor did not believe that Nogar had a specialized weapon capable of this damage. But he was still convinced that Nogar was pulling a prank on him and wanted to know how he did it. As Captain Captor got closer to Nogar, he threw the target at his feet then sternly said, "For damaging this practice target that before you has survived for thousands of years, I have decided to enforce my own judgment and punishment."

Captain Captor then rose into the air in order to position himself directly above Nogar. All of the Gunar lords including Nogar knew what Captain Captor was about to do. He was about to deliver a death pillar.

Gunar was instantly alerted to Nogar's situation and immediately relayed a message to Nogar's mind. His message was, *Nogar, form a fire shield.*

Nogar was scared and confused as he replied, "A fire shield? I don't know what that is, little alone do I know how to make one."

Gunar then said in all his wisdom, *Nogar, don't think, just do it. You're a dragon lord now. It's an ancient* defensive tactic. Only the truly gifted dragon lords can produce it, and you are one of them.

As Nogar meditated on Gunar's words, he stopped thinking about producing this fire shield but instead believed he could produce it. With this new sense of direction and understanding, Nogar then opened his mouth. This allowed fire to flow out freely. At first, the fire came out slowly, then it began to come out faster. Then the fire began to curve backward surrounding his body. The fire did exactly what Gunar said once it surrounded his entire body, it began to harden, forming a protective barrier like a shield.

No sooner had this protective layer of fire hardened, then Captain Captor delivered a death pillar hitting the shield hard but was unable to penetrate. Captain Captor forced his death pillar for over an hour which began to weaken him. While Nogar stayed protected under his fire shield, not even getting warm. This extended period of time not only weakened Captor but Nogar as well as Captor began to fall to the ground. Nogar couldn't hold his pillar back any longer as he collapsed to the ground as well. Captain Captor was still angry that he was unable to fully carry out his punishment as every single muscle in his body lost their strength. Nogar was the first to come to his senses as well as the first to receive his strength. As he did, he saw that Captain Captor's head was only two feet away from his. After a few seconds, Nogar used his weak muscles to crawl over to his aggressor until he was only inches from Captain Captor. When Nogar was over top of him, he could feel these ducts in the back of his throat begin to open, only this time, Nogar noticed he had complete control of the opening and closing of the ducts.

Nogar used this new tactic to keep the hot liquid from filling up the glands except for his right side. Once this spike had hardened, Nogar reached in and grabbed it with his hand, then he leaned over Captain Captor and waited for him to open his eyes. When Nogar could see Captor's pupils, he raised the spike high above his head then breathed fire on the tip, warming it up until it was glowing. Nogar wanted him to fear for his life. Nogar could see that fear in his eyes as well as in his trembling face. This sight pleased him.

Captain Captor knew his life would soon be over. It was at this time that Nogar slammed the spike downward toward Captor's head making him close his eyes. Captain Captor heard the loud thud of the spike hitting a solid surface, but much to his surprise, he did not feel any pain. Upon this discovery, Captain Captor opened his eyes and began to turn his head right until his head was quickly stopped by the spike lodged into the ground less than an inch from his head. Then Captain Captor turned his focus back unto Nogar. As he did, he said, "Why didn't you kill me? I tried to kill you. The law of the land states that kill or be killed even by your own kind."

Nogar looked down at him, gaining more strength he got enough to get to his feet. Once standing, he again looked down. While staring, he said, "Just because you tried to kill me without fully understanding the situation doesn't mean I should kill you. Plus, this army needs you, your strength, and your wisdom. I need you. You're also a captain. One does not achieve this rank without earning it."

Captain Captor couldn't believe the words he was hearing.

Nogar then proceeded to explain how he had damaged the target since no dragon lord has ever been ever did before. To further prove the truth of his story, Nogar opened both of the ducts filling his side glands then letting them harden as the stem bellowed out of his nostrils. Once the spikes had hardened, Nogar looked around to spot something to shot at, not wanting to destroy another target. Nogar spotted a large boulder across the field. He then asked some of the Gunar lords to move aside giving him a clear shot.

Nogar then began to focus on the boulder concentrating while he formed a fireball then shot the fireballs along with the two spikes. Everyone watched with anticipation as the fireball flew straight to the boulder. When the fireball and the two spikes hit the boulder, the impact nearly split the boulder in half. The two spikes passed completely through landing several feet beyond the boulder on the ground.

Captain Captor was speechless as again he couldn't believe his eyes. He then flew over to the boulder to fully examine and even found the spikes that had cooled down.

As Captain Captor wrapped his mind around what had just happened, he came to the conclusion that Nogar did not destroy the target on purpose. Captain Captor then got very excited as he rushed over to Nogar, almost knocking him down as he said, "We have to inform Captain Racklin right away. He will want to know about this powerful weapon. It just might be what we need to end this war."

Chapter 26

Captain Captor found Officer Zar amongst the group. In his excitement, he began to explain Nogar's weapon despite him witnessing it himself. Captain Captor further explained that he needed to take Nogar to Captain Racklin right away, so he left him in charge. After everything was arranged, Nogar and Captor then left the shooting range heading straight for the general's quarters where they planned to meet up with Captain Racklin. When they arrived, Captain Captor walked across a large room into a second room, leaving Nogar alone.

When Captain Captor entered this second room, he saw Captain Racklin sitting at a large stone table looking over some reports from different battle captains. Captain Racklin was overwhelmed with grief from this war. Captain Captor ignored his disposition as he felt his news would cheer him up no matter what. His excitement didn't even allow him to wait for Captain Racklin to address him as he rushed up to him. When he got up to him, he said, "Captain Racklin, I have some very good news concerning one of these new soldiers in training."

Captain Racklin looked up from his reports at Captain Captor and said, "Unless you have discovered a miracle that will aid in the ending of this war, I really don't want to be bothered. But since you are here, what is the name of this soldier you want to tell me about?"

Still unable to control his excitement and eagerness while smiling, he blurted out, "The soldiers name is R. Nogar, sir."

Captain Racklin's eyes widened upon hearing the name as he said in disbelief, "Captain, are you sure you have the right soldier?"

Captain Captor stood tall as he proudly said, "Yes, Captain Racklin, R. Nogar has been performing better than all the other new Gunar lords. Despite this, I have been on his case as has Officer Zar to make him pick his pace and the pace of the other Gunar lords." Then Captain Captor grabbed Captain Racklin's arm and began to drag him across the room. Nogar was sitting down until he saw Captain Captor practically dragging Captain Racklin toward him.

When Captain Racklin saw Nogar standing stiff as board, he said, "Hello, Nogar, I guess you have something to tell me. Captain Captor won't tell me what it is."

Nogar felt a little uncomfortable explaining why he was here, but he cleared his nerves before he said, "I can produce magnum spikes and shot them inside a fireball. The first time I did this, the spikes penetrated one of the practice targets. I also almost split a boulder in half with these spikes."

Captain Captor stood proudly almost boasting as he said, "Captain Racklin, when I saw him split that boulder, I knew you had to hear this and see it to believe it."

Nogar's anger began to boil as he opened his ducts filling his glands. Once hardened, he turned toward Captain Captor and said angrily, "You tried to kill me while I spared your life."

Upon hearing Nogar's words of Captain Captor attempted to kill him, Captain Racklin rose into the air, and in a matter of seconds, he had Captain Captor pinned to the ground. Captain Racklin stared deep into Captain Captor's eyes as once again, he feared for his life. Captain Racklin had to hold back his anger in order not to kill him as he said, "You did what? Captain Captor, you better answer my question truthfully. Even so, I may not spare your life. Now tell me, did you attempt to kill this soldier?"

With fear growing in his eyes as well as in his face, his voice began to crack as he answered, "Yes, I did, Captain Racklin. I did it because I thought he damaged the target as a joke."

It was then that Nogar stepped forward and said, "Captain Racklin, I was the victim. I also do not agree with Captain Captor's decision purely out of rage. I also don't agree with his following actions, but I was able to defend myself, but I wouldn't have to do it if I wasn't attacked. Captain Racklin, I am unharmed. I want to speak to you with respect. Captain Captor achieved the rank of a captain as such. He must be a valuable asset to this army."

Captain Racklin was indeed impressed with Nogar's forgiving nature as he slowly began to release his grip on Captain Captor. In his anger, Captain Racklin did not realize that his blunt force had not only knocked Captain Captor hard to the ground but also one of his claws began to dig into the back of Captain Captor's skull as he pinned him to the ground. As Captain Captor got up, holding the back of his head, he then turned around. As he was leaving, he was stopped by Captain Racklin's comment.

Captain Captor turned his head to hear Captain Racklin say, "Captor, your life was in my hands and was only spared because of Nogar and no other reason. But now, I need to evaluate your actions, and I might just have to reassign you to a different area, but for now, return back to the range and the training of the new soldiers."

At the end of Captain Racklin's comment, Captain Captor continued to proceed to leave Racklin's presence.

Nogar watched as Captain Captor left. He also turned to leave, but he too was stopped by Captain Racklin's voice. "Nogar, wait, I still have to talk to you. Come to me."

Nogar moved in closer. When he did, Captain Racklin asked him, "Are you all right, Nogar?"

Nogar then replied, "Yes, Captain Racklin. Gunar, my trainer, was aware of my situation. He told me of a defensive tactic called a fire shield. An ancient way that was lost over time. Thankfully, it was able to counter Captain Captor's death pillar just in time."

Captain Racklin let out a sigh of relief. He then said, "General R. Nogar, you don't truly realize the vast importance of your presence and leadership to this army, do you?"

Nogar looked at Captain Racklin as he said somewhat timidly, "I believe so. However, you think that I am destined for something, so can you explain to me why I'm so important?"

Captain Racklin then said, "You are our next commanding officer with the rank of general over the entire Gunar army. You will take on the responsibility once you have gained enough experience through your training and battle experience. Just as your enemy, J. Sparcan, who is also the general over the Wapec army, and Nogar, I can assure you that he has already taken his title enjoying his power."

Nogar began to shake at the mentioning of Sparcan's name as he was the last dragon lord that he wanted to think about right now.

Captain Racklin studied Nogar, then he said, "Nogar, I know why Captain Captor brought you to me."

Nogar, a little confused, said, "Isn't it because of my newly discovered weapon?"

Captain Racklin was smiling as he imagined this mighty weapon's power, then he said, "Nogar, your weapon is unlike any other in all of Dragtoneea. The combination of your magnum spikes with the hottest fireball so hot that it can melt hardest metals. This combination could tear through a dragon's skull like butter. It will be very handy in battle."

Nogar was having a hard time grasping Captain Racklin's words as he said, "Captain Racklin, I don't think that I am the Gunar lord to lead this army. I am way too young."

Captain Racklin understood his concern as he replied, "Nogar, I don't want you to worry, my young general. I am not going to dump all this responsibility on you until you are completely prepared for it."

Nogar let out a long sigh of relief and also releasing a built up large amount of tension in his body as he said, "You have no idea how much relief I feel. Especially since you told me that I don't have to take on that great responsibility, not giving it to me for several years if ever, and I believe I am going to choose not ever."

Nogar had a big grin on his face as he finished his statement, but his grin didn't last long as Captain Racklin had something to say.

Captain Racklin said, "Not years, maybe months and possibly even days from now."

Nogar was a little frantic as he said, "But, Captain Racklin, I don't know anything about war and battle or for that matter leadership."

Captain Racklin did not hesitate as he answered, "Do not worry, General Nogar. Soon you will. I will be right with you by your side giving you counsel. I will also be taking your orders as you give them to me as well as to the army."

Out of frustration, Nogar throw his hands up into the air, then he began to pace the room, feeling the stress building up again.

Captain Racklin could sense Nogar's frustration as he said, "General Nogar, I know of your frustration—"

Nogar stared him down with a combination of anger and worry in his eyes.

Captain Racklin continued, "I too was thrown into a position of responsibility that I too didn't want. I too didn't want to command an army. I would rather just be a regular soldier or even a guard."

Captain Racklin took a breath then continued, "But instead, I have been the commanding captain for 239 years. I have led this army to many victories. I have also been there when we have been defeated. I have lost and saved many lives. The Dragon Master and Gunar would not put their trust in you with this position. If they were not confident in knowing that you are stronger then you think being able to handle the responsibility to lead this army to victory over our enemies."

With Captain Racklin's positive reassurance, Nogar's stress began to melt away.

Upon seeing Nogar's relief, Captain Racklin then said, "Nogar, I will begin to train you personally. We have a short season of peace with the Wapec army. In that time, you will have the best training possible."

Even more of Nogar's stress disappeared after hearing that he would receive personal training from Captain Racklin. Nogar then said, "Thank you so much, Captain Racklin, for your willingness to personally train me."

Captain Racklin smiled as he said, "Nogar, go back to your training now, on the target range. I will join you soon, but first I have some things to finish up here."

Nogar did as Captain Racklin requested upon his leaving. Captain Racklin returned back to finishing up making preparation for the upcoming battle. Captain Racklin had a lot on his mind, knowing this season of peace was coming to a close. But also knowing that the Wapec army was already strong, but they received even more strength including their general.

As Nogar approached the shooting range, he saw Captain Captor harassing some of his fellow soldiers in the same manner that he was harassed. Nogar decided to take a stand against Captain Captor as he changed his course to land a few feet away from Captain Captor.

Nogar then said, "Captain Captor, if you wish to pick on someone then take it out on me."

Captain Captor had no idea that Nogar had combat foresight. Nogar could see Captor's every move of firing several fireballs and how to avoid them. Not only this but he also knew how to counter them by shooting his own fireballs each one hitting Captor in his chest and each shoulder after that Nogar was on his own. Soon, this foresight began to happen, and Captain Captor began to shoot his fireballs in sequence. As Nogar waited and watched the fire balls, he began to dodge first to his right then to the left then he leaned backward as a fireball barely missed his head. As he came up much to the surprise of Captor, he then shot his fireballs first hitting his right shoulder then his left one to his chest and a last fireball to his face.

This not only knocked him unto his back, but it also caused some brief blindness and confusion. Nogar then rushed in pinning Captain Captor to the ground much in the same manner that Captain Racklin did. As Captain Captor began to receive his eyesight, he was confident that the face he would see over top of him would be Captain Racklin.

But much to his surprise, the face he saw was Nogar, then he said, "This is the second time I have spared your life, and I can assure you there won't be a third."

Captain Captor knew that Nogar was serious about ending his life, and he would have to be careful as he knew that Nogar was stronger and more powerful than him. Nogar then released his grip and rose into the air as he knew he would have to keep a watchful eye on this unpredictable captain.

After his encounter with Captain Captor, Nogar waited for him to leave before he went over to his harassed friends and asked, "Are you all okay?"

Socer, one of the harassed, said "Yes, Nogar, we are all okay, thanks to you."

Then Socer said, "When Captain Captor returned without you, he was still furious, so he decided to take out his anger on us. We were the first Gunar lords he could find, and we don't even know why."

As Nogar continued to listen to more of the details from his friends, he knew they were telling the truth. He then began to feel the pain from his own encounter with Captain Captor plus this pain began to turn into anger very quickly.

Nogar suddenly spun around away from his friends as he began to search for Captain Captor scanning the grounds. As he did, he discovered Captain Captor resting in a shady spot away from the heat. Nogar began to move in for the kill, but he was soon blocked by Captain Racklin, and he had to use all his strength to hold Nogar back.

Captain Racklin then said with some strain in his voice, "Nogar, please stop and think of what you are about to do. You are about to let your anger take over and kill one of your own. That's the Wapec way, not the Gunar way."

Nogar's anger slowly began to go away as he made a promise to himself that if Captain Captor ever did something similar or worse, he would end his life. So Nogar would continue to keep a watchful eye on him just in case he would have to uphold his promise.

Captain Racklin came down not only to train Nogar but also the other new Gunar lords further in their training. After Captain Racklin calmed Nogar down, he found Officer Zar in order to be caught up on the training so far as well as Captain Captor's actions. Captain Racklin wasn't at all surprised to hear of Captains Captor's aggressive actions as he thought back on the reason he was transferred here in the first place.

Captain Racklin then told Officer Zar, "I had to transfer Captain Captor here in order to fulfill the empty position before that he was in a position that dealt more with battle and combat. I know he wants to go back to it, but his honor, duty, and pride wouldn't allow him to give up his post here until I find a more qualified soldier. I have been searching amongst the old, but now I must search amongst the new for the best qualified soldier as range master."

Captain Racklin took a brief pause before continuing, "Officer Zar, I need to check on all the new recruits, but my main focus will be on Nogar."

Officer Zar understood completely as he said, "I've been watching them very closely. They are all progressing very fast. As for Nogar, he is not only excelling in each task, but as he learns a task, he then teaches all the other new Gunar lords."

This news pleased Captain Racklin as he left Officer Zar in order to find Nogar. Captain Racklin found Nogar performing one of the most difficult exercises on the range—the rotating rings. As Captain Racklin continued to observe Nogar on the rotating rings, he noticed that Nogar passed through the rings with ease.

But the end was the most difficult part of all the moving targets. Nogar could hit one but was having problems hitting the second target. Captain Racklin watched as Nogar would rest at the end of the obstacle after a few failed attempts. Captain Racklin decided to give him some advice.

As Nogar was resting, he thought back on this obstacle that he has been trying so hard to complete wondering how he can successfully complete it. Nogar has figured out how to fly through the series of rotating rings by first going through the outer rings then the inner rings going in opposite directions.

The next series of rings were on a pole that he would fly through the bottom rings and move up until he got through all three rings. At the top, he would then dive to the bottom heading toward two moving targets. They were on a pulley system with two large boulders to counter the targets' weights, making them move. Nogar could always hit the first target but never the second one, and he didn't understand why.

In the middle of his frustration, Nogar began to think about his military position and the role he would have to take on. This was when he began to doubt himself, truly wondering if he was really qualified to be the general of this army. While still in his thoughts, he heard a voice said, "Nogar, are you okay?" This sudden comment startled him. When he calmed down, he saw Captain Racklin approaching him.

When Captain Racklin got closer, Nogar said, "Captain Racklin, how am I supposed to be a great leader in battle if I can't figure out this simple obstacle course?"

Captain Racklin chuckled as he said, "It's actually much simpler than you think. As dragons, we have a sort of aiming mechanism built into us that I just so happened to discover." Captain Racklin began to look around. As he did, he spotted a large circular boulder then he turned back to Nogar. As he did, he said, "Nogar, do you see that large boulder across the field?" Captain Racklin was pointing to the boulder about one hundred yards away.

Nogar looked in the direction he was pointing in, and he did see it. Nogar responded, "Yes, Captain Racklin, I see it."

Captain Racklin then said, "Focus real hard on it. As you do, you'll notice a white transparent dot out of the center of each eye." Captain Racklin then waited for Nogar to get to this point before he would give any further instruction.

As Nogar began to focus on the boulder, he thought to himself, *This is stupid.* But he trusted in Captain Racklin's advice. Slowly, Nogar began to see these two dots just as Captain Racklin said. He clearly saw almost invisible dot out of each eye. Nogar then said, in a surprised tone, "I can see the two dots, Captain Racklin."

A smile came to Captain Racklin's face, then he said, "Now I want you to focus even harder on the two dots. As you do, I want you to bring them together. As you bring them together, they will overlap until they become a single dot. At this point, I want you to place the dot unto the boulder then shoot a fireball at the boulder."

As Nogar began to focus on the two dots, he was able to bring them together—one on top of each other as Captain Racklin instructed. Nogar then took in a deep breath as he carefully took this dot over to the boulder. Then letting out the breath, Nogar focused in on a dark spot on the boulder. Feeling confident, Nogar then shot just a fireball just as Captain Racklin had requested. The fireball flew straight and on course at the boulder's dark spot.

After his shot, Captain Racklin said, "Nogar, do you remember the exact spot you were aiming at?"

Nogar turned looking at Captain Racklin as he said, "Yes, Captain Racklin, I do remember where I was aiming at."

Then together they flew over to the boulder to inspect the boulder. As they got closer to the boulder, Nogar could clearly see his blast mark from his fireball. As Nogar got even closer, Nogar noticed that his blast mark was in the exact spot that he was aiming at.

Captain Racklin flew a little faster to examine the boulder first. After Captain Racklin had finished, Nogar went to personally examine it afterwards.

Nogar turned to Captain Racklin in total amazement as he said, "I wasn't this accurate with the targets."

Captain Racklin was smiling as he said, "This tactic again is of the ancient ways lost over time. It will help you to be more accurate. I want you to use this skill to accomplish the final task of this obstacle."

Nogar looked at the rotating rings, and he realized that he was very close to the starting point of the obstacle. Without hesitation, Nogar lifted off the ground to try and accomplish the task put before him. Captain Racklin observed as Nogar again with ease accomplished the rings, then using the new aiming technique, Nogar was able to hit both targets with extreme accuracy. Nogar was beaming as he flew down to Captain Racklin.

Captain Racklin too was beaming as he said, "It won't be long now until you will be joining me and the rest of the army then leading us in battle."

Nogar was puffed up with Captain Racklin's encouragement but turned to him and said in a serious tone, "Captain, I am going to be completely honest with you. I am terrified. I am scared that when I do complete my training and join up with you along with my fellow soldiers, I will only join them on a bloody battlefield of death. Knowing I will only add to the death total and possibly even be added to the death total on the same field that I am defending. Plus, I still don't think that I am the right dragon to fill the general position. So if it's okay with you, Captain Racklin, as the acting commanding captain of this army. I will withdraw from the general position, leaving you permanently in command."

Captain Racklin let out a loud laugh that surprised Nogar, even startled him. Captain Racklin then said as his laughter calmed down, "Nogar, it wasn't me that handpicked you out of millions of leird candidates. It was the Dragon Master who did, and I have never seen her reverse any of her decisions, but I will tell you this for now. Focus, let's focus on your training. After the group catches up to the progress you have made, they you will join up with me on the battlefield. Until then, you all will be normal regular training soldiers. As I have told you, when you are ready, you will then take this command from me placing it upon yourself."

Even with Captain Racklin's reconfirming words, Nogar still had some doubt but decided to put it aside so he could focus on his training as well as teaching his young soldiers. Soon after Captain Racklin's counsel, Nogar and the rest of the group began to make great progress that really began to impress Captain Racklin. After a few weeks and at the end of a training day, Captain Racklin began to address the entire group.

He said, "I am proud and impressed with every one of you. You all have had great breakthroughs in your training. So much so that I have come to the conclusion that it is time to use your training in the ultimate test of battle."

Eager eyes dimmed at the thought of a battle challenge and the thought of taking a life or worse having their own taken. This particular thought concerned many of the young Gunar lords.

As Locur saw the life draining from out of the eyes of his companions, he courageously said, "Captain Racklin, sir, I don't think that I am exactly ready for combat just yet."

Captain Racklin let out a laugh before he said, "Locur, you have no need to fear for when we go to the battlefield, you all will watch from the protection of a safety wall. You will not be thrown into the fight this earlier in your lives and with no experience."

Several of the young Gunar lords were instantly relieved while others were a little disappointed.

As Captain Racklin observed the behavior of his young soldiers, he said, "Soldiers, just because you will be observing the battle, don't get too comfortable. For it won't be long before you all will be beside your fellow Gunar soldiers who will be fighting under my orders, then they will take orders from General Nogar and possibly even Captain Captor's. So I suggest you learn all you can that includes patience. But tonight, you need to get plenty of rest for tomorrow is going to be a very big day."

Chapter 27

It didn't take very long before all the new Gunar lords were talking amongst themselves after Captain Racklin had finished with his comments. Some of the more courageous ones even came to Nogar with their concerns. In the midst of all their commotion, one of the confused lords, Furton, boldly spoke up. "Tomorrow, what do you mean tomorrow, captain?"

This outburst caught everyone's attention as they all turned toward Captain Racklin eager to hear his reply. Captain Racklin was waiting for someone to bring up this exact point, waiting for all to give his undivided attention before answering. When he saw that they all were waiting on him, he said, "Tomorrow is the end of the peace treaty we established with the Wapec captains. So tomorrow, all of you, will be observing the upcoming battle. Which also means tonight, you will join up with all the other Gunar soldiers. We will gather around the battle fires. This is in preparation for the battle ahead of us to raise our courage and spirits."

Flowy was very nervous as she said, "But, Captain Racklin, how long after we observe the fighting tomorrow then when we will be thrown into the fight?"

Captain Racklin had given this speech many times and answered even more questions including this one. Captain Racklin calmly replied, "I would not throw any of you into the battle until I feel that you are fully prepared for the fight. No, my young soldiers, I will only have you join the fight when I truly feel you are ready and not a second sooner."

Garnar was sitting on a rock pondering when suddenly, he stood and said very loudly, "I have sneaked away from the dragon leird training grounds so that I could watch some of the fighting that has been going on. There is defiantly a necessary skill of flying required to be able to fight as well as to survive. Nogar, our noble great leader, is the only one who has successfully completed all the difficult flying and shooting obstacles. We have been lucky as he has been teaching us as what he learned, but I still don't think that we have trained enough for this air combat."

Captain Racklin understood their concerns as he said, "I have seen you complete the flying rings as well as the spin and shoot. These obstacles are specific for combat situations." Then Captain Racklin looked directly at Garnar as he said, "You will have to trust me with this. Plus, once you're in your first battle, your instincts will kick in as well the help of your trainers. But as I have said before, I will not put you into battle until I am positive you are ready for it."

The small group was still growing uneasy about this situation. Nogar, sensing this, decided to try and ease their minds. He did this by saying, "I know we are all scared about tomorrow, but Captain Racklin wouldn't put us in danger. I trust him. We all should trust him."

Upon hearing Nogar's words, they were still a little uneasy but were more willing now to obey the command of their captain and their general. When they all had calmed down enough, Nogar spoke once more. "Captain Racklin, we will be under your command and protection"—Nogar turned to the group then continued—"won't we?"

Everyone who had already calmed down, but now with Nogar's question not only addressed to them but to Captain Racklin as well.

Now they have a reason to be worried as they looked to Captain Racklin for his response in anticipation. Captain Racklin was looking out at all the young soldiers as he said in confidence, "I will be at first. But I cannot remain with you as the fighting gets worse. I will have to join the fight. As the battle continues, you will join in when you are ready. This could be during the first battle or the last you, will know when you are ready. From there, you will be evaluated by our seasoned veterans then assigned a battle position to best strengthen the army. You will then continue to train and improve on your fighting skills on and off the battlefield."

Nogar had listened very earnestly as he was pondering on all that has been discussed this evening after a moment in his thoughts. He then motioned for all the Gunar lords to gather together in order to discuss this future event amongst themselves. As they gathered around him, Nogar spoke, "Listen to me, I know that each of you don't feel like you are prepared for this is a very big challenge that has been placed before us. I know this because I don't feel ready myself, but if we govern ourselves with fear, then it is this fear that will kill us when we have to join in the fight. But if we trust Captain Racklin and learn from this challenge, then we can and will survive. I don't know about you, but I want to be around for a while, so I am going to trust him."

The majority of the group was in agreement with Nogar and wanted to know more about what would come next for them. But a few of them still remained skeptical about the challenge tomorrow but put their feelings aside deciding to agree with the rest of the group. Upon getting everyone's approval, Nogar then turned to Captain Racklin saying, "When do we leave?"

Captain Racklin smiled as he said, "Excellent. In order for a soldier to become a warrior, they must have war experience. Through this battle challenge, you will start to gain that experience as it is designed to strengthen the mind making a frail weak mind into a strong unbreakable one. This particular challenge will begin at dusk, so when we will leave, which isn't very far away, Nogar, I need you to start preparing yourself and the young Gunar lords under your leadership for I will call for you soon."

It was at this time that Captain Racklin left them and did not return until three hours had passed. During Captain Racklin's absence, most of the new soldiers were practicing their new skills on the stationary targets. Some were attempting the rotating rings as Nogar was coaching them while others were going through the flying rings and others were doing the spin and shoot. Captain Racklin then returned gathering all the soldiers together. Once together, he took the group to the battle fires but choose to select a few including Nogar to observe a small battle.

The battle was amongst a small group of Wapec soldiers who call themselves freedom fighters against the Gunar captains and selected Gunar warriors. In this small group also included Socer who was watching the epic battle from the beginning to the end. As the hated enemies dived and swooped at each other, it almost looked like a dance with fire. Until a Gunar lord delivered a death pillar which ended one of these freedom fighters which also ended the fight.

As this dead Wapec soldier fell to the ground, Socer turned to Nogar asking, "Do you think we will have to fight tomorrow?"

Nogar looked at Socer seeing fear sneaking into his thoughts. Nogar then put on a brave face as he said, "Captain Racklin has assured us that our participation of this challenge would only consist of observing the battle and not joining in it." Nogar took a brief pause before he continued, "But, Socer, I would always be prepared just in case something happens. In case we might have to be engaged in the battle."

After both sides separated, Captain Racklin gathered the eager new soldiers, not really sure why they had been picked over the others nor did Captain Racklin explained why he picked them. They all headed back to the other young Gunar lords to explain what they had observed as they could see them around one of the battle fires. When they arrived at the battle fire, Captain Racklin instructed Nogar to gather behind him. It was a simple enough task to follow. Once Nogar had accomplished Captain Racklin's command, Captain Racklin was ready to give him and the rest of the group some of his counsel.

When Captain Racklin saw that all the new soldiers were ready to listen, he proceeded to say, "I see that you have gathered as I instructed. But now it's time for you to mingle with the other older wiser soldiers. I would strongly advise for you to interact with them and learn from them. They are full of knowledge due to years of experience. Again I would strongly advise you to take full advantage of this opportunity. If you don't, your inexperience self will make you stick out like a sore thumb painting an easy target on your back where several of your enemy soldiers would gladly take advantage of it, rushing in for the kill."

Captain Racklin then walked in closer to Nogar as he continued to say, "I have talked with Nogar about a particular battle fire he knows how to get there. There are veteran soldiers with good battle experience that will give you their advice and share their techniques and experiences. They will tell you how they have survived for all these years, but only if you ask them. But be careful, just because it's night, it does not mean that there aren't any Wapec soldiers on the prowl. If there are, they will be looking to make a quick easy kill on some careless soldiers even more so because they lost one of their own today. Nogar, I am putting all my trust in you to get them all to that battle fire safely."

When Captain Racklin ended his speech, he then lifted himself into the air then turned as he headed in the opposite direction of Nogar's course, disappearing quickly. Shortly after Captain Racklin disappeared, Nogar looked in the sky in the general direction Captain Racklin headed in. As he continued to peer into the darkness, the sky began to light up with bursts of fire like a World War II movie. Nogar knew that Captain Racklin was fighting those freedom fighters in order to protect them. Nogar knew that they must move now as he loudly said, "My friends, it's time to follow me, and no matter what, don't break formation."

No sooner had Nogar gathered them all in formation behind him, then Nogar lifted off the ground followed by his troops as he led them toward their designated battle fire. As they were flying toward the fire making a great time, Nogar kept his eyes moving. As he did, he clearly spotted some Wapec soldiers that had gotten past Captain Racklin's forces. No sooner had Nogar spotted these Wapec soldiers, then they spotted the small Gunar group and began to stalk them. Nogar watched as the Wapec soldier's course of travel changed to their course of travel which made Nogar immediately change his.

In Nogar's mind, he could see the slaughter of him and his troops if was to stay on his same course as he saw them flying parallel with him. Nogar changed their course just in time as the Wapec soldier's began to close the gap as they began to mimic his every move. Nogar yelled out, "Dive!"

As they dove down, it was like they were flying next to a mirror as their every move continued to be mimicked as the Wapec leader suspected every rookie move Nogar made. Nogar had to use his newly acquired flying abilities of flying in a zigzag patterns while at the same time increasing his speed with no luck of losing the pursuing Wapec soldiers.

Nogar had to protect his young frightened soldiers while performing his acrobatic flight mimicked not only by his soldiers but also by the Wapec's. As he flew, he could make out at least three figures in the shadows. But Nogar was unsure if there were more hidden soldiers deeper in the shadows as Nogar continued to try and lose his deadly attackers. Nogar noticed that his decisions were not taking him and his soldiers closer to the battle fires but the opposite. So in a desperate attempt to save their lives, Nogar let out a loud distress roar, the same roar Gunar let out at Snow Mountain.

The Wapec soldiers were blinded with grief as they were too focused on pursuing the easy Gunar targets to realize that Nogar had signaled for help, alerting the entire Gunar army. As Nogar led his soldiers around a large rock structure, giving them some protection, he could see the battle fires in the distance. As the Wapec soldiers began to circle the structure, Nogar looked beyond them and could see a solid line of dark figures forming in front of the battle fires. Suddenly, four figures from both ends took flight in an attempt to get behind the Wapec attackers and rescue their new fellow soldiers.

As the Wapec pursuers continued after their prey, two of the three saw the line of Gunar soldiers and decided their life was more important and abandoned the attack. During their retreat, they ran into one of the pursuing Gunar soldiers. One of the freedom fighters dived getting under the new threat while the other ran into him and was defeated. But the lead Wapec soldier had his sight on the easy targets behind the rock, determined to end as many of their lives as he could before they could kill more of his own kind. This determined soldier was blinded by anger as he almost figured how to get to his abundant prey. He smiled at the fear he could see in their faces.

When the Wapec soldier saw an opening that he could penetrate to get to his quivering quarry, he was suddenly hit by a fireball to his face causing brief blindness. Shortly after, another fireball hit his right wing, ripping a hole through the leathery skin causing him to plummet to the ground. When he hit the ground, the broad tip of his nose hit first creating a deep trench before his forward progress was stopped by a large boulder almost knocking him out. Once he gained full consciousness, he was surrounded by five Gunar soldiers. He was unable to fully defend himself. It was at this moment that he knew his life would end shortly.

Nogar was still peering out from his hiding spot not fully aware of what was going on when his view was blocked by a large dragon. Nogar feared for his life and his friends. This dragon saw them backed into the corner trying to get away from a Wapec soldier that got through the Gunar defense.

The dark figure then said, "Don't be afraid. My name is Varznok. I am a Gunar soldier alerted to the distress roar. I am here to escort you back to the battle fires."

Instant relief could be seen on all the faces of the young soldiers as they slowly began to exit the secured rock formation. With this escort, Nogar once again gathered his group together as they safely headed toward the battle fires. As they got closer to the solid line of Gunar soldiers, a few stepped aside to let them pass. Once they huddled around the battle fire, Captain Racklin told them to go. They began warming themselves up. As they did so, they all except Nogar who were still unaware of the execution taking place.

But Nogar watched as the line stood tall despite his group was safely secured behind it, then just as earlier, a few stepped aside to let others pass. This same process happened several times to let a few pass in and out of the line. Amongst one of the small groups was Captain Racklin. Nogar saw that Captain Racklin was holding something in his hand, but he couldn't tell what it was. When Captain Racklin got to the battle fire, Nogar said, "Captain Racklin, I thought you were going to meet us here at the battle fire."

Before Captain Racklin said anything, he did a quick head count, then he let out a sigh of relief. Then Captain Racklin said, "When I left you, I took several soldiers to distract these freedom fighters. Then I heard your distress roar. I then turned from the fight. I hurried over to you to make sure you were okay. On my way over here, one of the freedom fighters that pursued you was caught, and I carried out the order to execute him for his crimes."

Nogar was happy that their pursuing attacker was caught and killed, but he didn't want to know the details of his execution.

After Captain Racklin did a quick inspection of the frightened new soldiers and seeing no injuries, he then let out a loud cheer celebrating their safety. In his joy, he exclaimed loudly, "We will all celebrate tonight feasting on the spoils of today."

Chapter 28

On the way to the feast proclaimed by Captain Racklin, Nogar began to recognize the course they were traveling along with the structure they were approaching. Nogar knew that he had been here before as they flew up the steep wall of the mountain. Upon entering the large banquet hall room filling with Gunar soldiers, the surrounding were getting more familiar. There had been several tables set up that had an abundance of food on them. None of the soldiers were eating as if they were waiting for something. Once Captain Racklin entered and walked into the center of the room, he raised his hands saying, "My fellow troops and friends, we have a feast. Eat while it's hot."

The hungry dragons began to devour the abundant food. Nogar couldn't help but think that it just might be meat from a marcouren. As it kind of had a rubbery chewy texture, but he really enjoyed the salty flavor. Once everyone's bellies were full, the old soldiers left the room retiring for the night. While the new soldiers began to look for a comfortable spot to settle down for the night.

Some of the exhausted young soldiers fell asleep right away while others were too anxious for tomorrow's challenge and had a harder time falling asleep. But a few were still terrified from their encounter today, afraid to close their eyes thinking that if they do, they might not open again being killed in their sleep. When Nogar awoke in the morning as a beam of light landed right on his right eye, he arose to discover that he was the first to wake up. As he got off the ground, he could feel a kink in his neck, and he began to stretch it out to try and loosen the tight muscles and release the built up tension.

As Nogar's tension began to wear off, he ventured around the room careful not to wake up any of the sleeping soldiers. As Nogar came around a corner, he saw Captain Racklin talking to Captain Captor in the same room that he was brought to after he tried to kill him. When Nogar saw them, he headed toward them eager to find out what they were talking about and also eager to know what they would be doing today. But his progress was stopped by Captain Racklin as he almost ran him over as he did not see him oddly enough he was looking for him.

When Captain Racklin realized who he almost ran over, he immediately said, "Nogar, just the dragon lord I need to talk to. I need you to gather all your new soldiers together very quickly. Then take them to the protective wall located directly below the entrance at the base of this mountain. From there, you will be safe. Nogar, I need you to do this with no questions asked. I just need you to hurry." At the end of his statement, Captain Racklin turned toward Captain Captor as they departed together but split going in different directions once they got closer to the ground. Nogar wasted no time as he began right away following Captain Racklin's instructions by first gathering the soldiers that were awake placing them by the entrance. Then waking the still sleeping soldiers which weren't very many and those asleep were about to wake up. As the group finally gathered together at the entrance, Nogar waited until he had everyone's attention.

Once he had all their attention, he said, "We all have to leave right now for the protective wall at the base of the mountain."

Porgan, who was still not fully awake, said, "So why do we have to assemble at this wall so quickly?"

Nogar was not in the mood to tolerate any unnecessary questions as he said, "Captain Racklin didn't give me any details. He also didn't allow me any time to ask questions. He only said to hurry, so my best guess would be that the Wapec army has arrived early to attack us, and we need to get to the safety of the wall as quickly as we can."

This was more than they needed to hear as Nogar's words answered any and all other questions they might have at least until they reach the safety of the wall. As they approached the entrance of the cave, Nogar looked down to see the wall that Captain Racklin spoke of. Nogar then looked back at the group saying, "Follow me." With that, Nogar then stepped over the edge letting his body weight turn himself into a dive just inches off the face of the mountain. Nogar free fall to the ground until he could see distinct detail of the ground that he was about to hit.

It was at this point that Nogar opened his wings lifting him up into the air then gracefully landing on the ground safely behind the wall. Then Nogar looked up beckoning the group to come down by waving his hand.

As Socer looked over the edge, he didn't want to do it at first, but digging deep for courage, he was the first to follow after Nogar, doing exactly as he did and landed just as easily. Soon after, all the other new soldiers followed after them landing perfectly without harm, ready to view the battle as promised by Captain Racklin as each of the new soldiers approached the wall to peer over the side. As they did, they gazed across the camp.

They all were surprised including Nogar to see most of the Gunar soldiers running in different directions in panic and confusion while yet others were taking flight toward the battlefield. Nogar instantly knew that this mass confusion wasn't due to the acts of the freedom fighters, but it was the entire Wapec army arriving earlier than expected. This act broke the conditions of the peace treaty that they promised to follow. Nogar's suspicions were confirmed as the first wave of Wapec soldiers entered into the camp causing multiple alarms to go off which only caused more confusion and panic. But despite all the confusion, the Gunar soldiers were able to line up creating a line of defense, but it didn't last for long. Several of the Wapec warriors broke through this defensive line heading straight for the wall, as if they knew that the new recruits were there. As the lead Wapec soldiers got closer, all the young soldiers ducked behind the wall hoping they had not been discovered. But Nogar had to be sure that they had not as he raised his head over the wall. As he peered across the camp, he saw the current battle taking place inside the camp.

In the midst of this epic battle, Nogar was scanning the ground looking for Captain Racklin, but he was unable to find him. But instead, Nogar was discovered by a couple of Wapec soldiers and not just any soldiers. One of these soldiers was a Wapec captain. This captain was in charge of leading and planning the current attacks and was looking for something. Upon seeing Nogar, he charged straight for him while letting out a terrifying war cry. Nogar knew his group would be slaughtered if he remained with them.

So without warning or letting anyone around him know what he was planning, Nogar immediately pushed off the ground rising in the air leaving the other soldiers speechless. Once Nogar was eye level with this Wapec captain, he felt like he needed to turn to his right. He decided to follow his instincts. Nogar darted to his right which was in the opposite direction of the current battle, hoping to draw this Captain to him and not to his soldiers he left behind. Nogar's decoy attempt worked perfectly as the Wapec captain followed after him with fire in his eyes as he pursued after Nogar.

Occasionally, Nogar would look over his shoulder to see how close behind his pursuer was to him to know if he was faster than him. Nogar would only be able to catch brief glimpses of him as he weaved between trees and rocks in order to conceal his exact location from Nogar. As Nogar continued on his course just in order to save his own life, he spotted several large rock structures, some of which had scorching brunt marks from fireballs of past battles. Nogar then turned his flight direction toward them struggling to reach the first of the many of these structures.

As he focused on this large rock pillar, he was trying to figure out the best way to maneuver around it. Nogar's thought process as well as flight pattern was disrupted by a hot bright burst of fire that just missed his head. Nogar then had to abandon his current plan and turn his flight direction upward in order to avoid the death pillar as well as the rock pillar he was about to hit. Nogar cleared the surface of the rock pillar by just centimeters. When he reached the top, he stopped to rest and see where his pursuer was at.

While Nogar was catching his breath and looking down, he saw this Wapec captain cautiously approaching this new burned mark looking downward for his dead victim. When he didn't see Nogar on the ground, he then looked up and soon spotted him.

This Wapec captain then dug his claws into the rock on each side as he began to drag himself up the rock with ease in a spiraling pattern. When this Wapec captain got closer to the top, he sternly said, "Boy, do you know who I am?"

Nogar had to turn himself around in order to address this captain. When he could see him, Nogar said nothing. He only shook his head in the negative.

The Wapec captain just smiled in delight before he said, "I am Waparan, the commanding Wapec captain. I have killed hundreds of your pathetic kind with no mercy, and boy, you are my next victim— an order from my general." No sooner had he ended his comment then he spread his wings, letting the warm air raise him high above Nogar.

Waparan then began to race downward toward Nogar. As he got closer, the only thing Nogar could think of was to shot several fireballs directly at Waparan. One of Nogar's fireballs hit Waparan in the face, distracting him enough for fire another fireball to hit his left wing toward the base. Both of these successful hits were a complete surprise to Waparan as he had to recollect his thoughts. When Nogar's fireball hit Waparan's left wing, it made him veer to the left while at the same time he was losing altitude.

Despite this fortunate event, it didn't buy Nogar much time to figure out an escape plan or even a way to fight back. To buy more time, Nogar immediately took off heading in the opposite direction of Waparan hoping to find a hiding spot or even an area where he can easily defend himself. As Nogar looked around, he couldn't find spot, a cave, or a large enough area to be able to conceal himself, little alone an area or opening to allow himself to escape. It was at this time that Nogar concluded that he would have to take a stand and fight back and kill or be killed.

While navigating through the rock pillars sometimes, he would barely be able to squeeze through some tight spots. Nogar would look down and found several small boulders that broke off the pillars. Nogar looked back, not to see if Waparan had found him but to look at the tip of his tail focusing on his tail flaps used for turning while flying. While moving the flaps, he wondered if he could use them as a form of a weapon against Waparan.

He also noticed that Waparan was having a difficult time trying to track and follow him. Nogar decided to use this time to attempt to pick up one of these boulders with his tail flaps while still in flight. After his third or fourth attempt, he began to notice certain things such as he was either going too fast and was stubbing his tail into the boulder or the boulder was too heavy to pick up. Finally, Nogar was able to judge the size he could lift along with the right amount of speed to make a perfect interception.

From this, he learned three very important factors—the speed he needs to maintain, the size and weight of the actual boulder, and lastly, the timing needed to scoop and pick it up. Nogar knew if he wanted his life to be spared, he must be able to master these factors then use it to defeat Waparan. As Nogar was piecing together a plan of attack, he got a sudden urge to move his body to the right very quickly due to the fact that he was suddenly covered in a blanket of darkness. As Nogar bolted to his right, he felt the familiar heat source of one of Waparan's death pillars. In his retreat, Nogar spotted the perfect boulder then timed it perfectly in order to scoop it up.

Nogar was then avoiding fireballs from Waparan as he carried the boulder in his tail. As he did, he thought, *I need to fling this boulder at Waparan trying to cripple him at the very least. Then I can move easily and finish him off, but how am I going to be able to accomplish this task?*

Just as Nogar hoped, he heard the familiar voice of Gunar as he said, *Nogar, do you see the rock pillar right in front of you?*

Nogar looked up seeing the pillar about twenty yards in front of him as he replied, "Yes."

Gunar then said, *Hurl yourself around it using your weight and speed. From there, I'll instruct you with the timing and speed to throw the boulder as well as the direction it will need to be thrown.*

Nogar trusted in Gunar's advice as he focused in on this pillar, he was trying to remember all of Gunar's instructions. When Nogar was within twenty feet of this pillar, he looked back and saw that Waparan was only thirty feet behind him and closing the gap. At the speed he was going, Waparan would be on top of him before he could reach the pillar. Gunar, sensing the danger, knew how to increase his speed and bursts enough for him to reach the pillar and accomplish his goal.

Gunar then spoke to Nogar saying, *Nogar, you still have a chance to reach the pillar before Waparan reaches you. You have adrenalin sacks on each side of your throat.*

Nogar began to feel his throat to try and find the adrenalin sacks. Gunar continued, *Nogar, if you tap into these sacks, you can gain bursts of energy and speed. But it will also weaken you if you use it too long. It could weaken to the point of killing you. I will tell you when to open these sacks and when to close them. If you follow my instructions exactly, this will save your life.*

Nogar was confused by this counsel as he asked, "Gunar, what's adrenalin sacks, and how do I use them? We haven't gone over this at all!"

Confident, Gunar replied, *It is easier than you think. All you need to do is think about this function. As you do this, instincts will naturally take over and the reserve sacks will open.* Gunar knew that he had to be smart with these reserve adrenalin sacks. Gunar then kept a close eye on both targets. As both Waparan and the rock pillar got closer, Gunar said, *Nogar, open your reserve sacks for a few seconds right now!*

This extra energy and burst of speed surprised Nogar as well as Waparan as Waparan had to exert even more energy just to try catch up to Nogar. With this new energy, Nogar has created an even larger gap between him and Waparan and was now only a few feet from the pillar. Once he was about to go around the pillar, Gunar instructed him to open his reserve sacks again for a few seconds to sling shot him around the pillar.

Once Nogar came around the pillar and was now facing Waparan, he was still listening to Gunar's every instruction. When Waparan noticed that Nogar was now heading straight for him, he thought, *You fool, you are heading directly at me. Once you are within range, I will hit you with one of my deadly fireballs. This time when you fall, I will finish you off for good and send your head on a stick to your pathetic Gunar forces.*

Meanwhile, as Nogar kept getting closer to Waparan on purpose, all he could think was, *I hope this works, and I really hope that Gunar helps me perform this perfectly.*

Chapter 29

Gunar was viewing Waparan, but he had to quickly reconnected into Nogar's thoughts just in time as he began to instruct him, *Waparan is really close to getting within range. I want you to wait to throw the boulder until he gets ready to shoot some fireballs. At that moment, I want you to dip into your reserve sacks right before he fires at you and hurl the boulder at him. When you do dip into your reserve sacks this time, it will give you extra strength allowing you to hurl the boulder with greater speed toward Waparan. Now, Nogar, after you hit him, you will need to finish him off very quickly. As Waparan has killed more than one Gunar soldier, and I don't want you to be added to his list.*

Nogar also didn't want to die. He wanted to live as long as he can, so Nogar decided to listen very carefully to Gunar's every word. Nogar knew that right now, he had to focus on every action that Waparan made as they were getting very close. Nogar suspected that Waparan was planning to carry out his own assault. He could see it in the pupils of his eyes. As both Nogar and Waparan were getting in range of each other, Nogar had a thought that ultimately would make his own attack more successful, but he would have to be patient.

Nogar proceeded on his designated course as he was waiting for the perfect moment to carry out his plan. This happened when Waparan began to open up his mouth mixing oxygen with his saliva to produce fireballs. Nogar knew of Waparan's deadly accuracy and even more of his potent fireballs. Nogar then watched as Waparan began to form a fireball. But before Waparan could shot any of his fireballs, Nogar shot one of his own. Waparan had to maneuver under it in order to avoid being hit.

This was exactly what Nogar predicted, and this was when he used his reserve adrenalin to fling the boulder knowing that Waparan would resume his same course. No sooner had Waparan lifted his head to focus on Nogar to deliver a deadly fireball then the boulder made contact with his head, slamming his eyes closed. Waparan then lost all consciousness and ability to use his muscles as he plummeted to the ground with increasing speed. Nogar wasted no time as he immediately dove after Waparan's body, getting ready to deliver his own death pillar.

When he reached Waparan's lifeless body, he then delivered a death pillar to the base of his neck, quickly ending his life. Nogar then landed next his body and saw his key claw glowing. Nogar then gripped it and noticed that it was loose as he wiggled loosely. Nogar's instincts kicked in as he pulled it off his finger. Upon moving his arm, he saw a leather bag around Waparan's neck. Nogar took the liberty to loosen the bag by unbuttoning a unique bone button attached to one of the straps that secured it around Waparan's neck.

After Nogar pulled the bag away from Waparan, he began to examine it. He discovered a fine workmanship covering the straps as well as the bag. It looked very similar to a native Celtic design. Nogar then thought to himself, *How old is this land to have Viking designs covering this bag?*

Gunar didn't comment as Nogar thought he would. Despite this, Nogar continued to examine the bag. He then found a flap and was kept closed by another unique bone button. Nogar pushed the button through the hole on the flap and opened it up. Inside, he found other key claws trophies of Waparan's victims that he collected throughout the years.

Nogar saw the greenish colored Gunar key claws of his fellow fallen soldiers along with reddish Wapec key claws. Nogar then thought, *It's ironic that Waparan's trophy bag would end up holding his own key claw.* Nogar then tossed his key claw into the bag. Afterwards, he slung the strap around his neck attaching it with the bone button like a necklace so it wouldn't fall off. Nogar then turned around to head back to the Gunar camp as Nogar glided in between the pillars. He began to form a story so that he could tell it around the battle fires of his victory.

As Nogar thought of his victory, it drowned out the memory of the second Wapec soldier that tagged along with Waparan. But as he continued to fly through the pillars getting close to exiting the pillars, he quickly remembered this second soldier. But as Nogar continued to getting closer to exiting this field, he didn't remember seeing two soldiers and must have disappeared before the attack. But Nogar put this second soldier to back of his mind as he figured that he would have ran into him by now and must have returned to his own camp.

Nogar was getting excited as the gaps between the pillars were getting larger which could only mean that he was almost out. But as he came a large pillar resting on a rock was the second soldier waiting for Waparan. Nogar hid behind one of the pillars and figured he must be waiting for Waparan to exit out as the victor. Nogar then began to come out from behind the pillar and as this Wapec soldier lifted his head and saw Nogar instead of Waparan coming out alive. This Wapec soldier sprung to his feet and then into the air preparing to kill this Gunar soldier.

This unknown Wapec soldier hovering above Nogar yelled down at him, "I don't know how you killed my captain, but I am going to finish what he started."

Nogar listened carefully to this soldier's voice as it sounded very familiar as he said, "Do I know you?"

At this point, the Wapec soldier was now flying toward Nogar as he replied, "You won't for long."

That last phrase was all Nogar needed to hear as he instantly recognized him right away. Nogar then said surprised, "Jeremy, is that you?"

His new attacker just smiled then said, "It's Dungar now. You catch on quick Gunar scum. Too bad I have to kill you now."

Nogar did not want to fight another Wapec soldier as he said, "Dungar, listen to me. You don't have to do this. You can go your way and I can go mine. Dungar, you also can have a change of heart and join up with me and fight for the Dragon Master instead of against her."

With a sympathetic expression on Dungar's face he said, "Really? I can leave the Wapecs and join up with you. I can really join the ranks of the Gunar forces because you know I didn't have a choice. I was forced to join the Wapec side."

Dungar continued to move in slowly as he got closer to Nogar. He really felt that he had gotten through to Dungar helping him join up with him and the Gunars. Nogar was a little more confident as he continued to say, "Yes, Dungar, you can, and I will help you through it."

Now Dungar was only a few feet away from Nogar as he said, "*No! Now you will die!*" Dungar then proceeded to shot several fireballs which Nogar was not fooled by Dungar's act as Nogar was preparing for the surprise attack.

Despite how close they were, Nogar was able to easily avoid Dungar's fireballs until one hit his left wing which didn't inflict any serious injury, but it didn't allow him to use his full wing strength. Nogar was still able to turn around and fly away from him, but due to his injury, Dungar was able to catch up to him as Dungar planned to overtake and kill him. Nogar knew even more so with Dungar than with Waparan that his timing would have to be perfect or it very easily could cost him his life. Nogar was putting a plan together when he saw large pillar directly in front of him and put it in his plan and would use it to his advantage.

Nogar continued on his course heading straight for this pillar, then he slowly began to turn over so that his back was to the ground so that he could see Dungar more clearly. Nogar watched as he could see the excitement in Dungar's eyes as he got closer. As he continued to inch closer, it was as if he could read Dungar's mind as he wanted to smash his head into the rock pillar they were heading for without slowing down. When Dungar got within hearing range, he yelled out, "You're dead, Nogar. There is no mercy in a revenge killing."

This is exactly what Nogar wanted Dungar to do as he began to increase his speed as he was carrying out his plan. Nogar had to be patient because if he started too early, it would alert Dungar of his counterplan. Nogar waited until Dungar was only five feet away from him before he started to go through with his plan. Once in this target range, Nogar began to produce a fire shield. As Dungar saw this, he thought Nogar was producing a fireball so he increased his speed. Seeing Dungar increase his speed was what he wanted him to do hoping that he wouldn't recognize that it was a fire shield. But just in case he did recognize it, he would fire magnum spikes into his throat.

Dungar was so focused on his revenge and how he would enjoy smashing Nogar's head into the pillar that he didn't see his reflection in the fire shield until he was a foot away. At this point, he was going too fast to be able to stop in time before long his head began to breach the fire shield.

All Nogar could hear was Dungar's yelling out in pain, "*Nooo…*" His screaming only ended when his tongue was incinerated, unable to speak.

Nogar observed the effectiveness of this fire shield when Dungar began to breach the shield. His scales instantly fell off turning into ash. The carnage continued as his flesh began to melt off his skull like butter. The intense fire then burned the skull as it looked like charcoal. Nogar watched the entire process as Dungar's momentum carried his body up to the second vertebra in the neck. Dungar's tip of his skull was just inches from Nogar's face almost touching the tip of his own nose.

It was at this time that Nogar disengaged the fire shield and turned to his left allowing Dungar's lifeless body to fall to the ground, grabbing his key claw before his body hit the ground. As Nogar placed his new trophy into his bag, he watched Dungar's body bounce off the soft sand surface creating a cloud of dust filling the air. Nogar decided to take a rest as he was exhausted from the two intense battles as he searched for a boulder to sit on. Nogar spotted a broken off pillar not far from Dungar's body and flew over to it. After he had rested for a minute, he looked down at the body of his second victim and wished that Dungar would have listened to him rather than attack him.

After another minute, Nogar couldn't believe what had just happened and even more surprised with what he had just done as he began to rub his eyes and face. Nogar was trying to convince himself that he didn't kill two Wapec soldiers, but if he didn't kill them, one of them would have killed him. Nogar wanted to take one last look at Dungar's body before he left, hoping that he wouldn't find anymore Wapec soldiers hiding anywhere. Nogar spent some time paying his respect to the two dead Wapec soldiers worthy adversaries before his departing.

But in the middle of his mourning, Nogar notice that the sand around Dungar's body was moving, rising, and falling—something big was moving under the sand. Suddenly, two huge sandy brown crablike pinchers shot out of the sand latching unto Dungar's lifeless body then slowly began to drag his body across the sand. Nogar looked over the arms of this creature and saw that it was covered with thick hairs allowing it to move rapidly through and across the sand. Then out of the corner of Nogar's right eye, he saw even more movement in sand. From the sandy depths emerged a massive brown thorny sand crab.

This crab had a dark and light brown camouflage. Nogar estimated that it stood as tall, if not taller than him, but had a much larger body than himself. Nogar noticed that the crab's arms were retractable as there were two tub-like budges on each side of its body. These arms allowed it to grab its prey from a farther distance then drag it back to its mouth. As Dungar's body got closer to its head, the crab began to nibble on the burned flesh with a tiny mouth.

Nogar thought that it will take this crab a month to eat Dungar's body, but after a few bites, a much larger second mouth swallowed the body whole. After the crab consumed its meal, it then began to burry itself underneath the sand waiting for its next victim to grasp in its pinchers. Nogar didn't even dare to venture back to see if Waparan's body met the same fate as he finally gained enough strength to be able to return back to the Gunar camp. As Nogar got closer to the camp, the sun was beginning to set. Nogar also noticed that the Wapec soldiers had returned to their own camp.

On his journey back to camp, Nogar reflected on his life realizing that his human life was but a faint memory. As he continued to camp, he reflected on how he had advanced from a dragon leird to a dragon lord and formed an inexperienced soldier to a worthy warrior. When Nogar was only a few yards out of camp, he decided to walk the remainder of the distance. As he did, one of the night guards spotted him.

The night guard then said in a demanding tone, "Stop, where you are and tell me your name?" Nogar was exhausted, and he was not in the mood to argue as he stopped and said, "My name is R. Nogar."

The guard turned from a defensive tone to a happy, even excited tone, as he said, "R. Nogar, you are alive. This is such great news." This guard then left his post and approached Nogar. When he got close, he looked over Nogar and said, "I see you have a small injury. Come with me, we will get that taken care of right away."

Nogar then followed the guard who was leading the way. The guard then said while walking, "R. Nogar, my name is Garmic, a fellow soldier. I am so glad that you are alive. We thought you were dead. I am leading you to the infirmary where you will get the medical attention you need."

Just as promised, the infirmary came into view—a large squared-rock structure with a single entrance. Garmic then returned to his post. Nogar entered the building. Once inside, he saw other soldiers receiving medical attention. Nogar saw one particular Gunar lord assisting the wounded soldiers while wrapping a serious burned with some kind of cloth. This Gunar lord looked up to saw Nogar.

The assisting Gunar lord said to Nogar, "I am sorry that I am not able to get to you right away. I see that your wound isn't too deep or severe. Your wound will be easy to heal, just sit down here and wait till I can get to you."

Nogar sat down where the Gunar lord instructed him to sit—on a large flat rock in between two soldiers, one with a severe burn in his neck and the other with a burn on his arm. Nogar didn't have to wait for long as the Gunar lord came over to further inspect his wound. Afterwards, he then left. Upon his return, he was holding a stone box with something moving inside of it, making a clicking noise as the unknown substance was bouncing off the walls of the box. Then the lid was removed, and the contents were dumped right unto Nogar's wound. It had a soothing, cooling feel.

Suddenly, Nogar knew that the substance was a type of insect as he felt the pinching of the insects eating away the dead flesh causing a worse pain. Nogar turned to the lord that infected him with the bugs and said, "Nurse, what did you put on me?"

The Gunar Lord just laughed as he said, "I'm not a nurse. I am soldier just like you. My name is Marbit. The common rule is any uninjured soldiers help the injured ones. To answer your question, what I put on your wound is an insect called a dragon beetle."

Marbit looked at Nogar's wound to see the progress of the beetles then he said, "The beetles eat away at the dead tissue. Then it will spin a cocoon around surrounding the wound. In a very short amount of time, the wound will be healed. While the scales begin to reform, the cocoon serves as the protective covering. You will have a battle scar, but we all have them."

While listening to Marbit's story, he was really impressed with these beetles even though he couldn't see the beetles at work. But Nogar could still feel some of the beetles eating at his flesh while others were beginning to spin a cocoon on the exposed tissue. In about an hour, Nogar's wound felt much better as if he had never been injured in the first place. Nogar knew that Captain Racklin must be worried sick thinking that he was dead, and knowing where to find him, he flew directly to the general's quarters.

As Nogar flew over, the battle fires to the large mountain's entrance. He wondered where his fellow soldiers at.

Once he entered the quarters, Porgan was getting some food and upon seeing Nogar exclaimed, "Nogar, Nogar, you're alive. Everybody, Nogar is alive."

Soon Nogar was surrounded by the other young Gunar lords. Even though he was glad to see them all, he was getting overwhelmed by all their concern and questions.

The sudden commotion alerted Captain Racklin who was mourning over some of the great losses which included Nogar. When Captain Racklin came around the corner entering into the next room seeing Nogar, his worry disappeared as a new feeling came over him—joy.

As Captain Racklin pushed through the young crowd to get Nogar, he noticed something hanging around his neck. Captain Racklin touched Nogar on the shoulder and motioned for the crowd to quiet down and said, "Nogar, we are so glad you're still alive. Come with me. We must talk."

Once alone in the separate quarters, Captain Racklin once again saw the bag as it looked very familiar as he asked, "Nogar, what is that bag around your neck?"

Nogar slowly moved his right hand to his newly acquired bag, grasping it protectively as if it was a great treasure. He then said, "It's a trophy bag that I acquired from around Waparan's neck after I killed him. Inside the bag are several key claws including the two Wapec soldiers I killed today."

Captain Racklin couldn't believe that Nogar had actually killed Waparan, but he was more interested in the bag still around his neck and the contents inside. Captain Racklin then beckoned for Nogar to hand over the bag to him, but Nogar was hesitant to hand it right over. Captain Racklin could see that Nogar was very attached to his newfound treasure as he said, "Nogar, come with me. I have something to show to you."

Captain Racklin then led Nogar over to a piece of furniture, one that caught Nogar's attention right away—a trunk against the far wall. Captain Racklin was standing by it as he opened the lid, inside were many other key claws.

# Summary

Best friends Ryan and Jerry were finishing up a normal day, completely unaware that their lives were about to change. In the dark night, they learned that they have been watched and followed by two reptiles not from their world. They learned that they were actually dragons came to recruit and train them to become like them. Ryan and Jerry along with other trainees were transported that night into a new world. In this new world, all the trainees learned that there was an ongoing war between the Gunars and Wapecs. But one of the biggest surprises that these friends learned was that their trainers were rival generals making them became the worst enemies.

About the Author

Trent R. Bingham was born and raised on a small farm in Idaho were he developed a vivid imagination. He is the only son with six sisters, so his imagination came in handy to play with a stick and a string and his made up friends. Over time, this imagination turned into ideas then into words then a story and now a book. He's happily married with three beautiful daughters, and each day, his dreams are continuing to come true.